THE
LANDWASTER

Chronicles of The Scraeling.
The First:

THE LANDWASTER

— a story of Harald Hardraada

M J Burr

The Publisher: ClioWrite Ltd
At: 36 Wairau Road, Oakura; Taranaki, New Zealand 4314.
mjb@cliowrite.com

Printed in the United States of America.
First Printing 2017.
ISBN: Print: 978-0-473-41124-4

This work of fiction draws heavily upon historical figures whose actions and philosophies were as I depict them. Any resemblance to any living person is coincidental

For Kath Arnold, Simone Betteridge and Vanessa Brown,

who have been with me from the beginning

and kept the faith throughout.

Thank you.

Contents

Prologue

Nidaros, Norway, Yuletide 1066.

And that needs to change soon. Yuletide in Norway must become Christ's Mass or the Feast of Our Lord at least, for since its last professed Christian monarch this land has lain under the hand of a known pagan, and before him a king much too busy for Christ. Yes – much must change, and if God will allow this tainted servant to do so I will bring about that change even as I brought about the destruction of the pagan and all he stood for. I, the cripple, once the lowest of the low; once a captive a trembling second away from the bite of the knife across my throat; once an object of derision and pity.

Like any other man's story, mine began in the blood and suffering of women; on a night when ruin and death burst from the sea to engulf a holy place where holy women practised love and service, to remind those who hide themselves away from the evils of this world that no refuge short of the Kingdom of Heaven is safe from Lucifer and his servant devils.

My story continued through more evil than is good for any man; through blood shed in battle and out, in greed, envy and ambition. It saw me become wealthy. It saw me in the company of the great ones of an empire, and in the bed of a queen, and in the confidence of kings.

On the other side of things, it led me into the blasphemy of believing that complicity in many small evils is excusable if it leads to the ending of a great evil. And, God help me, I played my part in the former so that I might boast of the latter.

So, from this moment I will make what amends I can and perform such penance as will ease my memories, salve my conscience and mitigate my debt to God. I will build where once I helped tear down; I will heal where once I wounded; I will lead and guide where once I schemed and deceived, and I will pass my life in love where once life only nursed and fed my hatred. And I will do

1

these things as much, I tell myself, for the good of my adopted country as for my own hopes of eternal life.

But if I am truly to atone for my past I must begin by confronting it; by living it once more, one single and last time. So, in these pages I lay it before you, as truthfully as it is already laid forth in God's great book.

And by that same care for truth I say that mine is not a pretty story, for it links with another's to tell of how I passed a life of treachery in serving a man I hated and feared. Aye, I served him in battle, in council, in murder and intrigue, always to one end. The end of destroying him and all that he was, for what he became mocked a God who had given him godlike stature, a clever and shrewd mind, great charm and a skill at arms that made him the foremost soldier of my time.

But the Devil gave him his soul, and in the end it outweighed the other gifts.

And in that end I served him his death in bringing him to drown in his own blood in an English meadow.

I am known to men as The Scraeling, and I served Hardraada, the Landwaster.

BOOK ONE

OF THE RAIDER

1031–1034

"At Haug the fire-sparks from his shield
Flew round the king's head on the field,
As blow for blow, for Olaf's sake,
His sword and shield would give and take.
Bulgaria's conqueror, I ween,
Had scarcely fifteen winters seen,
When from his murdered brother's side
His unhelmed head he had to hide."

The skald, Thiodolf, in 'The Heimskringla'.

The coast of Brittany, 1031.

There was menace in the air and the field-mouse could feel it in the moon that slid in and out of the clouds, dappling the land below with flickers of light and shade that spoke of movement where the land was rock-solid; of presence where there was no living soul and of nothing where there was indeed life. The shifting light held danger in the mystery of its shadows, and the tiny creature in the long grass at the edge of the clearing suspected it enough to flare pink nostrils to the sky in search of threat lurking in the dark.

But nothing moved at ground-level save the faintest of breezes and on it there was nothing but the faint scent of the sea a mile distant; nothing to alarm the rodent by sound, smell or vibration. So, hesitantly at first and then more boldly, it made towards the raspberries that clustered where the parent plant hung low in the deep shadow of a tree and there, its forebodings gone, the little creature began to gorge. So taken with its meal was it that it never saw the glint of moonlight on a silver streak of fur, and if it felt the air displaced by the armoured claw that smashed it into extinction it had no time to react to the presence of danger.

The badger dragged mouse, earth and berries towards its mouth and, in its turn, began to gorge. It was an old badger which had become so by being ever alert for the scent and sound of man, so even through the succulence of its second kill of the night the badger reared back and up as the faintest of vibrations rolled through the ground and registered in its belly. Sniffing the air just as the mouse had done, it caught a scent that caused it to move slowly back into the shade of the tree until a rear claw touched the lip of its sett and the thickset animal oozed slowly back over the edge of the burrow to lie hidden but for nose and eyes.

The vibration grew greater and the creature pressed backwards into its burrow as a shadow fell across the edge of the clearing. For a long moment nothing moved, then a low hiss whispered through the air and the shadow moved swiftly across the moonlit glade to be followed moments after by other shapes, with the shifting light gleaming here and there on the weapons they carried.

The shapes went to ground in the trees on the far side of the clearing, and the badger moved slowly backwards from the world of men and down into the depths of his own. Across the glade the thirty men from the sea grouped together, and although no word was spoken by any, a longer shaft of light from the moon lit up faces tense with expectation and alight with the anticipation of what was to come. Here and there a tongue moistened lips dry with excitement while broken-nailed fingers flexed and closed on the shafts of swords, axes and spears.

At length the scout returned, and spoke in a low murmur to one of the crouching men. He who was addressed looked about him, gestured to another shadowy form and swept a hand wide and to the right. At another hiss, ten men rose and moved off at a trot while the main body moved carefully and slowly through the trees until they thinned to reveal the outlines of several buildings clustering about a small and whitewashed church with a bell-tower at its seaward end. The leader gestured again, and two men turned to him.

"Church" murmured the leader, pointing. "That bell must not ring. Go." And the two men slid away, aiming to lose themselves in the shadows of the deep recess of the door beneath the bell-tower. The leader turned to the others.

"Bakehouse. Alehouse. Stables." Each was indicated in its turn. "Now there –" and a hideously-scarred arm lifted in the moonlight to a long and two-storeyed building "– there's where they sleep, and where we'll find them. Take your pleasure, but take it swiftly. And what you eat these next days will be what you take after, so if you would fill your bellies then, be quick about filling theirs now!" Muffled sniggers met this remark and the group parted for the leader to move through and to the right, in the direction of the sleeping-place.

But hardly had they begun to thread through the trees at the edge of the clearing when a dog's high bark of alarm sounded in the stillness and was immediately answered by several more. "Odin's balls!" snarled the leader, "Skallagrim's clumsy bastards've roused the dogs. On! On!" and twenty men broke cover to sprint for the largest building, brandishing weapons and giving tongue like hounds.

A door at the far end of the building burst open and a flying figure in a white shift burst from it and raced for the building the leader had identified as the stables. She skipped through a wicket door set into the larger one to hurl it shut, and the pursuers heard the thud of a heavy bar dropping into the sockets behind.

"The end, fools, the end!" shouted the leader, as those at the door swung axes and hammers against it but in only moments, and well ahead of the nearest raider, a door at the other end of the stables building crashed open and a horse erupted through it with a slightly-built figure stretched along its bare back. Under the rider's urging the beast went bounding forward on to the road that led inland past the end of the buildings.

"Leave it!" snarled the leader. "Leave him to Skallagrim! The church! The larders! The alehouse! Move, you droppings of the raven, move – but there! Look!" And as the moon reached into the stable a white shift gleamed in its radiance and two men sprang forward to wrench from the shadows the figure who had barred the other door in their faces only a moment before. It was a woman, long hair unbound and screaming her terror to the cold moon as the vikings yanked her forward.

"*Leder?*" asked one of those who held the struggling woman.

"No, I give her to those nigh as old and slow as she – you and Ulf. The younger ones are still abed! Come on!" and the leader raced for the door through which the woman had come and from which came a babel of cries as those within awoke to the peril that had burst from the night.

All through the buildings that comprised the convent of Les Trois Étoiles dark figures raced and swirled, smashing doors and shutters as they sought resistance and found none in that community of few men until they jammed, shouting and cursing, in the doorways of the sisters' dormitory. And then those who had given their lives to heaven found only hell itself, for when the raiders erupted into the sleeping-room some drove for the far door to bar and stand guard before it while their fellows did the like at the other end.

At that the sisters of the convent fell silent in pure horror and for a moment none moved as they stared wildly about them for deliverance from the nightmare of bearded faces, iron helmets and the rank odours of the male bodies that pressed in upon them. Then one young sister screamed, and the spell was broken.

A raider whooped and dived headlong at her, sending her crashing backwards over a cot and on to the floor beyond, where his weight drove the breath from her and pinned her helpless while he tore at the tarred rope that held up his breeches until the cloth came free. Then, seizing the front of the nun's nightshift in one huge hand and tearing it from her, he fumbled between his legs a moment, grunted and then savagely thrust his hips forward with a bellow of triumph that brought an agonised scream from the girl who writhed beneath him.

His fellows roared their acclaim and began to chant a count as his hips rose and plunged and rose again while he crushed the sobbing woman beneath his bulk and his hands mauled her breasts. At the count of twelve the man's eyes bulged as if they would start from the bearded face, he rammed his hips forward once more and clutched her to him, and he bellowed again as the seed burst from him.

And that began it. A chorus of screams echoed through the room as women were seized between two and three men, the clothing torn from them and they were cast upon a cot or upon the floor to be held by one while another drove into her without regard or pity for age or condition. Throughout it, the leader watched with his arms folded and his back against the door until he wearied and turned for the outside, crossing the yard to the church.

On the threshold he stepped over a male body still leaking blood and brains to enter the small church where, by the light of the votive candles, two of his men were collecting within an altar-cloth all that was valuable. "Only one?" he asked, and received a grunt in reply.

"Aye, the one. Went straight for the bell-rope. Never even saw us, I reckon. I tripped him an' Thorkill tapped him on the way down. How far's the castle then?"

"Two leagues. Bit more maybe; not much. Close enough if that bell had sounded – well done."

"That bugger on the horse – anyone get him?" asked Thorkill and the leader shrugged.

"If Skallagrim had the road cut by then. No-one else got out, and if he's got him, he'll be back with his boys wanting some loot and a fuck."

"Wouldn't mind a bit of that m'self" said Thorkill, and the leader smiled.

"Plenty of it over there. You finished, Sweyn?"

Sweyn hefted the altar-cloth over a shoulder and the three stepped out of the church to cross back to the larger building. The screams were dying through the dormitory, but in their place resounded the despairing sobs of the women who huddled together here and there throughout the long room, clutching at what remained of their clothing to cover their nakedness and their violation. Others lay unconscious while their violators sat or sprawled around the room in the slack-jawed stupor of their slaked lust.

The leader glanced about him. "Half of you" he said, "check the buildings and empty the larders. Pile all you find by the stables. The others – cut poles. Make stretchers. We carry or drag all we can back to the longship. The more we carry, the better we eat. Move! And you, Griss, get off her. If you haven't had enough by now, get more later. There's work to do."

Griss rolled from the woman and rose sullenly to his feet. Making no attempt to cover himself he raised a hand to point at the leader. "I do my share, son of Sigurd, and no man tells me when to take my reward. No man!"

"I'll tell you what I wish, when I wish, Bjorn's son" said the leader, and the softness of his voice failed to hide the steel within it. "I command here, and not by your leave. So don't point your cock at me, lest I cut it from you. And before you point your hand at me again, put a blade in it." The tension in the room could be felt, and even the sobs of the violated women died away.

"Get to work, and leave some for your brothers. There's always later." And Griss turned away with a growl and found his breeches.

The door opened. "Chief. Skallagrim's coming in" said one outside, and the leader stepped through the doorway to meet the party of ten which had earlier circled the convent to cut the road, noting the captive they dragged with them.

"The rider?" asked the leader, and the burly and one-eyed figure who strode in the lead nodded.

"Aye. Got him with a rope across the road. A real skinny little *scraeling*."

"And when the horse turns up at the castle?"

"It won't. Broke its leg in the fall. Snorri shut it up. How's it here?"

"All we thought it would be. Loot, women, food. In there, if you want some fun."

"Right enough, chief. What'll we do with this?" and he indicated the captive who stood, half-fainting, between two warriors. The boy – for he hadn't seen fifteen summers, the leader judged – was slightly-built with dark, curling hair through which blood still oozed to trickle slowly down his face. He stood awkwardly between the men who held him, and his head drooped.

"Give you some trouble?"

Skallagrim snorted "What, that size? Nah – did that in the fall. Came off the horse a good one; landed on his head. Rides better than he walks though" and for the first time the leader noticed that the boy's left leg was both short and hugely twisted, and that the knee pointed more towards the other than it did forward.

The leader put a hand under the boy's chin and lifted his head to look into eyes that even in the moonlight were clouded and dazed.

"Might's well cut his throat, eh?" asked Skallagrim. "You or me, *leder*? But quickly – I've got a hard-on fit to split my breeches!"

The leader smiled. "Then don't waste it. In you go. Leave this to us out here in case I think of a use for him." He casually lifted one brawny arm, smashed it backhand across the captive's head, and the boy flew backwards, hit the wall and slid down it to lie unconscious at its foot.

Skallagrim lifted a hand and hastened to the dormitory, while the leader turned to direct the gathering of the stores growing into a pile by the stables. After a while the man Griss lowered a half-carcass to the pile and checked to peer into the stable doorway.

"Freya's tits!" he chortled, "forgot about her! Hey, Ulf, you had this one eh? Well watch this – and ask her after who she enjoyed most!" And he stooped into the shadows to drag from them the nun who had been used by Ulf and his companion after the rider had broken clear. She shrieked from a mouth that still bled, and raised an arm to ward him off but he seized it and pushed hard backwards so that she staggered and fell upon her back.

Griss laughed. "Jus' you stay there" he commanded, "an' open good an' wide for my little friend here." He loosed his breeches to reveal a member hugely erect and throbbing with purpose. The raider grasped himself and stood over the woman.

"Look at this, you ugly bitch. I'm doing you a favour, right? You c'n have it rough or you c'n have it smooth" he gloated, "but if you ask me nicely I'll let you live to have my bairn, eh? Well, go on then, let's hear you—"

And then came a rush of wind and a loud and fleshy smack. Griss staggered, screamed, clutched his groin and collapsed. The vikings spun to see the captive, swaying still upon his feet but with a sling in his right hand and fumbling within his waist-pouch for another stone. The nearest raider leapt at him and clubbed him again to the ground, ripping the sling from his grasp and kneeling upon the unresisting body.

The leader strode to the writhing and screaming Griss, and stooped to peer at the egg-sized stone that protruded from his scrotum. "Told you that cock of yours would get you into trouble, Griss. Now it's got you an extra ball. Ulf, Asgeirr, get this free and see what you can do about the blood. Do whatever you must, but we can't carry a liability. Remember that." The two indicated knew in the instant what the leader meant and, nodding, they stooped over Griss while the leader moved to where the boy lay beneath the viking.

"Dangerous little bugger, aren't you, *scraeling*?" he remarked, but there was more thoughtfulness than malice in it. "Sling round your middle, holding up your pants. Dagger in your boot, yes?" Stooping, he turned back the cuff of the right boot and withdrew a bone-hilted dagger. He looked at the other leg thoughtfully, then balanced the dagger across a finger, lifted an eyebrow and commented to the viking who pinned the boy. "A *krøpling*, Askell, so he can't fight man-to-man, but he carries a sling and a dagger made for throwing. Bet me a gold piece he's handy with a bow too?"

He kicked the slight body. "Aye, *scraeling*? I wonder what else you can do. We'll find out. Askell, bind his hands behind him. He comes with us."

"Aye, son of Sigurd. And the woman here?"

"Griss' last stand you mean? You're a *skald*, Askell. What does a poet do with an instrument of poetic justice? Leave her be? Fuck her farewell? Cut her throat? Up to you. But bring the little *scraeling*."

The Chronicle.

*I*n truth, though, the stone that so took the leader's fancy and the viking's manhood had been meant for the man's skull, but my aim was not of its accustomed quality that night. All that passed since Sister Clothilde had burst in upon where I was sitting by a sick foal had passed in a blur or a daze, and sometimes both at once.

Clothilde, Clothilde. Sister to the convent of Les Trois Etoiles, mother to me and more. Older sister, carer, confidante, encourager, comforter. Healer of my body, and nurse of a mind often in torment as I grew, she who deserved the blessings of heaven suffered the torments of hell before she died, and I, who loved her, could not prevent it. Although I tried. As God is my witness I tried.

When she crashed through the stable door and spun to bar it, she was already screaming at me to loose Dancer, the black stallion colt who would suffer me and me alone upon his back, and she had run to the far end of the stables and swung open the door as I brought him from the stall. "The castle!" she had shrieked, "Raiders from the sea! Bring your father's men! Go, precious one, go, and tarry for none! In God's name, go, darling!!"

So accustomed was I to heeding her advice that I didn't argue or seek explanation, but swung to Dancer's bare back through a hand in his mane, dug in my heels and shot forward through the doors a scant few steps ahead of the shadows who leaped from the dark beyond them. And then it was away down the inland road in the moonlight, feeling Dancer's power below me as the great muscles gathered and stretched and gathered again until the moment there was a scream, a check, and all went black for me.

I next knew rough hands upon me, shaking me this way and that, and harsh voices speaking a tongue not known to me through the pain that bade fair to split my head. Then I was hustled away, back the way we had come, past a dark bulk on the ground that I struggled to identify through the stream of blood that ran down my face, and I knew no more until Clothilde's scream cut through the mists and I saw her flung to the ground and the raider standing over her. I struggled to my feet and none saw me for their attention to the scene before them, thus I was able to send my stone at his evil face with all the strength I could muster.

And then the darkness returned and I heard, saw and felt no more until I awoke with the world pitching and heaving beneath me so that the first thing I did was to ease a head that still throbbed by retching until my stomach nearly came through my throat.

Lake Ladoga, three months later.

"You betray me, Sigurd's son" said the warrior belligerently. "My brother dies and you forbid me to take the vengeance that's my due. You dishonour me and mine, and I'm telling you I'll have the body of this scraeling now.

It's past time for settling this.''

The leader sighed. "Galti Bjornsson" he said, "your brother brought his doom upon himself. As I've said, if he'd attended to his task and left his lusts until later, he might have enjoyed them until the last captive went overboard when none wanted her more. I told him that, but it was ever his way to think with his cock. And he paid the price."

Galti curled his lip. "And it's that price I seek" he spat. "My brother's price is his slayer. But you've taken that *scraeling* under your hand. To be your bum-boy in the night, more'n likely."

At that the leader flushed. "Careful, Bjorn's son" he snapped. I'm not as your brother was, careless of what burrow needed filling. Are you?"

"Enough, Sigurd's son. I've said my piece about this, an' you haven't listened. But for the good of our company I've held my hand while we crossed the whale's way, and now we've got easy sailing, it's time. I've waited long enough. I will have the *scraeling*, an' I'll prove my right to him through *holmgang*. Well? Do I get him, or do I get you first?"

In the deathly silence the sound of the river sliding past was clearly audible. Then Sigurdsson spoke.

"Galti, I'll meet you or any other under Odin's sky in *holmgang*. If you wish. But you are the thinker that your brother never was. Step back from this. Step back from it."

Galti held his leader's eyes a moment, then spat on the ground between them. "That for your word and your counsel, Harald Sigurdsson!"

"As you wish. Let the *holmgang* be prepared. Skallagrim?" Shaking his head, the one-eyed viking walked to the forest's edge to hew four saplings from it and to pace the nine-foot square of the *holmgang* while the two prepared themselves with sword and shield and the rest of the band drifted in around the square.

When they faced each other within the square Skallagrim stood between them, his weapon at shoulder-height while he spoke the ritual words of warning. "This need not be to the death. Let any who wishes step from the *holmgang* when he wishes, and let no more be heard of the matter that brought you to this. Begin!"

Bjornsson lost no time in launching a swinging cut that Sigurdsson caught high upon his shield, and he battered the leader's shield at every opportunity while warding off Sigurdsson's counters with apparent ease.

From where he stood, the captive caught a growled aside from Skallagrim. "Galti's going for Harald's left arm, the bastard. Knows it's still weak."

Askell spat. "Harald knows that too, friend. He's younger and fitter. A silver piece on him?"

"Nah. I wouldn't want to spend money I won on Galti Bjornsson."

In the ring the combatants had begun to weave and spin as the leader moved his bulkier opponent around and the clash of sword upon sword sounded ever louder. Of the two, Galti began to tire first even as Askell had forecast and, realising that, he flung all into a desperate assault with sword and shield both, seeking to drive the leader from the ring. But Sigurdsson would not meet his charges, spinning away from a shield-to-shield clash with his blade ever threatening Galti's face so that the heavier man was obliged to keep his own shield high, and when the end came it was as a result of that.

Charging in after a crashing blow upon the leader's shield, Galti thrust forward his own shield and toppled off-balance when it met no resistance. Sigurdsson had spun sideways before the impact and his blade bit deep into the back of Bjornsson's thigh as the man blundered past. He bellowed in agony as the blood burst from him, but such was his strength that he managed to turn and launch himself off his sound leg, point-first at his younger opponent.

But Sigurdsson avoided the thrust with ease, and as Galti went past the leader slashed backhanded and down with the full force of a muscular arm for the edge of his blade to take the man under the rim of his iron helmet, and when Galti hit the ground he lay still. The leader jammed his blade into the turf and signalled Skallagrim forward.

"You saw this done in fair fight, and you confirm that no blood money should pass from me or mine to him or his?" he asked, and Skallagrim grunted the ritual words "Aye. *Hagle, forfekte.* All's in order" and added, "he won't be needing it, and his family got no claim on it."

Sigurdsson pulled his blade from the turf, looked at the edge and stalked from the ring to pause where the boy stood. "Two men, *scraeling.* Two men you've cost me. Are you worth that?"

For all that the eyes stared boldly back, there was a flicker of fear in them. "You must make that decision, as you make all others. You say before all men that the first sought his own doom, and you, not I, killed the second.

Long may you continue to do so."

Others sucked in their breath at such insolence, but the leader flung back his head and laughed. "*Scraeling*, you amuse me. Long may you continue to do so, for when you don't – I'll feed you to the ravens. Now strip that arsehole yonder and bring his *byrnie*, sword and helmet to the ship. Pile them beneath his rowing-place, and when we leave you'll take his oar." He moved on to where Skallagrim sought him, as unconcerned by what he had done as if he had hewn wood for the fire.

Not, thought the *scraeling*, that Harald Sigurdsson ever hewed wood or fetched water. Since the night of terror and ruin three months before, he had seen Sigurdsson's authority questioned only once and he was now moving to where the result lay split-skulled in a puddle of blood and brains.

It had come as a shock to the captive to discover that the leader of the band of sea-wolves that had rent his world asunder was little older than himself. Harald Sigurdsson was already six and a half feet in height, broad of shoulder and long of limb with blond hair that was thick and full, but his beard was as scrawny as that of any other who had not seen eighteen summers.

Yet, mused the boy as he stooped over Galti and eased the helmet from the wound that gaped precisely under its iron rim, all deferred to him and if his own imperfect, but growing, grasp of the viking language were to be trusted, Sigurdsson had been a half-brother of the Norwegian king and had, only the previous year, taken a battle-wound that had nearly killed him in defence of his brother's claim to the throne. His brother, aye, renowned for his good works and his Christian piety, so what was – and as the *scraeling* heaved Galti over to roll up the heavy *byrnie*, the air trapped within the inert body surged forth in a groan that was part-belch, part-fart so that the boy sprang backwards in alarm.

There came a raucous burst of laughter from where three of Sigurdsson's band watched. "Good job the *leder* took care of Galti for you, *scraeling*! Scared you shitless jus' farting at you, didn't he? And him already kissing Odin's arse! What would he've done to you with his dagger?"

The captive stooped back to his task, and the tears came unbidden to his eyes as he contemplated what he had lost in the months since the destruction of Les Trois Étoiles. More than his work with horses, more than his studies in library and scriptorium, more than the loving kindness of the women in that closed community who made much of him, and more even than his freedom to rove forest and pasture with bow and sling. He had lost the right to eat as a human, to live as a human, to be considered a human. He was the *scraeling*, the captive, the *krøpling*, or cripple; suffered to live only as long as the leader's whim for keeping him alive.

And while it lasted, he existed among men who took lives as easily as they broke wind and with little more thought, who brawled as naturally as they breathed, whose speech was as rough as their clothing and their manners and who revered strength, brutality and cunning above all things.

"Mind you" came another, in mockery, "Galti would've had to get past his sling first, eh? Mind what he did to Griss?"

"Aye, but Galti would've had something more dangerous than his cock in his hand though" came back the first to yet more laughter.

"Maybe this little shit would've found the cock all the danger he c'd handle!" and the pack howled in laughter.

The captive gritted his teeth and got on with his grisly task, pretending he did not understand. *They're animals* he thought, *animals. And I'm not, so I'll outlast them. I'll match their mindlessness with cunning, their violence with soft words, their ignorance with planning and thought. I'll prevail, and if God is good to me, I'll destroy them.*

"Got him stripped yet?" broke in another voice, and the boy looked up to see that Sigurdsson had returned. "If he's not ready for the pyre when these idle buggers have built it, scraeling, I'm going to let them kick your arse a few times. Maybe something other than kicking it. Some of them aren't fussy. . ."

The Chronicle.

*T*he 'Scraeling' has been my name among my companions these many years, although I was christened Ranulf Denis Chrétien Nominoe de Lannion, first son of Ranulf, Sieur de St-Brieuc in that part of France that men call Little Britain and descendant, through my mother, of its ancient kings.

I would have been Sieur de St-Brieuc in my turn but for what happened just after my third birthday, on a day when my nurse took me to the stables to visit a strapping and handsome groom of her acquaintance. So engrossed in each other did they become that a child with more, perhaps, than his share of inquisitiveness wearied of the sighing, panting and fumbling so that when the groom backed the nurse up against a horse-stall and the sighs gave way to groans and gasps, the child rounded the corner in search of a more interesting animal than lurked under the groom's smock.

Alas. In that stall was a young destrier – newly-shod, part-trained and irritable because of the unaccustomed weight upon his great feet. When he felt his tail grasped and pulled, he gave vent to that irritation in a mighty kick that should have killed me, but which smashed my left hip and sent me hurtling across the stable. That I did not die was a miracle to my mother and a curse to my father, for the healers gave me over to God and He decreed that I should live with a hip that set as crudely as it had been bound. In my father's eyes, what emerged would never straddle a warhorse, lead a troop into battle for lord or Church, or sire an heir. So, persuaded that my injury would make me less than a Sieur de St-Brieuc should be, upon my fifth birthday he put me from his sight in the convent of Les Trois Étoiles. With time and the birth of three healthy sons who avoided such accidents even my mother, who had at first wept at the decision, came to think as he did. For had she not given a son dry of loins and thus empty of temptation to the service of the Church?

I knew none of this until Clothilde told me. Clothilde, who came to the convent when the Great Pestilence had left her widowed, childless, scarred of face and despairingly alive in a world now empty for her. Clothilde, who saw in a crippled and sickly child God's atonement for her loss. Clothilde, who loved me, mothered me, healed me when needful and explained the world to me without hesitation or evasion whatever my question. Clothilde, who encouraged me to be everything I could, and more than most of my age, despite my disfigurement. Clothilde, whose love for me was boundless and who spoke it in her eyes whenever they rested upon me.

I was fifteen when the raiders from the sea struck Les Trois Étoiles and Clothilde died when the ninth or tenth man to rape her cut her throat after, and my experiences of that night were as I have set them down. I did not know of her fate until much later when Askell, a gentle enough man and one closer to being civilized than most of his kind, told me from the depths of his cups one night among the domes and spires of the city at the end of the earth.

By then, though, there was no room for more hate in my heart because I had vowed it to the destruction of the man who, more than any other, kept the viking curse alive in God's world.

Somewhere along the River Dnieper, 1031.

Askell said, not unkindly, "Piss on them, Scraeling. Toughens y'r skin an' cleans the dirt from the cracks. But don't soak 'em in water – that just softens, not hardens. An' Griss had a wolf-pelt I got hold of after Galti stopped needin' it, so you can have that to sit on. Won't cure the blisters on your arse – oh aye, I seen the way you walk – but it'll stop you gettin' more, like."

The Scraeling thanked him gratefully, for such kindness was uncommon among the Norsemen, and looked ruefully again at hands cracked, blistered and raw from weeks of pulling at an oar. Had they truly once coaxed a pen along lines marked for him in faint charcoal? Had they ever really drawn notes from a harp? And were these the hands that had gentled Dancer into submitting to the ministrations of the smith when he had come from Lannion? Despite himself, the memories made his eyes prickle and smart so that he bent again over his hands.

"They'll get worse before they get better, Scraeling" came Sigurdsson's voice. They'll turn into man's hands, not priests'. That's what you were to be, yes? Well, now you're a *thrall*. My *thrall*, to do with as I wish. Don't forget it."

"What do you want of me, Sigurd's son?" asked the Scraeling, driven to defiance by his burning hands. "Why do you keep me alive? Must I thank you?"

Sigurdsson belched, waved the drinking-horn he carried, and became expansive. "You earned your own passage, *krøpling*, the night you sent a stone into Griss' crotch so he bled to death. He had it coming anyway, and in truth he came close to getting it earlier that night, from me. But you did it, and you did it well. Very neat. And very . . . poetic, I thought. After that, it was only a matter of time before Galti got sick of the sight of you and needed dealing with in his turn. Both the Bjornssons were trouble, and I'd had them marked since we began the voyage that brought us you. But you removed one problem and gave me an excuse to solve the other by letting him push me into a *holmgang*. Shame, eh?" He belched again, and the Scraeling caught the fumes.

"So. You could say you've outlived most of your usefulness now, 'cause you're a piss-useless oarsman. But you've got other talents. Convent boy, so you can read and write. You ride like a *valkyrie*, so you're maybe good with horses. Not that I need horsemen. Not now. But who knows, Scraeling, who knows? And you're not easily put off, 'cause I've been watching you suck shit these four months past. Oh don't worry – there's more of that to come. Much more. Maybe so much more that you'll forget about wanting to stay alive, and cut some throats? What d'you think, Askell? Eh?"

"Hasn't got the balls" returned Askell shortly, sensing his leader's mood, and Sigurdsson raised his horn again.

"Better not find any, 'cause that'll be the day I nail him to the dragon-post. 'Less I sharpen the sternpost instead and slip him on it like a glove." And he went off, chuckling at his own humour.

"Doesn't often get like that, Harald" muttered Askell, "an' best stayed away from when he does. Now, Scraeling – drop your breeches and piss on them hands."

The Chronicle.

*T*here was never any danger of Sigurdsson nailing me to any part of the vessel, but I came only slowly to realise that. Not that he cared for me in any sense – Galti's charge that Sigurdsson lusted after me could not have been wider of the mark, for his leader's tastes lay elsewhere, as I would see. But all in good time.

No – I was slow to realise that the man whom much of the world would come to fear and hate kept me by him as a talisman. I was, you see, what he was not and what he feared to become. Inasmuch as Harald Sigurdsson feared anything, it was being crippled, being reduced to something less than a man, for his pride in his own size, strength and vigour could not have been greater. When I knew him better I came to know that the arm-wound he had taken at Stiklestad in the service of his royal half-brother had nearly been his death, both then and later from the sickness that comes from a dirty and deep wound. There had even been talk of taking his arm and a hot iron to seal the stump, but he had sat up in his sickbed, raving as he was, with a blade in his fist to prevent it. And had he not won through in the end?

Thus, while I was a curiosity to him with my lurching and tip-toed gait I was his talisman, a reminder of what the force of his will had spared him. Aye, Sigurdsson's purpose in keeping me alive was first to justify his arrogance, and later to be of use to him in other ways. I can only guess at the thrill he gained *from the knowledge that he kept close one who had every reason to slit his throat as he slept.*

But if I was safe in his purpose, he was safe in mine – but he never knew that. His conceit blinded him to my purpose, and that was not merely to kill him, but to rid God's world of all his kind. This I swore on the banks of a river in the Kievan Rus and when I had sworn I felt all fear of the pagans and their ways drop from me. I had purpose even as he did, but my purpose came not from my own gratification; mine came from the way in which she who truly was mother to me had died, and in the way my world died with her and her sisters.

I was God's tool, and even though men soon came to nickname Sigurdsson "hard-raede" for the severity of his methods, there would come a day when I fancy he knew, in whatever corner of Hell his sins earned him, that in the end the Scraeling's word was harder and his purpose more fell and stark. Years on, and at his end when the arrow ripped out his throat and he began to drown in his own evil blood, he must have known that I, the Scraeling and the cripple, had wrought his doom after all. I rejoiced in the thought.

That, for Clothilde, Sigurdsson, and that, again, for the holy aunts of a crippled boy's life, and that, yet again, for Dancer. May Satan twist your bowels throughout eternity.

River Dnieper, above the city of Kiev, 1031.

The man called Thorkill snarled "Another bloody portage! Telling you, I've had my bellyful of them already – six so far, and still no fucking sign of this Kiev place."

"No choice" came his shadow, Sweyn, "what'll you do – sit on the bank an' moan about it? Harald can't shorten the distance, can he?"

"Wouldn't even if he could" grumbled Thorkill. "Jus' loves problems that one. Make us drag the longship fucking backwards jus' for a change, he will. Way it is, we're either rowing the bloody thing or dragging her. Dragon-ship? 'S a bloody dragging-ship, so it is!"

"I'm as much for soft beds an' willing women as you" Sweyn pointed out. "An' the sooner the better. So gimme a hand to get these *byrnies* slung to the poles, and we'll get 'em four at a time. You too, Scraeling. Shift your arse, eh?"

The Scraeling looked up from his perch on a bale of trade furs and got obediently to his feet. The weeks of tugging an oar had, after all, hardened his hands and brought a width to his shoulders that had not been there in his convent days, while exposure to the weather had darkened his skin also. He smiled easily, and spread his hands.

"Can't give you that long" he said. "Sigurd's son wants a list made of all these trade goods. Stops thieving bastards like you – so he said – stealing them as they're loaded and unloaded."

"What'd you call me, *krøpling*?" asked Thorkill, stepping forward. "What?"

"I call you Thorkill" said the Scraeling easily, "but the *leder* calls you a thieving bastard. Who am I to argue?"

The man subsided, growling, and the Scraeling stooped to pick up pen, inkpot and writing-frame before moving to another pile and beginning to scratch with his pen as he nodded and counted. In truth, he agreed with Thorkill, much though he despised the man, for he too was heartsick of the endless journey through the flat lands of the Rus.

From the land of the Finns, through Ladoga and into the interminable rivers by way of the Volkhov and the Lovat, they had traversed country that was sometimes wooded, sometimes swampy, sometimes under cultivation – but always flat and featureless. And here, in the Dnipro where at last the riverbanks promised some relief, there were twisting passages through shallow channels studded with sandbars that caused cruel toil at the oars when the *drakkar* grounded, as it did even under the most cunning of helmsmen.

And lately, to add to the increase in river traffic that the Scraeling privately thought betokened the nearness of a large city, there had been rapids – six of them, and today brought the seventh, each requiring an overland portage. Along the length of the dragonship men passed bundles from ship to shore where they were piled under the eye of six vikings, heavily armed against the possibility of a swift raid by the locals on such tempting prizes.

"Come on Scraeling" broke in Skallagrim's voice, "scrawl your runes and let's get started before fucking moonrise, eh?"

"Why start at all?" asked the Scraeling, scratching furiously. "Why load and unload all day like this?"

"To lighten ship, turdbrain. As you'll know when you drag it again, if you've forgotten."

"But look. Six men to guard the goods, right? Leaves twenty-three to drag and roll. Six to guard the ship beyond the rapids, leaves seventeen to carry everything round and pile it there again because they still need to be guarded while they carry."

Skallagrim frowned. "So? Can't be helped, can it?"

"Yes it can. Drag the ship fully loaded with twenty-nine. No need for a guard, with weapons within reach and the goods inside the hull, not out in the open. Then we do the portage once instead of having to make four or five more trips after we drag the ship round."

"Screaling, we never drag a laden ship. Men won't have it."

"They will if they know there are only two portages left, and they'll only have to do each one once. You ask them. And remind them they'll have to carry it all, sooner or later, anyway."

"Steering us now, are you? Screaling, stick to your scribbling!" and Skallagrim stalked off. But shortly after, Sigurdsson moved among the men and the order came to put everything back aboard after the log rollers, carried in the bottom of the ship, were broken out. And it proved to be as the Screaling had forecast, for six extra men made enough difference to keep the rollers moving smoothly from back to front and the dragonship moved swiftly enough along the portage track to still the grumbling that the thought of extra weight had caused.

There came the day when the prow of the *drakkar* nosed round a broad bend in a place where the river was quarter of a mile wide, and the reason for the increase in river traffic was revealed. Ahead lay a series of stone-built piers such as the Norsemen had never seen, and behind the piers rose the roofs and spires of a sprawling city, even to the scaffolding around a huge new dome away in the distance on a raised eminence.

"Kiev" announced Sigurdsson into the silence from his place near the helmsman. "Kiev, where my brother had marriage-kin among Yaroslav's family, and where they may receive us for his sake. But it's also whispered in Kiev that, in his younger days, my brother's belly-button knew the shape, depth and size of Ingigerd's, the queen. So let no man give offence to any here; no cause for affront to any of Yaroslav's laws. Pay on the barrelhead before you enjoy wine, ale or woman."

"We'll tie up here" he went on, "and I go ashore with those I name to find how we are received. If Kiev is as other places that sailormen haunt, there'll be drink and women near enough to hand. Let none go beyond the dock area, and let no man go ashore armed. This is my word and my will, and if any dispute it, let's hear it now." There was silence in the longship as it lay to one side of the stream, oars holding her still against the current. Sigurdsson nodded, then indicated a berth against a pier.

Two men rose at his gesture and went to him to confer briefly, then one of them turned and dropped a hand upon the boy's shoulder. "Here, Scraeling" he commanded, "to the *leder*" and he departed to fumble beneath his own rowing-bench.

"Scraeling" said Sigurdsson, "you spoke to Skallagrim of the portage of this ship, and your words had wisdom. Not all a warrior's weapons may be grasped in the hand or slung to a belt, *krøpling*, and you will come with us, with Ulf Ospaksson and Haldor Snorreson when they go ashore with me."

He thought a moment, then said, "You speak Latin and Greek, do you not? And French and Breton besides our tongue? Aye, and you have writing also. Yes, Scraeling, I can use you in many ways. Remember that your life ends the day you play me false. Now – get hold of something better than those rags, and ready yourself to face a prince." And with that he waved the boy away.

The Chronicle.

A nd that was a shift much beyond any that I had foreseen or even could have foreseen. From krøpling to confidant, from Scraeling to companion, you may think. But you would err, for my new station was no mark of favour nor reward. As with everyone in Sigurdsson's life and world, a man – or woman – was prized for the use that could be made of them and for no more. I was of use to him in the same manner, say, as the belt that held up his breeches, and I knew that even as I rummaged the ship for clothing that would suit our mission.

Nay – the surprise of that day for me was not my elevation, but the regard in which Sigurdsson was held in the court of Kiev. Once his name was given to the guard commander at the fine timber and stone building overlooking the main Dnipro basin we were received after only a short wait and shown along a broad and pleasing stone-flagged rampart to a great reception room with silken tapestries much beyond any I had seen at Les Trois Étoiles. Seated upon a carpeted dais at one end of the room and flanked by his ministers and courtiers with a boldly handsome blonde woman by his side, was one whom it took no great wit to conclude was Yaroslav, the hook-nosed Prince of Kiev.

Armed in a mail byrnie and helmet that made him taller than his six and a half feet, Sigurdsson stalked down the centre of what I surmised was the throne room, his lieutenants a pace behind him and I behind them again. He stopped before the dais and bowed low – and to my surprise Yaroslav smiled, rose and came down two of the dais steps to extend his hand and arm in fulsome and wordy welcome to the youth who yet towered over him.

And his wife, Ingigerd, arose also, and came down the steps to offer welcome – but behind her eyes was a look that I would see in many women appraising Harald Sigurdsson. Close to, her face belied the artifice employed in making her look younger, but she had once been a beauty nonetheless.

I was jerked back to the present by Sigurdsson's introduction of his two lieutenants, Ulf Ospaksson and Haldor Snorreson, and of his . . . writer, and Princess Ingigerd inclined her head to us and spoke a moment of the undoubted prowess of cousin Harald's sword-brothers in battle and counsel.

And in rape and murder, I thought, my eyes downcast. Would she have thought so much of them had she seen them bare-arsed and grunting like pigs among their fellows as they slaked their lust however they wished in those days following the descent upon Les Trois Étoiles when we sliced northward through the rollers of the Narrow Seas? Before their six battered and hopeless captives, who had been the most comely of the nuns, ceased to whimper in the agony of their bodies and the torment of their souls and quietly gave up their lives to be put over the side?

Aye, perhaps she would, did the look she sent Sigurdsson speak truly of her own appetites, I thought.

Shepetovka, Ukraine, spring of 1032.

Ulf went forward into his opponent's charge, swayed to the weapon-side and swept his blade low under the shield-rim and across the man's stomach. The breath came from the soldier in a whooping gasp and he doubled up, retching, to fall to the ground on his knees, his forehead touching the earth. Ulf waited patiently in the silence until the soldier had drawn his first agonised breath then stepped forward and drove it again from the man's body by slamming a heavy shoe into his side to send him sprawling along the ground before the still ranks of the Kievan soldiery.

"Told you, didn't I? Well didn't I, shit-for-brains? Told you that shield would blind you . . . fuck me, why do I bother? Good job for you I'm swingin' this bloody toy —" and the wooden drill-sword was hurled to the ground in disgust – "an' not The Serpent, 'cause you'd be gutted by now. Like a fish."

He swung his gaze upon the ranks of soldiery, none of whom would meet it, and raised his voice. "See that? One pass, one down, and you're on into the next one. Speed, that's what does it. Speed, and knowing what you're gonna do, and wanting it more than the prick facing you. Do it to him, before he does it to you!"

"Me" he went on, "me, I don't like a shield in battle. Fine if you're facing arrows, but you won't be once you're joined, so get rid of the bloody thing. Do the job right, and you'll have plenty to pick from later. Theirs. The other buggers what wasn't as clever or as nasty as you." His opponent struggled to his knees. "Fuckwits like this—" and Ulf's foot lashed out to send the man sprawling once more.

"Speed. An' thinking. An' wanting it – wanting to see the other bugger leaking guts. Right then, with or without shields – up to you, it's your arse – an' your girlie wooden swords, aye – into pairs. An' if I think you ain't taking this serious enough, you'll both face me. But I'll have The Serpent in my hand, an' I'll be looking for an excuse to sharpen her afterwards. Now then, on my word . . ."

The Scraeling turned away from what was happening in the early spring sunshine and back to the piles of stores that reached back into the recesses of the shed before him. Standing by one of the piles his lips moved as his pen flicked, tallying the items before him. He noted a number and moved on to the next pile, so engrossed in what he was doing that it was not until the huge shadow fell across him that he started and turned to the doorway.

Sigurdsson stood there, a long single-bladed axe in one hand and his arms bare. The scar of his wound showed white against his weathered skin and, despite himself, the Scraeling's eyes were drawn to it. Sigurdsson laughed.

"Aye, Scraeling – I carry the marks of my past too. But not like you – my wound doesn't hinder the warrior. In fact, I'm stronger and faster each day with The Nibbler here" and he raised the great axe in his hand.

"Clever of you, son of Sigurd, to avoid the weight of a shield on an arm that's taken such a wound" said the Scraeling. "Galti sought to use that against you, didn't he?"

Sigurdsson's face tightened. "There's no weakness in my body" he said shortly, "and Galti lies dead to prove it. But I killed him with a man's weapon. Not with a sling!"

"I use a sling, son of Sigurd" returned the Scraeling, "for it suits my preference of fighting, even as the axe suits your inability – ah, your preference – for not using a shield. Do we not all do what we can?"

Sigurdsson did not react to the taunt. "There are weapons" he said, "and there are weapons – even as there's fighting and there's fighting. As I've told you, Scraeling, you're proof. But you're useful to me in other ways, and that's why you stay here when we march to meet the Oguz invaders for Yaroslav."

The Scraeling could not hide his surprise, and Sigurdsson grinned, well pleased with his own cunning. "Why would I need you? For your strength on the oars? For your speed of movement? Should I make you Galti's successor for your prowess with sword and axe? No, Scraeling. For now, work on here. But come to the eating-place at noon." And he was gone, leaving the other to turn back again to his writing-frame and pen.

It had been a cold voyage from Kiev, with the snow still thick on the banks of the rivers they had traversed to come to the fortress of Shepetovka, in a basin where many rivers met. But the soldiers of Kiev had come in, sometimes two or three columns in a day throughout what was left of winter, quartered within the fortress and split into squads to be drilled in close-quarter warfare by those men set over them by Sigurdsson. And the longships loaded with supplies had also come down from Kiev and none, it seemed, knew where they'd come from before that. But come they had, each crewed by as hard and evil a set of sea-wolves as God ever turned His back upon, and these also accepted Sigurdsson's authority without question.

And while the soldiery sweated and winced under the lash of the vikings' tongues and sometimes their weapons, the Scraeling was told to see the burden of the longships transferred into the great shed, to itemise it, and then to apportion all of it into six piles. It hadn't been a task of great difficulty to the Scraeling, for all that he'd made it out to be so, and he had been checking the sixth pile for the third time when Sigurdsson had surprised him. What did it mean? What did the viking intend by his six piles?

The Scraeling found the answer to his questions at noon when Sigurdsson gathered his lieutenants about a huge chart pinned flat upon a table. "Ulf, Haldor, Skallagrim, Thorkill, Sweyn. And myself. You'll each take a dragonship up the rivers I show you in a moment. The ship'll be laden with your men and their supplies; you'll be guided by local men; you'll each be responsible for clearing the area on both sides of your river of any and all who don't swear allegiance to Yaroslav of Kiev. It's a simple task. Questions?"

Thorkill scratched in his beard. "S'pose we'd travel faster up and down the rivers. I see that, aye. What about where the rivers shallow?"

But before Sigurdsson could answer, Haldor Snorreson did. "Thorkill, your *drakkar* will float on the piss of ten strong men. When you've got less than that, come home!" And there was laughter, but Sigurdsson held up a hand.

"Get up the rivers and behind the Oguz. Pin 'em against the rivers, run them out of room. Get them to stand still – and smash them. Destroy their villages, leave 'em nowhere to go. Then get back in your *drakkar* and do it again somewhere else. But clear your river. Got it?"

"Prisoners?" from Skallagrim.

"I don't expect any" said Sigurdsson flatly. "What you do with the pretty ones is your business. Hostages, now – they come back here when you send for resupply. That'll be the job of my writer here." He swung to the Scraeling, who flushed despite himself.

"Him?" asked Sweyn in amazement, "the Scraeling? This useless bastard?"

"Only with a sword or an oar" returned Sigurdsson amicably. "But he's sorted out all you'll carry with you and checked it all. He speaks five languages, ours among them, and he speaks it better than you do. He can read and write, keep books, lists and accounts and he's well up to making lists of hostages and sending you what you need to stay fighting for as long as you need to. I need your cunning, your sword and the fire in your belly, Sweyn. But the Scraeling's got his uses, and I need them too."

"But can you trust him?"

"Where's he going?" asked Sigurdsson in exasperation. "From

Shepetovka, the arse-end of the Rus? Odin's balls, I can hardly even say it! No – all he can do to piss me off is get things wrong."

"How d'you know he won't, on purpose-like?" from Thorkill. "He's a smart little bastard."

"Aye, and he's smart enough to know Harald'll cut off his balls if he does" said Haldor. "Good enough?"

"Resupply?" asked Ulf, who was never given to long speeches, and Sigurdsson nodded.

"When you're ready, send the longship back here, with or without hostages, for what you need. The Scraeling'll fix you up. As Haldor says. Now – about the river network . . ." And he went on, using the chart to show how the network of rivers could be exploited to cut marching-time and to speed deployment so that the longship crews would always have the local advantage.

Sigurdsson's certainly a soldier, thought the Scraeling as his pen raced to keep up with what was said, *for he seems to have overlooked nothing*. And when his viking-led soldiers came to battle against the tribal invaders of the Rus, the result would be just as certain. He stole a swift glance up the table to see Sigurdsson, younger and taller than any there, leaning forward to deal with a question raised by one of his lieutenants and saw how his right hand flexed and clenched almost of its own accord as if it sought the haft of a weapon. *No,* thought the Scraeling – *perhaps more than a soldier, but less than a human being.*

Before long the meeting ended with Sigurdsson's lieutenants satisfied, and at the leader's nod Haldor broached a keg of the brown and bitter beer that the vikings preferred to all other drinks. The talk turned to the prospects of plunder during the spring campaign against the Oguz and it was generally agreed that they were scant, for the Oguz were herdsmen and shepherds driven, with other peoples, into Yaroslav's domains by the fearsome and devil-sent Tatars of the steppe.

"I hear they look just like their own sheep" remarked Skallagrim, "an' that's just the women. The men are even uglier!"

"Ugly women never held your pants up before" returned Sweyn, "an' if you get no luck with the villages, I wouldn't like to be the first Oguz man you come across neither!" There was a roar of laughter, and another when Skallagrim offered to find a pretty sheep for Sweyn and Thorkill to share.

They never change, thought the Scraeling, *never. Of all in God's wondrous world, only battle, plunder and women stir or move them —*

"Screaling! Re-supply! Now!" came a voice from the table, and the Scraeling took the vessels to the keg while their owners chuckled at one of Ulf's rare sallies.

The Chronicle.

*A*h, *Ulf. Didn't you and Ivarr beat Clothilde bloody because she fought your intentions for her there in the stables of Les Trois Étoiles? Then you used her and boasted later of how your tally exceeded that of Ivarr. There's a place in my thoughts and my intentions if not in my heart for you, you animal, but not now. Now I must be submissive; now I must become useful; now I must become trusted.*

Where was I? Yes — do none of these devils have a morsel of softness in them? The ten-year-old Elisabeth, daughter of Yaroslav and Princess of Kiev, is captivated by Sigurdsson. Over the winter she found one excuse after another to be near where the tall warrior was; one pretext after another to ask him of life in the far lands of the north. To be truthful, he treated her courteously in all my knowledge – but what would her mother's looks have got her, I wonder, had he come across her in a ravaged village and not in the palace at Kiev?

But the devil argues for his own within my head, and if I am to be just as truthful I must say that I have never seen Sigurdsson, the beastmaster of all these animals, lower himself to their level. Alone of all, his is the arse that I have never seen shine pale and white by sun or moon. But he urges the others to that – he controls them with promise of battle, plunder and rape while he keeps himself aloof from the last, at least. Aye, the others are animals but he is evil, for he uses their lusts as weapons to suit his own purposes. And as long as there are such men as Sigurdsson in the world, there will be men to do their bidding.

In the convent, Clothilde would oftentimes ask Sister Margarethe to read to me when the damp and cold of winter pained my twisted limb and made me fretful for lack of sleep, and Margarethe once told me of a many-headed monster of ancient times that men called the Hydra. The Hydra could never be slain, for it grew a new and more deadly head as quickly as one was cut off, so that all the champions of antiquity who came against it died in the attempt, for bravery was never enough. In the end, he who conquered the Hydra – and I have forgotten his name – did so by cunning as well as bravery.

Sigurdsson is the Hydra of my world, for through him evil will grow its deadly heads wherever he can gather the cruel, the greedy, and the rapacious to himself. Do I have the cunning to end the time of the viking?

The battlefield of Olevsk, 1033.

Sigurdsson scowled at his captains. "On my word" he said "and not before! Skallagrim, get your hand on those berserker bastards – two men of yours for every one of them; I want them useful – and all of you remember the rest of us're going straight for Wladyslaw. Me in front and you all up my arse in wedge, the banner in the middle. Keep it tight, because if we fall apart those Poles will eat us – they're four to one any way you look at it, so we all depend on each other. Never mind the berserkers; they're just a fucking nuisance to a commander, but they'll give the Poles a bit to think about while we kill their king. Questions?"

The Kievan army stood on the defensive where the road across the plain began to wind up into a low range of foothills, and no flank scout had reported any probing effort by the Poles to find a way around the host that awaited them.

"Good" Yaroslav had grunted in his tent that morning, "cheeky buggers are coming though us. They think. What d'you think, cousin?"

"I think this – Wladyslaw? – what a bloody name! – wants to settle it for good. Fine by me. Maybe he's right. Let's settle it – and him too" came back Sigurdsson. "From what I'm told, he's the one stirring up the Wends as well, so get him and we get peace on your border for – well, forever."

"Wish we could get him" mused Yaroslav, tapping his cup on the edge of the table. "Been a pain in the arse for years. I'd love to feed him his own hands."

"Can't promise that" rejoined Sigurdsson, "but we should be able to get his head. Listen — And what the viking had to say had determined the battle-order for the day.

Now, on the slope below in front of the Kievan battle-line, the berserkers had begun to stamp and howl and some to throw off their clothing as the battle-madness gripped them. Others clashed their weapons on the iron rim of their shield in counterpoint to the chant of their battle-songs, and already some were being physically restrained by Skallagrim's brawniest soldiers as their eyes rolled and the foam of their spittle blew from them.

"Come on, *leder* come on" pleaded Skallagrim silently, his eye upon the tall figure under the raven banner on the slope above, "come on – these bastards're dangerous, an' they ain't fussy who they stick it to when the fury's on 'em. Come on – my boys're shitting blood here – ahhhhh!! – let 'em go!!" And as his men dropped their grasp, a chorus of unearthly screams split the air and the berserkers leapt forward to hurl themselves, weapons whirling, into the ranks of the Polish army.

At the same time the cavalry on the flanks of the Kievan army broke forward with a blare of trumpets and a huge tumult of shouting, and as the Polish horse leapt to meet them Skallagrim rolled his eye up the slope to see the towering figure sprint down towards him, the mailed figures sliding in behind him in a moving, armoured wedge that swept up Skallagrim and his soldiery and buried them with shocking force into Polish ranks already struggling to contain the screaming berserkers.

The flying wedge cut through the Polish lines as swiftly and easily as their dragonship parted the waves, pausing only momentarily before the whirling axe of the figure that raged at their head opened a mighty gash in the ranks of Wladyslaw's bodyguard. Then, like a riverbank undercut by a wave, the guard rolled back from the royal standard and it collapsed as its bearer was cut down. Down, too, went the figure beneath the standard, a golden circlet rolling from its helmet as it fell, and then only the raven of Sigurdsson's banner remained waving over the spot where the Polish king had fallen.

A mighty roar went up from the Kievan army and it pressed forward, abandoning its positions on the rise of the hills to cleave deeply into the ranks of the Poles who, dispirited by the death of their king and now without any capable of directing an orderly retreat, milled aimlessly until they were cut down or dropped their weapons in haste. But Yaroslav's men were in no forgiving mood, for they had been made aware of Polish intentions for their land and city and they gave themselves up to blood-lust so that, in the end, it was Sigurdsson's northmen who turned upon their own allies and whipped them back from the cowed Poles as huntsmen whip hounds from the slain boar.

Later that afternoon Sigurdsson met Yaroslav on the field of Olevsk and held forth a leather bag. "As I promised, cousin. Oh, the gold ring he wore on the helmet didn't come through well. A bit dented. In fact, quite dented. Will you be wanting it?"

Yaroslav smiled thinly as he peered in at Wladyslaw's bloodless face. "No, cousin. Keep it. Your service today more than merits it; your northmen tilted this battle by themselves, and that's fitting enough for what you've done these two years past. The thieves and outlaws and berserkers and other hard men who've come to you in such numbers have given the armies of Kiev an edge they never had before. It was a good day that saw your longship nose round the bend before Kiev, Harald. Aye, the best of days."

Sigurdsson shrugged. "You took the chance, Yaroslav. Aye, you and Ingigerd made us right welcome." For a moment something flickered in Yaroslav's eyes, but the younger man continued, "And now your borders are safe. Or nearly safe. There's one more thing to do, and that's what I want to see you about. The prisoners. Have you thought about what's left of Wladyslaw's army?"

It was Yaroslav's turn to shrug. "Take the usual oaths of loyalty for the future" he said. "Back them up with hostages from the highest-born survivors, and let the rest go. What do you say?"

"I say no" said Sigurdsson. "You've got the chance here to secure your western border for your grandchildren and their grandchildren too."

"By killing them all?" said Yaroslav in amazement. "That'd create hatred that would last for generations, Harald. It'd ensure another army coming over the border within five years, man!"

"Not by killing them" said Sigurdsson. "What do you say to this . . ."

The result was a series of summonses for the senior commanders of the Kievan army to attend the royal presence the following morning. Another result was a scouring of the boatyards along the great Dnipro for all the pitch that could be had in a hurry, while grindstones flung sparks far into the gathering night.

"You all know" spoke the Prince of Kiev to his assembled generals and commanders the next morning, "that Kiev lives by trade along the water road between Gotland and Byzantium. What menaces that trade menaces Kiev. You all know, also, that Kiev didn't seek this fight. You also know that this fight with the Poles was not the first – but before the God of our new cathedral of Saint Sophia, it'll be the last!"

"I will have peace" he went on into the silence, glancing around, "a peace that rides on the back of terror if I can't have it otherwise. Let all men – Wends, Khazars, Pechenegs, Kipchaks and all others who would menace our land and our peace – know what befell the Poles. And when they know, let them tremble! This day will each surviving Pole who came in arms against us be punished by having his right hand struck from his body. Cousin Harald?"

"Lord Prince" said Sigurdsson, "what's a dead soldier but a memory to be avenged? And what's a one-handed soldier but one still alive, one who must be fed, one who can till fields and tend beasts only slowly and clumsily, one who'll never again bear sword and shield? Thus you gain your ends with no further loss of life. *Vess-heil*, Yaroslav the Wise! *Vess-heil*, I say!" And in a moment, the area before Yaroslav's tent erupted in approval.

Throughout that day, disarmed and captive Poles were dragged to the blocks to have their right hands severed, those who resisted the butchery being killed out of hand. Axes rose and fell to the screams of the maimed and fire-irons hissed as they staunched the blood of the maiming. A ladleful of pitch was slapped upon each stump and the sufferers left to walk, stagger or crawl to the west as best they could singly, in pairs or in groups.

Aye thought the Scraeling when he heard of the deed, *that was harsh counsel of a certainty. And Sigurdsson intended it all along, for that was surely why he had the northmen stay the hand of the Kievans on the field of Olevsk. Aye, he intended it as an example, a terrible example.*

He said as much to Askell, and the old *skald* nodded his head. "That" he said, "is Odin's way, Scraeling. Your God, the White Christ, speaks of gentleness and forgiveness. But Harald's a son of Odin. For such a one, vengeance and punishment ride the wings of the ravens that speak the Allfather's will. Aye. The counsel he gave Yaroslav was *hard-raede*. For such is what he is - a man of stern advice. But he lives by it also, and mark you, Scraeling – should the Allfather send him such a destiny, Sigurd's son will die as he has lived, and gladly."

The Chronicle.

*T*hus, on a bloody field in the Kievan Rus in the third year of his service *to Yaroslav of Kiev, did Sigurdsson come by the name that would ring throughout the world of men and warriors, Harald Hard-counsel, or 'hard-raede'. In time, and because those who did not know the Norse tongue heard it so, it became 'Hardraada'.*

But that nickname was little more than a fore-runner of a truly terrible one that was rooted in the single-minded ruthlessness that marked all his acts. Sigurdsson never defeated where he could annihilate, and he drew no distinction between enemy warriors and enemy wives, or enemy greybeards and enemy children.

Where the enemy moved too quickly for our columns, our soldiery used fire and flood to destroy all left behind that moved or grew, and conscripted labour to tumble the very buildings themselves, that those who had escaped us might be denied shelter of any sort among the lands whose ravaging witnessed our passing. For the most part, enemy civilians would be given to Odin among the ruins of their own homes, but on Sigurdsson's whim they would be spared to carry tales of the implacable Kievan columns and of the banner that preceded them. A banner bearing a raven that carried death, destruction and ruin on its wings. And because of it, gradually, that new and terrible name came to be whispered across the land on those bitter winds of the Kievan plains – 'The Landwaster'.

Aye, where The Landwaster passed, all threats to the western borders of Kiev passed also and the task was done. In truth Yaroslav owed Hard-raede much, and the viking was quick to grasp that.

That was why he sought the hand of Yaroslav's oldest daughter, Elisabeth, so causing his royal cousin a vexing problem. Yaroslav hungered to be the foremost Christian monarch of the eastern lands and that ambition now lay within his grasp. But the open paganism of the Landwaster sat uneasily with the status of royal son-in-law. So Yaroslav found a plausible excuse to deny Sigurdsson in his suggestion that his honoured relative seek the merit attaching to a Christian prince in the service of the Emperor of the East at Constantinople, thus proving himself on a wider stage and allowing the twelve-year-old Elisabeth to come of marriageable age. While much, of course, might happen to a soldier on an unsettled frontier in those years . . .

But it's true that Yaroslav may have had other motives. I heard whispers, but only whispers, that Ingigerd's taste for the children of Aasta, queen of Norway, hadn't ended with Olaf. As I've written, I know what I saw in her face on the day she met Aasta's youngest. And certainly, he of the 'hard-raede' had enough of the devil in him, and enough disdain of danger, to put horns on Yaroslav under his own roof.

However it all was, then, the world knows that Yaroslav of Kiev went on to become Yaroslav the Wise, the great spreader of Christianity throughout the eastern lands; a ruler who caused many books to be made and gifted, and churches and monasteries without number to be founded and endowed. With architects and builders from Byzantium he made his city as strong and as beautiful as the myriad buildings within it; he gave his state a code of laws both wise and fair and he gave his people years of lasting peace.

That these things rested upon the huge shoulders of a man as evil as Sigurdsson – or Harald 'Hardraada' as the world was now calling him – is one of God's delightful ironies. But doubtless He had his purpose, for aren't we cautioned against the sin of pride? And what makes a man prouder than constant success?

For the Landwaster, too, would have his triumphs even as Yaroslav had his. In fact he would go from one triumph to another in the Emperor's service, and each would persuade him that he was Odin's incarnation and might do whatever he wished. The Landwaster vanquished armies and fleets, humbled generals and kings, bedded an Empress and a princess, and became a king himself; and in all his life knew failure only once – and that at my hands.

And it killed him. Is God not good?

BOOK TWO

OF THE MERCENARY

1034–1040

"The king's sharp sword lies clean and bright,
   Prepared in foreign lands to fight:
   Our ravens croak to have their fill,
   The wolf howls from the distant hill.
   Our brave king is to Russia gone, --
   Braver than he on earth there's none;
   His sharp sword will carve many a feast
   To wolf and raven in the East."

The skald, Bolverk, in 'The Heimskringla'

11th century Constantinople.

Constantinople, 1034. The Imperial apartments.

The young woman took a deep breath, stepped across the threshold of the richly-furnished room in the imperial apartments, and took the outstretched hands of the two ladies who came towards her in greeting.

"Eudokia," smiled the first of them. "I am Isadora. How beautiful you are! Is she not, Anna?"

"Exquisite," said her companion. "And tiny! Welcome, sister, welcome to the inner circle!" And something about the manner in which she said the last two words caused Isadora to giggle, so that Eudokia glanced at her.

"Come," said Anna, turning. "Come and be presented to her Majesty." A flicker of nervousness crossed the newcomer's face, and Isadora murmured, "Don't worry, my dear. You're wonderful in every way, and I see you've dressed as you were advised". She glanced at the filmy skirt, and the half-shift cut just tight enough to emphasise the swell of small but perfect breasts. "Just . . . just be bold. The empress detests half-measures."

So I've heard. Eudokia took another deep breath and summoned all the confidence she could. *Remember why you're here.* She stepped forward with the two ladies-in-waiting to where a small woman reclined on a couch awaiting them.

The trio stopped a yard away, and Isadora and Anna stepped back, leaving Eudokia alone under the scrutiny of a pair of hazel eyes set in a heart-shaped face framed by thick dark hair that curled in ringlets about it. "Mmmm," said Zoe, empress of the Macedonian line for the six years past, "Lady Eudokia, isn't it?"

Eudokia curtseyed as deeply as she could. "Yes, Majesty," she said on arising, "and I thank you for the honour you do me and mine today."

"Oh, tush!" the empress said, swinging her legs down and rising to come forward. "Such talk among sisters! Eudokia, all here are . . . 'sisters of the inner circle', as we term ourselves." *There's that expression again thought the girl, and the others are smiling again. Can I guess why?* " . . . for do we not all learn from each other?"

Eudokia appeared nonplussed. "Learn, Majesty?" she ventured, and the empress sat again and patted the couch beside her.

"Yes, Eudokia. Learn. As you'll shortly see. But first – sit by me and tell us of yourself, my dear. All of us. Let me see – you come to us from the house of Vonskaya, do you not?" she said, naming a family prominent among Constantinople's Russian merchant enclave.

"Yes, Majesty," replied Kia, "I was named for your Majesty's elder sister, the Princess Eudokia, who has taken the veil. At my father's insistence my governess taught me, the descendant of foreign merchants, the ways and manners of polite society. On my eighteenth birthday she introduced me to the Comptroller of your Majesty's Household, who honoured my family in seeking my father's permission for me to join your Household, in what he termed your Majesty's, ah . . . inner circle of companions." *And I see none here are more than twenty-five* thought Eudokia. *Save the empress, of course, and if the rumours I've heard are correct, I can guess why.*

Aloud, though, she said, "My governess taught me to play the *lyra* and *shilyani* and to love learning. My father insisted that I learn to weave fine cloths, and especially silks such as these . . ." she gestured to her clothing, and the ladies gasped "and it's been my pleasure to do so." She paused, looked around, and pretended to falter. "Majesty, I wouldn't have you think me boastful . . ." *but it's all part of making an impression, and I'm certainly going to do that.*

"No, Eudokia," the empress said quickly. "Ah, that's too long a name for convenience, my dear, although it suits you very well. You shall be 'Kia' to us, even as 'Isadora' is 'Dora' and 'Anastasia' is 'Anna'. Over here – with an imperious sweep of her arm, "you see Xanthippe, who is 'Zana' to us, Dominica, who is 'Domi', Cleopatra or 'Patra', Herena, who is 'Rena', and Galla, who is the only sister with but one name!"

The ladies referred to smiled and raised a hand as they heard their names *And we're all girls together,* thought Eudokia, *and some of us much under twenty-five, now I look at us. Hmmm.*

"Then, 'Kia' I am, Majesty," she said, "and happily so, and happy to learn what the inner circle of sisters would teach me. When may I begin?"

"Why, now," the empress replied and this time there was a giggle, almost of anticipation, from her ladies.

"Majesty?" frowned Kia, and the empress waved a hand.

"Pay no attention, dearest Kia. You are the first to join our circle for some time, and the sisters always look forward to the occasion. Is that not so, sisters?" There came a chorus of assent. "Galla – fetch him."

A tall auburn-haired girl bobbed her head, got up and walked to the door and passed through it. "Kia. Do you know what is meant by the 'inner circle'?"

Kia looked blank. *Of course – I've been schooled by the best there is*, she thought, but she replied, "Your Majesty's most intimate companions, surely?"

"Aye," returned the empress. "We sew, weave and make music together. And occasionally, we . . . learn together. As I said, a woman's life, Kia, is more than mere domestic duties. Especially if her station in life is more than merely domestic, as is ours. My ladies can expect marriage to men high in our service and important to our designs; generals, admirals, legislators, provincial governors, nobles charged with work vital to me and the like. Men important to empress, City and empire; important enough for us to seek to control them and have them do our bidding in every way we can. In the way of which we will now speak, Kia, the 'inner circle' uses slaves to develop a particular talent."

And I think I know what that is, Kia thought. *So the rumours are true. But there's more to it than that, isn't there? Still – one fence at a time.* "Yes, Majesty?"

The door opened to admit Galla and, behind her, an immensely broad man of medium height, powerfully-muscled, bow-legged and bearing more scars on his body than Kia would have thought possible, and when he prostrated himself before the couch she saw that the scars extended up and down his back also. She opened her mouth, but closed it again as the empress spoke.

"This slave was wounded and taken in a raid upon one of our outposts. Just another wild Magyar horseman from the great plains of the northeast. But he proved an intractable slave, for they are a brawling and contentious folk even among themselves, and he bears the marks of all those who have tried to teach him better."

Kia nodded, fascinated by the man's scars.

"And one of my inner circle who saw him stripped naked to be flogged one day also noted an . . . outstanding attribute, shall we say? She purchased him, and made me a present of him. Rise, fellow, and prepare."

The Magyar scrambled to his feet and threw off the loin-cloth that was the only garment he wore and, despite herself, Kia gasped. The empress Zoe chuckled, and her ladies echoed it.

"Aye – an impressive attribute, is it not? And believe me, when it's wanted, it becomes a truly out-standing attribute!" and the comment brought outright laughter from the circle. "Because of what he was, we refer to him as the Horseman. Because of what he has we refer to him as the Horseman also! There are four such slaves, Kia, and we use them to develop those skills of which I spoke. Skills that a marriage-bed does not often teach, but often appreciates nonetheless. Skills that encourage men to do our will. What do you think?"

Kia licked her lips. "Majesty, wrestlers learn in their gymnasia and not in the match-ring alone, and soldiers train for battle, do they not? Is there a difference?"

The empress laughed and clapped her hands. "Just so! Just so, my Kia. Bravely spoken! Ladies? Sisters?" There was a chorus of approval. "Kia, last week three of your sisters rode the Horseman, one after another, for he has the trick of control that our service demands. He is yours to try if you wish."

"Three Majesty? Three?"

"Three. Anna, Galla, and Patra." The words hung in the air like a challenge. *Be bold* said Anna's voice in her head. *The empress detests half-measures.* Kia bobbed her head, and gestured to the slave. "Yonder" she said curtly, indicating a backless couch, and the man's lips parted in a smile of greedy anticipation as he moved to the couch and reclined.

The girl didn't hesitate, but mounted the couch, swung her hips across the man, grasped his now-erect member and inserted it within her. She took a deep breath and eased herself down the shaft until her shaven parts pressed against the muscular and scarred belly.

The Horseman let out his breath in a great gasp and then thrust savagely upwards hard enough to lift Kia's slightness from her knees upon the couch, and from where she sat the empress could see daylight between the bodies of her attendant and her slave. She chuckled as the crack of flesh meeting flesh resounded through the room and watched again as Kia was hurled upwards a second and then a third time. "Dora! Anna! Take her arms! Ride,

Kia – ride the Horseman!"

But before the other women could move, Kia sprawled down across the slave, seized his ears, and dug her nails in hard. He howled in pain and his rhythm broke long enough for the girl to whip a hand behind her and seize his testicles in a long-nailed, menacing grasp.

"You are here to serve, slave, and not for your sport." she hissed. "So show me your wares, and lie as still as you can while you do so, lest I take it into my head to harvest these plums. You boast of your control, yes . . . ?" And so saying she stretched up a moment, considered, and then settled herself watching his face the while. Her body never moved, but the Horseman's body did and it soon became clear that her internal muscles were hard at work, for the man began to grunt and writhe beneath her, faster and faster and ever more loudly.

When his eyes began to roll she waited a moment before jamming down hard upon him, while his frenzied grunts became a hoarse and muted bellow that was more bovine than human. If she felt pleasure at all there was no trace of it, for all the while the beautiful face registered nothing but concentration, and when she was sure he had finished she got off him with no further word. She cast an eye upon the Horseman's flaccidity. "My lady" she called across the room to Zoe, "I fear I may have broken the wild horse. Shall I find you another?"

A gust of laughter swept through the room, led by the empress herself who clapped her hands in glee. "Bravely spoken, dearest Kia, and even more bravely done! Come, these idle slatterns shall draw you a bath while we talk."

As Kia luxuriated in the steaming and fragrant sunken bath, the empress glanced from a seat beside it at the shining, youthful body with its perfect and doll-like shape. "Tell me how you ruined the Horseman, for I watched in amazement. Do tell me how it was done!"

Kia shrugged. "I milked him, Highness," she said. "A trick shown me by my governess." That made the empress sit up.

"Your governess?" she repeated. "Your governess? And what other things did she teach you, pray tell?"

Kia smiled at her. "Much, Highness. She was an excellent teacher, and had once been counted the best courtesan of Novgorod. Her skills made her many friends but more than a few spiteful enemies. One of them, alas, was her downfall and she fled to Kiev, where she has relatives among my family. Oh, she has much learning of the book sort, aye. Much learning. But she has other knowledge as well. Knowledge that can be of interest to the 'inner circle'. She taught me many things that I can show you – and teach you, if you are of a mind to learn."

The empress smiled and nodded "Oh yes, my dear," she murmured. "Yes indeed. As you showed us all, a woman's power to enslave can humble the mighty – and not only in bed. But tell me – why did you humble the Horseman?"

Kia shrugged again. "For his arrogance in seeking another triumph over another of your Majesty's ladies. All men think through their genitals, so all men are vulnerable and I thought it no bad thing to use him rather than please him. For his education in knowing his place, and our amusement in watching him learn it."

The older woman regarded her a moment longer, then smiled and rose from the seat. She looked down at Kia, who was rising in her turn. "We'll speak again, my dear Kia, and longer – but not of your governess' teachings alone. We speak the same language, you and I. And I have a problem, a most vexing problem, for a mind as direct as yours to solve, but I must think on it a little further."

Wrapped in a towel Kia still managed an elegant curtsey. "Majesty. My help is yours. Whenever, wherever, and however you wish."

The empress of Constantinople put her head thoughtfully on one side then murmured, "Yes, Kia. Yes, I believe it is. But enough of 'Majesty' and 'Highness' when we of the 'inner circle' are alone. As your sisters do, you may call me Zoe."

"Majesty" said Kia, "I thank you and would seek your wisdom. Was the Horseman mute from birth?"

"No, my dear. He was perfect in every way, for the 'inner circle.' Well, in all but one way. Given his exceptional attributes, the choice of which organ to lose was offered him."

Kia laughed. "His tongue or his balls, yes?"

"Exactly, my dear. Any attendant of the inner circle must never speak of what he sees, does or knows, and a moment's pain is little in the face of so much pleasure."

"Of course, Maj . . . Zoe. Why, what else could you do?"

Zoe nodded approvingly and smiled again. "Quite. I can see we'll have much to talk about."

Oh yes Kia told herself. *Much indeed. In fact, so much that you'll not need anyone else, Majesty.*

Constantinople, early 1034.

The Scraeling wandered the streets of Constantinople, his head in a whirl as he sought to comprehend the sights, sounds and smells that assailed all his senses at once. What was it about the masses of humanity that pressed him on all sides that was different? Pausing on a street corner he listened a moment to the voices about him, and his quick ear discerned almost at once the fact that at least half a dozen different languages were being spoken about him, and he marvelled.

Yet there was more; something else. Was it the regularity of the paved streets under his feet? Was it the absence of rubbish-strewn puddles despite the short and sharp downpour that had caused him to seek shelter only moments before? No, for his three wintry weeks in the capital of the world had accustomed him not only to the miracle of drains and sewers but to lights that lit the night streets that trading might continue until buyers and sellers both were sated.

There were great churches and cathedrals, any of which would have swallowed the chapel of Les Trois Étoiles, towering over him to the heavens. There were free-running fountains that tapped the giant cisterns fed by the aqueducts bringing water from the high places. And most of all the public baths that— and there, the Scraeling had the answer to his puzzle.

Despite the throngs that jammed streets and shops, he realised, there was less odour than he had known in Hardraada's *drakkar,* that which had brought them down the well-worn, weary river-road and across the Black Sea to the city that Norsemen termed Miklagaard, Romans called Constantinople, and the ancients had known as Byzantium. It seemed to the Scraeling that the smell of sweat, farts, fish and beer had been as much of his life as the oar he tugged day after weary day when the river was too narrow or too silted to take risks with the cargo of honey, wax, furs, amber and leather that lay within the shallow deck under the feet of the oarsmen.

But not here, despite the presence of more people than he had believed existed in the entire world. Here there was nothing to offend any nostril, and he sniffed deeply as he passed the stall of a perfume seller, and again a moment later as a seller of *kibab* fanned the coals of his brazier and the smell of roasting meat brought the spittle to his mouth.

That was it. The folk of this place bathed. They were clean, even the poorest of them, and that fact alone underlined the difference between the northerners and the Byzantines in a manner that stood for all other differences also. It was, he thought, a measure of their civilisation that they did not equate strength with smell and that, for them, hair worn long might be dressed and not merely matted. And here he was among them – surely at the ends of the earth itself, and a world away from the fields, woods and hedgerows of his former life.

"You like me, noble sir? You like Irena?" broke in a voice and he came back to himself to see the heavily-rouged woman who sat by the fountain where he had paused in thought. "For five *nummia* you can have me. Only five, young sir . . ." and she gestured to an alleyway across the small square where his steps had led him.

The Scraeling flushed with embarrassment, for although his grasp of the vernacular spoken in this place was far from perfect, it was good enough for him to understand what she offered. Quickly he turned away and limped for the larger street beyond, but her voice followed him.

"All right, three! Three *nummia*, and I'll suck you first as well . . . three! . . . ah, bloody cripple!" He did not turn but lurched on, his cheeks burning. How could he have missed the gaudy clothing that whores were required by law to wear? Not as if—

A shadow fell across him and a rough hand grasped his shoulder. He spun, the dagger sliding from its sleeve-sheath into his other hand, and a familiar voice said, "Whoa, Scraeling – put away your toothpick; you're among friends!" and he looked up into the dirty and bearded face of Hrani Haakonsson and behind it the grins of Skallagrim and another three of his cronies.

"'S going on then?" inquired Hrani, "why's she cursing you . . . ah, you never paid her! Cunning little bugger, you are! Hey boys, the Scraeling here just got a free one, I reckon! Good one, Scraeling! What's she like? Tell your shipmates!"

"Bit heavy-set for my taste" mused Skallagrim, looking at the whore who, seeing their interest and scenting business, had struck a pose with a hand on her thrust-forward hips and what passed for an enticing smile on her caked face. "Aye, big arse. What about it, Scraeling? Worth a couple of coins, is she?"

"He wouldn't know!" scoffed another. "Look at him. He never had her – he'd need a plank across's arse to stop him disappearin' in that altogether!" at which there came a mighty shout of laughter that left the Scraeling wishing the ground would open and swallow him.

"One way to find out" said Hrani purposefully. "Wish me luck. Whass' the deal then Scraeling – five, was it, or three? She'll bloody work for five, so she will!" And without pausing for an answer that the Scraeling was too embarrassed to give, he strode across to the whore who smiled up at him and led him away to the alleyway.

"Beer" announced Skallagrim, "or the catspiss that passes for it here. But hang on – I been in that place over there, an' it wasn't too bad. Come on – Hrani'll be a while, 'cause he likes his money's worth. Come on – you too, Scraeling, you'll just get into trouble 'f we leave you alone – get your hand in your pocket, Karl, it's your turn."

Inside the tavern the talk was of the wonders the vikings had seen, and it quickly became clear that they were impressed. "There's twelve miles – twelve fucking miles! – of walls" said one in awe-struck tones, and another came in with, "Aye – an' there's seven of 'em too!"

"An' they calls their navy 'the wooden wall' besides" said another. But Skallagrim was less ready to be astonished.

"I dunno" and he belched before continuing. "I dunno. 'F they're the hard men you say, why'd they need raggy-arsed bastards like us, Bergr? 'Wooden walls' my arse – I'd back us in our *drakkar* against any three of 'em at once."

"Me" said Karl, "I'm a seaman an' I don't give a shit about no seven walls – but I'd like a run at the seven palaces! An' the women inside 'em" he added.

"Some of them" said Bergr breathlessly, "some of them got fountains that piss out wine. All day!"

"Aye" said Skallagrim, winking at him, "but even the Scraeling c'd do that – if you let him drink enough of it first!" There was another roar of laughter in which even the Scraeling joined and lifted his cup, but even as he did he caught looks of what he thought was annoyance and even contempt on the faces of the Byzantines who sat around them. It seemed, he thought as he sipped, that some of their hosts held the shaggy barbarians in low regard.

And why not? For the most part those new-come to the ancient city came with the dirt of their voyage upon them, they were hairy and unkempt, they smelled, and most of all they were invariably loud. None saw any need to moderate or change their ways in any fashion, for most despised the Byzantines as the strong despise the weak and mocked them as soft. *Soft they might or might not be*, thought the Scraeling as he covertly watched the faces in the background, *but what's certain is there're many of them. And their city's existed for centuries, enduring much and outlasting all who would conquer it.*

". . . merchant. Well, he was once" Skallagrim was saying, "Though he don't do much haggling these days. Good friend of Yaroslav – name of Vonskaya. Well, Harald would've come with us, but for the message that says someone from the house'd come see him this afternoon. An' that it was important. So he stayed back – there, Scraeling, your free fuck might've impressed the *leder* himself. Have to make sure we tell him, boys!"

Again the Scraeling joined in the laughter, but even as he did the thought came to him that, here in a city that was old when time began and which contained all the wonders of the world, some of Sigurdsson's crew would always recall it only as the place where the Scraeling had supposedly cheated a whore.

The Chronicle.

*T*he manner of my acceptance by Sigurdsson's crew never ceased to amaze me. From the moment that Hardraada fought Galti Bjornsson for my life I was part of their crew and, though I remained a captive it was as Hardraada had once said – where was I to go if I ran? To Hardraada I was his thrall, and to the crew I was the leder's thrall also. And that was that.

It never entered what passed for their minds that I might harbour resentment or the wish for vengeance upon them for the manner of my joining their company. Nay – strangely, for a race that made so much of blood-feud and wergild, they assumed that I would accept my fate meekly and throw in my lot with them as *if I had never seen three of them take turns on the woman who had once read a sickly and crippled child to sleep. One of the many things I despised about them was the very manner in which they acted as though they had the right both to propose and to dispose, to wreak their will and to shape the destinies of all about them according to it. Aye, that was it – and the faces of the Byzantines in that tavern that day were witness to the viking disregard for the opinion of others.*

The curious thing was that I, a thrall and 'The Scraeling' was well accepted by them all – save Thorkill, who for some reason held me in a contempt that was certainly mutual on my part for his foul mouth and an even fouler and more evil mind – and the more often I spoke up for myself the greater seemed to be my standing among them.

In part that was, I think, because of Hardraada's known protection, and in part because my service to the Norsemen's cause during the Shepetovka campaign had made me a person of some consequence, regarded by many of that band of illiterate cutthroats as a man of dazzling learning. In truth, however, I served Hardraada's cause then because I could do nothing to avert it or turn its course, and I had an end of my own, an end for which I would assist in an evil much smaller than the great aim I clutched to me as a miser guards his hoard.

So I had served Hardraada as he swept first the Oguz and then the Pechenegs from the river-basins of Kiev. Where and when I could, I eased the burdens of those taken captive or hostage, and none thought to ask the source of the orders I gave in the great depot of Shepetovka, for it was assumed that I spoke in Hardraada's name. But I took care not to ease them too much, for that was never the leder's way, and I took care even more to have ready a convincing reason why I had done so should I be asked.

But I never was, for as months turned into years Hardraada's own arrogance convinced him that I was his man, and the faultless manner of the resupply operations no less than my comprehensive accounting of the booty that flowed in with the hostages and the growing numbers of captives destined for the slave markets as the tides of war swung against the invaders only seemed to confirm that I was his man.

When we arrived in Constantine's city, then, I was far more than the "writer" who had accompanied Harald Sigurdsson to his reception at Kiev. By then he had a new name – two new names - and a new substance, so he thought it fitting that he had also a secretary to make him as different from others as my deformity made me.

Thus I was not surprised when he commanded me, on our return that day, to make myself ready in all things to accompany him to the Imperial Palace the next morning. But I was surprised – aye surprised, amazed, and disgusted to boot – when I discovered what an empress would there ask of him.

The Chalke Gate, Augustaeum Square, Constantinople, the next day.

The guard before the side-door looked at us carefully, frowned and asked, "You are expected? The lady Eudokia knows of you?" The Scraeling translated for him.

"We'd hardly be trying to get into the Triconchus Palace if we weren't expected" said Ulf patiently. "Tell him that."

"Especially with such a big, strong fellow as him to stop us" added Haldor, notorious even among the vikings for his short temper, before the Scraeling could open his mouth. "Tell him that too. And if it's that fancy helmet that stopped him hearing the *leder*'s question, tell him I can help him off with it if he wants? And see if it fits any better up his arse?"

The Scraeling swallowed, and offered a less abrasive version of Haldor's remarks. The guard looked doubtfully at the three vikings and retreated within the gatehouse to be replaced a moment later by an officer who looked up at the three huge Norsemen and waved them through the gate.

"Bid them follow" he said and set off across a great green open area where grooms were exercising ponies at the far end.

"What is this, sir?" asked the Scraeling and, mollified by his tone, the officer grunted, "Emperor's polo ground, varanger. The Tzykanisterion. Those are the royal ponies. Over there's the emperor's zoo, the aviary – that's birds to you – and behind that, the pleasure-gardens."

Catching the lift of Hardraada's eyebrow, the Scraeling translated as he scurried along beside the officer. "Where's the throne-room?" demanded Hardraada, "Ask him if it's true there's a steel tree inside it."

"In the Sigma Hall" nodded the officer, "with mechanical birds that move in the branches. And under a roof of gold" he added as an afterthought.

"Bastard's lying" grunted Ulf when the Scraeling translated. "There's not that much gold in the world."

"There may be truth in it" returned the Scraeling, "I've heard that story before."

"They're pulling your tit, then" said Ulf, "wouldn't trust these pretty boys to lie straight in bed. Come on, Scraeling – if you had all that gold, would you put it in your treasury or on a fucking roof? Think about it!" Haldor grunted assent and the Scraeling fell silent, noticing that Hardraada had not shared his lieutenants' opinion.

They arrived at another door, where they were met by the guard of the inner palace, and the officer saluted them and returned to his post. The new guard – four of them, the Scraeling noticed – led them through a maze of light and airy corridors with statues of white, grey and black marble on either hand and thick carpet under their marching feet until they paused before a double door upon which the officer scratched lightly in preference to knocking. A woman's voice spoke from within and the man disappeared through one side, leaving guard and visitors outside.

"Look at that" breathed Haldor, and the others followed his gaze to a shiny frieze that ran all the way at ceiling-height around the anteroom in which they stood. "That gold?"

"No" said the Scraeling definitely, spreading his hands. "Not that. Can't be!"

"Why not?" frowned Haldor, "why can't it be?"

"Because you keep gold in a treasury, not on a wall or a roof" explained the cripple, with a guileless look on his face. "Ask Ulf. He knows these things."

Hardraada snorted in laughter. "He's too quick for you two" he said. "Odin gave him brains when he took the leg."

"Odin gave him a big mouth too" growled Ulf, "and he should watch how he uses it."

"Temper, temper" said Hardraada, who was clearly in a genial mood. "We need his mouth this minute. Unless you've learned Greek since we set out, he's the only man we've got who speaks it. But the court speaks it too, and I was told to bring a Greek speaker – however I got one. That suggest anything to you?"

But before anyone could answer, the door swung open and the guard officer waved them through. He gestured at their helmets and retreated, closing the door as he went. Bareheaded, the vikings stepped forward into the room and stopped as a woman rose from a couch.

"I am Lady Eudokia Vonskaya" she said. "You are Harald, son of Sigurd? Whom men call 'hard-raede'?" The Norse was slow, careful and awkward on her lips and Hardraada nodded.

"I am Harald Sigurdsson, aye" he said. "What men call me is more their concern than mine. *Vess-heil*, Lady Eudokia. The stories of your beauty do you less than justice."

For in truth Eudokia was beautiful. Tiny of stature as she was, her body was perfectly formed and the gown she wore was cut to show enough of the small and pert breasts to lead a man's eye to her narrow waist and beyond to the firm and shapely hips that curved beneath it. Her skin was the fashionable creamy pallor of the Court, and in her dark hair the light from the window picked out faint streaks of henna. She looked up at the towering viking and nodded her acceptance of his compliment.

"And should the stories of your prowess in battle be as true as those touching your height and strength, son of Sigurd, you will render this Court much good service, and fairly expect much in reward. My kinsman, Yaroslav, speaks well of his Landwaster – so well that the highest in the land would speak with you." Her tongue switched suddenly to Greek. "Which of your men speaks the language of the Court?"

Hardraada's gaze swung to the Scraeling, and he answered. "I, lady. I am lord Harald's secretary, and I speak the tongue for him." He translated for Hardraada, who nodded. Eudokia turned her gaze upon the Scraeling.

"And your name, secretary?"

"My name, highness? Ah – I am the Scraeling."

"The Scraeling? You have no other name?"

"No, highness. I need no other name."

She frowned slightly and the Scraeling saw the question in her eyes before she turned back to Hardraada.

"Son of Sigurd, I am to convey you to one who would speak with you. As you see, my grasp of the tongue that was my grandfather's is not all that might be wished. So, your companions will be offered hospitality here, while you and your secretary accompany me to where that person awaits you. Now. You may lay your weapons yonder." She swung back to me and inclined her head for me to speak.

Hardraada heard her in silence, slipped sword and dagger from his belt and gestured for her to precede them. She swept to another door, the stuff of her gown rustling, and Hardraada looked at her rump and leered a moment before waving Ulf and Haldor to seat themselves and following.

The door opened through unseen hands as Lady Eudokia approached, and the party passed through another room to enter a third, where Eudokia came to a stop once the door closed behind them, and turned to look up at Hardraada.

"*Varanger*" she said, using the term that denoted a foreign mercenary, "know that you go to meet the Empress Zoe. She's a remarkable woman, born to the purple as the niece of one emperor and the daughter of the next. Don't allow her beauty to blind you to the power of her mind, for many who have taken her lightly in the past have paid with their hands for deceiving her. And sometimes for failing her. She's no woman who hears only what she wishes to hear, but a monarch who hears much from many sources and who will have her way. Thus, speak honestly and openly whatever she asks of you. You understand?"

Hardraada spoke his assent and her eyes rested on the Scraeling again for a moment before she turned, walked to the door and opened it with her own hand to allow the two men passage into a richly-furnished room beyond. "Nay, dearest Kia" came a voice from across the room, "your sources are faithful ones – in truth, he is the biggest man I have ever seen! Come forward, *varanger*. Kia?"

The voice came from yet another tiny woman seated upon another couch, holding a cat on her lap. She put the animal aside as Eudokia stepped before us and announced, "Majesty, this is Harald Sigurdsson whom his own kind call Harald *hard-raede* for the strength of his arm and his conduct in war. He wishes to take service in your majesty's armies and to submit himself to your majesty's will."

The empress looked up at Hardraada. "Does he? There is always work for such a warrior in embattled Constantinople, Kia. Does he speak Greek?"

"No, majesty. His secretary speaks for him. Scraeling, tell your master that he may greet the empress."

But before the Scraeling could speak, Hardraada had dropped to his knees before the couch, saying "Scraeling, tell the empress Zoe that she shines like the sun over all things in her city, and that the swords of my soldiers are hers to command as she sees fit."

Zoe's gaze swung to the Scraeling as he did so, and she nodded before rising. She rose, stepped closer to the Norse giant whose height even on his knees was only a thought less than hers, and looked deep into his eyes. "Secretary" she said, "tell your master that I have many soldiers and countless swords. What I require is a man to do my bidding as I command. As I command in all things. All. Will he be that man?"

Hardraada heard the words without comment, then he bowed his head, reached down for the hem of the empress' gown and raised it to his lips. "Tell the empress, Scraeling, that some oaths need no words to give them life" he said, and stared forthrightly into Zoe's eyes again. "But aye – I am her man in all things. All. Tell her so."

Zoe listened, her head on one side, then reached out a hand and toyed a moment with a lock of Hardaada's thick yellow hair. "That is a mighty oath indeed" she mused, "and may require much of you. Much, aye, and in ways that have nothing to do with swords and soldiery. How say you?"

"I say – let her majesty command me" said Hardraada, "and prove me at the one time."

A look passed between the empress and Lady Eudokia, before Zoe put a hand under Hardraada's arm and urged him to his feet. She looked at the figure that towered over her, for she was only a thought taller than Eudokia, and said archly, "Hmm. Kia, I am tempted to 'prove' him in a manner he may not have considered. What do you think?"

Eudokia giggled. "Majesty, majesty – business first, pleasure after. Isn't that the way of it? And should he not earn any reward you may be considering?"

"No" said Zoe sharply, as Hardraada looked towards the Scraeling, "leave that, secretary. But tell me this – is your master truly named – ah, what was his byname, dearest Kia?"

"*Hard-raede*, majesty. It means 'hard-speaking' or 'ruthless' in the Norse tongue."

"Hard - raad - a" said the empress, whose soft and liquid speech could not encompass the throaty and guttural vowels of Norse. "Hard-raada. Tell me, secretary – is your master truly a hard man as he has been named?"

"Aye, majesty, he is. A hard man in all things" said the Scraeling and then, greatly daring, for his quick mind had caught the drift of the ladies' thinking, "and in all ways".

The women looked at each other and broke, as one, into peals of laughter. His patience at an end, Hardraada demanded, "Scraeling, what is this? Speak!"

"*Leder,* have patience for the moment." Mindful of how much Eudokia understood, he added, "Her majesty is considering the matter of your employment, and seeks reassurance of your worthiness. Lady Eudokia knows much of you, and is advising her."

Turning to the empress, the Screaling met her lifted eyebrow with, "Majesty, my commander would know what you wish of him. He is eager to serve you in any way you wish."

"Very well" said Zoe, clearly making up her mind. She waved to seats nearby. "Bid your master sit, and do so yourself. I commanded that a Greek speaker be brought because I want no error of understanding in what I would have him know. Speak faithfully and well, secretary, if you would keep your tongue." And in the instant, the face that had giggled in contemplation of testing Hardraada's manhood turned ice-cold, and the Screaling swallowed hard and nodded.

"Now" said Zoe, looking directly at Hardraada where he perched on a chair that creaked under his weight, "I am the descendant of emperors and have ruled in my own right these six years" and the Screaling murmured in his master's ear as she spoke. "My husband, emperor through our marriage, is old and cannot give me the child I seek to preserve the throne of my ancestors. I need a younger man. You understand, secretary? You take my meaning?"

"Majesty" nodded the Screaling. "I understand, and have spoken your words and meaning to my master here." Zoe contemplated him a moment, her face like stone, and went on.

"But, *varanger,* the man who sires my child must be of royal blood – either through a marriage with me or in his own right. And I cannot marry, for I am not a widow. The emperor, Romanos, is old, as I have said, and feeble besides. Very well. Let us come to it."

"*Varanger* – I seek a man who will make me a widow. Beyond that, I seek a man who will make me pregnant. He may be one and the same man, or he may not." Zoe leaned forward, and there was no mirth in her face as she asked, "How hard are you, Hard-raada? How hard?"

The Screaling's voice faltered a moment as he realised the enormity of the empress' words, and hastily he cleared his throat and continued. When he had finished, Hardraada raised his head in the silence left by Zoe's hanging question and said, "Tell her majesty two things, Screaling. Tell her that I'm half-brother to a king of Norway, and tell her also that I'm harder than any other servant she has. In any way she wishes – for as I said, I'm hers to command. And that's the word of Harald *hard-raede*, so speak it exactly as I have done."

Zoe clasped her hands together when the Scraeling fell silent and said "Then it is decided, *varanger*. Listen well. The emperor's skin pains him, for it is thin and chafes easily. Because of this he spends each evening in his bath before he retires. Nay –" she said as she saw the question form on Hardraada's lips "– we no longer sleep together, nor have we done these many months. It is his custom, when in his bath, to be attended by two manservants of the bedchamber who await his pleasure within call. His accustomed servants will become ill on the third day from today, and I will see to it that others are appointed in their place. As a dutiful wife should." She paused and glanced searchingly at Hardraada.

"You will come here in the afternoon of that day, attended only by he who is here now, and you will wait in a place to be shown you until the emperor goes to his bath. You will then be brought to the door of the bathing chamber, where none will see you or disturb you. When you have done what you are sworn to do, you will make your way back to your place of waiting. And, Harald my hard man, each day is precious, as I have said. You may look for the reward you earn almost immediately."

Hardraada inclined his head, and the Scraeling saw that he struggled to contain his excitement. "Majesty, all will be as you say, and I—" he said, but Zoe broke in on him.

"Hard Harald, are you Christian?" she enquired, and the shock on Hardraada's face was plain to see.

"Majesty . . . I . . . my mother, Queen Aasta, had me baptised. Aye. Why, majesty?"

Zoe waved her hand impatiently. "Baptism has little to do with anything. On what things do you swear, *varanger*? What is holy to you? The Bible? Nay – I have it. I know what things are holy to your kind, for my Kia here has made enquiry of her family's own kin in the lands of the Rus." She reached to a low table and brought from it a dagger curved after the Byzantine manner. She laid it across her hands and held them out to Hardraada.

"Swear, *varanger*, swear on steel and hilt that you will be true to me and to my charge given you. Swear this by your god." The challenge hung in the air of the room like thunder before a storm, and all in it held their breath.

Harald Hardraada reached out and laid a hand on the dagger held in an empress' hands. "On steel and hilt, by hand and haft, by edge and point I swear before Odin Allfather that I will keep faith with you in any and all matters of your service."

Zoe let out her breath in a long hiss. "Then it is done. Here, *varanger*, take this dagger and wear it that its sight may remind you of the moment you became the hard man of a queen. Until your queen reminds you . . . in other ways." Eudokia's smothered giggle broke the tension within the room and all laughed.

"Harald Hard-raada, remember this day always as that upon which an empress poured wine for you with her own hand. For the first time, at least. For I would hear of your campaigns for our dear friend Yaroslav, Constantinople's shield in the north . . ."

An hour later the northerners took their leave in charge of a silent and unsmiling manservant, and Kia turned to Zoe as the door closed behind the cripple. "Done, my queen?"

"Done, my Kia. Hardraada will not fail us. He will serve."

Kia smiled lazily. "Yes, Zoe – he will serve, because he sees himself serving you as a stallion serves a mare. You! 'I am half-brother to a king of Norway'" she mimicked, "aye, and doubtless he was as sweaty and hairy as the rest of them also."

Zoe yawned, stretched and reached for a rope pull on the wall behind her. Half of the thick panelling on the rear wall slid back and eight men of the imperial guard clashed to attention in an ante-room beyond as their officer stepped into the room and saluted. "My thanks, Isaac Comnenus" smiled Zoe, "but the talents of my loyal guard will not be required this afternoon. Your empress blesses you."

"Heaven-born one" said the officer, saluting again, "may you live forever" and he stepped backwards and closed the panelling on his handpicked squad of killers.

The Chronicle.

*A*t that time I had lived among some of the most dangerous and violent men in the world for over three years, and had my life at Les Trois Étoiles not tumbled into red and bloody ruin I would have taken the tonsure on my eighteenth birthday. Instead, I spent some of that day listening to a beautiful woman prove to me that evil is not the sole preserve of violent and pagan men, for in less than an hour of it the Empress Zoe – daughter, niece and wife of emperors as she was – had turned me into her accomplice in regicide.

For that is what it was. After all consideration of her reasons for wishing her husband dead was finished and done with, I could not rid myself of the truth that she proposed to kill her husband before God, and an emperor consecrated before the same God. And the tool she had chosen meant that the emperor Romanos was but a dead man walking, for on the day appointed, Harald the Ruthless would let nothing stay him from seeing that he died.

I had looked long and hard at the empress while she and Hardraada spoke, and I saw in her the same ruthlessness that drove the man I hated. For all that I had heard her reason for taking another husband, I did not believe it. No – she wanted her husband dead for her own end, and not that of her city and state, I was sure. And if that were true, then not only would Hardraada not sire her child, but he would be lucky to survive the murder of her husband – and I with him.

Now there was irony. My closeness to Hardraada would serve to place me near enough to destroy him with all his kind when the chance came, but if Zoe intended treachery she would destroy me also. And much I doubted if Hardraada would stop to consider that, for I had looked hard at him also as he knelt there before the Vixen of Constantinople and I saw clearly that he was thinking with his cock no less than had Griss Bjornsson. And that was not normally the way of Harald the Ruthless. But when a man sees himself either upon a throne or between a queen's legs, how "normal" is the prospect of both at once?

Why did I not merely stand back from this? Why did I not simply run, and leave Hardraada to suffer what I was sure would be Zoe's treachery? For it had occurred to me, certainly. But leaving aside my visibility as a foreigner and a cripple – even if I was surely not the only such in this teeming city – to do so would mean abandoning what I now saw as my life's work.

For if Hardraada alone died, another just as evil would surely come from a number that included Ulf Ospaksson and Haldor Snorreson, or even he whom

I thought of as Thorkill the Foul, and in such case the viking curse would still lie upon the world. And then, how many more Clothildes would follow? No. Hardraada was the key not only to his own destruction but to that of all his kind, and my task was as clear as it was twofold.

Somehow, I needed both to see him safely through the murder of an emperor and also to let him know that I had kept his back the while, for that would surely increase his trust in me. So I thought hard and spoke.

"*Leder!*" said the Scraeling, and Hardraada turned his head. "Aye? What is it, Scraeling?"

"*Leder*, humour me a moment." And in Greek, he commanded, "Fellow, hang on a minute! Come here!"

The manservant turned obligingly and stepped towards him, and the Scraeling spoke evenly in Norse – "Strike, *leder*. Kill this man now. Now!" and Hardraada gaped at him.

"Scraeling, are you mad? What . . . what . . .?" But the Scraeling's eyes were locked with those of the servant, and he shook his head.

"No, *leder* no matter. This fellow understands no Norse. Didn't even twitch." And he bade the guide sit before beckoning his giant master to one side and dropping his voice.

"*Leder*, this is dangerous. It's dangerous all ways. There's more in it than we've heard, and the empress is holding back."

"Scraeling, she wants her husband killed and I'm going to kill him. There's danger all right – danger for Romanos. Look Scraeling, it's easy. She's going to make it easy for us, so don't pee yourself. Ulf and Haldor'll tell you the same."

"That's just it, *leder*. If you'll take my advice, you'll say nothing to either of them."

Hardraada scowled ominously. "Nothing? To two of my most trusted? Why?"

"Because of what they might say to others, *leder*. Less said the better, yes?"

"Scraeling, those two would think twice about telling Odin what they didn't think he should know. As I say – don't pee yourself!"

The Scraeling shook his head. "*Leder*, I'm not saying they'd blab lightly. But just now, you spoke a name best left unspoken. And you didn't think twice about it, did you?" He spread his hands persuasively. "This bloke speaks no Norse, aye, but what if he heard a *varanger* speak the emperor's name three days before he gets topped? See what I mean?"

Hardaada frowned down at the Scraeling and turned to look at the manservant, who was back on his feet and waiting. "You're serious, aren't you?" he asked, and made up his mind. "Right – you and I talk this over later. Ulf and Haldor get told . . . for now, anyway, let's see . . . the empress wants to recruit a company of *varangers* for her own service. That do?"

"For now, aye *leder*. It would explain much of your later . . . closeness . . . to the empress."

Hardraada grinned. "And I'm looking forward to that, Scraeling!"

The Scraeling motioned to the manservant. "Lead on, fellow" and to Hardraada, "*Leder*, you do know she's fifty, don't you?"

Hardraada stopped and swung to the other. "Fifty? You joke, Scraeling. The woman we just left? Fifty? Never!"

"On my life, *leder*, Zoe the Macedonian is nearer sixty than fifty. In fact she's fifty-six years of age. Her father had two daughters Zoe and Theodora, and he wouldn't let men anywhere near them until he couldn't ignore the fact that he was dying. Well, would you, as an emperor who had no son? Ask yourself – what does a female succession mean? In practical terms? Eh?"

Hardraada frowned. "How do you know this?"

"I speak to people. And I listen when I'm in a wineshop or a bazaar, because you can't ever know too much about your enemy."

"Scraeling, these people aren't enemies. They're friends. One of 'em's just made me the kind of offer you dream about."

"Yes. Why? You think she hasn't got hard men of her own? That's what I want to talk about later. And as for them not being enemies – maybe they're not yet. But maybe they will be one day."

The manservant ushered them through a door and Haldor and Ulf looked up from the table where they sat. "Nearly came looking for you" growled Haldor. "I don't trust the scraelings 'n this place – they're all too bloody oily for me. Notice how they never look you in the eye?"

"Nay, Haldor – that's only because a big upstanding chap like you's got eyes so far above theirs" returned Hardraada, the picture of good humour. "Anyway – no way to talk about the folk who'll make you rich, is it? Come on – we're leaving. Scraeling, tell this whoreson to show us out."

The imperial apartments, the next day.

Zoe smoothed an unguent into the skin under her jaw, looked at Kia in the mirror and asked, "Is it really necessary my Kia? And him such a . . . such a hard man too? I wonder how hard he truly is?" and she giggled. "Don't tell me the thought hasn't crossed your mind, you minx! That I wouldn't believe!"

Kia grimaced. "Well . . . aye, Zoe. Aye, it did when I met him. He's very strong-looking – big hands, big nose, long fingers. Infallible guide, in my book" And she giggled in her turn. "But does it matter? When we've got the Horseman . . . in hand, so to speak? And the Norseman, like every other man, thinks through his cock."

Zoe laughed. "Aye, as you say and truly enough. But for all that . . . a change never comes amiss, does it? And there's the thought that he might be able to do more for me than the Horseman ever could. My intended's healthy enough, that's true, but Hard Harald is younger . . . ah . . . more virile? And you know why I do all this" she ended, wiping her fingers.

"Aye lady. You guard your youth for your city and your people, that you may produce the heir of Basil of blessed memory."

"Blessed by all except the Bulgars he slew in thousands" returned Zoe, unscrewing another lid and peering into a mirror at her eyes. "What do you think of this cream? It seems to work, but . . . oh, the smell! Still – smell shouldn't bother me if I'm thinking about bedding a *varanger*, should it?"

"Majesty" said Kia firmly, "You can't afford to let Hardraada live. He must die after doing what he's sworn to do. As we discussed. Comnenus and his guards will cut him down – just too late. And you know why!"

"Yes, yes" sighed Zoe. "Comnenus can't do this – although he would – because he's known to be my man. But a stranger, now, a *varanger* disappointed at not being offered the military appointments he thinks his fame and station merit . . . aye. I understand. But it's still a waste!"

"Just so. You're loved by the people, dearest Zoe, and rightly so. But they won't stomach the killing of an emperor, even a half-man such as Romanos. Not even by a niece of the Bulgar-Slayer and the daughter of Constantine. But be of good cheer, my lady. If thinking of Hardraada brings forth a . . . a royal itch, I'll have the Horseman fetched to scratch it. Shall I?"

And at a languid wave, Kia reached to a bell-pull. But the servant who appeared in answer bore a tray, on which lay a folded piece of paper.

"Lady" he said, bowing, "This was delivered a moment ago, for you. He who brought it awaits." Kia nodded, took the paper and read:

High-born One,
The secretary of one whom you met yesterday would speak with you on a custom dear to your grandsire's heart.

The Scraeling.

Kia frowned and turned the paper over. "There is no more?" she asked, and the servant shook his head. "Nothing, Lady Eudokia."

"This person" she said, "a *varanger*? With a twisted leg?" and at the man's assent she turned to the empress.

"Majesty, it may be as well if I were to see to this matter immediately. By your leave?" and on receiving it she instructed the servant to show the messenger to an ante-room and then to summon the Magyar to the royal presence.

"I can't imagine what this fellow wants" Kia said, holding out the paper to Zoe once the door had closed behind the servant, "but anything or anyone connected with what was discussed yesterday . . . ?"

Zoe nodded thoughtfully. "Even so, Kia. In your hands, then. See what he wants – and grant it. This job must be done."

Kia swept into the ante-room where the Scraeling waited, and the young man rose awkwardly to his feet.

"Lady Eudokia" he said, "thank you for . . ." but she cut him short.

"Yesterday, fellow, you were told to return in three days. Why are you here? And what did you mean by your note?"

"Lady, I could not risk your refusal. I referred to your grandfather to ensure that you would see me. Look first at this. I wrote it in Greek" and he held forth a scroll.

Kia looked at him for a long moment until he looked away beneath her gaze, then she took the proffered scroll, waved him to a seat and took one herself. Opening the scroll she found herself looking at a lengthy column of verse:

> *The king's sharp sword lies clean and bright,*
> *Prepared in foreign lands to fight:*
> *Our ravens croak to have their fill,*

The wolf howls from the distant hill.
Our brave king is to Russia gone, --
Braver than he on earth there's none;
His sharp sword will carve many a feast
To wolf and raven in the East.

Where Ellif was, one heart and hand
The two chiefs had in their command;
In wedge or line their battle order
Was ranged by both without disorder.
The eastern Vindland men they drove
Into a corner; and they move
The Lesians, although ill at ease,
To take the laws their conquerors please.

Before the cold sea-curling blast
The cutter from the land flew past,
Her black yards swinging to and fro,
Her shield-hung gunwale dipping low.
The king saw glancing o'er the bow
Constantinople's metal glow
From tower and roof, and painted sails
Gliding past towns and wooded vales.

Kia looked up, and her voice was sharp with anger. "What does this mean? Why are you wasting my time, secretary? And what is it?"

"Your pardon, lady. Your grandfather knew this as a saga; it's the way of the Norsemen to remember their deeds in song and verse. Especially is this so of their great ones – their kings and famous warriors. And last night I heard yet more, composed by their *skald*, but not written down, for that is not their way. But I have written it, lady. See – " and he held forth a smaller scroll.

Behind the walls of Miklagaard
Was offered work for a warrior hard
In service of a foreign queen
And she the fairest ever seen.
A king swore oath on haft and steel
To all her enemies would he deal

The blow on which feasts Odin's ravens
And bring home her cargoes safe to haven.

Before his axe did eagles fall
And feasted wolves and ravens all
Because his armies gave her sway
His queen would ever have her way
No man alive might stay her word
For fear of Harald's flashing sword
Thus did she of beauteous face
Reign supreme within that place.

"How" said Kia, her voice shaking with anger, "did your master's promise to my queen become known? How?"

The Scraeling spread his hands. "Lady, a *varanger* company is not as your army. It's a band of free men, all equal under *varanger* law, who freely follow any leader they wish. He has power over them so far as they wish to be governed, and if any don't then they leave the band and none may hold them. This is their way."

Kia frowned. "And? Answer my question!"

"Because this is so" continued the Scraeling, "not to answer the questions of such as the two lieutenants Haldor and Ulf – you recall? – who waited while the empress favoured us, would have aroused suspicion. So my *leder* sought my opinion and I counselled him to tell of an empress' invitation to him to form a *varanger* company for her use alone. And this was given out. The rest – the rest is the *skald's* imagination and his flight of fancy."

"It's dangerous!" snapped Kia, and she stamped her foot in anger. "When Romanos dies, any listening to this will know who, and why! *Before his axe did eagles fall* leaves nothing to anyone's imagination, you Norse fool! Can this . . . this *skald* . . . be silenced?"

"Not easily, lady. A *skald* is . . . forgiven much, for he is the good fortune of a warband. He's usually older, aye, and less of a warrior than the others. But he holds the stories and tells the legends for all to hear. But, after the deed is done . . . I hold some sway with him, lady, for like Askell I'm no warrior. Not as the others of Hardraada's company are. And as I say, after the deed, I can prevail on him – as will Hardraada – not to sing of this nor admit it to the others."

Kia said nothing, but turned back to the scroll. When she looked up, the glance she sent the Scraeling would have melted pitch. "Scraeling, no word of this must leak out – now or ever, through *skald* or drunken varanger or . . . however. Should it do so, agents of the lady I serve will find the source and silence it – together with kith and kin, family and friends. This I promise you!"

The Scraeling bowed. "Lady, I agree with you in all things. That's why I've come here today, not knowing if you would see me but trusting that you would. And if you would hear me a little further, I have an idea that may set your fears at rest . . ." and on receiving her nod he spoke on for a few moments before falling silent while she thought.

Eventually she looked up and nodded. "Yes, Scraeling. Yes. I like that. As will my lady. Make it so – just in that fashion." She paused, thinking, and then:

"My lady is . . . in audience . . . at this moment, and I will report this to her later. But for the moment – wine?" and an astonished Scraeling accepted.

Kia poured wine for them both. "Come here, secretary. I would know more of you. I would know how you are able to read and write our language. I would know why you don't smell of bears and fish, as do other *varangers*. I would know of your affliction. I would know all. So raise your cup, *varanger* who thinks before he acts, and speak."

The Chronicle.

*B*ut I took care to tell her only what I thought she might safely know, for from the moment of our first meeting I had believed Lady Eudokia Vonskaya to be one of the most dangerous of all the dangerous people I knew. For at our first meeting, and while Hardraada and his lieutenants offered her greetings and let their imaginations dwell upon what her clothing concealed, before I lowered my eyes as befitting one who knew his place, I had seen the flaw in her doll-like beauty.

Eudokia's eyes were black as coal and as hard as the flint we used to strike sparks from the steel in our fire-boxes. Recall that I, no warrior, had lived years among men of sudden cruelty and unpredictable violence, and believe that I had learned to see menace within as well as without so that, for me, the beautiful woman sitting across the low table was as a serpent whose venom might be no less fatal because of its small size.

So I told her a tale that was enough of a mixture of truth and fiction to withstand the scrutiny I thought she would give it. That I had been afflicted from birth and that because of God's palpable displeasure I had been given into the care of a monastery, where I had been mocked, humiliated and used as an example of the wages of original sin. That I had survived the viking attack upon the monastery because of the insistence of its brothers that I sleep in the stables and in no Christian building. That I had been suffered to learn to read, write and count only that I might one day know for myself the word of a generous and forgiving God.

And, I went on, being mindful of my dwelling-place I had been careful always to keep myself clean through bathing, even though the brethren saw, in that, further evidence of a wayward, wicked and sinful nature. Thus I had been glad enough to cast in my lot with Hardraada's band when chance offered.

Throughout my recitation of a story that I largely made up as I went, Eudokia's black eyes never wavered from me, and I grew uncomfortable under them. So it was with relief that I heard her ask me, again, what it was I did among Hardraada's band. I answered that I kept all manner of records, held and disbursed money among the men according to what each received and spent, and used a readiness to learn foreign tongues as the Norsemen would not, to help the band pass where it would. She considered that, nodded and a moment after, gave me the shock of my life.

"When you spoke just now of how it is among the *varangers*" she said, rising, "you spoke of 'their ways', of 'he' and of 'the others' and of 'them'. You are not Norse?"

And the Scraeling answered, dry-mouthed at that reminder of how dangerous Eudokia might be, "No, my lady. I was born in Brittany, a country of the Narrow Seas, and the band took me from there."

She nodded. "And you went with them out of hate for the brothers who had abused you. And you serve the band – but you have not become one of them, I think. Not yet." And he mumbled something, for she probed too closely for his comfort. At last she appeared to make up her mind.

"Scraeling" she said, the eyes boring again into me. "There are two doors from this room and one is locked. Go now and bar the door you were shown through."

Wondering, the Scraeling rose and did so, but when he turned back to the centre of the room he stood frozen in shock.

Eudokia had removed skirt and tunic while his back was turned and now stood before him in nothing but sandals, her naked body glowing.

"Come here, Scraeling" she ordered, and he could do nothing but move to her, dazed. "You have never had a woman" she said, and it was not a question although the Scraeling shook his head in answer.

She reached out and loosed the cord to let the Scraeling's breeches fall and when he saw her look, first, at his in-turned and twisted leg he turned away to hide it from her in some manner, but she stilled him by reaching for the member that had sprung rigid. She glanced at the Scraeling and licked her lips while he went scarlet with embarrassment.

"That is about to change" she said. "How perverse of God, first to punish you for original sin and then to equip you so wonderfully for committing it, Scraeling."

Hardraada's quarters.

The Scraeling sighed. "No, *leder*. Put it from you. Not a blade. Remember what we agreed on last night – how open we are to treachery? All Zoe needs do is set her bodyguard on us after you slit the emperor's throat and before we can get clear – then she has a dead husband and the bodies of those who murdered him. You and me that is. Dead, and not able to embarrass anyone, right?"

"Wrong" said Hardraada confidently. "She needs me for the second part – getting her with child. She's not going to kill me, is she?"

"*Leder*, I'll tell you again what I know from street gossip. Zoe is putting horns on her husband under the very palace roof with someone called Michael. Michael the Paphlagonian. He's the brother of the chief eunuch of the women's quarters, he's half her age and – the gossip says – hung like a donkey. *Leder*, Zoe might fancy a great big *varanger*, but she doesn't need him. She can use you any way she wants, get her way and get clear."

"If the gossips know all this" snapped Hardraada, "why doesn't Romanos?"

"Good question" returned the Scraeling. "I asked it too. What I'm told is that he doesn't want it to be true, and what an emperor wants he gets.

That's half the opinion. The other half is that he doesn't care who's fucking Zoe as long as he doesn't have to. He wasn't keen on marrying her in the first place, and they can't abide each other so he's making the best of a bad job. Take your pick. But when you think about whether or not Zoe'll keep her word, think about it from her viewpoint, not what we want to be true."

"You know, you've changed all of a sudden" said Hardraada, squinting down at his secretary, "never heard you say that before."

"Say what?" asked the Scraeling.

"'Fuck'" said Hardraada, "and 'hung like a donkey' come to think of it. Not like you."

"No mystery there" said the Scraeling, colouring despite himself. "I have to listen to Thorkill much more than you do. You can tell him to bugger off anytime you like, but I'm stuck with him and that other foulmouthed arsehole, Sweyn. Between them they'd make Christ get back on the cross of his own free will, wouldn't they?"

Hardraada exploded in laughter. "Convent boy, eh? Wish those nuns could hear you now!"

So do I, you thing, thought the Scraeling, *but not for the same reason.* Aloud, however, he said, "There is a way, *leder*. In fact, I've already fixed it and all it needs is for you to agree."

"Taking a bit much on yourself, aren't you?" said Hardraada, much less genially, "since when do you make decisions for me, *krøpling*?"

"As you wish" said the Scraeling, "but that's what assistants do. They assist. And's not as if I had anyone else to discuss it with. Want to know how I fixed it?"

"Go on then. But it'll need to be good."

So the Scraeling described how he had written five stanzas of a saga, making two of them contentious enough to cause the empress alarm ". . . because the people won't let her kill an anointed emperor. No – not even her, and they love her almost enough – but not quite" and blamed Askell for an excess of zeal that only Hardraada or himself could correct.

"If, of course, we live through the emperor's death" he finished. "But – and here's what got Eudokia interested – we can make it look natural, so there's nothing for anyone to answer to –" and he went on to relate the rest of his conversation with Eudokia. "So that's why, *leder* a blade of any sort won't do. Not even the fancy one Zoe gave you, see?"

Hardraada played with his beard while he thought. "So – Romanos dies and Zoe gets what she wants. I get what I want – Zoe on my side. I might even get Zoe on her back, because I still don't believe you, Scraeling. Which of these oily bastards wouldn't want a sturdy Norse child? And there's no risk; nothing for Zoe to play us false over, so she can keep her options as wide open as her legs. If I'm lucky. Yes, well done Scraeling – I like it."

Odd, thought the Scraeling, *how much like Kia he sounds in those words. But not so odd really, for neither thinks of any but themselves and their own ambition.*

The Chronicle.

My walk from the palace back to the tavern where Hardraada's crew had found lodging had been even slower than my shuffling gait would normally have it, but I have always remembered it as each of us remembers his, and probably her, first swive. For although Kia had sucked almost every vestige of strength from me, from the moment she had pushed me down on to the couch and straddled me until she commanded me to dress and be on my way, I felt still the buoyancy that goes with admission to a state once denied.

I was under no illusion, even then, that Kia had acted as she did from fondness for me. Oh no. She had admitted me to her body only in order to pry me loose from Hardraada's band at her will, and I knew that even as she reached for me. But she didn't know that I knew, and that was a measure of my triumph in deceiving her even as I was deceiving Hardraada. Kia would consider herself able to make Hardraada dance through me and that suited me well enough, for I would enjoy whatever measures we trod also. Her actions gladdened me in other ways also, for what she did suggested that her assassins would live beyond the deed. But more of that later.

"There" she murmured, bending low over me, "now we can begin" and I felt something inside her tighten hard around me before she began to move against me, squeezing and relaxing, squeezing and relaxing and refusing to let me go soft so that, as I looked up at her face above the taut breasts, in a few moments I felt myself quicken. She felt it at the same time and her face relaxed a moment, but I have always held that it was triumph and not tenderness, for to her it was only a well-practised result.

However it was, though, all my being seemed concentrated in my loins as a fire began there to send its heat throughout my body and it built and built until I forced my hips up, lifting her slightness into the air and forcing her to grab at the back of the couch where we lay. Yet the tempo of her squeezing increased until the fire racing up and down my throbbing member demanded release, and at the very moment I could bear it no longer I forced open my slitted eyes and saw, in an instant's clarity, that she was watching me intently. I opened my mouth to plead for release but my words were drowned in a great wail from her then all was fire again as I heaved her back into the air and spurted huge and helplessly into her very depths for long, long moments.

Kia collapsed across me, and neither of us spoke until she murmured, "Screaling, I give you to the world of women. But not yet. Not until I've felt the power of you again. And again. And yet again." And I might have believed her, had I not seen the calculation so clear in her face in the moment of climax.

Twice more did Kia 'feel my power' that day. I was young then, and the young do these things, but if I took anything from it beyond the pleasure, which was undoubted, it was the conviction – also undoubted – that the beautiful Lady Eudokia was a born, practised and enthusiastic harlot.

But, with all of it, Kia gave me my introduction to that particular pleasure of the flesh, and if only half of her protestations concerning her own pleasure were genuine, then our tryst was a good one for both of us.

But it was a long way home nonetheless.

The Chalke Gate, Augustaeum Square, Constantinople, two days later.

The Screaling announced to the Imperial guardsman at the entrance to the Palace that the Lady Eudokia had sent for his master and the man nodded.

"I remember your master" he said, "for he's not easily missed. Only two of you this time?"

"As you can see" returned the Screaling. "A quiet watch this afternoon, friend?"

"As ever" said the guard, opening the gate to let them through, "but better'n the ballot for service against the Turks out in the islands though."

"What islands?" asked the Screaling, who believed that no knowledge was ever wasted.

"Greek islands. Haven't you heard there's a war on down there?" returned the guardsman, waving another forward to his station and falling into step with the *varangers* as they set off across the courtyard. "It's all turning to shit though 'cause the Turks're giving Maniakes a real hiding."

"What's all that, Scraeling?" in Hardraada's rumble.

"Fellow here's telling me about the campaigns in the islands. Turks are winning against . . . ah, Maniakes . . . he the general?" to the soldier.

"Aye. But he's Romanos' man, an' fights Romanos' way. Useless as tits on a tomcat. Anyway – Imperial Guard don't go anywhere the emperor or empress don't, so I'll be seeing a bit more of you. Right – through that door over there, and they'll take you on."

When he was out of earshot, Hardraada muttered to the Scraeling, "Now, remind me, Eudokia'll meet us, making out that I'm her lover as far as the guard's concerned. So why're you here?"

"I'm the cover the guard will see right through" explained the Scraeling patiently. "That's why I'm carrying these scrolls. No-one in his right mind would believe that a big handsome *varanger* like you is actually going to spend a bit of time talking ship-building with a beautiful woman – but that's the story that'll 'explain' why we're in there for hours. Yes?"

Hardraada nodded, and a slow grin passed over his face. "And if I get really lucky" he said, "I might need all night too!"

Once again they were passed into the palace buildings by the inner guard until they came again to the ante-room where they were met by Eudokia. She came forward to meet them, and nothing in her face or greeting gave any clue of how the Scraeling had last looked upon her.

"Your purpose holds?" she asked, looking all the way up at Hardraada, and the giant nodded.

"Aye, lady. And the empress – does hers hold also?"

"Of course. Now – you have considered what the Scraeling and I discussed? Aye? Then recall, Hardraada, that if there's no reason for enquiry into the manner of the emperor's death, it will be well . . . for all." *And thus no reason for you to play us false, is what she's not saying*, thought the Scraeling, but in truth he had already decided that such would be the case, for if Zoe still contemplated treachery, Kia's performance of his last visit would not have been necessary. *Proof*, thought the Scraeling, *of Lady Eudokia's influence with the empress.*

"You'll wait here until this evening" continued the tiny beauty, this time glancing round to include the Scraeling, and the eyes were as hard and cold as ever, "when you'll be sent for. My lady and I will be visible, as always, so that none will later connect us with any of tonight's events. You are to follow, without question or speech, he who comes to lead you to the royal apartments. He's a low-born fellow, a slave of mine." And she looked directly at Hardraada again as she said those words, and he nodded at the Scraeling's translation.

"After" she continued, "you'll be brought back to a place where I will come again to you. Are there questions? No? Very well. Then – food and wine await you on that table" and she gestured to a corner. "Until later." And she was gone, an emperor's fate sealed.

Hardraada let out his breath in a silent whistle. "How'd you like to wrestle that, Scraeling? Bet she wouldn't let you get away without paying!" For the story of the supposed triumph over the whore of Ixos Square had gone the rounds of his band, to its great amusement and an even greater increase in the Scraeling's credit.

"No" he went on, "if I didn't have royal pussy waiting for me, I'd rattle her myself. Still – once Zoe's decided she can't live without what I can give her, I can put in a good word for my faithful secretary and Cunning Man, eh? Want her before or after Haldor? You know, you sometimes piss him off 'cause he's not as quick-thinking as you? You rattling her would really burn him, 'cause he's been talking about her since we came here last time!"

Under the circumstances the Scraeling found it quite easy to shrug his offer aside with some remark about Haldor needing the help more than he did, at which the viking roared with laughter. *If you only knew how little I jest,* thought the secretary, amazed at Hardraada's ability to dwell on such things in the time before he set out to kill God's anointed.

Suddenly he sobered. "Food, aye. Wine, no. Wine later – but we need a clear head now. What are these, Scraeling?" He indicated a chess set upon a side table, and the Scraeling explained that it was a game of warfare. That got his attention and, while he ate with an appetite that the other could not match, Hardraada examined the pieces as the Scraeling explained how they moved.

The scratch at the door came halfway through the third game, and despite themselves their hands went to their dagger-hilts as the door opened and a manservant appeared. "Lords" he said, bowing, "I am commanded to ask you to follow me".

The two *varangers* glanced at each other and arose to follow the man out and through a maze of corridors and rooms, in one of which he stopped and lit a taper from a votive candle burning in a wall-niche. The next doorway gave on to a stone-lined corridor where he took a torch from a sconce on the wall, lit it from the taper and set off down the corridor that led, clearly below ground level, for a hundred yards. At length he stepped sideways into a niche and cautiously opened a door within it after crushing the torch beneath his heel. The three men found themselves in a room identical to those they had come through save for a heavy door set flush with the wall and the guide looked round at the Norsemen.

"This is . . .?" murmured the Scraeling, and the man leaned closer to him.

"The royal bathing room, lord. I am to wait here for your return, aye?"

The Scraeling nodded and waved him aside. He stretched up to Hardraada and spoke softly in Norse. "We're here. Let's go in swiftly, for there may be a draught as we open the door. If we're betrayed, it won't matter how fast we go in, 'cause we're dead anyway."

"Right, Scraeling. Me first" came back Hardraada, and he stepped to the door. "Ready?" And on receiving the Scraeling's nod he opened the door as wide as needful and slid quickly through. For all his bulk, the Norse giant moved like a shadow and the Scraeling followed in his wake and drew the door to behind him, to find himself face to face with a heavy drape or wall hanging designed to keep out draughts. Hardraada held up a warning hand and both men froze, listening.

There was no sound in the chamber, and then there came a dry cough. The cough of an elderly man, followed by a faint splash and the squeak of wet flesh upon tile as he moved in the bath. The Scraeling saw, slightly to one side, the edge of a curtain and he nodded towards it. Hardraada nodded back, and the Scraeling moved the edge a fraction and peered cautiously round it.

In the middle of an empty room was the bath, set within a raised platform, and visible within the bath was the back of a head, an old man's head by the colour of the hair that grew sparsely from it. A robe lay on the floor to one side, and a pile of towels lay upon a seat, but there were neither servants nor other clothes on hand. And those three things, the Scraeling would later realise – the height of the bath that offered cover to an approach, the way the target faced, the lack of servants – combined to make Romanos' death as certain as anything that had happened to him since he burst from his mother's womb.

He yielded to Hardraada, who saw the possibilities at once and gestured towards the floor. Both men slipped through the curtains and fell noiselessly to their knees to cross the floor and they had covered half the distance when the sound had them snatching for their daggers. Then Hardraada lowered his head to the carpeted floor and the Scraeling saw, through the pounding of his heart, that his leader was fighting to suppress laughter and he realised, at the same time, that the sound was that of Romanos humming.

When the big viking had himself in hand again, they continued their stealthy approach until the head was directly above them and at that point Hardraada turned to the Scraeling, pointed emphatically at himself, and then at the Scraeling with an immediate dismissive wave that said, as clearly as words ever could, "I'll do this. Stand by". The Scraeling nodded once, took a small towel from his tunic and handed it to his chief.

Hardraada turned his attention back to the bath above, and the Scraeling watched, fascinated, as his nostrils dilated and the great chest rose and fell as the fingers flexed. He laid the Scraeling's towel across his right hand then, with shocking speed, Hardraada reared upright on his knees and his right hand, open like a claw, clamped down upon the emperor's head and hesitated a moment. A moment just long enough for the mouth to open in shock, before ramming the slightly-built body down into the bath at the same time as a huge left arm slammed across the emperor's chest to hold him back against the wall of the bath.

And then it was only a matter of hanging on to the edge of the sunken bath with elbows alone while Romanos fought for his life against the massive strength of the arms that girdled him and held his head under the surface. Once, twice his arms came from the water and flailed at the unseen power that had him in a vice, and once, twice, Hardraada buried his face in the emperor's shoulder and squeezed harder. A third time he tried, but his arms had scarcely cleared the surface when they splashed back, helpless, into it.

And that, thought the Scraeling, was the end of it but Hardraada held grimly on for moments longer after the last flurry of bubbles had burst on the surface. Then "Dagger!" hissed Hardraada, and the Scraeling drew Zoe's dagger from his leader's belt. "I'm going to let him go" came the instruction.

"Soon's I do, give me that knife. I'll stick him if I have to stop him yelling."

"Aye, *leder*" came back the Scraeling, "but if there is no need, keep your arms in the water a moment longer" and as Hardraada released the emperor's body he placed the dagger on the edge of the bath and made for the pile of towels. Seizing two he hastened back to where Hardraada gazed at Romanos' dead face and began to scrub at his master's arms.

"Carpeted floor. Needs to stay dry" he explained as Hardraada turned to him in annoyance. "How'd it get wet if Romanos had a seizure and drowned?"

"Thinking, Scraeling, thinking!" said Hardraada approvingly. "You're a cunning little bugger, aren't you? 'S why you're so useful to me. Bet he wishes you'd been on his side" he said, jerking his head at Romanos' body.

The Scraeling swallowed and did what he had no wish to do. He looked at the dead emperor and forced himself to sound unconcerned. "He's not looking happy" he said, "but you wouldn't if you had a seizure and it hurt. So no harm done. Well, some harm done – to him."

"Well said, convent boy" said Hardraada. "Ex-convent boy. You've done it now. That your first deader, is it? Aye, must be."

"No" said the Scraeling, "there was Griss. At the convent."

"Oh aye" said Hardraada, his eyes still upon Romanos, "but Griss doesn't really count. That was in hot blood, in battle you might say. This's different. You never set out to kill a man before?"

"I did, once" said the Scraeling. "Look, *leder* can we talk about this somewhere else? Romanos is about as good as he's ever going to be, no finger-marks 'cause of that towel, and who knows how long Zoe's men can keep this place clear for us?"

"Right" said Hardraada. "Check – no water on the floor 'cept what's normal, take these towels, aye . . . that's it. Back to my sweet Zoe's arms" he laughed. "Made her a widow, Scraeling. Wonder when I get to make her a mother?" And he slapped his accomplice on the shoulder.

The Chronicle.

Hardraada was right, of course. I was party, and even accomplice, to the murder of the Emperor Romanos Argyros and no two ways about it. What can I say? If I were Norse I would say that the wyrd – the great web that had woven into it the destinies of all upon earth – included the fact that I would one day assist in the murder of an emperor, and because of that weaving I could not avoid my fate. But I was no pagan – I was Christian, and could choose good or evil for myself, so before my God the wyrd was irrelevant.

My former argument that a small evil was acceptable if it led to a great good paled more than somewhat when set against the murder of an emperor anointed before God, and even the fact that I had laid no hand upon Romanus meant little in comparison with my help given up until then – and indeed after, for I come to that now.

No – I told myself then, and I clung to it with all my being, that I was among evil. Not only Hardraada and his crew, but Zoe herself who compacted for the deed just done. Not only Zoe, but those whose lust for power and favour led them to do her bidding.

And, ever and above all, Hardraada. Harald the Ruthless. Harald the Hard, who would not turn back from anything to which he had set his hand. Harald of the Hardcounsel, whose first and greatest concern was himself and his own desires.

I had – and I didn't know how, other than the way I had chosen – to rise above what surrounded me so that I might one day end it. But I reflected, as I followed Hardraada's broad back through the silent palace, that a favourite saying of Askell's was "Shit splatters". And I couldn't escape the thought that some of it appeared to be sticking where it splattered.

Kia's apartments in the Triconchus Palace.

Kia turned to the Scraeling, and her glance swept across the manservant also. "Wait here" she commanded, "for I shall shortly return." Turning to Hardraada she bade him curtly to follow, and with a wink at the Scraeling he disappeared after her.

The servant stepped to the table where wine and the remains of their earlier meal still lay, poured a cup of wine and offered it to the Scraeling, who took it gratefully and gestured to the man to help himself also. The servant politely declined and moved to stand with his back against the wall where he could see the first movement of the door through which Kia had taken Hardraada. The Scraeling paced the room, his mind full of what he had seen and done in the bathroom, while he listened for the tumult that would follow discovery of what lay within it.

When the door moved, the manservant jerked upright and bowed to Kia as she swept through it. "You'll be required again tonight" she told him. "Make yourself comfortable here and use this food and wine as you wish until then." The man assented, bowed again and seated himself.

Turning to the Scraeling, she said, "Secretary, you are to come with me. Bring your scrolls."

The Scraeling followed Kia to a room four doors down the corridor and as the door closed behind him she spun and threw herself at him, her arms reaching up to twine themselves round the Scraeling's neck and her mouth seeking his frantically as she rubbed herself against him.

"Is it done?" she demanded after a moment, "is all done as we wish?"

"Completely" answered the Scraeling, his back against the door and his front bulging despite his efforts to turn his lower body from the insistent pressure upon it.

"Aaahh!" The breath came from her in a long sigh. "Then tell me of it. All of it, for I want to know how an emperor dies".

The Scraeling flinched inwardly, but said, "As my lady wishes", for he could say little else.

"'My lady'? What's this of 'My lady', secretary? After what we've shared? And before what we're about to share?"

"Now?" and it came out as a startled squawk. "My lady – Kia – this palace must soon be turned inside out with news of the emperor's death!"

"The death of a man no longer young. A man worn down by failure in war, differences with the noble classes, and all the other cares of state. A man who had a seizure in his bath and drowned."

"But . . . but an emperor—!"

"An emperor whose quarters were sealed off from those of his wife by his own edict. An emperor whose ex-servant, now mine, led you to him there tonight. No word of what has passed tonight will come past the queen's own guard and she will not be disturbed until morning, nay not though Joshua's trumpet itself sounds the way! Besides . . ." and her voice became husky, "my mistress is . . . busy. Even now she receives report of the husband's end, and I, her servant, need to share that knowledge."

And whatever the Scraeling had to say was quite set aside as her hands undid the lacings of his shirt . . .

In the early hours of the next morning the servant came awake instantly as the door opened, and rose from the couch where he dozed. He picked up cup and wine flask and looked enquiringly at the Scraeling, who waved his offer aside. All he wanted was sleep, for Kia's energies had drained what the events in the royal bathroom had left of his. And, in the instant of thinking about her, she was there in the room followed by a Hardraada looking hugely pleased with himself.

"My man here will take you by a secret way to a dark street" she said, "where none will know you come from the palace. Your empress thanks you both. Look for further marks of her favour, *varangers.* Hold yourselves ready to do the royal will as well as you have this night." And it seemed to the Scraeling that her gaze lingered upon Hardraada a moment, before she turned and swept from the room, no vestige remaining of the woman who had seized him, clawed at him, ridden him and ruined him for half of the night.

"She's a cool one, that" commented Hardraada. "Sorry to keep you waiting" he said ironically. "Affairs of state."

"Successfully concluded?" asked the Scraeling, hoping that his weariness didn't show, and Hardraada smirked.

"I know someone who thinks so" he said. "Tell this fellow to lead on".

The path took them downstairs, upstairs and along a multitude of corridors until it ended in another long tunnel, at the end of which was a door that brought the party to the inside of a small and nondescript dwelling.

"Clever" commented Hardraada as he peered into the gloom of the street. "Scraeling, give this good fellow a little gift, would you?" And as the secretary fumbled for some coins and the man turned to him, Hardraada moved behind him, his right arm swept across the man's throat to seize his own left bicep and Harald the Ruthless wrenched viciously upwards and to the right. The servant's neck broke with a crack that the horrified Scraeling heard and could well-nigh feel, and Hardraada let him drop to the floor as his secretary stood paralysed, a hand still in his pouch.

"It's called covering your tracks, Scraeling" said Hardraada reasonably. "He's – he was – the only one with anything to gain by telling this night's story. Now he can't tell anyone."

"You could say the same of me" said the Scraeling, his voice shaking.

"When's it my turn?"

"Ah, but I need you" said his master. "I've gone past needing him. Look, don't go girlie on me, Scraeling. Eudokia herself gave me the nod to do this. She and Zoe play hard, and we're all aboard the same *drakkar*. Calm down."

"What about him?" asked the Scraeling, still fighting for control as he realised the significance of the look that Kia had given the viking. "We can't leave him here – he'd be bound to cause questions just by being in this handy place."

"Well done Scraeling – you're thinking again" rumbled Hardraada. "We take his purse, his shoes – they're quite good, but they won't fit me – and that fancy leather belt . . . ah, any jewellery on his hands or round his neck? Good, grab that too. Then we cart him down the street a way as long's it's still dark, and we dump him. Just another robbery, just another victim. Dangerous place, Miklagaard."

So they robbed the poor fellow, and the Scraeling half-lifted him from the floor until Hardraada could get a grip that slung the man over one huge shoulder. "Just open the door and have a look" instructed the chief. "Not too much to this – just look at people as problems, Scraeling. Problems are for solving. By the way – you started to tell me about setting out to kill someone. Back there in the bathroom, remember?

"Aye, that's right" said the Scraeling, peering round the partly-opened door, "it was just after I wounded Griss. I was going for another shot when someone flattened me, I remember."

"Who was it?" asked Hardraada, hefting the body more comfortably upon his shoulder, "Phew this bugger stinks. They shit themselves when the neck goes, y'know? Anyway – who'd have been your next target after Griss?"

"You" said the Scraeling as he stepped into the street.

The imperial audience chamber, Triconchus Palace.

The first minister of Constantinople was aghast. "Majesty, it's . . . it's unthinkable!" he spluttered. "But you did it! Aye, you did it – oh it's that Russian slut poisoning your mind! I really can't imagine why you let her lower you so, majesty – you, daughter, niece and wife of emperors. She's . . . she's nothing but a grubby little whore from the provinces with nothing to recommend her—"

"Except her willingness to serve me, John Orphanotrophos! To serve me in attempting to get your brother – your brother, fat man! – a throne that only one thing in his life fits him for! How dare you criticise my Lady Eudokia? How dare you? Kia knows of my dreams and my wishes, and she sets about making them reality! Do you? Well do you, eunuch?"

The eunuch gobbled in anger. "Dreams? Dreams, my lady? How does fornicating with a *varanger* before your husband is decently cold serve your dreams? While your betrothed, my brother, passes the night on his lonely couch!"

Zoe started from her chair on the dais as if she would fly at her minister and he backed away before the ball of spitting fury she had become. "Morality? You would preach to me of morality? You, a willing accomplice to the death of an emperor? Oh aye, well you knew of it! Well enough you knew of it for it was your advice, fat man, that saw me find a servant known to none to carry it out!"

John the Eunuch faced his mistress defiantly. "Aye, all that is true majesty. Just as it is true that he should have entered Hell straight after, and not the royal body! What were you thinking—" and he reeled as the full-blooded slap took him across the face.

"Eunuch, you presume!" said Zoe, and the icy hiss in her voice was more frightening than her fury. "You talk of entering bodies. Let me tell you of what I have in mind for you should ever you presume do so again. The Turks we fight in the Greek islands make a practice of impaling those who offend them. Have you heard of this practice, fat man?"

The eunuch wiped tears from his eyes and shook his head in terror but, sensing the empress' mood, he remained mute.

"Then let *me* presume to instruct *you*, lordly one. A man has his hands bound before him and is led to a stake set in the ground and sharpened to the finest of points. There, a rope is run through his bonds and over a beam. Three men – or say four or even five for a man of your stature – walk away with the rope, so lifting the man into the air. When he is at the top of the stake, John, two executioners seize his legs and engage the point – the *sharpened* point, recall – well in his anus. At the signal, those on the rope – drop it." She paused for effect, then, "I am told that an executioner's skill is judged by how near to the back of the head the point appears." By this time the eunuch was pale and swaying before her, but he could not tear his gaze from the beautiful and implacable face.

"Eunuch, should ever you speak so to me again of my trusted servants, any of them, I will see that point emerge through your neck. Know this – you're an administrator without peer, and this is why you've risen above merely supervising the ladies of the household to run my court and my government. It is your function to do this and not to instruct me unless I ask for instruction. It is your brother's function to get me with the child who will continue the Macedonian line. I will give him the imperial sceptre in return for his fleshly one, but know, eunuch, that to this date he has wielded it with me exactly forty-three times in three months, *and-I-am-not-yet-with-child*."

She leaned forward and tapped her minister on the chest. "Now the way is clear for me to marry, that sceptre will be used much more often. But last night I took the chance of a man, a chance offered me by Fate. A generous Fate, I may add, for he who filled me so well last night is young, virile and strong, of royal birth and not a Paphlagonian peasant. Therefore – a word of advice, eunuch. Know your place. Know what you do well, and bid your brother do what he does well also. And reflect upon the fact that, should the *varanger* get me with child, he may be able to get me another minister also. Now go – you have much to think upon. Go!"

A chastened John the Eunuch stumbled from her icy fury and as the door closed behind him, Zoe passed a hand over her forehead and called "Kia?" The curtain covering an alcove at the back of the room slid aside and Kia emerged and moved swiftly to her mistress.

"My lady!" she exclaimed, "My empress – Zoe my friend – that . . . that . . . creature should have his tongue torn out for his impudence in speaking to you as he did!"

"Nay, dearest Kia – offer me no advice, for I have had enough for today!" and Kia was instantly contrite. Zoe waved aside her apologies and reached for her hand.

"You heard all? Tell me – what did you hear? What was in his voice?"

"Fear, my friend. Fear for himself, certainly – but at the beginning, fear of Hardraada also. He fears our *varanger* and I believe he sees his doom, and that of his family, in Hard Harald. By the way – is Harald truly hard? How hard?"

Zoe laughed. "Hard enough, my Kia. You heard me tell John that he filled me well last night, and I tell you that he filled me often besides. Well

– I needed to seize that chance did I not? And I was acting in the empire's interests was I not? I would not have you believe that I acted for my own pleasure, dearest friend!" She fluttered her eyelashes in mock protest, and Kia broke into laughter.

"How fortunate that God made you an empress, my lady, for you cannot dissemble well enough to pass as a criminal!" and they laughed together before Zoe sobered.

"What am I to do with our *varanger*, Kia? Do I keep him here in my guard? And as my own secret bull? The prospect appeals. Counsel me, my friend."

Kia released the empress' hand and, standing up, began to pace as she thought aloud. "How long can we keep him secret? One who cares not what others think, so much of a warrior is he? What'll happen when such dalliance becomes known? Intrigue, feud, murder possibly. No, certainly, for the Norse are violent men who live violently. If the Paphlagonians fall because of feud with the *varangers*, who'll take their place? And if none steps forward, anarchy and ruin will follow. Yet if the incompetent step forward – the same, with civil war added."

Zoe sat unmoving except for the nodding of her head as she recognised the truth of the points she was hearing and Kia paused in her pacing, folded her arms and lowered her head pensively as she thought a moment.

"Now. Consider what is won by sending the *varanger* away." She unfolded her arms and held up one tiny hand. First" – and a finger rose – "my lady's plan goes forward as it was intended. Michael the Paphlagonian becomes your husband, you conceive his child and a lawful heir is born. Second – the *varanger* and his devils do your majesty's bidding in our wars with the Turk, say, or in such other place as you choose. Third – his talents and energies are better used at a distance than here, for if he had the influencing of state policy, war would surely follow. This one is a warrior born, and his men likewise. Fourth – if he goes to the frontier and dies there, no harm is done provided Michael wields that sceptre of which you spoke to good effect. If he does not – and Hardraada is accounted a formidable warrior by my grandsire's folk – then he can be brought back as openly or as secretly as your majesty sees fit. For whatever purpose your majesty sees fit."

"Kia, what is this of 'majesty'?" protested Zoe, and Kia came swiftly back to take her hand again.

"Zoe, I speak as a counsellor and not as your friend, for now!"

Zoe smiled. "Then it's settled, through your wisdom. Hardraada goes to war, and he may or may not have left me something. It's enough. For now. What is it, dearest friend?" For Kia was pensive again.

"Nothing, dearest Zoe. Not of Hardraada. But of one close to him. I speak of his secretary."

Zoe's brow furrowed. "The secretary? What of him? A cripple, is he not?"

"The same" said Kia, "but there is something about him . . . I examined him closely the day he came to us with a plan for the matter of Romanos . . . which I believe was his plan."

"Then we owe him much" said the empress, "for as we agreed, my dear – it was better than ours."

"Aye, it was" returned Kia, still pensive, "but he did not conceive it for our benefit. His plan had the merit of ensuring that the assassins survived, when we would have had them killed – if you recall. And the saga I told you of would have been easy for one of his skills to concoct. Aye, the Scraeling is clever. Far more clever than Hardraada, whose strength and prowess at arms means he need fear no man. But the Scraeling's mind is his weapon."

And Zoe, seeing how far away was her friend's mind, asked, "What does 'scraeling' mean, Kia?"

"Exactly, ah . . . 'native', or 'person of that place' It's not a polite term, for it indicates contempt – usually for a conquered or slave race. Shall I tell you his story? I've taken some pains to know it, for reasons that have to do with us . . ." and on receiving Zoe's nod she launched into the story of the Scraeling's origins and ended,

"Thus, I believe that the Scraeling – as he seems happy to be known – is coming, or will come to be, of some importance to Hardraada for he is a man of learning and prudence. As we have seen for ourselves. And that if we can have him do our bidding, Hardraada will follow."

"Why would he do our bidding, though?"

Kia waved a finger. "My question also, friend and queen." She paused, to choose her words carefully. "I don't believe the story I told you of his origins. Not all of it, but I told it to you as it was told to me. To begin with, I have the impression that he is with the viking band, but not of it. Why? Again – were his deliverance from humiliation the joyous thing he says, why would he continue to be known by a name that reeks of contempt?

No, dear friend, whatever put him into the hands of the sea-wolves is not a happy memory – but I've no proof other than a woman's intuition. And as I say – I've examined him closely."

Zoe sat bolt upright. "Kia, you've had him, haven't you? You minx! Tell me. Oh, tell me!"

"I deflowered him" said Kia, smugly. "On the day he came to me to speak of the supposed indiscretion of their *skald*. But I did so to make him mine, and thus ours. The day may come when you need Hardraada to do something he wouldn't do of his own accord, and then it'll be time to tickle the Scraeling's lust."

Zoe clapped her hands in delight. "Kia, you're surely the jewel in the imperial crown! Ah though – how did you spend last night when I was . . . in conference with Hardraada?"

"Why, in conference with the Scraeling, my lady." And as Zoe broke into laughter she added, "It was meet to discover what had passed in the bathroom so that we might, you and I, compare stories. And I tell you this besides, between we girls – only the Scraeling's leg is crippled! Now, majesty, upbraid me not" – and Kia fluttered her eyelashes also – "for 'I was acting in the empire's interests was I not? I would not have you believe that I acted for my own pleasure, dearest friend!' Not all of the time . . ."

The empress of Constantinople laughed until the tears came.

Hardraada's quarters, three days later.

Hardraada shook his head as he honed the edge of the dagger Zoe had given him. "I can't believe she's fifty-six, Scraeling. Never. She put me through my paces, and I don't mind saying so" he said.

"She is, though" said the Scraeling doggedly. "She's impressive, I'll give you that – what I'm told is there's rooms and rooms of the palace given over to producing creams, oils, lotions and potions for her to drink, sniff, rub on, wipe off, even bathe in. She's got an army of apothecaries working to find her the elixir of youth. And she does all that to stay young enough to produce an heir for the city. She's admirable, really. But she's definitely nearer sixty than fifty. Almost three times your age."

"Well she doesn't swive like it" said Hardraada. "She goes at it like a stoat. Do you know . . ." And he went on to tell the Scraeling something about the royal body that made him blush, for all his recent experience of Kia's favourite ways. "And I can tell you" he went on, "if this is what they mean by 'entering the royal service' I'm happy to give it a year or so. But what do we do— aye, Ulf?"

"Messenger in a fancy coat just brought this for you, *leder*" said Ulf, with a dirty look at the Scraeling. "Looked as if he had a bad smell under his nose, so I took the package and told him to fuck off."

"And?" said Hardraada, hefting the packet in his hand.

"And off he fucked" said Ulf. "Did I do right? You've not been around much to ask, lately" with another look at the Scraeling.

"Been trying to get you honest employment, haven't I?" said Hardraada. "Or at least as honest as an old rogue like you ever gets!"

"And how's it going, since we're speaking about it?" asked Ulf. "Does Zoe have work for us or not?"

"This ought to tell us" said Hardraada easily. "I'll have a look at it first though. Don't go too far away." The message was unmistakable and Ulf sniffed and turned away.

"They're restless" said the Scraeling, "and bored. That's dangerous – Haldor stepped in between Ivarr and Laurs yesterday, or there'd have been a killing."

"That Laurs's a menace" said Hardraada. "One, he's Danish and, two, he's a berserker. And that's always a bad combination outside a battlefield. Aye, he's a menace. But that's why Haldor, Ulf and Skallagrim are my right-hand men. Now let's see what Zoe has for us."

He slit the wrappings to reveal a heavy velvet money-purse and a folded letter, which he passed to his secretary. "What's this about, Scraeling?"

The Scraeling unfolded the letter, cleared his throat and read aloud:

To our trusty and beloved Harald Sigurdsson, greetings.

It pleases us to appoint you Hetaireiarchos of marines in our Aegean Fleet and to admit you to all the privileges and respect due to the holder of that rank. We congratulate you, noble Harald, upon this, your elevation to the nobility of our Court.

Your formal commission follows but we advise that, because of the dire need of our empire of a warrior so formidable, you are hereby requested and required to proceed with all despatch to where your command meets the enemies of our civilisation and the True Faith.

We further direct that this letter serve as formal orders and sufficient warrant for all men to know our love and esteem for you, Harald Sigurdsson, and we direct and command all owing allegiance to us in any manner or form to afford you such assistance in carrying out this, our will, as you may or shall need.

Given under the Great Seal of State and over our signatures,

Zoe, Regina Imperatrix   Michael IV, Rex Imperator.

He read it a second time, and when he ended Hardraada said "Michael? Who the fuck's Michael? And where'd he come from?"

"Paphlagonia, I would think – but don't ask me where it is" said the Scraeling. "I told you about him, remember? And you told me off for saying 'hung like a donkey', yes? Remember now? Well he is, according to gossip, and Zoe must like it because as far as I can see, this letter means he's Romanos' replacement."

"Thought I was supposed to be that" said Hardraada. "Little slut – squirming and gasping when she wasn't screaming her head off and clawing me bloody – then this! Odin's balls – what a bitch!"

"Not necessarily" said the Scraeling, who had been thinking hard. "You've got a commission out of it, and become a noble of the Court. That doesn't suggest she's going to send you anything nasty one dark night. And believe me, that happens here from time to time. Ask Romanos."

Hardraada waved petulantly. "I'll lose no sleep over it" he snapped. "Power's here, Scraeling. Here. Not in . . . in . . . where's the army anyway?"

"In the Greek islands, according to that sentry we met at the Palace, and getting a hammering too, from what he said" said the Scraeling absently, then "but hang on, *leder*. This might suit us very well. Look – we've climbed all over something that was going to happen anyway. Romanos would've got it courtesy of Zoe whether we gave it him or not, aye? And Zoe was always going to marry Michael because whatever heir she produces can't be a bastard. Now – nothing's changed."

"Not for you!" snapped Hardraada. "But she as good as promised me that she'd . . ."

"Well, no" returned the Scraeling. "As I recall it she said that the man who made her a widow might also have a chance at ringing her bell, so to speak. I know that, *leder* – as your interpreter I took some trouble over getting it right 'cause soon as I realised what she was driving at, it scared me shitless. I mean, you don't knock off an emperor every day."

"Won't be killing any more for that little slut" muttered Hardraada. "So, come on then – where's this leave us?"

"As I said" returned his secretary, "it leaves you a noble, a high-up in the army and someone who rattled Zoe hard enough and well enough to impress her, I think. She's sending you to war because – well, because that's where she needs the man who topped Wladyslaw and glued Yaroslav's arse to his throne. Oh aye, she knows about that. I'd say she knows, too, that you'd be trouble left here, and that's another reason. Y'see, Zoe's a woman—"

"Noticed that, several times."

The Scraeling smiled thinly. "—and she's got to work through others. She's working through the Paphlagonians and you've made that possible, so she'll not forget you. Now – she sends you off to where she can use you, 'cause it's good for her. But it's better for us, because Ivarr and Laurs can kill Turks instead of each other, Ulf and Haldor can get back to doing what they're good at instead of giving me shitty looks 'cause they know there's something going on that they're not privy to, and going to the islands will get you out of the way of a poisoned dagger in the street one night or one day. As I said, it happens here even if you're sure it won't happen to you." *And when it does*, he thought, *I want to be the one who makes it happen. Why should I give you to some faceless assassin when I've worked so hard on you?*

Hardraada pulled at his beard and looked at the Scraeling for a long moment. "Scraeling, you've been . . . different since we've been here. You talk sense, and I can't always get that from my captains. What's changed you?"

"Changed me? Nothing that I know of *leder*. Maybe I use my head where your other advisers use swords, axes and big balls. We look at things in different ways, that's all. But – if you could tell them what we know about the last week or so, I bet they'd agree that the best thing for us – and maybe the safest thing too – is to get back to what we understand. And that's kicking someone's arse."

Hardraada nodded, but the fierce blue eyes remained locked on the Scraeling. "And maybe we'll tell them when we get where we're going. And it's good advice. One other thing. Zoe can always get us back when she wants.

Or if she wants. I may even have done her business already. It's a funny old world. Time we saw more of it, right enough. Screaling, I did a wise thing in not feeding you to the fish of the Narrow Seas, I think. Call Haldor, Ulf and Skallagrim, would you? And come back with them yourself."

The Chronicle.

*W*hat changed me? Watching him murder a man then swing a leg over his wife – slut though she was – within the hour was a good part of it. Knowing that, if he lived until the stones of Les Trois Étoiles crumbled and fell, there was no hope for his blighted soul was another. But most of all, fearing that I would become like him if I didn't arm myself against his outlook by affecting the attitude that no part of his service troubled me.

Or perhaps it was Kia, and the way she used her body as a tool, that convinced me that much of the world Hardraada sought so hard to enter stood in falsehood and operated on deceit. Consider – Zoe used him to murder an old man and fake his death that she might play the cow to the Paphlagonian bull, and hedged her bets by bedding Hardraada along the way; Kia used me as a surety against some future need; I deceived him over my covering of her; and Zoe packed us off to the wars after enjoying his services in both senses of the term.

Compared with some in and around the Byzantine Court, I thought, even Thorkill sometimes looked gentlemanly.

The imperial base of Samos, 1035.

Ulf slapped the table for emphasis. "They'll just have to learn, then, *leder*. They can't walk on water, an' they're fuck-all use pulling faces at the pirates. Surely you can get archers to train 'em? I mean – those orders of yours'd get us into a convent-full of nuns if the Screaling's right, so getting a couple of squads of archers ought to be easy?"

"Ulf's right" rumbled Skallagrim. "'S the way to do it quick. Look at the difference we made to Yaroslav's army 'cause we got amongst 'em ourselves. You can't make archers out of footsoldiers 'less you know what you're doing, an' none of us do. We can make 'em soldiers good as any, but we need help with making 'em archers."

Hardraada held up a placatory hand. "Agreed. I need to get us . . . say fifty archers. Scraeling, write it down. Then get moving on it – let me know tomorrow where I get them."

The Scraeling blinked, his pen poised over the paper. "Me? Why me? I haven't the first idea. I'm a secretary, not a bloody drill-sergeant!"

"Three reasons" said Hardraada. "First, you're a cunning little bugger. Second, you've never let us down yet. Third – as Ulf says, we need to get to grips with these bastards any way we can and as soon as we can. They won't line up and offer us their throats, so we need to beat them on the water, and that's why we're using *drakkars* too. But when we close them, getting over the side to board could level things out a bit. Those dreamers who write orders can call our soldiers 'marines' as much as they like, but from what I've seen so far, they're the sweepings of every poxy little fort and camp in the Empire."

"So there you are, Scraeling – make us some archers" said Skallagrim again. "The other thing is, this is the last thing standing between us and a beer, and we want it out of the way. You'll think of something. Won't he?" he asked the others, and they slapped the table in acclamation.

Not that their acceptance of me's ever caused me anything but work, thought the Scraeling bitterly. But in all of it they were unaware of the determination burning within him, and he hugged that knowledge to him as he cleared the table of lists, orders and the other debris of getting a military command under way, to make room for the beer-jars.

"What's a *hetaireiarchos*, anyway?" enquired Hardraada of no-one in particular. "Odin's balls and belly – it hurts my tongue just saying it!"

"I know that" said Ulf smugly, "Means you're in charge of a thousand men. Lowest rank a noble can hold, besides."

"That right?" mused Hardraada, "that's – ah, Scraeling, we've got fifty real men. How many scraelings is that to each one?"

"Twenty" replied the Scraeling, with a faraway look on his face. "That for training, is it? And you did say fifty archers, didn't you? One archer for each squad of twenty makes a thousand all up. Right. Tell you about it tomorrow. You'll get your archers, but it'll cost."

The talk turned to Hardraada's charge of ridding the Aegean waters of the pirates who rampaged virtually at will along the supply lines of the hard-pressed Byzantine army of the islands. Greek though they were, they took full advantage of the power vacuum created by the empire's mighty struggle with the Arabs of Sicily and North Africa to prey on far-stretched imperial supply lines. Attempts to use a traditional convoy system had been unavailing against the sea-wise corsairs, who had simply banded together in numbers sufficient to overwhelm the escorts.

"No good" Hardraada had pronounced to a meeting of his lieutenants, when he had consulted as widely as he could. "Convoys're defensive, and we won't settle these buggers like that. Not while they can sail the arse off any escort the empire can put up. We know that better than anyone else, eh?"

"So. We're going to do it again, with bigger convoys than ever. No more small convoys, 'cause they're too hard to protect – but we protect these new convoys with all we've got every time. And we might have more than the pirates reckon we have. Ulf, you're a salty old bugger – what do you think of these screeling sails? You know, the three-cornered ones?"

"I like them" grunted Ulf. "Don't matter where the wind is with those things, you go forward no matter what. Why, *leder*?"

"How'd they suit a *drakkar*, in your mind?"

And that made Ulf sit up. "A longship? What for?"

"Never mind what for" said Hardraada testily, "would it work or not?"

Ulf stroked his beard while he thought. "Can't see why not" he said at length. "Give you one bloody fast *drakkar,* though, on any point of sailing. That what you're thinking?"

"It is" said Hardraada. "And we're going to have five or six 'bloody fast *drakkars*'. That's the way we'll sort these buggers out. Nothing I've ever seen's quicker than a *drakkar*, and we're better seamen. We'll have all the longships we can muster from Constantinople, and Kiev too if we need to, and we'll crew them with our own and any other who fancies sailing with us. And we won't just wait for them – we'll go looking for their bases, of a dark night. Be the Rus all over again, eh?"

So Hardraada waved his orders at Stephen Palaesostom, *strategos* of the Aegean Fleet, and the admiral undertook to have as many longships, together with their crews, as could be found in the city sent for with all dispatch. In the meantime, Hardraada summoned the Screeling.

"Now. The *drakkars* are coming. What about my archers?"

"They're coming too. Or they will be as soon as news of your archery tournament gets about to work them up."

"What archery tournament?"

"The one you'll be hosting, and betting quite heavily on, to rub in the fact that your marine archers are the best in the Aegean Command. In about two weeks, and just before the *drakkars* come from Constantinople. That one."

"Scraeling" said Hardraada ominously, "what, by the extra ball of the bastard king of Scania, are you dribbling about?"

"That's how you get fifty of the best archers in the Command under yours, see?" explained the Scraeling. "You hold a competition, you lose, you pay up and look gracious – I thought a half-dozen gold pieces and three or four jars of Falernian might be quite tempting as prizes – and at the end of the day you've learned your lesson and everyone agrees that these marines are good fellows, if a touch boastful at times. And you never know – one of ours might – just might – win it, so we'd make on our wagers at least."

"But anyway – a couple of days later, you wave your orders at their commanders and require the fifty names I give you to be transferred to the marines. That's it – fifty of the best bows in the Aegean sailing with us. Easy!"

"Not as easy as just grabbing them in the first place" argued Hardraada, "and cheaper, too" and the Scraeling rolled his eyes.

"*Leder*, what would we get then? We'd get delays while their commanders appeal to the admiral and then some more while he tells them to transfer the men and look happy while they're about it. But the commanders know that, so what'll they be doing while all that's going on? Why, what would you do but sort out the ones you most wanted to get rid of? How did I hear you describe our marines? 'The sweepings of every poxy little fort and camp in the Empire' wasn't it? Something like that anyway."

Hardraada thought for a moment, then he grinned. "Agreed, and well done. Scraeling, I took you from that convent instead of slitting your throat because I liked how you put Griss Bjornsson away. You've got brains and you've got balls, for all you're a *krøpling*, and I said then to Askell that you were a dangerous little bugger. I was right, wasn't I?"

Believe it, for one day you'll find that out personally thought the Scraeling, but aloud he said only, "Ah . . . entries to be made with me personally, so I can get the names . . . and I've used a bow more than a bit, so I'll sort out the men we want, and match names to faces."

"Fine, fine – it's all yours" said Hardraada. "Oh, one thing though."

"What?" asked the Scraeling, and Hardraada frowned down at him.

"Put on an entry fee" said the towering viking. "Might as well get some money back."

The Chronicle.

*I*t *worked as simply as I had planned it. For half a dozen gold pieces and a few jars of wine, Hardraada not only had fifty of the best archers in the Command by the time five more drakkars and their cutthroat crews arrived from Byzantium, but he had them hard at work sharing their talents with men who, it had to be said, proved apt and willing pupils.*

It must also be said that during this time I came again to realise that, evil though he was, Hardraada was a military colossus in ways that had nothing to do with his stature. Under his direction his lieutenants had their marines training carefully and precisely for the sort of fight they would be waging – one in which they would use the confines of a ship's deck as an arena where they would use their big and heavy shields to press their adversaries against bulwark, mast and bulkhead while their spears and short stabbing-swords - "grazed" was the word I heard Haldor use – between the shield rims to find their mark in men fighting to get a foothold on an unfamiliar deck.

By the time, then, that another convoy was assembled at Samos for the Peloponnese, Hardraada's command was as ready as training would ever make it and it was time for the test of battle.

Off the Cyclades island group, Aegean Sea, 1035.

Hardraada shaded his eyes and peered into the sun. "Can't be one of ours. Not from that direction. Master – get a man up that mast. And tell him to stay there until I know what he knows."

A seaman climbed reluctantly up the *dromon*'s stout mast to perch in the angle between it and the yard. "Sail" he called down, and a second later "another behind it."

"*Leder*" said the Scraeling, "look there, to Ivarr" and Hardraada followed the pointing finger away to the right flank and beyond the wallowing merchant convoy to where Ivarr's *dromon* was flying a red flag.

"Master!" snapped Hardraada, "tell your bird up the mast to break out the blue flag." The Scraeling translated and a moment later the flag was streaming from its lanyard. Eyes back on Ivarr, the Norsemen saw his red flag bob once and then descend to halfmast and climb again four deliberate times. "Someone over there's got good eyes" muttered Hardraada.

"Deck!" from the masthead, "Four more sail behind the first!"

"Nine sail" said Hardraada, "they're definitely not ours. Coming north and nor'-east. Scraeling – get those flags down. Send "Close on me" to the *drakkars* – tell that scraeling what the signal is – and order the stand-to. You might need to teach me their tongue after all, eh?"

Not before time thought the Scraeling as he bellowed for the shield that lay at the foot of the mast to take the place of the flags, for he considered the viking reluctance to put themselves out in learning any other language to be a startling flaw in people who plied their trade among foreigners.

The shield soared up the mast on the lanyard; the six *drakkars* sailing on the left-hand immediately hauled on their steering-oars and turned to come under the lee of the bulkier *dromon*, and their oars came out as the ship twice their size took their wind. The activity had not gone unnoticed aboard the *dromon* immediately ahead, for it came up momentarily to spill its wind and allow Hardraada's ship to catch up, reducing the sailing-distance between them and forming a screen for the six lean shapes that came racing close into them.

"Good lad, Arngeirr. Say what you like about Icelanders, Scraeling – they can sail, though!"

"What'd I ever say about Icelanders—?" returned the Scraeling, but Hardraada was demanding that he badger the lookout for numbers and courses again. For moments more the convoy held its course and then a figure appeared at Arngeirr's rail and waved before, imperceptibly at first, his vessel began to bear away to the left, away from the menace of the oncoming sails on the horizon.

"See 'em myself now" muttered Hardraada, shading his eyes, "*Qaribs*, and bloody quick. And they've got the wind. Hope they think we're running."

"We'd hardly do anything else, would we?" asked the Scraeling, and Hardraada puffed out his cheeks.

"A normal convoy would" he said, "but they've got to have seen we've got more *dromons*'n they've ever seen in one place. So why're we running?"

"Because we're not confident about beating them, perhaps?"

"That's what we want 'em to think before I slip Skallagrim, Ulf and Haldor" returned Hardraada, peering again into the sun. "Come on, you arseholes, come on! We want them close enough to catch between the *drakkars* and the *dromons*. These things aren't as quick as longships, Scraeling, but they shift along if they're handled right. And if our scraeling doesn't handle this one right, I'll feed him his own toes. Still on his feet. You might tell him that?"

But the Scraeling contented himself with making sure the man understood the importance of reacting immediately to any command he received from Hardraada through himself, and ended, "Now – look frightened!" and the man obliged.

The oncoming ships closed fast, and their intentions were clearly to be seen from the way they held a course that would drive them through the middle of the convoy, and under that threat the curve set by Arngeirr tightened as the convoy bore away. Then Hardraada said, "Scraeling, tell the master that when I blow this he needs to get speed off her quickly, or we'll go straight up Arngeirr's arse. And if that happens, he'll get something up his, too." And he unhooked an ox-horn from his belt, waved once to the *drakkars* foaming along on the left hand, took a deep breath and raised the horn to send a blast pealing over the water.

The foresail came down with a rush and the *dromon* checked like a reined-in horse before sliding on through the water. At the same time a chorus of shouts arose from the longships and they surged forward under oars, past the forefoot of Arngeirr's vessel, across the front of the convoy and out in an arc that took them across the rear of the onrushing corsairs. "Hard right!" snapped Hardraada as the *drakkars* vanished around the front, "All sail!" and the *dromon* spun on her heel through the convoy, chose a gap and shot through it to confront the pirate that lay, low and threatening, beyond.

The leading corsair arrowed straight for the two *dromons* on the near side of the convoy while its fellows made for the bulky merchantmen in the middle. The sudden appearance of three *dromons* from the far side of the convoy took them momentarily by surprise, but they had no hesitation in offering battle. The Scraeling nocked an arrow to his bow as his eye took in the waving blades and his ears the battle-shouts of the garishly-dressed hordes that filled every cranny of the long and low craft that leaped towards him.

Then a horn-blast split the air and a storm of arrows flew across the water between Hardraada's ship and the two nearest corsairs. Gaps appeared in the dense ranks aboard her, but were widened again and yet again as a second and then a third volley of shafts tore into them before the two separated to lunge at each bow of the *dromon*. Grapples flew and a wave of screaming pirates surged over the bulwarks.

The horn screamed again, twice, and the first rank of marines waiting amidships dropped their spear-points and charged into the left forequarter of the ship, followed a moment later, on the right by the second rank.

"That's it, Scraeling – time to feed the ravens!" Hardraada caught up the long and single-bladed axe from where it leaned against the rail beside him and hurled himself down the steps, along the deck and into the fight that boiled in the *dromon*'s forward section.

Deciding that it would be no bad thing if the fight were to be kept there, the Scraeling made it his business to pick off any pirate who broke from the mêlée. Time after time the curved Turkish bow flexed in his hands to send shafts flickering fifty yards along the deck to bury themselves in the bodies of men who were, for the most part, unarmoured.

The tides coming over the bows faltered and fell back before Hardraada's terrible axe, and the marines pressed forward in his wake to send them reeling back aboard their own craft where they sought to cut the lines that held them to what they had supposed would be their prey. Then the Scraeling took a hand in aiming successive shafts into the figures he could see at the steering-oars of the two corsairs, dropping each one as swiftly as he appeared so that the pirates hung irresolute.

The marines pressed forward on all sides, and such was their blood-lust that the pirates found it difficult to surrender, many raising empty hands in futile attempts to ward off sword or spear-point. There came the moment when no pirate lived on the deck of Hardraada's *dromon*, and the huge figure waving an axe red to the hand-grip leaped nimbly to the gunwale and then to the deck of the right-hand *qarib*. The marines raised a cheer and swept after him, and again they took no prisoners. The Scraeling lowered his bow and for the first time looked about him.

One *qarib* had broken free from the press and was clawing its way back to the north with all speed, while three others were each board and board with a *dromon* like mastiffs in a bear-pit. Beyond them the remaining three corsairs were rafted together into a circle by the *drakkars* that prowled round them like wolves round a sheepfold, and within the circle the Scraeling could see nothing alive, such had been the speed and ferocity of the longships' attack from the cover of the convoy. Even as the thought registered, two *drakkars* broke from the circle to take the remaining corsairs in the rear.

No corsair had penetrated the convoy, and it lay five or six bowshots away under headsails alone, the big boxlike shapes rolling in a gentle swell while Arngeirr's *dromon* cruised up and down between them and a battle now coming rapidly to an end.

Hardraada came striding back to the command deck, red to the elbows with his mail flecked and stained the same colour. "Good shooting, Scraeling" he announced. "Saw you at it – kept them where we could reach 'em. Tell this bugger to get his men throwing that pirate trash back in their ships, will you? In their ships, mind you – not over the side. And while that's happening, pass the word for all my captains to board here soon's they can."

When his wolves were assembled Hardraada spoke his thanks and commended them for their prowess. "Now" he went on, "that's half the battle. For the rest of it – Ivarr, where'd you say this scum came from? Their bases I mean?"

Ivarr rummaged in a matted beard. "Well" he said, "those charts you showed us had a group of islands about there –" and he gestured to the north-east "– an' that's where they came from, I reckon. Why, *leder*?"

So Hardraada told him, and after a moment of startled surprise there was a mighty shout of laughter. "And that's just the beginning" noted Hardraada, "because there's no money in chasing pirates. So we'll have done with that, soon's we can, and show them the Empress' peace besides. Or something like it. Now – *drakkar* captains take a boatload of corpses with you. Take some seamen to work the *qaribs* until you get close, then ship a tow so the *drakkars* can take 'em right into the surf. Then chop a few holes in the bottom, cut 'em loose and deliver them back to their womenfolk. And don't forget – use the trip over there to cut the balls off each deader an' stuff them in his mouth. Just to show that piracy isn't something they should go on with, right?" He looked round at the wolfish faces alight with glee, and the Scraeling struggled to suppress a shudder. "Questions?"

"Prisoners?" from Thorkill. "Can we use 'em to work the ships?"

Hardraada frowned. "Why've you got any? The orders were to spare no-one who hit our decks!"

Thorkill shrugged. "Dunno, *leder*. Some of the marines are a bit old-fashioned about that."

"Then teach them better!" snapped Hardraada. "We won't fix these bastards by being nice to 'em. I want everyone in these islands to shit themselves at sight of an imperial ship. At sight! You hear?"

"Fine, fine" said Thorkill hastily. "Can I have them?"

"No fear" said Hardraada. "Seeing we've got them, they'll pay us back for our trouble at the slave block. Use the seamen – and any pirate wounded you want. Nail the wounded to the mast or the deck or whatever, before you cut them loose into the surf. You know what to do – get on with it. No more fuck-ups, Thorkill. And no prisoners, either."

And as the dragonships cleared for the north-east with their grisly cargoes, the convoy got under way with hoses aboard the *dromons* sluicing blood and brains from their decks as they took station on the ungainly merchantmen.

"Good result, Scraeling" said Hardraada, elbow-deep in a pail of water and scrubbing busily at his naked torso. "Those archers we got 'cause of you did a marvellous job with the men – we got three flights away by my count, and slowed 'em boarding because of it."

"Think it'll be enough?" asked the Scraeling, "Today, I mean?"

"Nah. Never" said Hardraada. "It'll take time and a few more todays, I think. But when the convoy's safe to harbour, we're coming back here. Over there –" and he jerked a massive head in the direction of the dragonships' wakes.

"We'll spread a bit of piracy of our own – make a few widows, snatch a few slaves, share a few women just to keep the boys happy. Be like old times. The pirates'll learn, one way or another, and we can get the fuck out of here and on to where a man can win a bit of loot. I'll make you rich yet, Scraeling!"

But riches had to wait until the band was finished among islands that, for all the beauty of their setting in a sparkling blue sea, the Scraeling could never recall without a shudder. What he was part of there haunted his dreams for many a year after he left the Cyclades.

The hard-raede of Harald.

Hardraada kept his promise to return, and he did so within a week when he led three longships back to the scene of the victory over the pirates, there to cruise up and down below the horizon until darkness fell. Led by Ivarr and Thorkill, the dragons crept inshore at the islands under that covering of cloud kept by the devil for those who do his work, until the thunder of surf was loud in their ears and the guides could see the river outfalls that they had noted on their last venture there. An urgent whisper brought the raiders round to the mouth of the largest and, bent to their wrapped oars and muffled rowlocks, the crew sent the sleek and deadly shapes gliding into the river like hunting serpents.

Kneeling in the snarling prow of the leading dragon, Ivarr sniffed their road – and before God the Scraeling could account for it in no other way – up the deep-water channel however it bent and twisted, with his murmurs relayed back down the length of the ship to the steersman. At length he held up both arms in the loom of the starlight, and a sharp hiss from Hardraada kept the oars in the water where their drag was enough to hold the longship against the slight current. "Woodsmoke" came back from Ivarr.

Hardraada put over the steering-sweep and ordered them into the bank, where cloak-wrapped mooring-picks were hammered into the ground and an anchor-watch of three men per *drakkar* was set before the wolves took to their trail. Scouts were sent away and it seemed only moments before a murmur passed. "Village." Swiftly the crews of the longships padded away into the darkness and the Scraeling followed, and if proof were needed that the devil rode abroad that night it came in the shape of a high and proud moon riding clear of the clouds that had hidden it until the moment of the attack.

Across the bend in the river was a narrow stretch of woodland and lining the near edge of the river were the frames where the folk dried their nets. Further along the edge their fishing-craft gleamed in the moonlight and beyond them again the shapes of dwellings were black in the shadows.

All this the Scraeling saw in the moment of arrival, for he had been among the last to come up and, even as he took in the sight of the sleeping village before him, the first shape left the cover of the woodland and flitted across the moon-washed space to the dwellings.

It was followed by another four or five, and those by another cloud of men, and then another and another until the space between the beach and the dwellings swarmed with dark and deadly menace. Still no dog barked, and he realised that the same breeze that had brought the scent of wood-ash down the river yet blew their scent from the village. But at last a dog, perhaps awoken by the chink of metal on stone, gave tongue and was swiftly joined in chorus by others.

But the warning was too late, for the village was doomed and death waited at every corner and doorway. To the bellows of the vikings as they kicked open the cottage doors was shortly added the screams of those within; man, woman or child mattered not as the people of the village were torn from their beds and hustled to the square at its centre. And whether they cursed their attackers, or railed at them, or sought God's mercy mattered no more, for they were as doomed as their village. That came to the Scraeling as he hastened through the village and across the now-empty spaces beyond to push through the crowd.

When all were gathered within the square, Hardraada stood before them and demanded to know who spoke for the village. One man of about forty drew himself up and, in a voice that he could not keep from trembling, admitted that he was the headman.

"How many folk? Scraeling?" and he looked about him. The Scraeling translated, and all eyes swung to him.

"Five score, great one. All loyal subjects of the Emperor Romanos – long may he live and prosper our empire" came the reply, and Hardraada snorted.

"Then where are they, headman? Where are your men? Why are there no more than four *qaribs* on your beach? Is their fishing so cunning that you need only four vessels to feed so many? Again! *Where-are-your-young-men*? Scraeling, bid him speak the truth or I'll cut out his tongue!"

So I did, but it helped the man nothing, for his next utterance was, "Lord, there has been much sickness ... we have no physician, nor ... for it has pleased God ... aye, lord, much sickness ..." And it was obvious even to those who did not understand him that he was temporising and lying.

"Karl, Sweyn – grab him, hold him up!" commanded Hardraada before the Scraeling had finished and, stepping to the held man he drove a knee hard into his groin. A dagger appeared in his right hand as his huge left hand clamped and held the jaw that opened in a scream of agony, and in a flash the blade was thrust into the open mouth and something flew from it. The vikings let him go and the man collapsed, screaming.

"You should always keep your word. Wonder if his balls hurt more than his tongue?" mused Hardraada, "Reckon he c'n feel both? At the same time? What'd you reckon Karl? Anyway – pick me another. Any one'll do."

Another was thrust forward, and Hardraada said "Right, Scraeling – same questions an' remind him— Freya's tits, Sweyn, shut that bugger up, eh? – remind him I haven't got all night to wait on him." Even as the Scraeling spoke Sweyn thrust downward, once and hard, and the shrieking ended in a rasping gurgle.

Yes, it emerged, the young men of the village had been taken in piracy and killed. Yes, they had been joined by young men from the other villages on the island. Yes, they of the village had taken riches and loot from imperial ships in the past and the speaker would gladly show the noble lord where it was.

Hardraada looked at him from his great height and the man dropped his gaze. At length he said, "Skallagrim, take ten men and this piece of shit to wherever he wants to take you. Send back to me what the loot is and how much of it there is to carry. Scraeling, you too. Ulf, Haldor, Thorkill – separate the women and kids; put 'em in those hovels over there. Rest of you – on my word, drop the nearest villager. Quick as you like; we haven't got time to amuse ourselves with them if you want the women after, 'cause we've got other places to go tonight."

The Chronicle.

And all happened as the leder commanded. It happened there, it happened again at the next village and it happened throughout that summer on every inhabited island of the Cyclades group. It was, indeed, the Rus all over again, even as Hardraada had said; wherever he struck, Hard-Counsel left some

alive to carry the tale and spread the terrible legend of The Landwaster on a tide
of savage reprisal, razed villages, wholesale rape and exemplary slaughter.

But by summer's end the Aegean convoys sailed in peace.

The Imperial palace, winter 1035–1036.

The fat man paced the floor of the opulent office, his chins on his chest as he chewed his top lip. "Are you sure you're eating right?" he asked "The augurs told you what to eat. Do you stick to it? Consistently?"

"If I see another green vegetable this week" said the other, "I'll have the man carrying it whipped. And anyone within ten yards of him. Consistently? Yes, brother John – I consistently follow the augurs' advice. And before you ask, I back it up with seafood, spider-webs, fungi – and even bull's blood. I eat, and drink, and exercise according to every crack-brained, half-formed idea my imperial bedmate comes up with, and some of them— never mind. You don't want to know."

"Yes, I do" snapped the eunuch. "I want to know about everything that keeps us indispensable to her, and it seems to me that there are worse ways of getting on in life than pleasuring an empress half-silly! Just get on with it!"

"Pleasuring?" exploded the Emperor Michael, "What's pleasant about stud duty twice a day – minimum, I might add – indoors, outdoors, standing up, lying down, by a fire, between two torches, in a bath, by a river – even under a bloody waterfall once! I might also mention – under a full moon, a crescent moon, no moon at all, on top of a pharos, to music, with and without chanting . . . it's bloody hard work! You should try . . . ah, sorry."

"But none of it works. And you know what? I doubt if it ever will. For all the wild ideas she listens to about what to eat, drink, rub on, take off, paint her face with, put inside her – Zoe's just too old, brother, and that's it. All of it."

"Not necessarily" argued the eunuch. "She's got the finest minds of the empire keeping her young! It could be you, you know."

"Brother, from Bithynia to Constantinople there are at least sixteen people alive today who can call me father. And they're only the ones I know about, because Zoe's fire-iron has been tempered in lots of forges. Zoe's fifty-seven this year. Most women her age are grandmothers, or even great grandmothers. Listen carefully. *It's-not-bloody-me!* And if you want more proof, how about that bloody *varanger* who rattled her after he topped Romanos?"

"Keep your voice down!" snapped John. "What about the *varanger*?"

"Well, didn't you say he banged her most of the night? And what came of it? Nothing! Suggest anything to you?"

"No, but it obviously does to you. What?"

"Zoe's had the best of both of us. She's not fertile, John. She's past it. Face it. Bring back the *varanger*."

"What on earth for?"

"So he can give me a break! And so she's got someone else to blame when the time comes – because it will come, John. Believe me. Bring him back."

"No chance in a thousand. He's wintering in Kiev among his barbarian friends, and he can stay there a bit longer. Shouldn't you be off to eat something sustaining? Zoe's probably wondering where you are . . ."

The North African coast, Spring, 1036.

Hardraada scoffed at the request. "No chance in a thousand. We were here first; we've made our camp and we're not moving. Tell your master to go fuck himself if he's got nothing else to do."

The messenger blanched as the Scraeling translated, for although Hardraada had spent part of winter becoming conversant with the Byzantine vernacular, he had no head for Greek and was content to leave official dealings to his secretary.

"Noble *hetaireiarchos* . . . I . . . may not take such a message to the Lord Maniakes. He . . . he is the *strategos* chosen of the emperor himself!"

"Ah, I see!" said Hardraada ominously. "That changes things, of course" and the messenger brightened visibly. "In that case, ask him to *please* go fuck himself after you remind him that my *varangers* owe allegiance to the imperials themselves and not to any of their pot-lickers. I'm relying on you, mind, 'cause if I have to tell him myself I won't say please. Got it? Now fuck off yourself!"

But the Scraeling added "Bow to my commander and then enter the tent with the writing-table outside it. Wait there for me. Look unhappy!"

The messenger had little trouble with that, at least, and retreated through the crowd around Hardraada.

"So" said Haldor, "you were saying about Serkland?" By which he meant the coast of North Africa.

"Other end of the pirate problem" said Hardraada, waving an ale-horn expansively into the distance. "Same problem we tidied up among the Cyclades. But this time our orders are to use such means as I see fit to put an end to 'em. 'Such means as I see fit.' That means by land or sea."

"And the orders come from the top?" asked Ulf, holding out his horn to a servant.

"All the way" said Hardraada. "That's where I was summoned to when we came back through Constantinople from Kiev. Now admit it – you thought she wanted to kick my arse, didn't you?"

"Never" said Skallagrim. "Well – she might when she hears what that Maniakes has to tell her."

"What I told that screaeling was Odin's own truth" said Hardraada. "I answer to Zoe, and nobody else, because she told me that as a mark of her favour over the pirate business. And maybe other things too" he sniggered. "Anyway – once we've sorted out this problem, we're going back to the City and into the Varanger Guard. The Guard itself."

"Impressive" said Skallagrim. "I c'n see why you told Maniakes how to spend his morning. Think he'll wear it?"

"If he doesn't" said Hardraada, "he's welcome to try shifting us."

The Screaeling slipped from the crowd and made his way to his own tent where Maniakes' staff officer waited, looking unhappier than ever.

"You've got a problem" said the Screaeling without preamble. "What's Maniakes likely to do when he hears your message?"

"Two things" returned the other. "First, he'll break me back to the ranks for not being forceful enough, then he'll come up here and kick your man's arse all the way down to the river flats."

"Neither appeals as a good way to begin the emperor's business" remarked the Screaeling. "This is the muster camp and we haven't even seen an Arab yet. It's no time to be falling out among ourselves, and if Maniakes tries what you say he'll try, I wouldn't give shit for his chances of surviving, let alone getting a campaign under way. Hasn't had much to do with *varangers*, has he?"

"Jesus" muttered the officer, "why couldn't I have gone sick yesterday? In fact, why couldn't I have joined the fucking navy?"

"Never mind" said the Scraeling. "I've got an idea, but whether or not it works is up to you. You can read and write, of course . . .?"

Later the same afternoon.

Five minutes after Maniakes' liaison officer had gone, the Scraeling was arguing with Hardraada. "*Leder,* it just isn't worthwhile pissing Maniakes off by defying him. He must be seen to get his own way, because everyone knows he's the boss. Whereas only we know that you're Zoe's man and answerable to her."

"I don't give a pinch of raven-shit" retorted Hardraada, "and I'm not backing down. We got here first, and took the risks of an unsupported landing on an enemy shore. Loki's arse, man, we covered the army as it came ashore! Why should we move? Not that we're going to!"

"We don't have to" said the Scraeling, "so long as we make it easy for Maniakes to back down. Give him an excuse. And we can. What do you think of this . . ." and as he spoke one bearded face after another broke into wide smiles, for the Norsemen prized cunning even above bravery.

"You've got it then?" asked the Scraeling, "because Maniakes'll be here soon wanting to know why you didn't fall about doing what he wants. Now for fuck's sake, *leder* don't let him needle you. Just remember who's going to win. And win without bloodshed, or feud, or holding up the army, so we can get on with enjoying that place in the Guard, eh?"

And Maniakes did arrive within the hour. He was a man of just less than Hardraada's own height with a black and bushy beard, and the Scraeling was glad to see the figure of his previous messenger among the half-section of cavalry at his back.

"What's this about you wanting to see me over our campsites?" he demanded when greetings had been exchanged. "Straightforward, isn't it? I want the high ground up here, and there's plenty of room on the river-flat for you and your thousand, *hetaireiarchos.* I wouldn't be here now if your message hadn't asked for my help. Do I have to do everything myself?"

"And good of you to answer my request, *strategos*" answered Hardraada, aware that some of his lieutenants were finding it hard to contain their mirth. "The problem is that our holy man—" and he took Maniakes' arm and drew him aside, lowering his voice confidentially, "and my *varangers* are a superstitious lot, most of 'em pagan – our holy man has pronounced this to be the place where the gods will speak to him. Higher up, see? And they set great store by it."

"You got me up here to listen to some pagan claptrap about campsites?" demanded the empire's most senior soldier; "I'll kick his arse for him, and yours too, Hardraada, before either of you—"

"Hang on, Lord Maniakes, hang on. My men are likely to be important in this campaign. The empress thinks so, because she told me two weeks ago, right? After all, we kept your armies fed and supplied by cleaning out the Cyclades pirates only last year – so let's not be hasty. This is important to my men, and you're spoken of as a fair-minded man, so I'd like to offer a demonstration of what this holy man of ours can do. What'll it hurt to watch? You might even be impressed."

And Hardraada was the soul of reason, so at length Maniakes agreed, grumbling at the time wasted over a perfectly straightforward matter, and allowed himself to be led to a tent where the Scraeling himself sat by a burning brazier, garbed in a bear-pelt and his face streaked with wood-ash and soot.

"Now" said Hardraada, "ah – I see your man there, your messenger, aye. Can he write?"

"All my staff can write!" snapped Maniakes. "That's one reason why they're staff!"

"You're so fortunate" murmured Hardraada. "Right – let him go around and write the names of a dozen or so men – your men or mine, doesn't matter – on those bits of paper, one name per paper; fold 'em tight as you like and the gods will reveal the names to our holy man without him reading them. Not that he can read in the first place, mind you. I'm not as lucky in my staff as you are."

Once that was done, the folded papers were put into a helmet before the Scraeling, who raised his eyes heavenwards and spread wide his upturned hands a moment before settling himself again, his eyes going blank. Askell stepped forward, selected a paper, and held it to the Scraeling's forehead.

"Iannos" pronounced the Scraeling, and Maniakes' messenger called "Here!" Askell inclined his head and handed the paper to the Scraeling, who opened it and offered it to the sky in acknowledgement before letting it fall into the brazier. Askell reached for another paper and laid it again upon the Scraeling's forehead.

"Leo" and a cavalryman called "Aye!" and to a murmur of amazement Askell handed the paper to the Scraeling who offered it to the heavens, dropped it into the brazier and readied himself for a third.

"Ivarr"

"Alexander"

"Leo Kouradis"

"Sweyn"

"Staurakios"

And each name was answered as the Scraeling read each paper through its folds, faultlessly, while the murmurs of astonishment grew.

"See?" asked Hardraada in an undertone, "He's important to us, and that's why what he says goes. You and I, of course . . . but my men depend on him y'see?"

"Oh very well!" snapped Maniakes, "But if these . . . these pagans of yours don't perform – and they'll be up front in every engagement, Hardraada – there will be some arse-kicking, and I'll be doing it! Have your campsite!"

Constantinople's land *strategos* strode back to his horse, mounted, kicked the beast hard in the ribs and clattered away down the hill, followed by his mystified staff, while the vikings on the crest of the hill burst into long-suppressed laughter.

"Don't ever dice with the Scraeling" gasped Skallagrim, wiping his eyes.

"Not without looking in his sleeves!" whooped the normally dour Ulf.

"Beer!" chortled Hardraada, "Beer for the Scraeling! Beer for all of us – to drink to what a fucking simpleton our noble *strategos* is!"

"And the health of Iannos, his messenger" said the Scraeling, "who made all things possible and all names known, by answering first!"

The Chronicle.

I was proud of my performance, for two reasons. First, it saved Hardraada from a clash he would eventually and surely have lost – and that would have suited my purpose not at all. Second, the Norse love of trickery and subterfuge came to confirm my standing among the cut-throats as a fellow of infinite cunning, and that suited me much better. If Hardraada were Odin, as I sometimes thought he saw himself, then I was Loki – prince of tricksters and the arch-deceiver. That was how even Hardraada's lieutenants came to see me but their arrogance, like his, lay in the assumption that this Loki would always work for them as the real Loki worked for Odin and Thor. He should have listened more thoughtfully when I urged him to 'remember who's going to win'.

What I could never get over was the way that he, so far-sighted and clever in war, showed no such foresight in ordinary matters. His determination to have his own way in all things may have made him Harald the Ruthless, but it was also like to be his death – much before I was ready to make it so, for I knew that Maniakes would eventually discover how he had been duped. The natural talent of the Norsemen for bragging would see to that, and what I had heard of the strategos' similarity to Hardraada in the matter of exacting revenge for insult offered or imagined persuaded me that our victory was likely to prove expensive.

As it was God must have been keeping him for me, because all that campaign season while our forces rolled back and forth along the top of Africa crushing cities, villages and ports from land and sea and teaching soldiers and common folk alike the hard-raede of the Landwaster, Maniakes' concerns with the armies of our Arab foes kept him separate and apart from those of his 'hetaireiarchos of marines'. By land and by sea, as I say, we kept help and succour from the Arab armies and reinforcements from their kin battling our forces on the island of Sicily.

But Sigurdsson was no good and faithful servant in that, for much spoil fell to us while we were about it. Every strong place we took was scoured clean before it was reduced to rubble, and the forcing of treasuries large and small was reserved to Hardraada's oldest wolves and his secretary, who listed their contents straight after, and sometimes while the clangour of battle still resounded outside.

So loud and far did the Landwaster's ravens scream that Arab resistance crumbled before us – and Maniakes took the credit for that to himself, aye so much so that he launched a subordinate on a half-cocked invasion of Sicily the following year and watched the fool's arse well kicked by Abdallah-ibn-Muizz for his pains. And when we did get round to sorting out that particular mess, all it got us was more of Maniakes' jealousy. Well, as they say – if you can't take a joke you shouldn't join . . .

Kiev, winter 1036–1037.

Yaroslav's eyes slid away from those of the taller man, and it didn't go unnoticed. "I'm not opposed to it altogether" he said, "but it's not quite that straightforward, you see."

"No, I don't see" said Hardraada. "She's of marriageable age, surely? And you sent me away to prove myself – well, ask the pirates of the Cyclades about me. If you can find any. And even that loudmouthed prick Maniakes admitted that I'd hauled his arse out of the fire in doing it. And he got all the glory for taming North Africa, aye, but ask him who held the sea-lanes to Sicily and smashed the Arab embarkation ports so he could bring their armies to battle? And my men fought a few of those, too. What else must I do to win your daughter?"

"Well, cousin, she is a princess. Yes, yes, I know –" and Yaroslav held up a hand – "you had a lot to do with ensuring that, and Kiev is grateful. And you've taken enough from the infidel to ensure my daughter won't starve, at least." Hardraada didn't respond to the feeble joke, and Yaroslav went on, "Y'see, you haven't exactly got a position, have you? Granted you're a soldier that no enemy wants to meet – but if you were to win yourself a state, now …"

"Yaroslav, that's bullshit and we both know it. Correct me if I'm wrong, but it's less than two hundred years since your ancestors were hairy-arsed *varangers* too, and I've done more, faster, than they ever did. And as to having or winning a 'position', whatever that is – my marriage to Elisabeth would keep your Kiev safe for my lifetime and your son Izyaslav just as safe on his throne after you go. And let's not forget that my mother was a queen."

But that's just what you don't want, thought the viking as Yaroslav pretended to think about his words. *You don't want me anywhere near your spineless idiot of a son – any of the four've them, matter of fact – in case I take his crown and his head with it. As I might, just to piss you off in your smug Christian heaven.*

"There's one thing more" said Yaroslav slowly, "and it's a problem. Elisabeth's the daughter of a Christian house, and – how do I put this? – she needs a Christian husband."

"I'm baptised!" snapped Hardraada, "and men already refer to my brother, Olaf, as a fucking saint, for Christ's sake!"

Yaroslav winced. "That's what I mean" he said, "baptised, yes, fair enough – but you have the odd lapse, Harald. Don't you? I mean – there's the raven banner, and I hear things about your campaigns from Shepetovka – offerings to Odin and the like . . ."

"You didn't mind at the time, did you? Not with a throne to secure, Yaroslav. It was a weapon – all part of convincing the scraelings that the Prince of Kiev was the man to back. Anyway, if you want the truth" returned Hardraada, "saintliness came late to my brother, and that's well-enough known. What of it?"

"Just two things, Harald. Carve yourself a niche. Somewhere other than here. And show me – show all of us – some sign of Christian piety. You said people were already referring to Olaf as Saint Olaf. Well, they're already calling me Yaroslav the Wise, and I won't – I can't – give my daughter in marriage to a pagan soldier. Humour me, cousin."

Constantinople, early spring, 1037.

The Scraeling shook his head, openly just hanging on to his temper, and reached out to wrap the amber in the soft cloth on which it lay. "I can't be bothered with idiots, and if you're not an idiot you're a thief" he said. "Never mind – your loss and someone else's gain. Never fear – I'll come and see you again when I've shit to sell rather'n the real stuff, 'cause you're only offering shit prices!"

"Hang on, hang on" protested the other, "don't be hasty. We're still—"

"Hasty? Hasty?" snapped the Scraeling, "I'm not being hasty. What I'm being is completely pissed-off with you wasting my time. You're wasting my time, friend, and I've got better things to do, with real merchants. Last chance – three *solidii* for each of the lumps in the top row, two for the next row, one for the third-rate pieces beneath. What part of that you having trouble with? Eh?"

"Three *solidii*'s a lot of money" protested the merchant, a hook-nosed Armenian in a greasy shift, "and I'm not sayin' your stuff ain't good, but I've seen better."

"Only in your greedy dreams" retorted the Scraeling, "and by the way, three *solidii*'s not a lot of money because only about a fifth of it's gold. Largely thanks to bastards like you who clip it, melt it, re-smelt it and re-stamp it. No, don't bullshit me – we can always call that coinage inspector over here? Dealing with doctored coin gets the same penalty as doctoring it. Now – as I said before – last chance. Want it or not?"

"I'll take all the top row" said the Armenian sullenly, "and I'll take the second, too – if you'll give me four for three in the third row? Look, you've got more amber than a bull can shit and there's a lot of it about. I'm taking a chance, here."

The Scraeling let out his breath in a long hiss. "A chance? A fucking liberty's what you're taking, friend! All right. As I said, I've got other things to do. Four for three in the third row. But you buy all of it, yes?"

He spat on his right palm and held out his hand. The Armenian did likewise, and ran a dark eye over the spread-out contents of the cloth roll before fumbling in his robe for a purse while the Scraeling carefully rolled and wrapped the bundle of amber pieces. Moments later the transaction was complete, the Armenian had gone and the Scraeling rose stiffly and awkwardly to his feet.

"Get your price?" came Askell's voice.

"Yes." said the Scraeling as he stretched his twisted leg, which had never become accustomed to the squatting position. "Oh yes. That one came down in the last shower, and helped me get rid of all my rubbish. Greetings, Askell."

"Rubbish? Looked all right from where I was standing."

"Ah – you'd have been looking at these pieces in particular?" and the Scraeling shook several large and glowing lumps of amber from his sleeve and held them out to Askell, whose eyes widened.

"How'd you . . . I saw you . . . aaahhhh – when you rolled them up, aye?"

"Just so" said the Scraeling as they moved off. "Wide sleeves're a real good idea. I'll sell these to someone who appreciates good amber. And speaking of clothes – you make a convincing coinage inspector. He stopped arguing, just about the time I threatened to call you over to look at his coin, so we need to find a tavern on the way home, 'cause I owe you!"

Askell shook his head in admiration. "You're a bloody handful, Scraeling. Cunning as Loki an' you miss less than Odin's ravens" he said, "but how far'll he get before he checks?"

"Oh he's got the right number" said the Scraeling. "I just swapped a couple here and there to match the sort of money he was offering."

"Shit!" said Askell. "I was watching you an' I never saw a thing I shouldn't have seen! The boys're right – I'll never dice with you!"

"Friends're quite safe" chuckled the Scraeling, "They come in handy now and again – just like you did! But did you just happen by, or were you looking for me?"

"Harald sent half a dozen of us out after you. He's got a palace summons for tomorrow" said Askell. "Wanted to make sure you wouldn't spend all night an' half the day aboard a whore an' come back with a hangover. Or a cracked head from her pimp 'cause you bilked her."

"Has he though?" said the Scraeling thoughtfully, "wonder what sort of trouble that'll bring us? Ah well – that's tomorrow's problem. In the meantime, that wonderful smell's coming from a tavern, my friend. Food and beer too . . . let's spend some of the Armenian's money."

The imperial palace, the next day.

Hardraada clashed to attention, a gleaming pillar of steel with his helmet in the crook of his arm, and inclined his head. "Majesty."

"Welcome, *hetaireiarchos*. And it is time we received you at Court. Had it not been for our urgent need of you in the war zone, you would have been presented to us long since" said the emperor, looking at the Norse giant with his hooded eyes while the Scraeling translated, and thinking *So you're the killer of emperors and the tupper of empresses? You're a big bastard all right. Should I have you killed?*

"Your majesties' fights are my fights, and your majesties' enemies mine" said Hardraada, "and I am a soldier. Thus the war zone is where we belong, my men and I, and we seek no more." *And you're the Scraeling's human donkey, are you? Hope your cock's harder than the rest of you, friend, because you're going to seed. Overmuch good living and couch drill by the look of you.*

"*Hetaireiarchos*, your troops are among the best in our service. What you did in the Cyclades and in North Africa is known to me. And I have a task for you that is worthy of such a man." *Not to mention the other thing I have in mind.* "Tell me – you are Christian, are you not?"

What the fuck's going on? First Yaroslav, now this suety bastard – "Aye, majesty. I was baptised at birth" *And what that's got to do with anything?*

"Colonel, you will not return to North Africa in this campaign season.

We would have you lead your regiment to Jerusalem, in our service. And we would have you leave at once."

A month later, Palestine.

The Scraeling glanced at the high ground. *They're up there all right* he thought, *because every now and again they let themselves be seen on the skyline. No accident, that – it's just to keep us on edge.*

"Seen the last of them, I think" came a voice from his right and he turned to the young Guards officer who ambled up beside him. "Haven't seen one for half an hour now – should think they've realised we're no ripe and tasty caravan, eh?"

"You think so?" said the Scraeling doubtfully and the officer mistook his doubt for fear.

"I know so" he said, and smacked the Scraeling heartily on the shoulder. "Don't worry – we're looking after the ladies – and you too!"

"That's all right then" said the Scraeling, "but who's looking after you?"

The soldier frowned. "What? What's that mean?"

"Just that. Someone needs to if you think the Bedu've gone, friend. Since we've been talking, I've seen two – up there, on two different places on the skyline. They want us to know they're keeping an eye on us. Got it?"

The guardsman looked down his nose. "They tell me you're the secretary of the *hetaireiarchos*. So you're not a soldier, are you?"

"Stumbled into it" said the Scraeling, "same way as he did. Do you need a fancy uniform to be a soldier, or what? But since we're asking questions – is it true that the Household doesn't usually move outside Constantinople?"

"Generally" admitted the guardsman proudly. "Only on the most important duties, and if the Family's involved."

"Which it is" nodded the Scraeling. "So we might say that the Bedu are new ground to you too? Thought so. Well if you don't mind a non-soldiering secretary giving you advice, keep watching the skyline. Because they're there all right. May not want our ladies – although I bet they do – but they want lots of things we've got – 'specially our horses."

"What makes you such an expert?" demanded a very nettled guardsman.

"A deep interest in my fellow man" returned the Scraeling amiably. "Especially my fellow man who might want to kill me for my possessions.

And the advice I take from those who know better, of course. But then, I'm just a non-soldiering secretary and not a cataphract of the Guard."

The guardsman scowled and hauled his mount aside for less criticism elsewhere, leaving the Scraeling to settle back into the easy rhythm of his own mount as it plodded on up the valley twenty yards behind the horse-litters bearing the royal party.

He cast his mind back to the audience in the Triconchus Palace and the barely-concealed air of malevolence he had detected in the words and manner of the First Minister, who had outlined and amplified the terms and purpose of their journey to Jerusalem as escort to the caravan that even then snaked ahead of and behind him. What did John the Eunuch have against Hardraada? The Scraeling thought he knew.

Zoe's not pregnant he thought. *And she isn't going to be, not at her age. But she might turn to Hardraada, because she's probably desperate. And John's desperate too – desperate to keep his place in the saddle. That's why he's sending the troublesome varangers away. Yes. Makes sense.*

So, and following the conclusion of a peace treaty with the Caliph of Egypt, it had been agreed that the road to Jerusalem might be opened again to Christian pilgrims. Michael IV had decided to commence the new era by sending a body of skilled masons to the Holy City to rebuild and repair the holy sites, and Zoe's sister, the Princess Theodora, as pious as she was plain, had consented to accompany the mission as Constantinople's emissary and ambassador. Which had necessitated the addition of five hundred cavalry of the Imperial Guard to the two hundred *varangers* and three hundred infantry already under Hardraada's command, and fairly unhappy the Guard were about it too.

But the movement of so many from Constantinople to Akko, on the coast of the Holy Land had shown them all what they could come to expect as direct servants of the imperium, and Hardraada had been obviously and visibly impressed. Nothing that might have added to their comfort or smoothed their path had been left undone, and even the weather itself had co-operated by providing the smoothest of sailings.

So there they were – a month out from Constantinople and winding down a valley that was about to emerge from the sheltering arms of a low range of craggy hills, and even as the Scraeling looked ahead to where the valley floor widened out, he noted the movement of the heavily-armoured cataphractoi horsemen as they closed a little upon the caravan. And here was Hardraada himself – not at home on a horse, but making a reasonable fist of things with his long legs dangling nearly in the dust, Skallagrim by his side looking just as uncomfortable.

"Eyes open, Scraeling – we're coming from the valley soon, and who knows?" called the viking and the Scraeling raised a hand.

"They've been with us for two days, *leder* and they'd be silly to try anything out in the open where the cataphracts'll chew them up."

"True enough, true enough. But watch it anyway. That's a cunning saddle."

For the Scraeling had had a saddle made in Constantinople after his own design. Deep in the basin, it was cushioned by a folded and stuffed wolf-pelt but what made it more unusual still was the presence of two stout leather horns, one at the apex and another at the left front. With such a saddle the Scraeling could loop his right leg around one horn and tuck the foot behind the other, and he was rock-solid in the saddle as a result. So mounted he could hope to use the long cavalry *spatha* that hung from his left hip to best effect, while a round shield was fastened to the right side of his saddle and the bow that was ever part of him when action offered was already strung and in his hand.

"I see you're looking dangerous anyway" added Skallagrim.

"Someone has to impress the ladies" returned the Scraeling with mock hauteur, "and you look like a sailor on a horse."

"I am a sailor on a horse" admitted Skallagrim, "and my arse wishes I wasn't. Honest, *leder* I'd be much happier on foot, with the boys. We're marching easy as it is."

"True – we're in no hurry" admitted Hardraada. "But I'd like to settle with those bastards . . . what are they, Scraeling?"

"'Bedu', they're called. It just means 'desert-dweller' and they're dirt-poor. That makes us, or anyone, a good target. And I think they're going to need settling, 'cause I can't see 'em just going away. They haven't these two days past."

"Let me think about that" said Hardraada. "In the meantime, keep closed up. And behind a cataphract if you can – they're expendable!" And he trotted on down the column.

The midday halt passed without incident, but the Scraeling was surprised when the evening camp was made earlier than usual and the unsaddled packhorses were herded into a small *wadi*, or depression, located a little further from the main encampment than was usual.

"Why's the camp so far away?" he enquired of Haldor, who smiled and laid a finger against his nose.

"Don't want some nasty sneaking up in the middle of the night, do we?" he returned, "Need plenty of space round about. In fact, we're so worried about it that we're pulling in men who'd otherwise be guarding the horses. Common sense, see?" and he would say no more.

But as the short desert twilight rushed into night, the Scraeling happened across half a dozen *varangers* wrapping axes and swords in cloth before slinging them across their backs and securing them tightly. "What's going on?" he asked, and one flashed him a wolflike grin.

"Going out" he said. "Fast and far, soon's it's dark enough. Don't want anything rattling or shining, do we?" and the Scraeling saw that, other than his weapon, the man was carrying nothing extra by way of mail or helmet, and even his clothing was dark-coloured and kept to a minimum. And the camp was suddenly filled with other dark shapes, Hardraada looming huge among them.

"Right then" came from the darkness. "Twenty of you, all chosen 'cause you can run. We're going to circle wide out, back and around this *wadi* and camp, now it's dark enough to do it without the Bedu seeing us, an' we're going to slot anyone we find on the way. And 'specially over towards the horse-lines. Haldor's boys're on their way over there now. No noise, an' run far enough apart not to trip over each other. Questions? No? Right, follow me." And he was gone, a shadow merging into deeper shadow.

Skallagrim moved through the encampment, warning those at each fire to keep to their usual evening routine but to take a sword to their blankets. "Nothing different now" he urged, "jus' let the fires die down natural. Sentries're set an' patrolling, same as always, so just forget about it until you hear all hell going on at the horse lines, eh? And even then – stand to, an' wait for orders. Got it?" And all did just that, although not many slept.

At some time after two in the morning, so far as the Scraeling could judge, Skallagrim's hell broke loose in a confusion of shouts, screams and clash of steel on steel from the direction of the wadi. A detachment of Byzantine heavy infantry came trotting up, armed and ready, their officer said, to relieve the watch – did the *varanger* officer have further orders for him? The Screaling turned to Skallagrim.

"Aye" said Skallagrim, "walk over to the *wadi*. Walk, mind, 'cause Haldor's over there an' if he sees armed men running towards him your man here'll find out what dealing with a bear with its arse on fire's all about. Tell him, Screaling – real careful, eh?"

The detachment vanished into the dark but returned almost instantly in groups of two and three, each dragging a prisoner to the torch-lit space before the watch-tent where two armourers flung him down, fitted a leg-iron and hammered home an iron shackle-pin before standing up, loosing a hearty kick and turning for the next until fourteen ragged and wounded Bedu lay on the ground before the tent.

Moments later Haldor and Hardraada came trotting in at the head of their men. "Hold there, Screaling" ordered Hardraada when he saw the medicine chest. "These buggers won't be needing help beyond tomorrow, and if any die tonight, well … save us the bother! And the medical supplies."

The Chronicle.

Hardraada left a strong detachment of cataphractoi at our campsite to deal with the prisoners, and if their officer's face was grim after he received his instructions it was grimmer still when the detachment caught us up two days later.

Was it really necessary to order the removal of each man's eyelids after they'd been spread-eagled and staked in the sun? The scavenger ants weren't slow to avail themselves of the bloody feast on offer throughout the day, but what was worse for the men charged with this act of barbarity was listening to the sounds from the darkness as the striped hyenas and jackals disputed for the bodies of the dead and the one or two left alive after a day in that furnace.

The point? Terror, pure and simple. The Bedu had never heard of The Landwaster, but they would learn. Aye, they would learn as easily as had the survivors of their raiding party, looking impotently down from the hills. As would others in the Holy Land.

Jerusalem.

The Scraeling spoke up confidently. "The Antonia Fortress, I would think Highness, and beyond it part of the old city wall. Both remind us of how well King David chose his city for protection of its holiness, for this is the only side which has no natural defences."

Theodora turned a rather protruding blue eye upon him. "Surely you have been here before, Secretary?" and the Scraeling blushed.

"No, Highness, but I've spoken much with those who have and I've read in our City's Great Library of this place, that I might be of use to you and those of your train who would know of it, for it has many wonders of our faith within it."

Zoe's sister clapped her hands in delight. "Then thrice welcome, secretary. I shall speak to your master concerning your services without delay!"

You're likely to have more need of me here than pagan Harald does thought the Scraeling, but in that he was eventually proved wrong. In the beginning, though, Hardraada did not trouble him greatly and in fact spent much time closeted with the officials who ran the city for the far-off Caliph of Egypt while his *varangers* grew increasingly bored in a city without taverns or whores and his Byzantine troops tried to ignore the presence of their traditional Arab enemies.

Thus, beyond a minimum of liaison with those officials responsible for the buildings on the emperor's lists – all of whom, noted the Scraeling wryly – had Greek better than his Arabic, he was able to put himself at the disposal of Theodora and her ladies, and with them he walked the breadth of the city in both directions, along the Cardo from the Holy Sepulchre to the Nea Church, and the Decumanus both.

They visited the Basilica of Constantine, where Theodora prayed, and then wept for the piety of her great ancestor, climbed the Mount of Olives and walked in the Garden of Gethsemane. And to the Scraeling's amazement, this second lady of the empire insisted upon honouring the other faiths to which the city was holy by walking to the Dome of the Rock and the Western Wall of Herod's Temple. Day by day his respect for Theodora grew, and for her part she seemed to regard the Secretary's opinion as infallible so that his was the first ruling sought in regard to any question that the religious riches all about them brought forth.

The day came when the Scraeling realised that he had not seen Hardraada for the better part of a week, and on making inquiry of Askell he discovered that the *leder* and his chief henchmen had ridden forth some days before, taking with them almost a hundred of the *varangers* – to where, or why, he did not know. "He asked for you, right enough" noted Askell, "but in the end said you were well enough where you were, keeping her Highness busy enough not to miss him."

The Scraeling frowned. "He put it like that? 'Not to miss him'?" And on receiving the *skald*'s assent he fell to pondering over what the viking was up to that he did not want the princess to know about.

Hardraada was gone for the better part of a month, and on his return he informed his secretary that his *varangers* had taken over the policing of the roads most travelled by pilgrims of each of the three Faiths that held Jerusalem holy. "Aye, close your mouth man" said Hardraada testily, but obviously hugely pleased with himself. "Isn't this what the emperor's about? Restoring the Holy City so our pilgrims can take advantage of the peace to visit? And what's better than keeping one set of pilgrims happy? Keeping three sets of pilgrims happy, that's what. Especially when they pay you for escorting them!"

And that, it seemed, was what he had been doing for the month of his absence – clearing the roads between Jerusalem and the coast as only the Landwaster could. The Scraeling would later find, to no great surprise, that he had left behind a bloody trail of dead men, gutted 'bandit' villages, wailing women and warnings nailed to trees by their hands.

"And it's steady business, Scraeling," said Hardraada enthusiastically as he paced up and down, "because, as Fayeed says, each village along the road'll pay for protection from the bandits besides – and that's regular!"

"Hold on" said the Scraeling, "what bandits? You've just cleared the country, you told me. Where're they coming from? And who's Fayeed?"

Hardraada laid a finger by his nose and winked. "You never know" he said, "some might come back, eh . . .? And Fayeed – well, Scraeling, he's a sort of local version of you – a clever bugger who doesn't have to trip over a chance to recognise it. He's dealt with *varangers* before and even speaks good enough Norse to get by. But I want you to meet him, because the two of you need to draw up the details of our little . . . ah, joint venture."

It transpired that Hardraada would leave behind a group of *varangers* sufficient in number and ferocity both to guard the pilgrim road and to exact tribute from the villages along it in consideration of their freedom from attack. Fayeed would forward the moneys to Hardraada in Constantinople by courier after deducting "fees and expenses". With the details agreed, went on Hardraada, it remained only to put them in writing "and that's where you come in. Now – what else've you been up to?"

The Chronicle.

*I*f I was surprised to find Hardraada so interested in my journeyings around *the Holy City with Princess Theodora, I was amazed to hear him proclaim the intention of accompanying us from then onward. But of course I didn't know of his wish to commend himself to Yaroslav, and would not know until he told me of it later. And as he noted then – if he were to become an avid pilgrim, who better to attest to it than Constantinople's second lady?*

So we did it all again – Theodora in raptures and Hardraada the soul of interested curiosity. The Bethesda Pool, the Mount of Olives, Gethsemane, the Temple Mount, Hezekiah's Tunnel next to the Pool of Siloam, the King's Garden, and all the rest. He excelled himself in suggesting the walk along the Via Dolorosa, though, for Theodora found this "wish to relive Our Lord's travail on His last day of life" an indication of the deepest piety. From the Mount of Olives to Holy Sepulchre and the seven Rests in between – "How does Our Lord's passion soften even the fiercest of natures!" she noted to me – and Hardraada's large and ostentatious gifts of money to the guardians of the holy places we visited likewise impressed her. Would she have been quite so impressed had she known that every penny would be recouped in being wrung from the folk of the Jerusalem road?

But the master-stroke was surely bathing in the waters of the Jordan before giving a feast to mark what he called his "confirmation" as a Christian. How God resisted the temptation to hurl a bolt from heaven at such blasphemy is known only unto Him. Perhaps He sought to lead the pagan on in his arrogance and conviction that he could do no wrong, to where I, His servant and weapon, would one day wait. Could I be so fortunate?

And the crowning touch – his suggestion that the piety of the noble Yaroslav, he whom men now called "The Wise", would surely welcome her account of the wonders to be seen in the Holy City. And that Hardraada would be pleased and honoured to be the bearer of such a tract when he wintered in Kiev, as we were in the habit of doing.

Suffice to say that the campaign in the Holy Land was at least as successful as the more conventional campaigns he had undertaken, and when we wound the road back to Constantinople there was enough in our coffers to make the voyage back to safe storage in Kiev almost as worthwhile as the year before. More, Hardraada returned with an augmented reputation as a man who got things done and also with a name for deep and generous piety.

How long and hard he must have laughed.

The Empress' apartments, the imperial palace.

None of her ladies would meet Zoe's eye as she paced the room like a lioness. "You heard me threaten that . . . that thing with impalement, my ladies" she snarled. "I should have had it done! Too late! Too late, now, for after he disbanded my guard on the pretext that his brother's army was more than capable of guarding my person, he has turned my husband against me."

"Majesty, for the empress of Constantinople it is never too late" said one, greatly daring. "There are men loyal to you who would do your bidding – whatever it is. This I know, on my life!" And the others murmured agreement.

"Sweet Isadora" said Zoe, "as you say, there are those who would do this – but at what cost? We are at war in the west and in the north, my husband is ill, and I dare not risk the civil war that would come through the murder of the first minister. Dearly though I wish it. No – I must find another way. With my own eunuchs dismissed and only my faithful maids-in-waiting left to me, I must find a way."

"And there may be one" said Anna thoughtfully. "For diversion, once, and to while away the year he was obliged to wait for a naval command, my brother studied the writings of Galen the Egyptian. That led him deeper into medical study, and a good friend of those days is now one of John the Eunuch's physicians." She let her words hang in the air, and for a long moment no-one spoke.

Then "And where is your brother stationed at the moment?" asked Kia

Vonskaya, her obsidian eyes offering no hint of her reason for asking the question.

The Gulf of Catania, Sicily, 1038.

Patience exhausted, Hardraada snapped "Take us in, man! There's no help for it – we've got to get ashore or we'll still be sailing up and down next bloody week!" He drummed his huge fists on the rail of his *dromon* as he looked to Maniakes' flagship, but there was no sign from there that the invasion fleet would do anything but plough up and down the Gulf of Catania as it had done for half the day already. "Scraeling, you're a horseman – how good're those cavalry screws going to be after this?"

The Scraeling pursed his lips. "Horses don't like this kind of movement" he said. "We're lucky it's not worse, I suppose, but . . . no, they won't be fit for much till they've got their land legs back."

"Well, the sooner they start . . . that's it. Master – signal my captains to heave-to, and then take us out of line. Soon's they acknowledge, signal 'Close on me'. Got that? Ulf – get as many archers as you can into our *drakkar*, but don't crowd 'em because we'll be relying on them. Come on, Maniakes, you arsehole!"

With his four marine-carrying vessels rafted two on either side, Hardraada gave orders that saw archers presently scramble into the *drakkar* that each *dromon* had towed across the Straits, and a double file of marines follow for their protection.

"We're going in there" Hardraada had said, pointing to the stone jetty that stuck out from the centre of the shoreline like a pointing finger, "and those buggers'll have something to say about it" – for beyond the jetty the foreshore was black with armed men – "so I want as many shafts as you c'n put into the air. You can't miss – not even you hopeless bastards from the Bosphorus fleet – 'cause the dragons'll take you right into the white water where you can get two with one shot if you're any good. Aye, I'll show you how next time" – that for the good-natured jeers that had greeted his earlier remark – "but we're relying on you, right? We're going alongside two and two, and we won't be fucking about when we hit that jetty – *varangers* first an' then the marines. So take plenty of arrows an' keep 'em coming."

And as the laden *dromons* stooped towards the jetty, the *drakkars* slipped and raced into the very surf, where they swung broadside to answer the hail of missiles from the shore. "Get us in there fast as you can, master" commanded Hardraada, his eye on the rapidly-closing gap between bulwark and jetty. "Don't care how ugly it is – just get us touching shore."

Hardraada's *dromon* forged through a storm of arrows stolidly deflected by the interlocked shields of the marines, to hit just ahead of Haldor on the other side of the jetty and Hardraada vaulted ashore to lead his *varangers* in a wild charge up its length. Haldor was only a step behind him and together the two Norsemen cast aside their shields and ploughed headlong into the massed ranks of the Arab army, axes whirling. At which there came a mighty shout from their troops and the twin streams funnelled into the hole carved by the raging figures who led them, while the archers in the dragonships, now almost stationary in the surf, and those aboard the first two *dromons* loosed into the Arab host as quickly as they could nock and draw.

From the *dromons* heavily-armoured marines poured ashore, shuffled into rank and set off up the jetty at a smart trot, shields held high against the arrows that persisted from the front and sides, until they too smashed into the Arab host and slowly began to roll it back. There came a moment when, with the Arab army pushed back from the landward end of the jetty, it threatened to outflank the Byzantines and in the very moment when the issue hung in the balance the scream of a horn announced that Hardraada and Haldor had broken through the far side of the Arab battle-line and turned to come in from the rear.

The Scraeling seized the ship's fascinated master and bellowed "Pole off, master! Pole off! Make way for the *strategos*!" and shook him until the man tore his eyes from what was happening at the end of the jetty and began to bawl orders. The Scraeling turned to the after-rail and gave the same command to the *dromon* behind him and scarcely had he done so when he felt the ship heel beneath him and saw the headsail quiver as it bit into the offshore breeze. As the bow came round it revealed the flagship standing purposefully in for the jetty and the other vessels forming line to come in behind it and into the other two jetties in their turn.

After that the issue was never in doubt, for men and horses flowed from the transports and into the town precincts of Catania even while the first of Maniakes' own troops stormed up the jetty to catch the Arabs between themselves and Hardraada's force. To their credit the Arabs died hard, refusing surrender and selling their lives as dearly as they might, but before the inevitable end the ox-horns had screamed and Hardraada disengaged to turn the battle over to Maniakes' troops.

Soon after, a *drakkar* slid alongside and the Scraeling was hailed by Skuli, Ivarr's lieutenant. "Fetch your rune-things, Scraeling, and climb in – we're off into the city before anyone else. You know why!"

Indeed I do thought the Scraeling as he slung the leather case over his shoulder and his bow and quiver on the other, *and I hope the bey's soldiers all died on the beach because thirty men – even varangers – isn't an army.* Skuli had with him an enemy youth whose gashed head told its own tale, and as they hurried through the winding streets the Scraeling ventured his Arabic. "Lose your helmet, did you?" and the youth looked his amazement.

"Aye, lord, and my senses left me when the blow came from the big man with the red beard." Haldor himself, then, who rarely struck a blow that wasn't fatal. "When I sat up, the fight was over and one of yours would have slain me but for this lord here –" indicating Skuli "– who stayed his hand and spoke of me to the big barbarian who led you."

"And you are to show us the location of the bey's treasury and war-chest?"

"For my life, yes, lord." The boy's voice was bitter, and the Scraeling understood at once the difference between a young man's visions of the glories of battle and the reality of having his throat cut like an animal, for hadn't he once been within seconds of such a death himself?

"And a good bargain. His treasure will profit the bey nothing now, and it was never yours. But if it can do good by preserving your life, why not? *In sh'Allah.*"

"*In sh'Allah*, lord" echoed the youth, glancing sideways in wonder. "Down this street."

Hardraada's headquarters.

The jewels sparkled in Hardraada's huge hand. "Good one Scraeling!" the viking said, "and well done to think of getting all this away before Maniakes' men turned up." He was looking at a small chest of jewels, a respectable collection of gold plate and a sack of gold coin.

"What Maniakes doesn't know won't hurt him" said the Scraeling, "and this is the best of it near as I could judge in the time we had. I had to leave some for the official looters to find."

"Fine, fine" said Hardraada. "We'll get an official share of that. Seal the place, did they?"

"Tight as a herring's arse" put in Skuli. "Guards on the door and all. We had this lot in a handcart by then, with stuff covering it from a house we turned over two streets away. So we went back for a look; Maniakes' boys'd got there by then and wrapped it up tight, an' when we asked them what was up they said, 'Fuck off with your miserable rubbish.' So we did." Hardraada and his henchmen roared with laughter.

"Tell me, Scraeling" went on Skuli, "would you really've used that toothpick of yours?"

The Scraeling smiled. "Let's be glad we never found out, Skuli. No offence."

"Eh?" asked Hardraada. "What's all this?"

"The Scraeling pulled a knife on me" said Skuli without rancour. "Over the Turk. When I told Snorri to cut his throat, this bugger had his knife out of his sleeve and in my face in a flash. Then he yelled something at the Turk – in screaling, like – and he shot off quick-like. What'd you say anyway?"

"I told him to run far and fast if he wanted to live, and to get going" said the Scraeling.

"Why'd you do that?" asked Hardraada curiously.

"Someone had told him he'd live if he showed us where the bey's treasury was" said the Scraeling doggedly, "A bargain's a bargain, and he kept his end of it. Didn't you say yourself you should always keep your word? When you cut out that pirate's tongue, before?"

Hardraada shrugged. "Well, no harm done. You're a bit soft though."

"You ever pull a knife on me and you'd better mean it" said Thorkill malevolently.

"The day I pull a knife on you, shit-head, you'll be in no doubt of my intentions" said the Scraeling, and the lightness had gone completely from his voice.

"You fucking little –" began a crimsoning Thorkill, but his step forward was halted by Hardraada's bellow.

"Enough! I need both of you, and there'll be no bloodletting until I say you can! Got it? Got it?? Whatever there is between you two can wait!"

The Chronicle.

A ye, a commander's task is never an easy one. But vikings are the strangest of men, because they see nothing amiss in killing others for their possessions while insisting on fairness for their own. Just the arrogance I've written of before, I think, but my insistence on fair dealing with the Arab youth was approved of in no small measure among that band of cut-throats. As to the other - my own dislike for Thorkill the Foul had simply boiled over in that instant, and I think all realised there would be a reckoning between us one day. But the very next day brought a summons from the strategos which Hardraada answered with two of his lieutenants and his secretary, and what I saw and heard then convinced me that the great have problems no less than the humble – and often of the same kind.

Catania, Sicily, 1038.

The orderly led us to what had been the bey's audience-room, announced us to the group of figures therein and retired, closing the double doors. Maniakes, tall, black-bearded and imposing as I remembered him from the year before, turned from the map spread out on the table and regarded Hardraada a moment before he spoke.

"Hardraada" he said, "There's probably a reason for your action of yesterday. I'd like to hear it."

Hardraada frowned. "What action you talking about, *strategos*?" he asked, and Maniakes looked black.

"Committing the army to landing where it did" he snapped, "by your action in seizing the centre jetty. You were perfectly aware that my plan called for assaults on all three jetties at the same time. And that the assault would be made by heavy infantry. What made you decide to act on your own?"

Hardraada sighed. "A few things" he said, "The way my beard kept growing and tripping me while I waited for you to get your plan under way" he said. "Sailing up and down with horse transports that'd already crossed the Straits an' needing to land the horses our cavalry'd rely on. Watching the Arabs on the beach deciding by the minute that we didn't know what we were about, an' hoping our men didn't feel the same way. You can't hold men at the 'ready' forever, *strategos*."

Maniakes wasn't pleased. "That's my decision" he snapped, "not one for a subordinate commander. You barbarians've never appreciated the need for all parts of an army to work together. It's time you learned better!"

Hardraada snapped back. "That so? Is there anyone around who can teach us better? Us 'barbarians' got your army up the beach yesterday, Maniakes, and we took casualties doing it. That's the second time in two campaigns we've covered your landing while you got your head out of your own arse, and there won't be a third!"

"Don't threaten, Norseman. Neither you nor your *varangers* are indispensable!"

"Really? The emperor thinks we are. That's why he picked us for his pet project in Jerusalem last year, *strategos*. You remember last year? The year you sent that fuckwit Constantine Opos to get his arse kicked doing the job you're having to do all over again now? Face it, Maniakes – my marines are the best soldiers you've got, and that's because my *varangers* – that's *my varangers,* you listening? – have taught them to be."

For a moment I thought Hardraada had gone too far because Maniakes looked as though he would burst. But he turned away to the table while his staff looked the other way, took a deep breath and turned back again.

"*Hetaireiarchos*, I warn you formally not to depart again from my orders or my plans. Whatever your opinions of them. I will have order, discipline and system within my command. You may go."

Hardraada put on his helmet, turned on his heel without a word and led us to the double doors where he turned.

"*Strategos*" his voice boomed down the length of the room, and Maniakes turned to look up.

"No need to thank us for getting your army out of the shit yesterday. It's a true pleasure to be associated with such brilliant planning. No, really."

The Chronicle.

*T*he trouble was, of course, that Hardraada and Maniakes were too much alike. Both were used to being the biggest men – in every way – in any gathering, both liked their own way, both were fond of their own opinions and in different ways both were both excellent soldiers.

That was the rub. Maniakes was a careful general whose subordinates were frequently not up to his own levels of excellence in planning, preparation and fighting ability, whereas Hardraada's ability to look ahead, to identify weakness and to exploit it was turned into success by the fighting qualities of his lieutenants.

The other way in which they differed was the Norseman's readiness to depart from a plan when opportunity presented itself, and in that his own formidable prowess in battle was so often a vital factor in achieving success. For me, that made the giant varanger a better soldier than Maniakes or, indeed, anyone else.

But it also enabled me to kill him.

The Triconchus Palace, that same day.

Kia stretched lazily beneath the covers and murmured "Well, darling. If that's a sample of your bedside manner I'm horribly jealous of your other patients!"

"No need to be" said the physician between gasps, "they're mostly men and rich old ladies. Not at all like you. In fact I've never met anyone like you."

"Let me see if I understand" said Kia. "The eunuch requires frequent purging. Why's that, did you say?"

"I didn't say" said the physician, nuzzling her ear and sliding a hand over her breast. "But, speaking medically, he's a big man and very much obese. Not to mince words, my lovely, he's fat. And I've noticed – professionally – that fat people's bodies often work differently from normal-sized people's. In fact, I — oohh! What's that about?"

"Just checking how yours works" said Kia mischievously, her hands busy. "Seems very normal – oh yes – but you're not at all overweight. Go on about why he needs purging? You explain things so well; doctors don't often do that you know."

"It's my opinion" said the physician, "that his stomach muscles are too overstretched to do their job properly. He can't get rid of . . . his body wastes, you see? So he needs purging, to help him . . . ah to help . . ."

"To help him shit." said Kia. "Oops. Do I shock you?"

"You're a bit different" admitted the physician, "but then I don't know many court ladies. And I had no idea why one of them wanted to see me today. As you probably know, I'm not on that side of things."

"Mmmm – you will be from now on if I've got any say in things concerning the court physicians" said Kia. "And I've got a fair bit of say, because I work for someone very important, who can get me what I want. And at this point I want more of this . . . lots more . . . aahhh . . . lie still, I'll do it."

"I'm not sure this is professional" said the physician faintly.

"Why not?" said Kia, sliding across his chest. "I didn't ask you here because I'm sick. I asked you into my bed, not beside it, because I've been interested in you for a long time. So when I found out you knew a friend of mine . . . oohh! Is that really what they call 'the healing staff'? But before you make me forget – don't you have to be careful with those purges? I mean – what happens if you mix the wrong strength, for instance?"

"Do we have to talk about purges now?" gasped the physician.

"Of course not, darling . . . let's talk about stretched muscles . . . yes, yours. It stretches so wonderfully . . ."

Agira, inland Sicily.

Hardraada scowled thoughtfully up at the castle battlements. "Hard to see how" he said in response to Haldor's remark. "Thick walls – high too – from what I'm told there's a strong garrison inside and none of Maniakes' forage parties have found any provender for miles. Countryside's bare. And I can guess where all the food is."

Haldor spat. "Maniakes'll never let us leave this place in our rear" he said. "It's too strong. We can starve it out I suppose – but how long's that going to take? The walls – well, they'll take a power of cracking, an' that Byzantine bastard's got all the engines. By rights this place should be in his sector, not ours."

"Don't hold your breath" said Ulf. "Our *strategos'* got no interest in making life anything but difficult for us since Harald got into him at Catania."

"So they won't come out . . ." mused Hardraada, "and we can't get in . . . how can we change that?"

"You can't" shrugged Ulf. "Unless you grow wings and a tail. Birds're the only things that go in an' out there."

Hardraada stared at him. "What was that?" he asked, "What'd you say then?"

"Eh? I said . . . ah, 'Birds're the only things . . .'"

"You're right" said Hardraada. "Ulf, you're right. Now – what do you know about catching birds . . .?"

And the result was that for two days scores of bemused men wandered the woods and pastures of the Agira countryside trapping and netting birds, while others shaved twigs down into tinder and tied it into balls with thread and yet others hacked wood from trees and scraped the resin from it.

"What's a bird look for when it's in trouble?" asked Hardraada of no-one in particular.

"Its nest?" guessed the Scraeling, and Hardraada smiled.

"And where do birds build nests?"

"Anywhere cats can't reach?" hazarded the Scraeling, light beginning to dawn. "Ah – roofs, lofts?"

"And roofs are thatched. Lofts're built of timber" said Hardraada smugly. "What happens if we have birds carrying burning tinder into the city?"

"Never!" exploded Ulf. "Not as long as your arse points downwards. They'll die first. Bet you."

"I'll take your bet, too" said Hardraada. "Have you had a good look at how many birds come out of that place first thing in the day? Well, we've got over a hundred birds, and tomorrow we tie fireballs to their legs and let them go. If only half of them reach their nests in those roofs and lofts . . . Now show me your money, friend Ulf. Anyone else?"

To the Scraeling's amazement and the chagrin of those who had money invested in failure, the release of the fire-bearing birds had the roofs of the castle's buildings in flames by mid-morning of the next day. At the same time the scaling-ladders broke from the cover of the woodland and advanced under and behind the locked shields of marine detachments to find their place against the walls. Up the ladders under a withering hail of arrows that swept the battlements went a mixture of *varangers* and marines and within ten minutes of the first of them setting foot on the battlements, the great gates swung open and the rest of Hardraada's force charged into an inferno of smoke where men struggled, shouted, cursed and died amid the clang of steel on steel and the ravening crackle of fire.

Once the gates were open the result was never in doubt, and throughout the courtyard of the castle where smoke roiled and swirled the defenders threw down their weapons and held out empty hands to the figures that loomed through the smoke. Some were fortunate and others were not, and it was not until Hardraada's horns blared the command to break off that the killing ceased everywhere and section commanders got their men under control.

"The strongroom?" shouted the Scraeling to a Hardraada wiping the blood from a long blade, and the viking shook his head.

"Not till the fire's out" he bawled above the crackle of flames, "or we have to pull back. The strongroom'll be stone-built, never fear. Get anyone you can find to the well over there – buckets, helmets, anything!"

But the task was hopeless from the beginning, and soon the horns pealed again and all left alive retreated through the gates to watch and listen as the flames consumed every timber building within the castle.

"There's one problem less for the *strategos*" said the Scraeling as they watched, little realising how wrong he was. "And we'll clean out the strongroom as soon as we can get to it?"

"I've already started" said Hardraada. "Ulf, you owe me some money."

The audience room, imperial palace.

John's chins wobbled with the force of his emotion. "It's an outrage, majesty!" he said. "It's more than that – it's tantamount to a blow at the throne itself! An attempt on the life of your first minister is an attempt on the monarchy! On the monarchy, I say!"

"Then we must be the more grateful that God protected you, my worthy John" said Zoe. "But tell me again – how was this – this abomination prevented?"

"A servant, majesty" said John, mopping his forehead. "The servant of one of the court physicians who was to administer me a – a medicine. It was the servant's nightly duty to mix the physic for the day ahead, and two days ago he went to do so. But he found the jar with my name upon it already full, lady, when it should have been empty. Oh, it was the correct medicine, but he swore there was more in it than the physic for, thinking it odd, and being a good and careful man he tried it upon a scrap of meat which he fed to an alley-dog." John paused and wiped his brow again, for effect, Zoe thought.

"And . . .?"

"The beast died in convulsions!" John announced. "In agony, in fact, for its bowels burst!"

"Then this physician has a matter or two to answer!" said Zoe decisively. "Let him be questioned most directly and severely. I would know what he says."

"Not possible, majesty" said John, black with anger. "Not possible, for the servant – a good and true man – came directly to me with his story. The physician discovered what he had done, and took his own life with one of his devilish potions. He was quite dead, with the poison still in his mouth, when a detail of the palace guard came to claim him for questioning."

Zoe nodded, regretfully. "Then bring me the servant, at least, that I may reward his honesty and his courage, John."

John looked blacker still. "Would that I could, majesty. I instructed him to keep himself close until I had considered this – but none has seen him since he left my bedchamber after reporting his suspicions yesterday morning. And I was so . . . so distraught, majesty . . ." John paused, gulped and brought himself under control, "so distraught at such treachery . . . I did not at first notice his absence. And now he cannot be found."

"What? What?" snapped Zoe, rising to her feet. "A man I would reward cannot be found? Nonsense! Use the bell-pull by you!"

The man who stepped into the room at the summons removed his helmet, saluted Zoe and bowed to John before advancing into the room and kneeling before the tiny figure who came to the edge of the dais to greet him.

"Heaven-born one" he said, lifting the hem of her robe to his lips, "How may I serve you?"

"My faithful Isaac" smiled Zoe down at him. "Lord John here has mislaid a servant whom we wish to reward. You have never yet failed me – will you and your men find him, pray you?"

"Majesty" said Isaac Comnenus, "if my lady wishes to speak with him, then the empire itself is not big enough to hide him from me. Live forever, my queen." He stood, bowed over her hand and saluted Orphanotrophos.

"You are hurt, commander" said the eunuch, nodding at the bandage on the soldier's hand. "A sword-cut?"

"Nothing so honourable, lord. I breed war-dogs for my amusement . . . and one with which I was careless did this. It is only a bite."

The Chronicle.

I was wrong in my belief that Maniakes would be pleased at the reduction of the castle at Agira. In fact he was much less than pleased, and said so quite clearly and loudly, for it seemed that the taking – not the destruction, but the taking - of the castle had been a key part of his strategy for holding the island. But we, of course, did not know this for Maniakes had neither consulted nor informed us of it. Not unreasonably, Hardraada pointed this out at some volume.

In fact, watching the clash of two angry men it was clear to me that they would never get on and that, were both to serve the same master it needed to be in different places. It must have been clear to Maniakes also, for after that came the orders detaching us to operate independently in the northern part of the island. In that, I believe, Maniakes showed a greater wisdom than Hardraada – but on the other hand he may merely have wanted to discover if Arab treasuries and strongrooms captured in our absence would prove to have more in them than those taken by us. Who knows?

The Emperor's rooms, Constantinople.

Scowling, the eunuch bit into the sweetmeat. "It's that little slut Vonskaya" he said malevolently. "She's in it somewhere, I know she is. There's a pretty strong rumour – I can't prove it though – that she was screwing the physician Diogenes, who was all set to poison me. But as I say, I can't prove it."

"Wouldn't mean anything if you could" said Michael IV wearily. "She's screwed half the Court at one time or another, and sometimes at the same time. God, I'm tired. And my head aches."

"You caught it a fair old crack when you fell during your last attack" said John. "If you'll take my advice, you'll get into uniform from now on."

"Uniform?" asked his brother, "what on earth for?"

"Two things" said the Eunuch. "It underlines your love for the army. And it gives you an excuse for wearing a helmet without looking weak about it. Being eccentric's one thing – weakness is another. What do you say?"

Michael passed a hand over his eyes. "I'll think about it" he said. "Did you ever find the servant who tipped you off about the physician?"

"I didn't" said John thoughtfully, "but that Comnenus fellow did. You know, the ex-commander of Zoe's bodyguard? He's devoted to her and she won't part with him – not at any price."

"I know him" said Michael. "Gave up a regular career to be her right arm. He's a killer, that one; wouldn't think twice about topping anyone she wanted topped. They're close all right."

"Really?" said John. "You don't think they're –?"

"I doubt it" said Michael, "but if they are – good luck to them. Good luck to anyone who keeps her out of my bed. But you say he found the servant? What's he say?"

"That's the problem" said the Eunuch. "Unfortunately, Comnenus only found the body. Someone'd slit his throat."

Zoe's apartments, the Triconchus Palace.

Gloomily, Zoe said "We've failed, my Kia. The eunuch is as strong as ever, and still I do not see my husband, so the work of getting an heir languishes. Kia . . . Kia . . . do you still believe . . . is it possible, do you think?"

"Have courage, dearest Zoe. The courage of a queen. We have lost little. Consider – your Isaac's men took the servant from under the very nose of the eunuch, as swiftly and expertly as they cancelled Diogenes. You are well served, my lady, and not by Isaac alone."

"Aye, Kia. In you and my remaining ladies I am fortunate indeed, and . . ."

"Nay, Zoe – not in us alone, but in others also. Do you recall the *varanger*, Harald the Hard? Let us talk of him a moment . . ."

North Sicily, late summer.

Hardraada shaded his eyes as he peered into the distance at the castle. "Castelbuono, is it? Well, we can't go round it 'cause I'm not leaving that behind to cut us off from the coast. We'll have to take it. It controls this whole area."

"And they know we're hereabouts" said Skallagrim, "unless they're blind. We've done a power of burning lately."

"So we can't sneak up on 'em" said Ulf, scratching in his beard. "We can make siege engines from the forest, aye – but what a pain in the arse!"

"Not to mention the time it'll take" mused Hardraada. "Any good ideas? Scraeling? You're a cunning bugger – what'd you reckon about this one then?"

"Not a lot" replied the Scraeling, also shading his eyes. "You summed it up quite nicely. Walls're high and thick. No direct approach on any side. Not overlooked anywhere an engine can throw a boulder from . . ." but as he looked at the castle that dominated the valley, something prickled at the back of his mind. But try as he might, it would not come to the front.

And in the back of his mind it remained until the early afternoon of that day when, after eating, he walked over to a tree in the forest that concealed their force to relieve himself. "Funny, isn't it?" he remarked to Skuli, who was on the same errand, "We've got a whole island to piss on, but what do we do? Why we pick a tree and two of us share it. Why pick on the same tree? Why pick on a tree at all? Why not piss on nothing?"

Skuli laughed. "You're a funny bugger, Scraeling. Must be all that education. What's it matter where a man pisses? You've got to piss somewhere—" but the Scraeling never heard the end of Skuli's philosophy on relieving himself, for at his words the idea that had eluded him before was now bright and clear in the front of his head.

"*Leder*" he said to Hardraada, "this our camp for a while?"

"Might as well be" said Hardraada, "till we sort out what to do about that place."

"That's what's bothering me" said the Scraeling. "I might have an idea – dunno without checking on something. I want to get a look at it from higher up."

"Fine" said Hardraada. "Take an escort – you never know." And he watched the Screaling signal to six troopers and heave himself into the saddle before turning back to his meal.

When the Screaling returned he slid from his horse and grinned broadly.

"What you looking so pleased about?" demanded Skallagrim. "Found another whore to cheat, have you?"

The Screaling rolled his eyes. "You're never going to let me forget that, are you?" he said, for he had long since stopped attempting to deny it, "but look – get hold of this . . . where's Harald?"

"Just called us together" said Skallagrim, "an' you're in time to join us."

"Well?" asked Hardraada, "What took you an hour?"

"Something Skuli said" replied the Screaling. "He asked why it mattered where a man pissed. And then I realised what'd been bothering me since we looked at Castelbuono this morning. I noticed it without noticing it."

"Eh? Screaling, what's in your water bottle?" demanded Hardraada.

"*Leder*, come and look for yourself" the Screaling returned. "And I'll help you. When you look at Castelbuono, what don't you see?" and they set off to the forest edge, where the Screaling waved at the bulk of the castle down the valley.

"What don't you see? On the walls?" he demanded again, and there was silence until Haldor said, slowly, "Jakes. There's no jakes on the battlements, or anywhere else come to that."

"Exactly!" said the Screaling. "Don't these Arabs shit? Have they mastered the need to piss? Of course not! So where're their jakes?"

"Round one of the other sides?" suggested Ulf and the Screaling shook his head.

"Thought of that" he said, "so I rode up to the hilltops and round the two sides we can't see. No jakes on any side."

"Would someone tell me why the fuck we're talking about where Arabs shit?" demanded Skallagrim.

"The Screaling's done it again" said Hardraada. "Skallagrim, castles have jakes just like we do in the *drakkars*. You know, wooden platforms hanging out from the walls where you go for a shit. Now, Castelbuono doesn't have any. What's that mean – they live in their own shit d'you think?"

"'Course not" said Skallagrim. "I mean – you wouldn't, would you?"

"So—?" prompted Hardraada, with a wink at the Screaling.

"So" said Haldor, "Their jakes are all inboard of the walls. And if that's so, there must be a bloody great drain leading out, somewhere along the walls. Eh?"

"Right" said the Scraeling. "It's round the north side. No, I haven't seen it" he said, forestalling Ulf's question, "but from the tops on that side you can see how green and lush the grass is at the foot of the castle mound. Quite different from the two sides you can see from here. So I think it's there. And it's a way in, because there must be a way of cleaning it out from time to time." He watched light dawn in Skallagrim's eye and slapped him on the back. "Tell me again, comrade. Go on" he said.

Skallagrim chuckled. "You're a cunning little bugger, Scraeling. Odin's ravens miss more than you do; fuck me if it ain't so!" he said admiringly.

That night.

Fifteen feet up the narrow stone shaft, Karl bowed his cowled head and tried to close his mind to what had just bounced off his shoulder. Taking a deep breath, he placed his hands behind him against the wall and pushed hard to the full extent of his arms. Then he placed the heel of his right foot in front of the toe of his left and levered upward. *Three more* he told himself – *hands–back–feet; hands–back–feet; hands–back* – he bowed his head again against the deluge of water that thundered down upon him as the man above emptied the water in which he had rinsed the sponge he'd used to wipe his arse.

The viking pressed hard back against the latrine-shaft wall and brought his hands round to wipe them carefully upon the heavy cloak he wore. *If I slip* he told himself, *I'll take Asgeirr and the others with me. Question is - will the fall kill us or will that thigh-deep pile of old shit we forced our way through save us? Or choke us maybe?* He fought to suppress a giggle. *'S not that funny* he thought, *what's the air in here doing to me?*

He took his weight on his hands again and cursed the throwing-axe strapped to his chest by the belt that girdled the heavy cloak to him, for small though it was he didn't really need the weight as he inched up the narrow latrine shaft. Hands-back-feet; hands-back-feet; hands-back-feet. Must be nearly there. He blinked cautiously upwards and decided he could see the soft gleam of light. *'Course* he realised, *that scraeling's arse isn't blocking the hole. His hole's not in the hole* – and again he fought the urge to giggle.

Get a grip he told himself. *That light – either there's no door in the jakes or it's open. Either way, you need to get through the seat quick and quiet an' pray to Loki that no-one else wants a shit before I'm ready to deny him that last pleasure.* Karl gritted his teeth and fought the shrieking torment in shoulders and legs to drive his way upwards in a haze.

He reached the top and paused a moment to steady himself. *Odin's balls – we must be thirty feet up. Thank the Allfather there's a jakes on this floor – I couldn't have gone another one.* The wooden seat felt smooth and strange to hands roughened by the stone of the latrine shaft, so he took a firm grip on the edge of the hole and pushed, praying it wouldn't squeak or thud against the wall. When the weight came off he rested a moment – *get out, get out, don't push your luck* – then grasped the stone edges of the shaft and levered himself out backwards, arms screaming.

There was a door, and it was ajar. Karl closed it softly and reached a trembling arm back into the hole to haul Asgeirr through and wave him to the space behind the door. The other demons climbed from their own fouled underworld after him, and perched on the edge of the jakes while they stripped off their cloaks and woollen leggings, balled them and dropped them back down. There was no need to send warning to the noses of those they would need to kill.

Karl eased open the door and looked out upon a corridor that was curiously empty given the noise that was coming from somewhere. Weapons in hand and naked, the four of them slipped down it and into a long and darkened four-sided gallery that ran round the top of a hall where a meal, or even a feast, he realised, was in progress. Asgeirr leaned close and breathed in his ear.

"Good one Karl! This must be most of the scraelings – an' they're not armed! Fuckin' marvellous!" Karl nodded, looked around a moment and made up his mind. Gesturing with his axe he led them in the direction where he had decided the gatehouse lay, and as the four figures flitted silently through the gallery he muttered a prayer of thanks to Loki for empty corridors and a garrison that had chosen to ignore the army it must know was in the area.

Their arrival in the gatehouse was sudden and violent, and the three men on duty died still lamenting the foul luck that had placed them on duty during whatever occasion was happening in the great hall.

"None for you, Bergr!" panted Karl, wrenching his axe free of the chest where it was buried. "No – leave the main gates – no time to bugger about with those pulleys. You an' Asgeirr get the wicket open – Harald an' the storming-party are under the mound an' those scraelings up top might catch a glimpse. Go! Quick!"

The wicket gate had opened scarce halfway when a rush of dark figures poured through it into the deep shadow of the gatehouse. "In the hall, *leder*" whispered Karl to the huge shadow that sought him, "some sort of carry-on – feast, maybe? Anyway – what looks like most've the garrison're there. Have we got—" but he was cut off by the scream of a horn, another and then a third from the walls above.

"Haldor's broken cover!" snapped Hardraada. "Time to feed the ravens – through the door in pairs, then right and left inside. Follow!" and he sprinted across the courtyard towards the door of the great hall. It opened just as he reached it and the big *varanger* smashed his way over and through the men in the doorway, and his vikings hit the opening two at a time behind him so that none jammed in the doorway. Once inside they fanned out immediately to right and left, each man sprinting into the attack and screaming at the pitch of his lungs.

Unarmed as they were, those within the hall went down like corn before the scythe, and it was over in six or seven bloody minutes. Only later would it emerge that those in the hall were the officers and under-officers of the Arab garrison, feasting in the expectation that the castle would soon be invested by the imperial army known to be in the area. Thus the carnage in the hall was wrought upon the very leaders of whatever resistance Castelbuono might have offered so that, by the time Hardraada and his lieutenants had their troops under control, there was little enough left of it. For their part, the soldiery awoke in their dormitories to find grim-faced marines and *varangers* at the doorways with naked blades in their fists, and there was no resistance.

Dawn found the fortress of Castelbuono firmly in imperial hands, and a genial Hardraada faced his lieutenants. "I'm offering a prize of ten gold pieces" he announced.

"What for?" someone wanted to know.

"For anyone who can guess how we've pissed Maniakes off this time!"

The Chronicle.

*H*ardraada *wouldn't have missed ten gold pieces from what we took at Castelbuono, or even fifty. That castle was the kingpin of North Sicily's defence and only the great fortress of Palermo was of more importance. And it had been done by four brave men and a storming-party of thirty. It was the stuff of sagas, of course, and Askell did us proud in that, even if he did invite the world to believe that Hardraada and his heroes tunnelled under the castle foundations and burst from the very floor of the dining-hall. Well, wading through shit isn't in the tradition of heroes, is it?*

But more to the point was what came from the strongroom. I was into it before the last defender had been shackled, and I didn't emerge until full daylight when my escort was yawning with boredom and urging me to hurry up with my bloody runes so they could break their fast.

The strongroom held gold and silver coin – sacks and sacks of it, obviously intended for disbursement among Abdallah's armies in one way or another, and more money than I'd ever seen or could ever have imagined existed. As I said when I had a moment alone with the leder *it was a dangerous amount of money. Its size would tempt him, I knew, but if he made away with all of it he'd spend the rest of his life defending it and I was fearful that he'd try. For if he tried and failed, another would do what I had sworn to do and that suited me not at all.*

No – I argued hard that, while such an amount couldn't be hidden, its size could be lessened by a fortune, with none the wiser. No discrepancy would ever arise, I maintained, for the only record of what came from the dungeon would be that made by the secretary to the emperor's faithful and valiant hetaireiarchos. *Who'd captured it and turned it over, right? And should any discrepancy ever come to light – and I could see no manner in which it might – it could be blamed upon the carelessness or the venality of its original guardians.*

Quick to see how he might emerge with both wealth and credit, Hardraada agreed with less fuss than I expected, and not even Maniakes could take the shine from this triumph. Perhaps that pleased the Landwaster more than anything else about Castelbuono, because the strategos had to invite him to his headquarters, eventually, to pass on the imperial thanks in person – and the taste of ashes in his mouth must have spoiled his food for weeks.

So that year Ulf and a strong varanger *escort took more than one heavy chest on from Constantinople to distant Kiev, there to winter and to return in time for the spring campaign. For the first time in Hardraada's service to the imperium he didn't winter in Kiev, for other matters in the imperial City claimed his attention.*

The Court, Constantinople, 1039.

Zoe drew herself up to her full height. "Kneel, *varanger* who was once fit to be a *hetaireiarchos*! Kneel before your empress, I say!"

Hardraada cast a wild glance at the Scraeling, who looked equally stricken as he translated, while behind him Ulf and Haldor tightened their grasp on their hilts.

"Kneel, barbarian!" came the voice again, and Hardraada sank slowly from his great height to his knees, his face betraying the emotions churning through his mind.

"You are no longer *hetaireiarchos*, by my edict and command!" The voice was icy and the tone perfectly level, as the Scraeling moistened dry lips. Who had Zoe been listening to?

"Instead, Harald son of Sigurd – whom men call Hardraada in token of your prowess in war – instead, you will rise a *manglavites* of the imperial Varanger Guard. Take this, with your empress' thanks and devotion for your mighty deeds in our service, against those who would overturn our peace and threaten our realm!" And at Zoe's signal a footman brought forward a velvet-covered tray on which lay a collar made of gold chain with, at its middle, a small version of the imperial seal. Zoe reached for the chain and placed it around Hardraada's neck, waving away the footman and fastening the clasp with her own hands.

"Rise, *manglavites* Harald! But before you do – know that this title, and the badge it carries, are the reward of a grateful state. This is the gift of a queen for her most redoubtable warrior." And the empress of Constantinople leaned forward and stretched to kiss Hardraada's cheeks, first one and then the other while a murmur ran through the multitude in the throne room at such a departure from all tradition and protocol.

"I thank your majesty for this great honour" said Hardraada slowly and thickly in Greek, and he touched first one cheek and then the other, "but your own gift is greater by far. *Hard-raede* is your majesty's man, now and forever." He paused, searching for words, and then, "Your enemies are mine, and my axe ever between you and them. *Vess-heil*, Empress Zoe!"

"*Vess-heil! Vess-heil!*" echoed Ulf and Haldor, and the courtiers erupted in applause at the famed *varanger* honour salute while Zoe bent forward again to speak a word into Hardraada's ear before drawing him to his feet and inclining her head at his bow.

"Secretary" she said, her voice as clear as a bell, "bid your master assume his duties as a *manglavites* of my Guard at once and take his station behind the throne, where he is evermore entitled to be and required to be. This is my word."

The Screaling spoke and Hardraada marched forward, helmet in the crook of his arm, to take up his post and the audience continued.

Zoe's bedchamber, that night.

Chuckling, Zoe murmured "You should have seen your face", her head on Hardraada's chest. "Thought you were in trouble, didn't you?"

Hardraada chuckled in turn. "So did Haldor and Ulf, and they're not easily impressed. But yes, you had me going" he admitted. "You can be a right little ball of fire at times."

"Mmmm" murmured the empress of Constantinople. "You should know, lover. Oh, you don't mean just in bed? How disappointing . . . I thought you were getting ready to make me the happiest woman in the world again . . . ah, you may be, soldier. Unless you've brought your sword to bed, part of you's on parade already, I see. When are you going to learn Greek properly, anyway?"

"Do I need to for this?" demanded Hardraada, his hands busy. "The Screaling's got me sorted out with the common tongue. What do I need Greek for?"

"Because your little ball of fire can't abide speaking the common tongue" returned Zoe, "and you'll need Greek – and good Greek at that – when you come back to Court. As you will soon, and I wish you could stay here now. Especially if you keep doing that . . ."

"Why can't I stay now?"

"Because with you beside him to be brilliant, George Maniakes might – just might – settle that business in Sicily. And I want it settled, before trouble blows up somewhere else."

"Why're you worrying yourself about that?" demanded Hardraada.

"by Freya, you're tiny. Here, worry about this . . ." and Zoe lost interest in Maniakes, Sicily and Greek for a while.

But she returned to it later. "I concern myself with that" she said sleepily, "because I need to concern myself with everything. The emperor has the Sacred Disease, the falling sickness, and the best physicians can't arrest it. His brother the eunuch knows nothing of military affairs and is scorned by the army; the top commanders aren't as they were in Basil's day, and Maniakes is – was – the best we've got. Until you, my hard, hard man. But you're going to make everything better."

"Ah" said Hardraada. "Maybe not. You should know that Maniakes and I . . . we don't work together that well. Fact is, the further we're apart, the better things go."

"I know that" said Zoe. "Your respective camps aren't as tightly sealed as you like to think, and I've got people in both. One of the reasons you became a *manglavites* today is so that I can send you here and there as I want without even consulting Maniakes, because your new commission isn't in the *varanger* mercenaries, it's in the imperial Varanger Guard. Now, Guard regiments don't often leave Constantinople, but Basil set the precedent years ago when he switched his élites around as he wanted. And the Varangers are the élite of the élite. Basil was a soldier above all else, and there hasn't been a real warrior's backside on the throne since."

"Dunno" said Hardraada, "you sit on it, don't you?"

Zoe smiled and nibbled one of Hardraada's fingers. "I was born to the purple" she said. "Basil's blood's in my veins too, and I'm not some blow-in or usurper. But there are some things I can't do, hard man. But you can. One of them is to be the power behind the throne because with Michael the way he is – and he'll be much worse soon – I'll need some. You heard me say today that your station entitles and requires you to be behind the throne at all times. That wasn't a figure of speech, lover. The other thing is – to get me pregnant. I'm the most powerful woman in the world, but I can't do that myself either."

Hardraada was silent and Zoe went on, "I don't know what you had in mind when you came to Constantinople, Harald, but it's all within your grasp now. Power – enough of it to make wealth irrelevant. An empire. Marriage to me. By our Church ordinances, I may marry three times. I'm on my second, and it's not going to last. Make me pregnant, warrior from the snow and ice, and if Michael's still alive when you do, we'll divorce immediately and send him to end his days in a monastery."

The Chronicle.

*A*nd as Hardraada boasted to me, Zoe's plan was to send us back to Sicily to seek a quick end to a provincial war that was draining the empire of funds and men to no great end. But as 1038 became 1039 and then 1040, the war in Sicily turned into a grim and bloody struggle in which neither side could gain a decisive victory and towns were taken, lost and retaken. We might have won it for the emperor, even if Hardraada would not have won it for Maniakes, for wherever the Landwaster raven flew over a battlefield our forces swept to victory; and where it stretched its wings over an area that needed to be subjugated and crushed, Arabs and native folk alike trembled at its passing and spoke in whispers.*

But Maniakes would not loose Hardraada as Yaroslav had had the sense to do. Jealous of anyone who might eclipse him in battle, it was never his way to delegate either responsibility or power. And because what the strategos could not do himself was left undone, Abdallah the Great Turk lived to fight another day – and another and another until Maniakes' inability to finish him, and his reluctance to let us do so, wearied Hardraada of a long-drawn war fought in a land now stripped of opportunity and empty of plunder.

However, as his star rose, that of Maniakes seemed to wane. He forced Abdallah into battle at Traina with a masterful campaign that denied the Arab any other option, but it was the charge Hardraada led, the charge of the Varanger Guard, that isolated the Arab general and drove him from the field even as his personal guard fell in windrows under our axes to buy him the time. Abdallah took ship that day and managed to evade the inshore blockade of that same Stephen Palaesostom, the naval strategos of the Aegean Command under whom we had served in our pirate-chasing days.

Maniakes did not receive Stephen's news calmly or well. In fact his fury knew no bounds and he seized the nearest thing to hand – a horse-whip as it turned out – and beat Stephen round the head with it. It took four aides to separate them, but only one messenger to report the matter to Constantinople and an interested emperor – whose sister was Stephen's wife.

But Maniakes might have survived that had he not attempted to swindle of their agreed wages and booty the three hundred Norman knights who had decimated the Arab cavalry at Traina. The trouble was that, unlike Hardraada, he wasn't a greedy man and so had no idea how to go about swindling anyone successfully. And then, of course, there was Arduin, leader of the Lombard mercenaries, whom he had flogged through the camp because of his presumption in refusing to make over a captured Arab stallion Maniakes thought he should have had first option upon. As Hardraada gleefully pointed out at the time, the problem with honest and upright men is that they tend to lack subtlety.

What really topped it off, though, was Hardraada's withdrawal of the Varanger Guard from Maniakes' battle order over the treatment of the Norman and Lombard mercenaries. In that, I have to agree, the viking was right. Maniakes was a straight-line, by-the-book soldier who went close to brilliance. On a personal level, though, he knew nothing about what drove a mercenary and he wasn't disposed to learn even though almost a third of his army was composed of men who fought for money and loot. Hardraada used that to pay Maniakes back for all his previous slights, real or imaginary, and that's why he took the Guard out of the line.

Anyway – orders summoning us back to Byzantium came in at just the right part of 1040, because Bulgaria had gone up in flames and Zoe had need of someone who could put out fires in her empire as well as in her bed.

BOOK THREE

OF THE VARANGER

1040–1042

"Harald the Stern ne'er allowed
  Peace to his foemen, false and proud;
  In eighteen battles, fought and won,
  The valour of the Norseman shone.

"He who the hungry wolf's wild yell
  Quiets with prey, the stern, the fell,
  Midst the uproar of shriek and shout
  Stung the Greek emperor's eyes both out:
  The Norse king's mark will not adorn,
  The Norse king's mark gives cause to mourn;
  His mark the Eastern king must bear,
  Groping his sightless way in fear."

The skald, Thiodolf, in 'The Heimskringla'

Thessalonika, Greece, 1040.

Hardraada waved his hand expressively. "Of course the garrison knows we're here. If we can see them, they can see us – and if you're standing siege you look at the horizon harder than Hrani looks for whores in a marketplace, and more often too. So they know we're here all right. Question is – can we rely on them?"

Haldor scratched, and spat. "I wouldn't" he said. "How long've they been penned up?"

"A month, near as I can judge" said Hardraada, "but word from the City was, they weren't driven in there – they went in in good order, so a month ago they weren't desperate."

"A month ago don't matter" replied his lieutenant. "'S how they feel about it now that's important."

"Right" acknowledged Hardraada. "And we can't find out any better, 'cause there's no way of getting word in or out. Screeling – anything clever?"

The Screeling shook his head slowly. "Not that I can see" he said. "Scouts reckon twenty thousand Bulgars between the city and us, so it's sealed tighter than a herring's arse, as Skuli would say. And no shithouse to sneak in through either –" and that raised a smile among the hard-bitten crew in the forest glade – "so, sorry *leder*, cunning won't serve. If you're asking me – we'll have to go through them."

"With twelve thousand against twenty" mused Hardraada. "Hard going."

"You're getting old, *leder*" scoffed Ulf. "Our twelve're Varanger Guard, the Guards infantry, five squadrons Guard cavalry and the field engineers – an' they're trained as soldiers first an' engineers after. Then there's the marines we trained, three regiments of them, and a couple of hundred *varangers*. Against what?"

Skallagrim stirred. "Ulf's right" he said. "Them Bulgars're a rabble, not an army. Our scouts didn't bump into them at all – they haven't got any, I reckon, so they don't know we're close."

"But they will" put in the Scraeling, "when we start foraging. We can't hide twelve thousand men then."

"So what you're saying" said Hardraada, "is that if we're going to take them it should be soon?"

"It should be now" said Haldor. "Freya's tits, man, the old Harald would've had his axe bloody by now. All that shagging on soft couches getting to you, is it?"

The Scraeling sucked in his breath, but there came a shout of laughter at Haldor's remark and Hardraada grinned as widely as any.

"I can afford lots of shagging on soft couches, you old bugger – I've got years on you. Bet I get into Thessalonika before you do?"

"You're on" promised Haldor, "but I won't be slowing down to give any young bugger a sporting chance!" And the planning began in earnest as the Scraeling, who did not expect to take any part in it, glanced round at the hard, intent faces and let his mind roam over the events that had brought the imperial armies to Greece.

Imperial tax demands had been seen by the Bulgars as more evidence of Byzantine hatred and contempt for the nation and race that Zoe's uncle, Basil II, had annexed within living memory. Whatever the rights of it an ex-slave from Constantinople, one Peter Delianos, had raised an army on the strength of his claim to be the illegitimate grandson of the last tsar of Bulgaria, and had used it to set Bulgaria aflame. Throughout the land imperial garrisons caught unawares had been slaughtered to the last man, settlers butchered on their farms and merchants burned among their trade goods as a whole generation of hatred found expression in women violated, children murdered and dwellings razed.

To make things worse, the conflagration in Bulgaria happened against a backdrop of disaster in Sicily as a series of reverses there undid all that Traina had achieved at the same time as Maniakes, architect of that victory, was recalled to Constantinople to account for his treatment of Stephen Palaesostom and to suffer imprisonment for it.

Hardraada had been more than pleased to witness Maniakes' humiliation from behind the throne, standing impassive as the disgraced *strategos* had appealed to him for first-hand corroboration of the difficulties of dealing with mercenary troops before commenting that he, personally, had not encountered any such difficulties that would not respond to order, discipline and system.

Leder, leder thought the Scraeling as he saw the gall in Maniakes' eyes, *hope that you never come within the length of Maniakes' arm in future . . .*

But in the absence of any commander of note, Sicily was well-nigh lost again – and worse, the Normans had seen the weakness of the Byzantines there and decided to seize the island for themselves, with the result that imperial troops and imperial generals had suffered a series of bloody and humiliating defeats at the hands of those ruthless and efficient horse-soldiers.

But Hardraada's forces had arrived in Bulgaria in time to follow the rebel armies to Greece and to catch up with it outside the city of Thessalonika. Now they had the chance — but his thoughts were interrupted by the crash of a fist on the table.

"No!" exploded Hardraada. "We're here to teach these scraelings a lesson, and that's not to rebel against the empire. Part one of that's about feeding their army to the ravens, and part two is about doing the same to their countryside – and then taking compensation for the damage they've done and tribute for their good behaviour in future. Me, I don't want to come back here, so I'm going to make fucking sure we don't have to! Remember Shepetovka? Well then – when you go to your divisions, tell your officers it's the Rus all over again, and tell 'em how much fun it'll be!"

The meeting broke up and his lieutenants drifted away to hold their own with their divisional officers. Hardraada sighed and nodded the Scraeling towards the large crystal wine flask on its silver table. "Might as well use the gift of a grateful empress" he said. "You too, if you want."

The Scraeling inclined his head and poured two goblets of the sweet red wine. Hardraada grimaced and pursed his lips. "I'm getting used to it" he said, "but I'm a beer man at heart. Now – there'll be more loot lying around today than you might think. These buggers've hit one imperial fort after another, an' each one of them had a strongroom where the garrison funds were kept. So, if this Delianos is worth a fart in a gale he'll have got hold of all that himself, 'cause he sees himself as a future king of the Bulgars and kings need treasuries. But there'll be other kinds of loot – they've knocked over the odd church, even though they're Christian too, an' the number of settler homes they've looted is anybody's guess. So there'll be a bit of that too, but a lot of it'll need to wait until we go over the bodies later. As far's the money's concerned, it'll be in what passes for a baggage train, and that'll be in their centre more'n likely." He paused, and the Scraeling nodded.

"So" resumed Hardraada, "you're going in, mounted, with a hundred men to find Peter's secret stash and throw a ring round it. And they'll be a hundred hard men too – forty *varanger* axemen and sixty marines from the old days, and two squadrons of Guard cavalry to punch the hole that takes you in. Got it?"

"Got it" said the Scraeling. "We'll grab the train, set up a perimeter and hang on until it's all over. Prisoners?"

"Nail 'em to whatever's handy" said Hardraada, "but save yourself the bother and don't take any." He raised his goblet. "Luck, Scraeling, for the first time you've commanded in battle. Always said you were a dangerous little bugger."

A valley behind the battlefield.

The cataphract officer leaned forward and shouted over the roar of battle, "Ready?" and the Scraeling swallowed and nodded.

"Right" said the other, "I'm leading, with half a squadron. The other half's behind us, and the second squadron's on the flanks. All your men in the middle, and try not to fall off! We'll be tight, because it's speed and a big hit we're after, yes? We know where it is – I've had a look – yes, right in the middle."

He sounded inhumanly cheerful about the prospect of spearing into the heart of a rebel army from the flank, thought the Scraeling and as if the cavalryman had read his mind he added, "Don't worry – they're foot, not dug in, no stakes, no cavalry support, no nothing. This'll be easy" he bawled, "just don't fall off! I'm off up front. You'll hear from me!"

The Scraeling nodded and moistened his lips, hoping that the axemen who rode on either side of him felt more confident than he did. Beyond them he could see a Guardsman tapping a fist on the horn of his saddle as he waited for the call that would send them forward at the walk, trot and eventually gallop. The man's body bespoke only tension and the wish to be loosed, and the Scraeling took some confidence from that.

A trumpet pealed above the clangour, a shiver ran through the mass of horsemen and it moved forward in answer. The pace quickened and someone bawled from the flanks "Close up tight! Tight! Get close! Closer, fuck you!" and the Scraeling could see the heavy Guards chargers pressing in from the flanks as the speed picked up another notch. Then the column bent and he realised from the increasing volume of noise that they were passing round the hill that screened the main battlefield.

Then they straightened, the trumpet pealed and suddenly they were flying, the footsoldiers' mounts swept along by the excitement they could feel from their bigger and heavier cousins as the commander launched them in the charge. Steel appeared in the fists of the cavalrymen on the flanks and then they were cleaving into and through groups of men on the ground, men who flung themselves aside from the path of the thundering hooves and the glaring eyes, careless of the long gleaming *spathae* slashing at unguarded heads and limbs.

The trumpet screamed again and the body of men divided to right and left revealing four wagons in front of them, their teams unharnessed and the yokes resting on the ground. Men spilled and swarmed all around the wagons but even as the Scraeling dragged his horse to a standstill he was conscious of the long sabres rising and falling again and again until none was left standing. Then the Guards officer was back.

"Here you are!" he bellowed, "Let's get your men dismounted, sharp-like, and set. You've got these wagons – now you've got to hold them!"

The Scraeling slid down and handed off his reins to a cavalryman, then scuttled forward in his lurching run to where the axemen gathered around Karl and Skuli. "Half each side, as we agreed!" he snapped. "Hold the ring against any who break through the marines. You support, not attack. Got it?"

"Aye *leder*!" came back the response and Karl's group broke for the far side of the baggage-train as the Scraeling looked around to see the last of the marines' shield-wall slipping into place to form a steel ring round the four wagons. It had all gone so well, he thought – it was almost as if they hadn't been noticed, but common sense told him that a hundred men punched deep into an army by forty heavy cavalry wasn't likely to remain invisible for long. Then where was the rebel counter?

On the heels of the question came "Sir!" from the marine commander, "About to get busy sir!" And beyond him the Scraeling could see a huge knot of rebels gathering about a tall figure in mail and conical helmet. For a moment he watched the man haranguing his followers, whipping them up to follow, and then he leapt for the driving-board of the nearest wagon and stood above them all as the rebels broke towards the waiting shields like a wave upon a beach.

The sling came off the Scraeling's waist in a flash and a stone went into the pouch as quickly, and as the mass of attackers flooded forward, the sling began to whirr by his side although his eyes remained fixed upon his target, the tall warrior who was so plainly a leader of some reputation.

His chance came as the man turned his head to shout encouragement to those behind him and for a second his face came from behind his shield rim. In that second of exposure the Scraeling sent his stone into the gap between shield-rim and helmet-brim as the head came round. The warrior dropped shield and sword and swayed as a bloody hole appeared where his left eye had been, then he toppled over.

"Mine!" bellowed the Scraeling. "First kill! Mine, you *varanger*s – mine, you marines! Who'll match me?" There came a mighty shout from the imperials as the front of the Bulgar charge leaped at the shields that awaited them, but the line held firm as the short stabbing-swords slid past the edge of the curved torso-length shields to find their mark in men who could not manoeuvre for the press from behind.

In the centre the *varanger* axemen stamped their feet and roared encouragement as they held their ground unwillingly, while above them the Scraeling sent missile after missile beyond the shield-wall, and at every cast a man fell. Soon enough the marines had built a knee-high wall of bodies before them and at the moment when the Bulgars drew back there was a roar in the distance and a mighty surge away from the small group around the wagons.

The Scraeling drew himself up as much as his vantage-point would allow and strained his eyes into the distance. "Banners" he announced to the upturned faces. "Banners, aye – Jesu, the garrison's come out! – it's come out!" At which the *varangers* clamoured even more to be loosed, and the Scraeling felt it timely to exhort them to stand fast in their mission. "You four!" he demanded, "into these wagons and break open every chest you see! Make report to me of what you find – aye, move before these bastards come back!"

But the rebels never returned, for they were caught between a garrison seizing the only chance left to it and an imperial army led by the fury of the Varanger Guard, and the combination more than made up for the disparity in numbers.

"Through them like a streak of hot shit!" crowed a Haldor still drunk with slaughter when he came back later across a battlefield where the only things moving were soldiers looting the dead and dispatching the wounded. "Them inside came out just at the time it mattered – took the rebels off us something beautiful. Get your wagons, Scraeling? Good, good! Harald'll be pleased. Another trip to Kiev this winter, eh?"

The Chronicle.

I estimated that the rebel army suffered around fifteen thousand casualties in what developed into a great slaughter. Faithful to Hardraada's command, the imperial army spared none it could reach and only my suggestion that further killing was a waste of marketable slaves sent the order to hold pealing from the trumpets and ox-horns.

His pleasure at the destruction of half the rebel forces in Greece and Bulgaria was matched only by his delight at the contents of the four wagons we seized and held. Hardraada's instinct for loot had triumphed once more, for the wagons contained many chests clearly marked with the imperial double-eagle which were, just as clearly, spoils of rebel descents upon Byzantine garrisons. Those, he decided, were to be ostentatiously returned to the imperial treasury after the army paraded in triumph through the City – lightened swiftly and secretly of half their contents, naturally.

Once again I found myself at the centre of the ravens' nest, as the imperial columns pushed back into Bulgaria and the Landwaster banners spread retribution and terror wherever they flew. Hardraada encouraged our troops to outdo each the other in the excesses of the conqueror for, he vowed, the Bulgars would become good and servile thralls of the empire, both as a people and a nation. So the columns burned, maimed, raped and slew from one end of that tortured country to the other until Delianos, Alousian, and all others with any pretence to leadership had been taken, betrayed or turned from in a nation that lay supine at the empire's feet.

Loot, slaves and all manner of booty poured back to the depot we established at Plovdiv on the Maritsa River where it took a team of literate captives to record it all under my supervision, and the years 1040 and 1041 ran their course in a welter of bloody retribution that continued even during the leder's frequent journeys back to the capital for "consultation" with the great ones of the Court. Yes, he was the hero of the hour; the man of 1041, and all lay before him.

Until the emperor died in a wet and stormy December.

The Triconchus Palace, Constantinople, November 1041.

The eunuch tapped his head to make the point. "Continuity, majesty" he said "Stability, more of the same at this time of trial – especially since the brilliance of the *manglavites* Harald has brought us such success among the rebels. Emperor Michael is sinking fast, and I fear that not even the best of our physicians can lessen the force of God's call. Indeed —" he added in some haste, "as can none of us. Now, my nephew – the emperor's nephew also, be it remembered – offers these things in full measure. With him as your heir and your majesty therefore able to assume a lesser burden as Dowager Empress, much may be accomplished whilst other things remain constant."

"Such as . . .?" returned Zoe, and Orphanotropos warmed to his theme.

"An emperor will remain on the throne, as is the custom hallowed by antiquity and the people's preference. Has not your majesty married twice to provide her people with that?" John paused a moment to savour his own logic. "Further, the direction of the empire may remain in the hands favoured by your majesty these many years past. Abroad, the noble Harald remains your majesty's sword, shield and strong right arm, and may even again conquer Sicily as he has reconquered Bulgaria. And finally you, blessed mother of our state, freed of the burden and the worry of a husband's illness, your majesty may even marry again and become the devoted wife of another. A young, strong and virile consort . . . and God's will may thereby be done at last." He bowed, straightened and mopped his forehead.

Before God, you disgust me! thought Zoe. *Your concern for yourself knows no bounds and to serve it you will twist any matter to your own use. If I didn't need you so much . . .* But aloud she said only,

"John, your counsel in our time of sorrow is as constant and wise as ever, and we find much truth in it." The eunuch bowed again in gratification, and

Zoe continued, "We will think upon your words. Bring the young man to Court that we may meet him."

She stood, and her courtiers rose with her. "Now – all of you – we are weary and have much to think upon in the illness of our beloved Michael, and we would be alone." She motioned to Kia to stay as the room emptied, and as the last door closed she spun savagely round.

"The fat fool!" raged Zoe. "He little knows just whom I have in mind to be my 'young, strong and virile consort'. Or perhaps he does, and would have him constantly on the frontier? No matter – I'll see to it that he isn't! But I need the fat one for the peace of my empire as much as I need my hard man for the defence of its frontiers – for now. And should Harald's seed find root within me, the eunuch's prickless nephew will be disposed of no less easily than his uncle would have been!"

Kia walked to the queen. "Zoe, dearest friend and queen – don't think of that now. You're tired. It's too much. You need do nothing for the moment – Hardraada guards the frontier and the eunuch, as he says, runs all within it."

But Zoe slumped into her chair of state and put her face in her hands as the tears came. "Oh Kia, my Kia – good and faithful friend . . . it begins again. All I want of this throne is to produce an heir for it, and I'm tired . . . so tired . . . of living under the curse of barrenness. Before God, I'll take the veil and leave this cursed chair to any who wants it. For God hasn't heard me, my Kia – He's turned His face from me and will not now send me a child. Aye – the veil befits me!"

Kia raised Zoe's head and took her face within her hands. "Zoe – queen, empress, friend. We have known despair before, haven't we? And haven't we always found the strength to go on? And won't we always? Courage, my queen!"

Zoe put her hands over Kia's. "No, Kia. Not again. Dearest Kia, I'm three-and-sixty years old. My courses have long dried up, and I'm a withered old woman who should be a grandmother. What chance have I of motherhood? What chance have I ever had?" Two great tears rolled down her cheeks and neither of the women moved to brush them away. "It's over, Kia, finished. Let the eunuch's nephew prevail. Let him take the throne, for I've failed it."

Then Kia produced a filmy kerchief and carefully wiped Zoe's cheeks. "Zoe, there may be a way. There will be a way if you command it." She paused to choose her words. "Isn't it strange that you, who wish to conceive, cannot, while I, who bed more men than I can count, must take precautions to ensure that I don't?"

Zoe flinched. "Kia, don't mock me!"

"Dearest friend, nothing's further from my mind. What I'm saying is – if you wish it . . . I can have the child you want. I can have a child for you, my friend and my queen. If it helps fulfil the destiny of Zoe the Macedonian, Empress of Constantinople. Yes, I know . . ." she said, the words tumbling from her, "the child won't be a Macedonian, but he won't be a Paphlagonian either, and if there's a disputed succession, or if the eunuch's nephew rules after you, there'll be a change of dynasty anyway, won't there? And . . . and this way, we – you and I – we can control it, and see it done our way! Majesty? Will you, queen and friend – will you think about it?"

Zoe looked at her in wonder. "You'd do that for me?" she asked, "you'd have the baby that I can't?"

"For you. For Constantinople. For what's right. Yes – and yes again if necessary."

"No. No – it can't work. No-one will believe it – there would be doubt, always – perhaps worse than doubt. There could be civil war. People know, you see, my Kia – I've been deceiving myself all this time. I see that now, I see that I was never going to become pregnant, I'm too – I was always too—" but Kia laid a finger across the royal lips.

"Hush, my queen. Consider – who'll challenge the pronouncement of the Patriarch of Constantinople that you, empress and queen, have been chosen by God to bring forth a child of your later years, even as Mary was chosen of the Holy Ghost to bring forth a child of her virginity? Who'll challenge God's mind to make miracles? *Who's ever done it and lived??*"

Zoe was silent for a long moment, and then she said, slowly, "Dearest Kia. Blessed Kia. We . . . we must think of this carefully, you and I. And we must talk of it again when we've done so. But now . . . now, my dear, my heart is so full . . ." The tears came again as she slid from the chair to kneel before the younger woman and press her face to Kia's stomach.

Kia folded the queen's head in her arms and pressed it to her as she smiled a slow, secret smile.

The Chronicle.

*H*ardraada didn't go to Kiev that winter, for it was one of crisis in the imperial capital as an emperor died and his widow professed herself not minded to take another husband. Instead, she announced on 12th December to the crowds who still adored her that she, Zoe, would step aside and assume the title of Dowager, leaving the throne and its burdens to the young and vigorous nephew of her beloved Michael. He, in token of a cherished kinsman, would rule as the emperor Michael V, and "his sword and shield shall be the manglavites Harald Sigurdsson, Commander of the Imperial Varanger Guard, who is today raised to the noble and exalted rank of Spatharocandidatus of the sixth degree of nobility at our Court."

Varanger Headquarters, the Brazen House, 20th December 1041.

Hardraada sprawled on the couch and rolled the word in his mouth. "*Spatharocandidatus*" he said with relish. "Not every day you commoners get to sup wine with one of them, is it?"

"I can't even say it" grunted Ulf. "Took me a week to learn '*heterairearchos*'. And this commoner'd rather have a beer anyway, so you c'n stick your wine same place as your your. . . whatever you call it . . . where's the Screeling when you need him for a bloody good insult?"

"Ah" said Hardraada, who had had more wine that night than any of them, "ah yes. Think the Screeling's got a lady friend. Checked out with me earlier on –" he belched, paused a moment and farted, "aye, earlier on – off like a rat down a hole."

"'S right" said Haldor, "Passed him coming back from the bathhouse, eh?"

"You had a bath?" asked Ulf in amazement, "What for? 'S bloody dangerous!"

"Not me" snapped Haldor, "the Screeling. Had a big cloak on, but I could see his legs bare beneath it. 'S if having a bath wasn't bad enough, he smelt like one of them knock-shops in Galata. Had that look about him too."

"He looked like a knock-shop?" asked Skallagrim, and belched. "You want a bit more water with that, friend."

"Fuck me, you're thick!" snarled Haldor. "All I said was, he'd that look – like he has, you know? – when he knows something you don't. You know?"

"That's 'cause he does, more'n enough times" said Hardraada. "He's a clever little bugger. An' let me tell you – every last farthing'f what we got held in Kiev is down there, black an' white, so we c'n all see – you c'n all see – what you got from Constantinople. Screaling did all that. Ev'ry farthing!"

"I like the Screaling" said Skallagrim. "Remember I wanted to cut 's throat real quick when I picked him up from that horse." He blinked in the light, frowning. "Can't think why I never. 'Member that night at the convent?" he appealed to the others.

"Anyway. Shooli – Skuli – told me the Screaling did real well at that place – Thessalonika – sent the *varangers* off, got the wall up real tight, jumped up'n a wagon an' dropped a Bulgar with that bloody sling of his – neat as you like with fuck-all of a target, straight through an eye. Slotted half a dozen more to follow an' dared the marines to do better. He's a bloody handful, Skuli reckons, cause when him'n Karl was havin' trouble hangin' onto the *varangers,* one roar from the little bugger on the wagon kept 'em sweet. Skuli reckoned he'd've as soon used the sling on the *varangers* as on the Bulgars."

"Aye" Hardraada waved his goblet. "I'd b'lieve that all right. Ask Griss Bjornsson!" and there came a howl of laughter from of his lieutenants. "To Griss!" roared Hardraada, raising his goblet, "Who traded us the Screaling for an extra ball!"

The second roar of laughter was lost in the crash of the door exploding inwards and before any Norseman could move the room was full of mailed men with steel in their fists. "Still, *varanger!*" came the cry, "Still! Hands flat on the table!"

"Fuck –" came Haldor, heaving himself across the table where he sat, but the invader on the other side hesitated not an instant before driving a mailed fist squarely into the viking's face to send him flying backwards to bounce from the wall and slide slowly down it, his eyes glazing. Of them all he had been the only one to react and the others sat and goggled foolishly at the blades thrust into their faces.

"What the fuck—" roared Hardraada. "D'you screelings have any idea what you're doing or who you're—" but he fell silent as a voice spoke from the doorway.

"They have every idea, *heterairearchos*, for they know of order, discipline and system. You remember how we've discussed that? Two or three times, I think, in places here and there – and now it seems that I'll have the last word!" And George Maniakes stepped forward from the doorway, a rolled document in his hand and a wide smile on his lips.

"Explanations, my drunken warrior. First, these are my men – the Scythian Guard. Second – at this moment, the *varanger*s all over this city are being rounded up. Third – I may have your rank wrong, but only technically because it's moot whether you lose your title before your eyes and balls or vice versa. This warrant from his Majesty Michael V empowers me to take you into custody."

"On what charge?" snapped a Hardraada now completely sober.

"Any of several" mused Maniakes. "What about: theft of imperial moneys, misuse of imperial resources – remember that castle you burned? – disobedience of orders in the face of the enemy, murder whilst collecting the emperor's taxes, furnishing the Kievans with information about our military – you're bound to have done that when you wintered in Kiev –and so on. Oh yes – and levying an illegal tax. On the Jerusalem road. Yes, we know about that – you do recall what I mean? I mean, I'd hate you to feel we're doing this unjustly or anything like that. Now come along."

"That warrant'll not stand up. The empress'll . . ."

"The empress has no power, Hardraada. No real power, that is. None that'll help you. God Himself can't help you now. Tell you what – why don't you resist arrest? Then we can get it over with and you won't have to watch the headsman get ready to cut off your nuts. I always think it must be terrible to have that as the last thing one sees before the needles in the eyes. No? Ah well - where there's life there's hope I suppose. If it comforts you. Let's get on, then. Manacles."

One at a time and in complete silence the four Norsemen were manacled, then Maniakes spoke again. "Look, Sigurdsson, if you want I can arrange things so you're blinded before you're castrated. Not much in it, I know, but for old times' sake – comrade in arms and all that – mind you, you'll have to ask me nicely."

Hardraada drew himself up to his full height and stared down at his rival. "And give you the satisfaction? That's the trouble with you short bastards – you have to have attention all the time. Maniakes, I wouldn't give you the steam off my shit if you were freezing to death in a snowstorm!"

Maniakes flushed. "Talk's cheap, *varanger*" he snarled. "Wait'll the headsman's got your balls in his hand and you're wondering when he last sharpened his knife!"

The Chronicle.

he messenger found me the day after the emperor's funeral, and confessed that he had been stalking me for two days awaiting a chance to speak with me alone, as he had been bidden most strictly to do, but had been frustrated in that by the fact that I had scarcely been from Hardraada's side in that time. And that caused me some puzzlement, for the man came from the Lady Kia Vonskaya, partner in no small crime of us both.

Varanger headquarters, the Brazen House.

The message the man carried was unsigned and brief enough. "*I would speak further of sagas with you, and soon. Tell he who bears this message how soon he may bring you to me.*"

"You're of Lady Eudokia's household?" the Screaling asked, and the fellow smiled and shook his head.

"I serve the heaven-born one. The Lady Zoe" he said, "under the centarch Isaac Comnenos, who's her man unto death. And we, my comrades and I, we're his in like measure. I'm not boasting, *varanger*, just letting you know how much the Lady Eudokia wants to speak with you."

The Screaling made up his mind quickly. "Come back in the early evening then, so I can bathe first. Unless you think I should come now?"

He smiled again and bowed. "No. Evening's better – prying eyes are everywhere, and that's part of why she wants to see you. Have your bath, *varanger* – I'll find out where I'm to take you to her, for it won't be the palace. Things are going on – still, she'll tell you herself. Want to burn that note? Until later then" and he disappeared, leaving the Screaling to the most thoughtful bath he ever took.

Later he was led through the evening shadows to an unremarkable house not far from that from which he and Hardraada had once emerged bearing a dead body. The guide knocked on the door before letting himself in with a key he produced from his tunic, and as it swung closed a movement from the room beside it brought the Scraeling's head round in time to see a tall hard-faced man sheathing a short sword with a click that sounded loud in the silence of the house.

"A friend" said the guide. "But just hope he's never an enemy. No, we won't bother with names. Stay here please – I'll tell the lady you're here" and again he disappeared, leaving the Scraeling with his hard-faced and silent comrade. He returned in a moment and nodded. "Through there, end of the passage."

Kia was waiting in the room there, and he saw right away that she was in a state of some agitation. She came swiftly forward – and to his surprise she embraced him. "Where have you come from?" she asked, and the Scraeling saw the shadow in her eyes.

He frowned. "The Brazen House. The Varanger Quarters. Why? And why are you here, my lady – have you . . . fallen from favour?"

She brushed the question aside, and asked, "And is all at the Brazen House as it should be? Are the Varangers sent here and about, or are they still quartered there? What troops are on the palace gates?"

The Scraeling's frown deepened and he opened his mouth to demand her reasons for asking, but she forestalled him with a desperate "Please, Scraeling! I must know these things!" so he shut it again.

"There's nothing amiss at the Triconchus Palace, or that part of it known as the Brazen House and given over to the quartering of the Varanger Guard" said the Scraeling. "Likewise, the movements of the Guard are normal, for Hardraada dictates those and only the Commander may order their dispersal. As you must know? And the gates and doorways of the Palace are kept by the heavy infantry of the Imperial Guard, just as usual. My lady, what's going on? Why these questions?"

She sighed, and took the arms he held out to her. "Scraeling, my lady has eyes and ears everywhere. Some of those eyes have seen documents prepared secretly, and some of those ears have heard a fragment of command here and a morsel of conversation there. Do you know that George Maniakes is to be released? Or that the Scythian Guards are being readied to take over the functions and duties of the Varanger Guard, and to guard the Palace? It is so – on my life and yours, it is so."

"Then, Kia, why have you delayed in telling us of this?" he demanded, "when warning might have . . ." he stopped as the thought took root in his head.

"Might have enabled your leader to strike first?" she finished for him, "By killing the empire's foremost soldier in his cell and slaughtering the Scythians in their beds? For he would do so – as you know. What does that gain except civil war, with the armed forces choosing sides?"

"And what's gained by allowing Maniakes to do the same?" the Scraeling snapped back.

"Maniakes is freed by the emperor's command" she returned, releasing his arms and beginning to pace, "and his actions are warranted. Michael is the law, Scraeling, and Zoe is now but . . . the Dowager. She could not prevent Maniakes' release."

"Stop." said the Scraeling. "Stop there. Michael is the eunuch's nephew, son of John's sister Maria and her husband Stephen. Stephen Palaesostom. Aye, that very Stephen whipped royally by Maniakes, and a great part of the reason why Maniakes is in prison now. And that same emperor will release him? Why??"

"Who knows?" asked Kia, and her mouth twisted. "All I know of our new emperor is his determination to reverse all that his predecessors did, to overturn their policies, to imprison their friends and to free their enemies. The fifth Michael will be, he boasts – for I have heard him – like no other emperor before him. He will be the new Constantine – oh aye, I have heard that too – on the backs of the Scythian Guard, beholden to none for advice or assistance. He, and he alone, will rule. And were I his uncle John" she added as an afterthought, "I would even now be giving thought to my choice of monastery to retire to, lest a worse alternative befell me."

The Scraeling was silent, stunned, and she went on, "All we can do is warn your master to be on his guard, and this warning comes from my lady, she who will ever guard him so far as she can. Tell him that when you tell him all else."

"Why did your lady hold so long?" asked the Scraeling curiously, but he thought he knew.

Kia began to pace again. "Many reasons. She thought the boasts mere wind and piss at first, the posturings of a young fool swept away with his elevation – but when the reports came to her from those eyes and ears

I spoke of, she knew them for something else. And when Maniakes was released . . . aye. But she would have Hardraada know of this through you, for I . . . I advised her so."

"Why, my lady?" asked the Scraeling, and Kia turned those fathomless eyes upon him.

"Why? Because your first reaction will not be to reach for an axe. Even though the axe may settle things in the end we think, my lady and I, that through you, other options will be considered first – and the mother of this nation will not have civil war if it can be avoided! No – we know, Scraeling, and we needn't speak of how, we know what you are to Hardraada and the *varangers.* And we know whence came the . . . alteration to our plan for another service you and your master once did us. But we don't blame you – no, we esteem you and your cunning, my lady and I. Go now to your master, and between you, save this City and this empire again. And the *varangers,* whether mercenaries or Guard, will not find my lady ungrateful. And you, Scraeling, you in particular." And, coming close, she stretched up and kissed him.

"Ah" said the Scraeling, confused. "Is there a back way out of here?"

"No need" smiled Kia, "nobody followed you here except the four of Isaac's men whose task was to discourage other followers."

"Very thoughtful, my lady" said the Scraeling, "but forgive my suggestion that we haven't done too well in avoiding surprises so far. You're known to be the empress' right hand, and anyone watching you's going to find out who the fingers on that hand are, in no time. And you had to get here somehow. No – I'm going over as many walls and through as many dark streets as I need to on the way back to the Brazen House. Can I have that man of yours again, d'you think?"

The Chronicle.

I had much to think of on the way back, for if one thing was clear, it was that all would turn on the issue of authority. It would be the new emperor against Zoe, the queen and empress beloved of the people of Constantinople for being the niece of a warrior emperor, the daughter of another and the wife of two more. Aye, born to the purple indeed. I was confident, as we skulked from shadow to *shadow, that if the empire's leading and most celebrated soldier were asked by the Dowager Empress to take safe charge of her person and realm, all the armed forces except the Scythians would rally to him, as would the people.*

Of course, I didn't know that Hardraada and his lieutenants – which would have included me but for Kia's summons – were even then being carted through the streets to a prison tower near Hagia Sophia, and it was only when we saw parties of armed men with torches at the intersections of the main streets did I realise that faces were being scrutinised and affairs investigated. And I had been seen often enough by Hardraada's side for my deformity to be memorable.

"Look at those helmets" breathed my guide into my ear, "those bastards are Scythians all right." And the distinctive comb on top of the helmets was clear enough in the torchlight for me to agree. "And they're smack in our path" he went on. "That way – over there" and he pointed to a deeper patch of shadow – "that's a ladder-street. We'll go down and along, then back up three levels and come out round the eastern side of the Brazen House?"

"Right. Whatever you say" I muttered. "Glad you know what you're doing. Look, we need to get back – there's so many Scythians about, they may've made their move already. Hardraada needs to know."

And the two of us glanced up and down the street before skipping across it and diving into the patch of shadow.

The Kadirga District, Constantinople, 20 December 1041.

Haldor stretched even further up on Hardraada's shoulders to peer from the slit window.

"See anything?" demanded Hardraada.

"Aye. That's Hagia Sophia to the right – know the dome anywhere, no error, even in moonlight." He snuffed, coughed and spat blood into the street far below. "Help yourself, you Scythian bastards" he said with feeling.

"Right? Then we're not far from St Mary's. Get off – you're heavy!" And Haldor sprang nimbly from his chief's shoulders.

"Well, fuck me – weren't you telling us how much fun it was to be a . . . what was it again?" said Skallagrim.

"A *spatharocandidatus*" said Hardraada, "and the good bit is that I still am. As a noble of the Court I can't be done to death in a dungeon, and since you're with me, neither can you. I must be tried if I'm accused of a crime."

"Sounds's though you're going to be accused of plenty, don't it?" observed Ulf and Hardraada smiled.

"None I can't explain" he said easily. "Everything that Greek prick mentioned can be explained in terms of how I serve the empire."

"Yeah?" asked Haldor, "How about the Jerusalem tax?"

"Who guards the Jerusalem road?" said Hardraada, and looked about him. "Anyone?"

"Well," began Ulf, "Bergr and his boys o'course. That's why we left them, isn't it?"

"Wrong" said Hardraada, "Fayeed guards the Jerusalem road. Bergr's contracted to him. Didn't you know?"

Ulf's forehead wrinkled. "Who's . . . Fayeed? Who?"

"You remember" said Haldor, "the screaling we did business with around those villages. When we were in Pala-es-Tina. The bandits. The Bedu. Remember now?"

Ulf's brow cleared. "'Course" he said. "But Bergr looks after the villages. And collects their money for it."

"Only for Fayeed" said Hardraada patiently. "It's his operation. We – us *varangers* – we only hire out Bergr's services. Look – Fayeed and our Scraeling sorted it all out legal. Fayeed offers the villages and the Jerusalem pilgrims protection, see? And they pay for it. We can't protect them; 's not the empire's territory. It's the Caliph's. The Caliph of Egypt" he added.

"Now. We do all right out of that operation. But that's a matter of business. See, *varangers* take service with me – I take service with the emperor, and put as many men as we agree at his service too. But it's my decision, right? Some *varangers* I put other places – as it suits me and them. And as his majesty's soldier I'm carrying out imperial policy by co-operating with the Caliph's forces in the Holy Land. And we're charging a fee for it so there's no expense to their majesties, see? Ask the Scraeling sometime."

"That's bloody cunning" said Ulf admiringly, and Hardraada grinned.

"The rest of it isn't bad either. When our day in court arrives" he said, "that Greek arsehole'll find out just how useful the Scraeling's been to us. And so will you. Until then, we're not too badly off. We know where we are, we're together, an' this place isn't the worst we've been in. I reckon our fuckwit emperor's in over his head, and Zoe'll give him just enough rope before she pulls the noose tight."

On a street-corner not far away, the same night.

The Scythian squad commander was enjoying himself. His centarch had come round only three days before with the red ribbon of a pentarch for ten of the longest-serving privates, and the hulking farmboy from Dorohoi had been one of them. He glanced proudly down at where it adorned his tunic and foresaw a glittering career for himself.

"There's a lot on, these next few days" the centarch had confided in them. "Get it right, an' this'll only be the first step. Long last, we're going to see an end of them *varanger* bastards. That's what I hear, and whether they go or stay, real Greeks'll be top dogs from now on. So get it right – gimme all you got and a bit more, keep your men moving, follow orders smartish – an' the next ribbon you get'll have a blue stripe on it, guaranteed."

And tonight's orders had included the disarming and detention of all *varangers* on the streets, so the squad had gone at it under his direction to such good effect that the carts had removed eight barbarians in total already, some of whom had provided excellent sport for his men before the carts turned up.

And this one had been more of the same. A tall and wide-shouldered barbarian with an accent you could cut blocks out of, who'd taken unkindly to being shoved against a wall and having his hands bound. That was at first, but he hadn't had much to say for himself since two of the boys had grabbed his arms and the farmboy had softened him up a little, just to show the two new men how these things were done by keen soldiers and leaders. No, not much at all – possibly the sight of his own blood from the smashed nose had calmed him down a bit. It often did, mused the pentarch, and in this case they hadn't had to bind him after all.

He yawned. Nine in all – be good to get the round ten, he thought, but with all the other squads blanketing the streets, the competition was fierce. So, what would a good keen soldier do? Go looking for the bastards of course. Standing there under the lights wouldn't bring them any. "Boys. We're moving" he announced. "Over to the foot of them stairs, an' we'll keep it real quiet. Wanna get ten if we can – twelve would be a bonus, an' maybe a piss up. Bring him – an' Janni, jus' hang back a bit an' look out for the cart, right?"

Five minutes after they moved into the shadows at the foot of the ladder street, one of the new men whispered "Boss?" and the pentarch nodded. He had heard the scuffing of leather on stone too. *Someone up there moving slow an' careful* he thought, and murmured into the other's ear, "Two anyway. Back against the wall. Wait for me." And he pressed another man back against the same wall as the first, and drew the other back beside him.

The footsteps came closer, moving fast, and now the pentarch could see two shapes faintly in the starlight from the level above. Aye, someone who didn't want to be stopped he decided, and he had opened his mouth to bawl a challenge when a voice roared from behind him, "Watch out, *varanger*, watch it - danger!" and there came a crack followed by a loud scream and again, "Watch out!"

Despite himself the pentarch looked back, and by the time he spun round again the dark figure from above was upon him and he was a lifetime too late to block the dagger that slashed across his throat. His last thought as his knees buckled was how salty blood tasted in really large quantities, and he never saw the second dark figure charge past him and towards the scuffle going on in the street.

The Scraeling was a step behind his guide as they fell upon the knot of struggling figures and he had the presence of mind to bawl *"Varanger, speak!"* in Norse, and one of the men heaved another from him to land screaming at the Scraeling's feet and yelled "Here!" The guide shifted target quick as light, and a bubbling scream from the shadows bore witness to the speed of his dagger. The Scraeling kicked out hard at the white blob of the face at his feet and the man's head flew back for the helmet to ring against the cobblestones.

Another clang resounded from the side of the alley as the last of the four dropped his sword and ran for the corner, but the Scraeling took two steps and swept his throwing-arm over, hard. The man checked, staggered and sank to his knees, his legs still going until he pitched forward, scrabbled a little more, and lay still.

"Varanger, with us!" snapped the Scraeling, and the guide rasped, "Down here – to the corner and right! Quickly!" and they burst away from the place where three men had died in seconds, down the alley and round the corner.

"Five!" shouted the stranger, "there were five. One back there at the—" and an arrow zeeped past his head as he spoke, from the man the pentarch had sent to watch for the cart.

"Spread!" rapped the guide, "Keep moving right – over there, see?" but the words were hardly out of his mouth when the Scraeling cried out and fell.

"Ah, fuck!" snarled the guide and turned to him, but the stranger scooped up the Scraeling almost without breaking stride and dragged him bodily to the shelter of the shadowed archway the guide had indicated.

"You hit?" gasped the stranger and the Scraeling leaned wordlessly forward against him to show the shaft of an arrow standing from the back of his shoulder. Without hesitation the stranger took the shaft in two big hands and snapped it; the Scraeling's eyes rolled up in his head and he fainted. The stranger caught him neatly as he fell, slid an arm between his legs, stooped and straightened effortlessly with the Scraeling over one big shoulder.

"Right" he said thickly to the guide. "let's fuck off – that hero with the bow won't come nearer by himself, but he's likely got mates. Yes?"

"Yes" said Comnenos' man, eying him in amazement and some respect. "You're fine with him?"

"Him and another two his size" said the stranger. "Where're we going?"

The week before, in the Dowager Empress' section of the Triconchus Palace.

Zoe smiled tremulously at her lady-in-waiting. "Yes, my Kia" said the Dowager Empress of Constantinople, "yes. If you're still of a mind to . . . you recall what we spoke of during the emperor's last illness . . .?"

"We spoke of your majesty's baby" said Kia, "Of the crown prince of Constantinople, born to the purple as was his mother; born of his royal father's last strength and a conception sent by Heaven. That's what I remember we spoke of, my queen and my friend. Have you thought on it then?"

"I have, I have, and yours is the only counsel I have taken. You, who are closer to me than a sister and who will be closer yet. Yes, Kia – we'll do this, but we must do it soon if I'm to discover that I am with Michael's child."

"Yes" said Kia. "If Michael the Great made you pregnant with the last of his life force . . . what a legend that will make, dearest friend! . . . then you will not discover it until Ianuarius at the earliest, and then Februarius will confirm that. And Zoe – the child will be born in September. Think of that!"

The empress clapped her hands. "The New Year!" she exclaimed. "Kia, it's perfect! A crown prince, the posthumous gift of Michael, born at the beginning of a new year. A legend in himself, and none will question that he was born of the purple and to the purple! Oh Kia, hold me close!"

The two women hugged, and then drew apart as the same thought occurred to both of them. "Who . . . who will –?" said Zoe; "Have you—?"

"Who would your majesty have as the father of her child?" asked Kia. "A Roman? A *varanger*? A Greek? My body is yours, yours to command as you wish. Zoe, my friend, the man we choose is just a man. He'll serve his turn – and that's all. In fact, in many ways, as the baby will be Michael's and none other's . . . in many ways it's better that there be no complications. You follow me?"

"Aye" nodded Zoe thoughtfully. "Kia, I'll not command you in this. For the sake of my ancestors who sat in this chair, I would that the father of the child you give the empire have royal blood, or at least that he is not base. But, my Kia, because I can never honour you publicly for a gift such as this . . . I leave the choice of father to you. Know that in this you rule a queen and empress, for I'll never ask nor seek to know who sired him. That is yours and yours alone. Kia, Kia, make me a mother!"

A house in Constantinople, 20 December 1041

The guide ended. "And that's it, my lady. Couldn't think of anything better to do than come back here, because one gets you five the Palace's crawling with Scythians."

"You did well, Leo" Kia assured him, "as always. But who's this? - aye, cut the secretary's tunic and shirt away – in fact, strip him off altogether."

"Penda Raedwaldsson, my lady" said the stranger, his hands busy with the Scraeling, "of the Dokeianos regiment of *varanger* mercenaries. From England before that."

"Dokeianos' regiment?" asked the guide, peeling off the tunic, "Wasn't that . . ."

"Yes – cut up and wiped out in Sicily. I'm one of forty who weren't ridden down by Norman cavalry or drowned in the Ofanto River" said the Englishman.

"So you're not attached at the moment?" asked Kia, and the big Englishman bowed.

"My regiment's broken, my lady" he said, "and no-one knows if it'll be re-formed. Half a dozen of us got back here to Constantinople on a transport."

"Well, you're attached to me now" said Kia. "You don't need to know who I am, but I'll pay you, feed you and house you. All right?"

"Much better than all right, my lady" said Penda, "I'm delighted. And thank you."

"Good" said Kia, absently, "then these two needn't cut your throat. Look, that wound's already inflamed!"

"Scythians!" said the silent doorkeeper, "they're dirty bastards – sorry, my lady – and they sometimes use poison on their arrowheads."

"Think you're right" said the stranger, "he went out real quick, and didn't even twitch all the way here. Shoulder-blade isn't the least painful place to take a shot. Want me to take that arrowhead out, m'lady?"

"Let's leave it for the surgeon" said Kia.

When the physician arrived he proved to be a leathery man of middle age and, at first, few words. He ordered water to be boiled and cloths made ready, and listened in silence to the guide's account of what had passed while he bent over the Scraeling's form, sniffing the wound for the first scent of corruption before taking a keen knife and extending the arrow-wound top and bottom and on each side.

Then he took from his bag what looked like two long-handled spoons, hesitated, looked again into the wound, replaced the spoons in his bag and took firm hold of the broken shaft. "Hold him" he instructed, "and pull against me when I tell you." Penda the Englishman and Leo took hold of shoulder and arm and nodded; the doctor pulled sharply and the arrowhead made a hideous sucking sound as it came free.

"Not barbed" said the physician. "Good – put him face down" and he cut still further into the exposed flesh, baring it to the light.

"Irrigation" he said, as though the idea were familiar to the surprised faces that looked back at him. Then he took a bottle of clear oil, wiped the wound clear of oozing blood and poured a few drops of the oil into what was now a large and open wound. He called for the cloths, soaked them in a dish of hot water and laid them directly on top of the wound, and the

Scraeling cried out in his unconsciousness.

"Right" said the doctor. "Your man's in shock. His body's shut itself down, in part because of the shock of the arrow wound. But it's not very deep – it ran up against the middle of his shoulder-blade – so I think there was something on the tip that's now in his body. The heat should bring it out, and the oil I poured in will kill the poison. I hope. I'll stitch the wound and dress it but lady, I'd like you to remain and the others to go until we need him turned over again. *Varanger*, I'll look at your nose on the way out."

When they were alone, the doctor bent again over the Scraeling but, to Kia's surprise, ignoring the arrow wound in favour of exploring the Scraeling's crippled leg. "Tell me what you know of this man" he said, his hands roving swiftly over the leg, kneading and squeezing and slowing only when they came to the hip-joint. *It's if he's seeing under the Scraeling's skin with his fingertips*, thought Kia, and she told him what the Scraeling had told her, of his having been born crippled and how he had endured a lifetime of ridicule because of it.

"I know nothing of his parentage" she ended, watching him dig his fingers in until their first joints almost disappeared, "whether they were rich or poor, devout or no. But they were surely cursed, and the curse came out in their child, so they gave him to a monastery that was later attacked by those who brought him here."

"Never" said the physician, "Not the bit about his birth, anyway, and I'd stake my reputation on it. In fact, I do stake my reputation on it, right here and now."

"He was born deformed" said Kia, "He told me himself, man!"

"I can't answer for that" said the physician doggedly, "but what I can answer for is that bones that've been broken and reset show thickening at the joins. Raised ridges, like cement that holds two stones together if you like. And you can feel that. I did feel it, just now."

"And" he said, his voice rising as he made his point, "my old master, the doctor who taught me all he knew, had a pelvis in his storeroom that'd belonged to a dock worker clumsy enough to get a load dropped on him at the docks of this very city. He was bound up – not very well as it turned out – and lived to die of drink thirty years later. My master got hold of the skeleton - and we don't need to talk about how, any more than we need to talk about how your man got a Scythian arrow in him – and I've held that bone in these same hands that just examined your man. And I'm telling you that this young man's had a dreadful accident at some time in his past."

"All right" snapped Kia, "Save the lectures for your students. Anything else you can tell me?"

"Ah . . ." said the physician, "where's he from?"

"Frankland" said Kia, "the Narrow Seas, he told me. Know where that is?"

"Yes" said the doctor, "and that only supports what I say. There's not much learning there, and they value cattle more than human life. Because, I suppose" he added as an afterthought, "you can't eat humans. Although with that lot you never know. Anyway, m'lady, I repeat – this young man's been dreadfully knocked about, to the tune of a shattered pelvis. The pelvis has been bound, and not bound too well. Oh it knitted right enough, but at the cost of an induced deformity of the left leg, the hip-bone and the socket, not to mention precipitated thickening of the fracture sites. If he was born deformed, my lady, I'll walk home on my hands."

"Thank you, doctor" said Kia. "I'm grateful for your attention and your advice, but it's dangerous for both of us to have you coming here so I'll contact you again only if things turn bad. Please, speak of this to no-one."

"Young lady, I've been a Court physician for many years, and it's not my practice to discuss my patients with anyone" returned the doctor, applying himself to the arrow wound again. "I know who you are and I know whom you serve, God bless her, and you can take that as another reason why I'll hold my tongue."

"Now – take these salves and medications. They'll see your young man over the poison on the arrowhead. It hasn't got too far into his system as far as I can see because of how quickly he got here. The man who carried him did a fine job. You see how I apply the salves?" and at her assent he added "Then you'll have no problem I can foresee. He's young, looks fit, and he's got shoulders like an ox."

"He may rave – in fact I'll be surprised if he doesn't as the poison fights with the healing oils I've used. Just let him rave, keep his body bathed and cool, but keep him restrained to give the stitches I'm putting in now half a chance, and if you need to summon me, do. In her service."

Kia thanked him and waited in silence for him to finish, then rang for the silent doorkeeper and turned the doctor over to him, her mind full of the Screaling. *I don't believe the story I told you of his origins* came back her own words to Zoe, *and whatever put him into the hands of the sea-wolves is not a happy memory – but I have no proof other than a woman's intuition. But I'll find out*, thought Kia, *one way or another. You're no sweaty axeman, my Screaling – you proved that when you came clean and scented to me tonight. There's a tale to tell of you – and I'll have it out of you one way or another.* And she giggled to herself, for she had had an idea.

The Chronicle.

I remembered the searing pain of the shaft hitting my back, but I never had any memory of fainting or being slung over the big Englishman's shoulder. What I do remember, though, are the dreams because they filled me with a despair that was both endless and hopeless.

And though all the dreams were the same, I knew that there was more than one because in some the face bending over my bed belonged to Clothilde, sometimes to Sister Margarethe – ah, and I knew then that I was sickly or in pain, for she would smile at me and hold up a scroll – and at other times the face belonged to a woman whom I did not know but who had the same dark eyes and brown curls that the precious looking-glass in the convent dormitory had shown a sickly child when he was permitted to look into it as a treat. And she did not often smile, but there was a world of sadness in her eyes. And once or twice the face looking down at me was that of Kia, and I would try to reach for her as my loins stirred, but I could not lift my arms for their great weight.

I asked all who came to my dreams if they would release me from the prison of my body, even for the shortest of times, but I could not make any – no, not even Clothilde – understand that I had a task to perform that would not wait, that I needed to send Hardraada and the scourge of the viking kind from the world of men, and that because I was krøpling I couldn't fight Galti Bjornsson hand to hand, especially since Thorkill the Foul waited behind him, humming one of Askell's sagas and sharpening his sword. In every dream I would explain all this patiently and even offer them my finest pieces of amber, but each of the figures would eventually smile as if I asked too much and fade away while I could not follow for the force that held me to my bed. And, frustrated, I would sleep again.

But the figures in the dreams I knew I had within my sleep were Hardraada and his lieutenants, and they sat at a great table with drinking-horns in their hands and about them, about their shoulders like a cloak, were the wings of Odin's ravens.

"Scraeling!" came Hardraada's voice like the thunder of Thor the Hammerer, "why do you deceive me?" And sometimes I would deny it and turn his enquiry with clever words and questions, and at other times I would reply that one who scorned no deed nor weapon in forcing others to his will could expect no better than deceit, lies and treachery. At this he would rise and come towards me, remarking that the nine by nine area of the holmgang ring would not allow me to use my sling before The Nibbler would find me. And then I would awaken, or seem to awaken, but soon enough I would dream again.

But when I did awaken, it was to one of the figures in my dreams. Kia was there.

Three days later, 23 December 1041.

The Scraeling had always enjoyed swimming, for water made movement a light and graceful thing and not the scuffling, dragging progression it was on land. He had dived deep today, down to the riverbed where he had picked up four smooth round stones for no reason other than that he could, but they would go into his pouch for the sling just the same. He kicked for the surface and made his way up through light that grew ever better until his head broke surface. He shook the wet hair from his eyes and Kia leaned forward from her seat beside his bed.

"You're awake" she said. "How do you feel? Thirsty?"

The Scraeling realised where he was and let out a croak, and Kia nodded as she looked searchingly into his eyes.

"The physician said you would be" she said, holding a soaked cloth to the Scraeling's lips for him to suck. "But your eyes are clear – first time in days, eh Penda?"

Another, and larger, form moved into the Scraeling's line of sight. "Good morning" said the form in Norse, "and welcome back".

The Scraeling closed his eyes. Yes. The thickly-accented voice he had last heard after the fight in the street. "The *varanger*" he croaked, and "More water, please, my lady."

"This is Penda Raedwaldsson" said Kia, squeezing the cloth for him.

"He carried you after you took a wound, and my man Leo brought you both back here. It seems you did the Scythians quite some damage, between you. Do you remember?"

"His voice" rasped the Scraeling. "No more."

"Well, let's tell you a story, if you're up to it" said Kia. "Then perhaps you can tell us one? Free his hands, Penda. Scraeling, you've a good-sized wound in your left shoulder and it's stitched. You've been tied down these two days and three nights to stop you tearing the stitches because you've been . . . somewhere else, and rather excited. But we'll come back to that. Here's what's been happening . . ."

And she outlined the events of the past three days in the city for the Scraeling, beginning with the arrest of Hardraada and his lieutenants, "– and you'd have gone too but for our meeting here –" and the disarming of the *varangers* of both kinds. The Scythians had taken over the functions of the Varanger Guard, and a freed Maniakes was the supreme commander of the state's armed forces of land and sea.

"And your chief's imprisoned, hard by Hagia Sophia, charged with a variety of offences that'll get him blinded at least. But not arbitrarily – he'll need to be tried and convicted. And that's not likely, for Zoe will protect him. You know why" she ended, putting a cup in his hand and holding up his head. "Penda?" And the big *varanger* stepped forward, reached for the Scraeling's right hand and shook it.

"My thanks" he said in careful and precise Norse, "for my rescue. The Scythians broke my nose," and both his eyes were blackened, the Scraeling realised, "and might've had further sport in mind for me. But you and your man took me from them, and I thank you." He reached behind him and brought from his belt a bone-handled and leaf-shaped dagger. "This is yours" he said, "I took it from where you left it in the alley. A cast of wondrous skill in such poor light, I thought. I've cleaned and sharpened it" he added, laying it on the table by the Scraeling's bed.

"Now" he began, and glanced at Kia, who had resumed her seat by the bedside. "As I've told my lady Eudokia, I am Penda, son of Raedwald, an earl of the realm of England. As young men will, I journeyed from my homeland to see the world and took service with the *varanger* mercenaries, in the Dokeianos regiment to be exact. The regiment was broken in battle by the Normans your general offended in Sicily, and some of us survivors made our way back to the city for lack of any better notion. Three nights ago, I was rounded up by the Scythians and beaten after I put one on the ground for handling me. Me – the son of an earl, and a *hus-carl* in my own right! When I saw the chance to warn you, I broke the arm of he who held me. We dealt with the Scythians and you were hit as we fled the scene – which was wise, from what my lady here tells us. I picked you up, and my lady's man Leo brought us here. You have understood?"

His accent was thick, and made more so by the way he wheezed through his nose, but the Scraeling nodded his head for he had the gist of it. "I owe you my thanks, Penda Raedwaldsson, for it would've gone hard with me had I been found with the dead Scythians." He drank again and turned his head to Kia.

"What's since, my lady?" he asked, and Kia shrugged her slim shoulders.

"As I told you" she said. "I'm told the Scythians sometimes use poison upon the tips of their arrows, and so it was. Penda and Leo brought you here to medical help so quickly that you've been ill and no more these two days. But you raved greatly, and were elsewhere in your dreams, and what we heard, Penda and I, has made us . . . curious, for you said some things that I found interesting. As it happened, Penda was with me when you began to rave – in fact, he's scarcely left your side these days past. He recognised your words where I didn't, for you spoke in the language of your childhood and in French, both tongues unknown to me"

"But known to Penda? An Englishman speaks those tongues?" the Scraeling asked sceptically.

"Raedwald is my father" spoke up the Englishman, "but my mother is Anne, second daughter to Guinclaff of Finisterre, and a woman of strong mind. She married a tall and handsome Englishman who came first to her family's home as a castaway wrecked upon a cruel coastline. In their home in England I grew up speaking both Breton and French as well as Latin, and I've spent much time among my cousins in Little Britain. Yes, my friend, I'm half-Breton. As it was plain you were troubled in your illness, I translated your words for the Lady Eudokia who shelters us. If I did wrong in that, I ask pardon."

"But I ask things other than pardon" said Kia, smiling a smile that didn't reach her eyes. "Will you tell me of them, Scraeling?"

The Scraeling passed a hand wearily over his eyes. "Aye, my lady.

What would you know?"

"Many things" returned Kia, seating herself again and waving to Penda to do the same. "Tell me of them as you wish, but tell me of them all. Tell me – of Clothilde and of Margarethe, whose names you cried out most. Are they your women? A wife? A mother? Tell me what Les Trois Étoiles is. And why you'd kill he whom I know as your master and your general."

"Is 'the foul curse' to do with the man known as Thorkill the Foul? Tell me why you rage at a man named Griss and why you feared one Galti. Which ancestor was Nomenoë; tell me of Le Brieuc and of the horse called Dancer."

"Tell me your real name, Scraeling, for I've often wondered. And finally – tell me why you told me none of this when first we spoke alone, you and I. Take your time – but tell it completely. And remember that Penda, here, has told me of some of it and recall that you don't know what, so speak the truth, Scraeling, for much may hang on this. When you're ready . . ." she ended, composing herself.

Many thoughts tumbled through the Scraeling's mind as he sought for a beginning. If Hardraada and his lieutenants were taken and in such peril as Kia suggested, it was the end of his design and the work to which he had vowed his life. In such a case there was nothing to prevent his telling Kia everything, but a habit grown over ten years died hard, and he hesitated. But suddenly, whether through despair or weariness or a mixture of both, he decided that none of it would matter thenceforth so he drew a deep breath and launched into his story.

"My name? I haven't heard it these many years, but once on a time it was Ranulf Denis Chrétien Nomenoë de Lannion, and I was first son of the Sieur of Le Brieuc, which place Penda surely knows . . ." and he spoke on of his accident, of his life in the convent, of the family that had turned its back on him, of Clothilde, "who was truly mother to me in my despair, my pain and my sickness and who had none of her own to call her such"; of her sisters in Christ who had raised and educated him for the Church while they vied with each other to spoil the crippled boy with what they could make or find. Of his work in pasture and stable as well as his learning, and of the life he had led in woodland and stream "until the night death and worse came from the sea to be visited upon these women who sought only a life of goodness, caring and service under God."

And Kia's eye met Penda's unseen by the Scraeling, for he was far away in another time, and gently she held out a cup of water that was taken and drained, also unseen. "I slew the man who would have raped the woman who was mother to me, mother above she who birthed and then betrayed me, and I was struck down because of it. And though I hoped not to, I awoke to a life among those I feared then, but have come since to hate and despise ever more as I've brought them to trust me."

And, he went on, the 'foul curse' was the world of the viking and what occurred within it, and his intent was to end it with the death not only of Hardraada but of enough of his kind to ensure that their world passed with them. Although, he admitted, seeing Hardraada rise in the world made him question how such an end might be achieved.

"I smile at him, flatter him, counsel him and plan for him so that he may lean on me as upon a staff. And one day his staff will turn in his hand and kill him and his as they killed mine."

And the ancestor Nomenoë? An ancient king of Brittany from whom his mother was directly descended, and because Penda spoke at that moment to claim Nomenoë also as an ancestor, neither of them saw Kia sit up sharply.

"Then we're probably related!" said Penda, holding out his hand again. "Well met, cousin!" but their laughter had more to do with the release of tension than humour, all the same.

"And I told you a little of this, lady, when we spoke" resumed the Scraeling. "But only enough to make it ring true, for even then deceit was my shield against the foulness I live with. It still is. Although" he said wearily, "if an imperial headsman takes Hardraada from me, another will take his place in the ice castles of the Norse lands until the day when the foulness bursts forth again and all will be as before."

The same day, in the Chrysotriklinos throne room.

Emperor Michael V sighed wearily. "No, uncle, it won't do. It's tempting to point out that everyone ought to be allowed to make his own mistakes; unfortunately that's only for ordinary people. Emperors aren't permitted the luxury of mistakes; too much hangs on them."

"Of course!" said Orphanotrophos eagerly, "That's just what I've been saying. The sort of experience I have – gained over all these years of service to the Dowager Empress – that's exactly what you need!"

Michael frowned. "Need? Need? I need nothing, uncle, and especially nothing that was of service to the hag Zoe. As I was saying – emperors don't make mistakes. Did Constantine the Great make mistakes? Certainly not, because he was divine. And, as I've already determined that I'm going to be like him, it follows that I need no advice either. You follow?"

"Er – yes, nephew, yes. I see what you mean, and if I may, I'd . . ."

"You'd like to suggest something. Uncle, when will you realise I mean what I say? I need nothing, uncle. Not you, not your advice, not Zoe."

"Nephew" said John determinedly, "you never know, and it seems. . ."

"How dare you?" snapped Michael, his voice rising. "I do know, just as Constantine knew, and for the same reason! Nothing is hidden from me, and because of that, all my decisions are correct and will not be challenged!"

"Of course, of course!" said the perspiring Eunuch, "but I . . . ah, I see a place for me still, as . . . as an advisor. To be consulted . . . used, even, when your majesty wishes . . . should you wish . . . to sound out an idea, perhaps?"

Michael V lost patience. "And why would one anointed by God ever want to seek opinions from commoners such as you?" he snarled, "You're not dealing with a hysterical old woman now, you know. Think on that where you're going – you'll have long enough. The rest of your life I should think!"

"Where . . . where . . .?" stammered the most powerful man of the last two reigns, "where has . . . your majesty decided I may . . . may best serve . . . you and the state?"

"An island" said the emperor Michael V. "Monobatae. No, I've no idea where it is or how big it is. My requirement was that it be far, far away, and I believe it is."

A house in Constantinople, 24 December.

Kia sat in the gathering shadows, lost in her thoughts. Beyond her windows the short winter day was nearly at an end and the people who moved briskly past were closely wrapped against the keen wind. It took the soft knock of the silent door-keeper and his apologetic enquiry as to whether or not she would like a lamp lit to rouse her.

She rose and began to pace. The decision pleased her, for she could see no flaw and the issue needed to be addressed soon. Very soon, she reflected, for there were limits to people's credulity and if her scheme were to go ahead, matters could not be long delayed.

The burst of spite that had seen Michael hurl Hardraada into prison had, she reflected, saved her from the choice she had been unwilling to make. She knew that Zoe would have had her bed the giant *varanger*, but she had been less keen to do so. He wasn't unattractive, she mused, at least not physically, but there was a hardness about him that had given her pause, hard-minded as she was herself.

Hardraada would always put himself and his own interests first, and if he saw personal advantage in proclaiming to the world that Zoe's child was a Norse bastard and not God's benison upon the Macedonian dynasty, why he would trumpet it from the rooftops. He might even, she thought, do so for the sake of it, for if her intuition was as keen as she thought it then he was a man given to seeking and facing down challenge of all sorts, one who was never happier than in staring danger and even death in the face for the thrill of mastering it.

Aye, that was it. Cunning, deceit and boldness were the Norse virtues, but they held little appeal for Hardraada unless an audience knew and appreciated his use of them. Cunning, deceit and boldness – but those attributes also belonged to another. Another who was as unlike Hardraada as might be. Another, who had vowed his life to ending that of Hardraada and all his kind.

Kia shivered momentarily at the memory of the look she had seen upon the Scraeling's face when he had spoken of the night of horror and ruin at Les Trois Étoiles. She herself was a woman whose short life had seen her master emotion for the superiority it gave her over those who, lacking her strength, gave way to weakness, and in the Scraeling's face she had seen an implacability to match her own. Yes – the Scraeling had the qualities Hardraada had, but he had more.

He had that iron self-control that came from a lifetime of adversity, from quarter of a century's battling against a world that had crippled him but had never been able to demean or defeat him. Linguist, scholar, organiser, planner as he was, he had managed still to prove himself in battle, and she could only guess at the courage and resolve that had sustained him through his ten years in a life he hated among men he despised.

Kia shivered again, and made up her mind. Yes. It would have been so in any case, but the revelation of his descent from the ancient kings of Brittany had settled it, had been almost a sign, she thought. The Scraeling would father her child – Zoe's child.

The Chronicle.

*T*hat was a time of great darkness for me, for reasons quite apart from the reluctance of the poison to leave my body. In truth that took long enough, but as Penda pointed out one day when I railed against my weakness, from what he could make out of city politics I was well enough where I was for a while at least, for there was nothing to do for Hardraada and his leading men. Maniakes had been thorough in casting his net, and it was Kia who brought me the news that I, "the secretary" was still being sought to complete the round-up of Hardraada's lieutenants.

But while I could appreciate the advice of a man whose company I greatly enjoyed there was more to my darkness than my wounding. It seemed to me that all I had worked for and all for which I had blighted my soul during my years in Hardraada's service was in danger of collapsing around me. For it was as I'd said – were Hardraada to die here, and even were his evil henchmen to die with him, another would take his place and sing the sagas that would doubtless be written about he of the 'hard-raede', and nothing would change for the weak, the helpless or the godly who lived in places such as Les Trois Étoiles. Angrily I told myself that I could do nothing to alter what would happen in any event and despite me, but it is hard to sit by and watch the work of a lifetime totter towards ruin.

I told myself also that as I had no idea in any case of how I was to bring an end to the viking scourge, the imperial headsman might as well have Sigurd's son. Aye, that would avenge my mother and my aunts of Les Trois Étoiles, but how would it keep others safe? In the depths of my despair I did what I had not done for many years – when I could leave my bed I ventured out by night, my tell-tale twisted leg bound up behind me under a shabby cloak and replaced by a crutch to make me one of the city's numerous and faceless beggars – to a church and there I sat before the altar and opened my heart to God.

"You" I prayed, "You who know all; You know of what my work must be in a *world where the devil triumphs through the deeds of men. Where were You when Clothilde and her sisters called on your name to shield them from unspeakable horror? Am I all that You sent them? Am I? If so, then I pray You send Hardraada safe from his ordeal that I, and not another, might one day wreak Your vengeance and Your will upon him and all his. And with him safe, send me, I pray You, a sign of how I might best do Your will and encompass his ruin, that Your world may be one where goodness reigns and evil perishes."*

But I felt no better, I realised, as I swung homeward with the crutch chafing my armpit and I struggled with the despair in my heart. Nor were things better the next day, nor the day after that nor yet the week after that, so that I despaired anew.

Yet God's will is ever hidden from us, and especially from those who doubt. Had I only known it, the second step in God's plan for me – for all of us – was being taken even in those days of my despair and Hardraada's captivity. I say the second because the first had already occurred when Penda, son of Raedwald of England entered my life.

Truly, God is good. Even when we, his creatures, don't see His design.

A house in Constantinople, that evening.

Kia dropped her robe and slid under the covers. "It's the time of year for gifts, and you've been too sick lately for this one in any case. Mmmm – you're so warm – I hate the cold" she said, winding herself around the Scraeling.

"What if Penda comes by?" asked the Scraeling, "He often does, just to check."

"Well, he won't tonight" said Kia. "I've sent him out with Leo to find a tavern, because he hasn't been near one since he brought you here. In fact, it's been hard to get him away from this bedside at any time. So I've told him I'll look after you tonight. Just me. And I'm going to. Believe it."

"So, all the more reason for him to look in when he gets home" persisted the Scraeling.

"If he does look in" said Kia patiently, "he won't get past the door, because I locked it. Any other problems?"

"He sleeps next door" said the Scraeling. "Won't he hear the noise?"

"Think you're going to make me squeal all night, do you?" asked Kia archly, "Such great conceit – hold on though! Well – here's part of you that doesn't share your reluctance. I do believe you're becoming an upstanding citizen . . ."

"I'm not reluctant" protested the Scraeling, "but it's been so long that I—" but she cut him off with a chuckle and, "– and getting longer as we waste time, I see. Now I'm warmed up, can we get on with it, d'you think? No, lie still – you're an invalid remember – let me—" and the Scraeling was soon in a condition where he wouldn't have noticed Penda's late regiment outside the door. Or cared.

Some time later Kia raised her head from his chest and said, "You remember I said you were being hunted for through the city? I doubt it it'll last – it's only Maniakes' spite. He's no reason to hunt for you, has he?"

"Perhaps . . ." said the Scraeling. "I made him look stupid the day we met" and he related the story of the campsite on the African shore." When Kia had finished laughing she said, "Aye, he'd remember that all right. He likes to be the one to stand out in a crowd – but not for reasons such as that. He's like Hardraada in that – they both think of themselves before anything or anyone else. Just the same – Maniakes will have guessed that Harald would never have thought that up on his own. You're clever, Ranulf de Lannion. In fact you're devious."

The Scraeling's eyes jerked open and he went rigid. Kia lifted her head. "What's the matter?"

"No-one's ever called me that" he said slowly, "no-one. The sisters at the convent called me 'Sparrow' because, they said, I was forever darting around like one. And Hardraada's men have never called me anything but 'the Scraeling' because that's how they referred to me after I killed Griss. And it stuck, I suppose."

"Why've you kept the name?" asked Kia curiously, "It's not complimentary, is it?"

"It'll serve" said the Scraeling. "It reminds me of what they are and of how they once saw me. It reminds me of how arrogant and unfeeling they are, it keeps my hate for them alive and it keeps my purpose before me every time one of them uses the name. Aye, it'll serve."

"And . . . Clothilde? What did Clothilde call you?" asked Kia, but the voice beside her in the big bed took so long to come from the dark she thought for a moment she had gone where she should not.

"Clothilde called me 'darling' always, except when she wanted to tease me. Then it was 'mannikin'. The night she died . . . I was sitting up in the stables with a colicked foal. 'Go, read to your foal rather than your Clothilde then, mannikin' she teased me before I left. But she sat up to get me something to eat after my vigil . . . and I've often thought she must have seen the raiders in the moonlight."

His voice died away and Kia found herself holding her breath before, "And she might have run for the church and the bell-tower. But instead she ran for the stables, to scream at me to ride to the castle, for my father's men."

"That was surely sensible?" ventured Kia, and in the darkness she felt rather than saw the slow and despairing shake of his head.

"The castle at Lannion is two leagues from Les Trois Étoiles" said the Scraeling, his voice blurred. "There was never a chance of my getting there, even on Dancer, getting my father roused and getting back in time to stop anything that was going to happen. No. Clothilde saved me rather than the convent. She got me away, knowing what would happen, but not knowing that Hardraada was too good a soldier not to cut an escape route."

It was Kia's turn to fall silent. Then she said, "I understand . . . much that I didn't before. Thank you. Thank you for speaking of it. Clothilde must have loved you very much."

"With her life" came a choked whisper. "She loved me enough to die a hideous death under a smelly, sweaty animal for the sake of keeping my life. I prayed that she died believing I had got clear. I still do." And after a moment, "But why did you ask?"

"I had a reason" answered Kia, "but it'll keep. For now. . . for now, come deep into me and be my man" and as he drove hard and far into her, Kia found a moment to realise that she might not, after all, have mastered emotion as completely as she had thought.

The Triconchus Palace, March 1042.

"It's not good" said Zoe, reaching again for her goblet. "The skinny whoreson had the gall to defy me. Me! 'You would do well'" she mimicked Michael's high-pitched voice, "'to remember that the barbarian is an accused enemy of your very own state, and to have no contact with him until your courts have heard him in examination.'"

Kia grimaced and raised her eyebrows. Zoe continued, "'And you would do well to remember' I said, 'that you've just admitted that both state and courts are mine. I determine who's broken the law, and I define treason also!'"

"'A figure of speech, aunt' said the little bastard. 'The running of the state is now in my hands. Was that not what you said in laying down the burden . . . so publicly?' and, my Kia, I was minded to slap his sneering face as once I slapped his uncle's!"

Michael, she went on to explain, was immovable on the subject of her continued visits to Hardraada and his lieutenants in the Kadirga tower, saying that it showed division within the royal family 'at a time of uncertainty for us in Sicily'.

"And who's he sending off to regain Sicily?" she snorted, getting up, "but the very fool whose arrogance and high temper lost it in the first place. And who's he got locked up? The general who retook Bulgaria and hauled Maniakes' arse out of the fire in Sicily. As I told him – if I could weep and spit at the same time I'd give him the benefit of both!"

"But still –" said Kia, "– no thank you, no more wine; more than one cup makes me gag these days, however fine. Ah, still – if Maniakes is to return to Sicily so soon, the case against Hardraada won't be pressed so vigorously. You know how they dislike one another."

"There's that" said Zoe thoughtfully, "and if we can keep hard Harald alive until we've seen the back of Maniakes, he may be spared for . . . other duties" and Kia caught her drift at once.

"Zoe, dearest friend and sister – too late, for our enterprise is afoot, and I may even say it thrives! I am with child, and he is in his third month."

Eagerly Zoe seized her hands. "Oh Kia, darling and beloved! Is it truly – when? Where? Who? . . . ah no! I said I would never seek to know, truest friend and sister, and I won't ask!"

Kia laughed and squeezed the royal hands. "Don't worry my queen, my friend, my sister. Your child has royal blood in his veins, and no drop of barbarian blood at that. But come – we've much to discuss, for now that I'm sure, we may plan when I disappear to my relatives in Kiev –"

"And when I begin to wear clothing padded ever more by the month –"

"Now, my disappearance. I'd thought I might fall from your favour – perhaps I bed someone you don't approve of and we fall out?"

"Yes, I might get jealous, good – but, let's see . . . I miss you so much, and I can let it be known that men aren't worth it . . . well they're not, are they? . . . and so after a token period – six months ought to be about right - you pop up again, restored to the warmth of Zoe's smile . . . to serve Zoe and her miracle child. Yes!" Zoe clapped her hands. "Excellent! And of course we must speak with the Patriarch concerning the period of thanks-giving for the miracle of Michael the Good – shall we make that Michael the Wise, do you think? Perhaps even Michael the Donor? – no? We can think about that; but yes, we must speak with the Patriarch concerning the announcement. And it should be soon, do you think . . .?"

"We can leave it a little longer, Zoe dear, because you wanted to be sure and three months is such a difficult time for an older mother – yes, it comes together. Fear not – our plan's off and running, and if we can keep our two fighting-cocks at the enemy's throat instead of each other's, who knows what'll come to pass for you, my lady and my queen?"

"Kia" said the empress, looking at her friend fondly, "clever and determined Kia. You, who see so much and so clearly – you're fit, yourself, to sit on a throne."

Kia spread her hands in denial. "Dearest friend, such isn't for me" she said, the modest lowering of her eyes serving also to hide their sudden gleam.

The Chronicle.

*T*he early months of 1042 were, as I've written, dark ones for me and I recall how I used to wish away the short day so that I could get out at night. Penda, that best of companions and friends, set himself to endure the daylight hours with me because the width of his shoulders made him almost as noticeable as my leg and limp made me, and although he was ever ready to game with me at chess, dice or backgammon he could always discern when I wanted to be left alone. Well as we came to know each other in that time, Penda never made mention of his opinion regarding what he had heard from my sickbed and the nearest we came to touching on it was his descriptions of his visits to his mother's Breton home.

One day in February or March Kia came home from the Palace and joined us, insisting that Penda continue telling me of his father's position at the court of the English king Edward. That very night she suggested to me that I ought to write down the story of my own life and upbringing, and I found the suggestion curious at first, for I'd never seen the Kia I knew as in any way concerned with the past.

But, she argued, were I to do so it would serve two ends. It would lend some purpose to my days while we waited upon events concerning Hardraada, and it might, she said, reveal some way or manner in which my purpose concerning the man I hated might be brought to pass. And if I'm truthful, I admit that I didn't want to push her into one of the sudden outbursts of bad temper that had become part of her for about a month – although to be just as truthful, she always apologised moments later and again during the nights together that had become commonplace since my recovery. All in Zoe's much-reduced entourage, she confided, suffered as she did in protecting a visibly-ageing dowager empress from the petty spite of Michael, whose airs and follies grew more outrageous by the day, and thus she made light of the headaches and fatigue that came to plague her. So, then, although I had never contemplated using a pen for more than drafting instructions or making lists, I began to make notes of this and that as they occurred to me.

Kia never slept at the palace in those days, but at the comfortable home put at her disposal by Zoe. This was, she told me in answer to my question, a sign of the importance Zoe put upon my continued liberty as the one person who could attest and prove that what Hardraada had done in the imperial service was just, legal and above reproach. For Maniakes had made one mistake in an otherwise flawless swoop – doubtless carried away by his success in netting his rivals so successfully, he had omitted to secure my archives from the Brazen House, an omission that Isaac Comnenos and Zoe's bodyguard had taken advantage of to such effect that the archives now reposed secretly in the dowager's quarters, the large book that contained them built completely into a heavy wooden table.

As the only man alive with full knowledge of what each archive contained, I would be vital to Hardraada's hearing in producing and speaking to the documents and records I had so carefully sanitised over the years. Michael's case, resting as it would upon undocumented statement and the prejudice caused by Maniakes' demonstrable jealousy, would inevitably collapse. Thus both Zoe and Kia were confident of the outcome – provided always that nothing happened either to the Scraeling or his archives. To ensure that, I never stirred out of doors even at night without Penda's bulk looming at my shoulder; the pair of us in clothing remarkable only for its shabbiness and I, as before, one-legged and becrutched. In fact my escort usually included at least two of Comnenos' wolves trailing us but as God is my witness I never saw any, well though I knew at least three of them.

So Kia stayed in the house that had become my prison, but I'd known more onerous confinement for she slept in my bed every night. Little wonder, I suggested, that she was fatigued, for she was an inventive and skilled lover and she proved it nightly. Before long she abandoned her practice of returning to her own bed in the small hours of the morning and I noticed that Penda, an early riser in the first weeks of our confinement, became less so in order, I thought, to give her time to return there without the embarrassment of meeting him. Although any embarrassment would have been Penda's rather than Kia's, I suspected.

March passed with no sign that Hardraada would shortly – or at all – be arraigned or brought to hearing, and it was in April that things exploded.

Kia's house in Constantinople, 18 April 1042.

The Scraeling rubbed the end of his nose with the pen and reflected on how difficult it was to write about oneself. It was, he thought, a question of balance between what had happened in his life and how he felt about what had happened in his life, for too much of the first would quickly become boring, while an abundance of the second would seem opinionated. But no, he thought, not so – these things might occur to a reader, but that wasn't the point. He would be the reader, because if he'd understood Kia correctly, the point of the exercise was to help him discover something in his past that would help him achieve the task to which he had dedicated his future.

Ummm. But if he were to be the reader – was it truly necessary to write down what he already knew? Yes, Kia had argued, because people thought only of one thing at a time - especially men, she had added with a knowing lift of her eyebrow – whereas many issues could be explored on one page of writing. Anyway – what else did he have to do? And so, impressed by her logic as always, the Scraeling found himself setting to work.

But it wasn't going well today. His mind kept wandering to what he knew or had been able to glean about the new emperor. Michael was the nephew of the Eunuch, right enough, but that hadn't stopped his sending John into exile within days of assuming the imperium and replacing him as first minister with yet another of Michael IV's brothers whom he had made take the name of Constantine – so that, Kia had reported Zoe as saying, Michael V could measure his growth towards greatness by occasionally over-ruling him. The Scraeling shook his head at what that suggested about the emperor's mental state but it was, he thought, of a piece with what else he knew about Michael V.

The man seemed to have no policy other than to reverse the edicts and policies of past rulers of the City. He had turned the City's administration upside down in replacing the magistrates of each city ward with his own nominees, he had taxed the nobility and the merchants and he talked of sending each male below thirty into the army or the navy for seven years so that all foreign mercenaries could be dispensed with. He would also – but the Scraeling shook himself and reached again for his pen before turning again to the first of the neatly-written pages that lay under a weight on the table where he worked.

If it is true, he read, *that what we survive makes us strong in the same manner as repeated heating and hammering tempers a blade, then adversity is to be welcomed and I must include within these pages my belief that I have known more of it than many others . . .*

Pompous, he thought as he scanned the words. *But leave it, because it's a start, and it can be rewritten later. Whenever 'later' might be. What else? 'I have been 'the Scraeling' among my companions these many years, although I was christened Ranulf Denis Chrétien Nominoe de Lannion, first son of Ranulf, Sieur de St-Brieuc in that part of France that men call Little Britain and descendant, through my mother, of its ancient kings . . .'*

The Chrysotriklinos throne room, at the same time.

"It's an insult to his rank, sire. It's against the laws of our state and common justice besides. An accused has the right to confront his accuser before the people of our realm, and this—"

"—that's my realm, aunt" interrupted the emperor. "Just so we have it straight" and some of the courtiers sniggered.

Zoe took a deep breath, and many present thought they had never seen her look more like a queen.

"In your realm, then" she snapped. "And now his chief accuser has returned to Sicily to resume a career that's been much less than glorious so far, leaving Harald Sigurdsson rotting in prison! When will this man - who bears the rank of *spatharocandidatus* I might add, and so is of higher rank than his accuser – when, I ask, will he have the chance to face his accuser in open court? How much is enough, Michael? How much?"

"About that much!" shrieked the emperor, and a hush fell over the Court. "Aye, about that much! I'm sick of hearing about it, aunt, and I'm sick of you!" he yelled. "This whole court knows why you want Sigurdsson released! You want him released because you can't do without his big barbarian cock in you, night after night! You're worse than a Galata whore, because at least she needs the work, while you do it for fun!"

Zoe stared at him, her face draining and her eyes huge.

"Aye, that's stopped you! That's stopped your foul mouth!" shouted Michael, spittle flying from the corners of his mouth. "Think I didn't know, did you? Zoe, the whole world knows of your taste for pork and the size of your appetite for it! You shagged my good and kindly uncle to death, you old slut, and he wasn't cold before you were panting and gasping under the big barbarian! Whore! Slut! Filth!"

Zoe flinched, but drew herself up and snapped, "I am the dowager—"

"You're the dowager harlot!" snarled a Michael now plainly out of control. "I know all about you. Nothing – nothing! – is hidden from me, you old foulness, for the divine Constantine visits me and offers me all the guidance I need as emperor. And I have decided what to do with you." He looked all round the hushed Court, pausing to enjoy his moment before fastening his gaze upon the tiny woman who stood before the chair.

Zoe the Macedonian straightened her shoulders, looked up at him and spat, "Calaphates, your father started life as a dock-worker, and you foul the memory of Constantine the Great in mouthing his name, let alone in comparing yourself to him! There is nothing you can do to me that I fear" and her voice fell to that icy hiss that had terrified John Orpanotrophos, "but do what you will do completely, prickless one, else I will one day pay a headsman to tear your entrails from your living body and burn them before me."

And for a second even Michael blanched before her, then he shrieked "Whore, you shall be degraded before our world and our people! This very moment! From this moment you are no longer of the royal family, by my decree! Your head will be shorn and you will enter a convent where there is no male thing, nay, not even the beasts in the field! Hold fast to your memories, harlot, for they must sustain your carnal appetites for the rest of your life. Take her! Strip this bitch of the imperium she may no longer wear! Take her, I say!"

Two Scythian Guards stepped forward and seized Zoe, one by each arm. She said nothing, but turned her gaze upon he on her right and the fellow dropped her arm as if it had been hot. She dropped her head to look at where the other clutched her arm and raised it again so that her eyes bored into him. He stepped back, releasing her arm, and he and his companion came to the salute before the whole Court.

"Majesty" said the first, falteringly, "majesty . . . by the emperor's word, majesty …"

Zoe stepped past him as his voice tailed away, and she began to unfasten the heavy brocaded robe, stiff with gems and cloth of gold, that she wore. Button by button she cursed Michael V, Calaphates, in the present and in the future, waking, sleeping, eating and fasting until the robe hung from her shoulders and open at the front. "Only a low-born churl such as you, Calaphates, would confuse this rag with majesty" she hissed. "Take it, commoner, and welcome."

Then she who had ruled the Eastern Empire shrugged her small shoulders to let the robe fall to the floor, and stood before the nobles of the Court in her shift and undergarments. There came a great sigh and a ripple and a movement around the room as some dropped to a knee with bowed head, for none doubted that they were in the presence of majesty still.

Michael broke the spell. "Guards! Take this slut away and shear her head as befits a strumpet, even though she is clearly no penitent. Then take her to the galley, that she may journey to where she will learn penitence. Go! And you others – arrest all upon their knees and deliver them to the magistrates on charges of . . . of . . . treason. . . aye, in that they denied my decree concerning the ex-empress Zoe the Harlot. Now!"

Zoe turned and walked between her guards to the exit doorway. "Behold your emperor and rejoice!" she called, high and clear, and her laughter rang out behind her down the hallway.

Later the same day.

The stranger came swiftly through the doorway and dropped his cowl to look curiously about him as the door-keeper closed and barred the door. "So this is the Lady Kia's lair" he said. "No, no man - stand easy, Cosmas. Fact is, there's never been a worse time for ceremony. Now – the secretary's here? Hardraada's man? Tell him I'm here to see him."

The Scraeling was fetched from his labours over the story of his life and Comnenos – for the stranger was none other than Zoe's bodyguard – spoke urgently to him for five minutes, and what he had to say drove the blood from the Breton's face.

"She must know" he said. "Kia must know at once. I'll rouse her myself."

Comnenos nodded his agreement, even while his mind registered the omission of the honorific 'Lady'. "Agreed, *varanger*. We must take each other's counsel and determine what courses of action are open to us, and the sooner the better."

The Scraeling went swiftly to the room where Kia had taken to resting by day, and woke the sleeping woman. "Kia, there is a messenger from the palace" he said. "Isaac Comnenos. Can you arise my lady?"

"Comnenos? Comnenos? He never leaves – Ranulf, what is it? What has passed?" She swung her legs from the bed and swayed as she attempted to stand. The Scraeling steadied her and said gently, "Your sickness is still with you, Kia. Don't move so quickly, eh?"

"Comnenos isn't used to carry messages, Ranulf, so there is need for urgency. But . . . hold me a moment . . . good – my shawl there please? I must look a sight . . ."

"Only the kind of sight men love to see" the Scraeling assured her gallantly, and she managed a weak smile before preceding him through the door.

Comnenos rose to his feet as she entered, and bowed.

"Isaac" she greeted him. "How is it with my lady?"

"I regret" said Comnenos harshly, "that my lady and yours has been taken by the Scythian Guard to be sent to the convent on Pityoussa Island" and in three or four sentences he outlined the scene in the palace of earlier that day.

"And outside the chamber I was removed from the side of the heaven-born one" he said bitterly, and the Scraeling was shocked to see two great tears slide down the cheeks of one whom Kia had once described to him as 'the hardest of men', "and for the sake of the audience my lady bade me make no dissent. It was my place, my duty and my honour to defend her with my life, and had I but been in the throne-room—" but he was interrupted by Kia's great gasp as she crumpled to the floor, a fall that the Scraeling only partially arrested.

The two men lifted Kia between them on to a couch, and the Scraeling called for the door-keeper and commanded vinegar. "Lady Kia's been ill these days past" he explained, holding a vinegar-soaked cloth under her nose, "and unable to keep food down. That's why she hasn't been at the Palace, and why she wasn't there today. But what . . . ah, she's with us again."

Kia's eyes fluttered open, and only the Scraeling's hand prevented her sitting up.

"Let me up" she commanded, and the Scraeling pressed her gently but firmly back down; something else that wasn't lost on Comnenos.

"No, Kia" said the Scraeling. "You can't help Zoe when you're sick yourself. Comnenos here couldn't, and nor can we. Not this way. But there will be a way, so calm yourself."

What's going on? Comnenos asked himself; *no-one's spoken like that to Kia in all my knowledge of her and the heaven-born one. What's this little cripple got? Or can I guess? Interesting . . .*

"Why are you here?" the Scraeling asked Comnenos, and the bodyguard understood what was behind the question.

"To plan" he answered at once. "Our interests are the same, secretary. We both serve those who are now in danger, and the safety of one's the safety of both. Secretary, I'm here to work out how we can get your master and my mistress freed. What do you suggest?"

The Scraeling looked at Kia. "Force won't do it" he said. "Cunning won't serve either, because both are too closely guarded, and by the time the empress isn't, she'll be far away on an island."

He paused and scratched his head, but it was Kia who spoke next. "This is serious" she said, and her eyes were distant. "If Michael can act so in setting aside the woman who gave him the throne, there's no saying if he'll hold back from anything. He might even decide to solve the problem of Hardraada, just for the fun of taunting Zoe with it. Ranulf, we can't wait – we must do something at once."

"The only force we have" said the Scraeling, "is Comnenus' bodyguard, but . . . no it isn't! No, it's not the only force at all. Zoe's beloved of the people, isn't she? Well, can we rouse the people? Not many'd know of what's happened today, would they?" He swung round on Comnenos.

"How many loyal men can you command? Because we might . . ." and he spoke for several minutes, at the end of which Comnenos nodded.

"A slim enough chance" he said, "but it's bold enough to be the best we have. Yes – agreed, secretary. All I've heard about you's right."

"No time for that" said the Scraeling. "Get them all together, at . . . at somewhere else. Not here. Kia's house must remain our last refuge. Can you find another?"

Comnenos thought a moment and nodded.

"Good" said the Scraeling, "then have your men assemble there, just before dusk. I'll speak to them, give them their instructions and send them to their areas. Send back for me when the men've been summoned. Now – as well as that, get me what money you can from the palace, but don't stay there too long – there's every chance you'll be picked up as a known Zoe's man. All right? Let's get on with it, eh? But Kia – back to bed with you. You can rest even if you can't sleep, and there's no knowing when or how fast we may have to move."

The Chronicle.

*T*he darkness that had been with me for weeks dissolved like morning mist in the face of something positive to do. At dusk of that day I went with Penda and Comnenos' escorts to the address provided by their master, a large suburban house. There I met with some twenty others, to whom I dispensed the money Comnenos had brought from the Palace, and called for silence.

The evening of 18 April 1042.

The buzz of conversation ended when the Scraeling moved to the front of the room and raised his hands. "We've only one shot at this" began the Scraeling, "so make it count. You're sworn to Isaac, and he to the empress. I'm sworn to the *varanger*, Hardraada, and both are in danger – my boss of blinding, castration and death, and yours of blinding at least. Tomorrow may be too late – next week certainly will be. We need to turn this round tonight, and the people of this city are the only means we have of doing it." He glanced round the big room to see all eyes on him, some wondering, some doubting, some disbelieving. He took a deep breath and continued.

"You'll spread out over the City, and you'll have all the news that's hot. The empress is deposed, yes. She's exiled, certainly. She's been degraded and had her hair shorn – absolutely true. She's in danger of her life after a decent interval since her banishment. Well, we don't know she's not, do we? Lay it on thick. Make it up if you have to. And buy ale or wine with this money. Buy it for whoever you're talking to – you're leaving the City, 'cause you can't see Michael being any good for any kind of stability – trade, religion, politics – you're getting all your money out and going to Kiev. Or Nicea. Or Trebizond – wherever. And you can't stay long in any aleshop, 'cause you're saying goodbye and you've lots of friends." He spoke on in that vein for a good five minutes before he looked around the room.

There seemed fewer doubters – many were nodding and one or two smiling.

"One other theme – and it's up to you to get it in if you possibly can – '*Who the fuck's this Calaphates person anyway? We know who Zoe is. She's the daughter, niece and wife of emperors. Real emperors, not some prickless, nancy-boy product of a knee-trembler between the eunuch's sister and a dockyard worker against a wall on some dark night long ago!*'"

That time there was a guffaw, and the Scraeling concluded, "Pile it on. Stir it up. As I said – this is it, and you carry the last chance for Zoe and Harald, her general. We want the streets alive by midnight. Penda, there, has my list of where I want this message spread. Go!"

The room emptied, and afterwards Comnenos and Penda looked at the Scraeling as if he had two heads. "I've never seen anything like that" rumbled the Englishman.

"Me either" said Comnenos, "and I'm bloody impressed. Where do you want me, secretary?"

The Chronicle.

*A*nd our men did handsomely. Midnight saw the wide streets of the city *alive with crowds marching upon the Palace, itself already standing in a sea of besieging citizens who chanted the empress' name. The Scythian Guard was conspicuous by its complete absence and the streets were given over to a citizenry that got angrier and more frustrated by the minute, not least because there was nothing for them to vent that frustration upon. Faced by the weight of citizen opinion, the government did what governments in that situation have always done, and probably always will. They simply retreated into their palaces and buildings, locked and barred the doors, manned the ramparts – and waited for hunger, boredom and the demands of everyday life to ease the situation.*

19 April 1042.

Shaking his head, the Scraeling said "It's not enough. What I saw last night was a start, but no more. The government just shut up shop and waited for things to settle down."

"Right" said Comnenos. "We've got to make them accept the people are a threat."

"But are they?" asked Penda, and the Scraeling glanced sharply at him for the big Englishman had often enough shown a fine intelligence.

"What do you mean?"

"Well" said Penda. "In the palace's place, I'd do nothing. As you just said, this thing'll blow itself out. People must eat, so they need to get back to work. And they've got their own lives to lead. Face it – when's it ever mattered whose arse's on a throne? To most people, emperors and kings're faces on coins. Who really cares? We need to make 'em care, and I hope one of you's got more idea of how we do that than I do!"

"I think I do" said Comnenos after a moment. "Michael's going to do away with the ward magistrates, isn't he? Well, they're known to the people. They're the very leaders we need – if we can get them where they're able to do most good, because Michael's capable of having them all executed for speaking treason. And that'll only make his plans easier. How can we get them on our side?"

"Theodora!" said the Scraeling suddenly. "Zoe's sister! Respected for her piety – almost a nun, in fact. Turned her back on Court affairs after she came back from Jerusalem, remember? Michael won't dare degrade a princess of such high standing and reputation – not even him. Yes – Theodora's where the people's leaders can go. If we can get them there! Yes – come in, Leo. What is it?"

"Just had word that Anastasius the Serbocrator's going to speak to the citizens in the Forum at noon today" he said. "It's pretty reliable. What do you think?"

What they thought was that they dared not miss whatever it was the Serbocrator, a traditional mouthpiece of government, had to say and so late in the morning the Scraeling and Penda left the house in their habitual attire with Comnenos, leaving Kia in the keeping of Leo and Cosmas.

They found the Forum crammed solid with angry humanity, and the Scraeling took much heart from the sentiments expressed around him. "Talking to a bloke last night" was one such, "lived here for just on twenty years, employs seven joiners'n his business, an' he's off to Nicea. Why? Can't see a future under the new tax laws, he says. Whassat do for seven families? Eh?"

"Not much that's good" said the Scraeling, "but then I s'pose emperors don't have to consider things like that"

"Well mother Zoe would've considered it!" said another, "I'd a beer last night with a guy who told me what that fucking mummy's boy'd done to Zoe, God bless her— hey, d'you know they've cut her hair off? Her bloody hair I'm saying! What's that all about then?"

"'S 'cause he's queer" said the first. "Known for it he is – I heard another bloke say so last night. Got rid of his uncle the Eunuch 'cause he got no interest in sex, y'know? Well they don't do they? Anyway, this other bloke had it from a fellow who's related to a footman in the Palace – Michael's slipping it to this new bloke, Constantine. Or Constantine's slipping it to him, or whatever. It's fuckin' disgusting's what it is."

"And that's running our City" said the Scraeling sympathetically. "Real shame, eh? Thinking about leaving myself, friend."

But a trumpet fanfare from the dais before the Forum steps hushed the crowd, and Anastasius the Serbocrator stepped forward holding a scroll. Anastasius was a man of some sixty years of age and he spoke through one of the imperial heralds, a man with a barrel chest and lungs apparently of brass who told all, at Anastasius' prompting, that the Dowager Empress Zoe of the Macedonian line had, by the grace of God, been taken in the act of conspiracy to poison the emperor Michael V.

That Michael, of his goodness and Christian forbearance, had determined not to put the said Zoe to death as the attempted crime of regicide deserved, but to banish her to an island convent that she might there repent of her crime and commend her life and her soul to God.

And finally, that the emperor would offer thanks for his deliverance with gifts of bread and wine at street corners to all who wanted it throughout the following week. Anastasius rolled up the scroll in the hush that descended on the crowd after the herald's last pronouncement, and then he glanced expectantly at the crowd.

"He can stick his bread and his wine right up his arse – if Constantine's not using the arse!" bawled a voice from the middle of the crowd that was immediately followed by cries of approval.

"Who the fuck's this Calaphates anyway?" came back the Screeling's own words of the night before, followed by cries of "Aye!" "Answer that!" "Well spoken!"

Anastasius gamely stepped forward and gestured to the herald. The crowd fell silent, the Serbocrator murmured to the herald and the man raised his voice. "Michael is of the imperial line and wishes only to be the father of his people. His love for you all is undoubted, and he is willing to make the City what it has not been for these many years, and if—" But he got no further, because the crowd erupted in a collective roar of fury.

"Imperial line? Fuckin' washing-line's more his place!"

"Queers won't father anything!" and "Don't want the bastard loving me!" and the herald glanced helplessly at Anastasius.

Then a white-haired citizen stepped from the front of the crowd and turned with upraised hands, and gradually the voices were stilled.

"Andrew Kouriados" said the Screeling's neighbour, and in answer to the Screeling's look of enquiry he explained, "Ward magistrate for twelve years. Good bloke, honest."

"Serbocrator" came Kouriados' voice, the voice of an educated and cultured man, "you miss the point. We, people of Constantine's City, want our mother Zoe, the queen of all the imperial family, the rightful heir to the empire, whose father was emperor, whose grandfather was monarch before him – yes, and great-grandfather too. How is it this low-born fellow dared to raise a hand against a woman of such lineage?'

"Get through the crowd!" hissed the Scraeling to Comnenos. "Soon's he's finished speaking, line him up to meet us with as many other magistrates as he can raise, right after this. Won't be long by the sound of things. Go!" And Comnenos wriggled away through the crowd as the Scraeling gave his attention back to Kouriados, who had been joined by another man of similar bearing stepping forward beside him.

"I endorse all my fellow-magistrate Kouriados has said" he cried, "and I add this. We people of this ancient and Christian City don't want this blasphemer Calaphates as our emperor, but the ancestress of all true citizens, our mother Zoe. She who alone is noble of heart and beautiful of purpose, she who alone of all women is free, the queen of all the imperial family, the rightful heir to the empire. Zoe, our queen!"

At which a mighty roar erupted from the crowd and they began chanting "Zoe!" "Zoe our mother!" "Zoe our queen!" and the Scraeling could see Comnenos amidst a knot of men at the front.

The Serbocrator judged it wise to retreat at that point, in the face of the shaken fists and bawling mouths, and the dais emptied of his staff and soldiery to the jeers and taunts of a crowd conscious of having just delivered a powerful message.

The Scraeling watched for a moment, then turned to Penda. "That's a beginning" he said. "Michael will hear of that within the hour. Now, cousin Penda, let's see if those big shoulders of yours'll get us through to Comnenos and his new friends."

The Chronicle.

*O*nce *persuaded of their duty to act as the voice of the people, the twenty or so magistrates Kouriados had hauled from the crowd were quite ready to approach Theodora, Zoe's sister, and one of them even volunteered the information that the devout and pious princess had taken up residence in the convent of Petrion.*

At the convent, the princess – as tiny as her sister, but much less ostentatiously dressed – greeted me with every expression of welcome as a cherished friend, as she put it, of her visit to the Holy City. Thus she greeted Kouriados warmly and listened attentively as he outlined the magistrates' concerns and suggestions which centred around restoring civil order and quelling the rioting.

At my suggestion she watched me write, and then signed, an order that Harald Sigurdsson be released immediately, and another appointing him Guardian of the Peace for the City of Constantinople and its environs.

The Kadirga Tower 19 April 1042.

The clashing of nailed boots on stone echoed down the corridor and the four men within the large top-floor room tensed as it halted outside their door, but relaxed as the flap at the bottom of the iron-shod door creaked open and a large tray with a pot on it slid through the opening.

Haldor grabbed the flap to hold it open and called, "Hey, Poxy! What's all the fucking noise about? Can't you backblocks arseholes even keep the place quiet at night so's a man can sleep?"

"Don't worry, *varanger* pig" came back a voice from the corridor. "We're working on it, jus' for you. We're going to fix it so you won't be disturbed no more. We're gonna top you any day!"

"Not you nor four more softcocks like you" retorted Haldor, "an' when the courts turn us loose, I'm coming back here to kick your arse so hard you'll shit through your teeth for as long's I leave you alive."

"Be quick then" came back the Scythian, "cause you won't be going to court. What you heard las' night was Zoe the Harlot getting turned into a nun. Woo-hoo, how's that then? An' today she's off to a nunnery far, far away, 'cause the emperor's workin' his way through the leftover business. I hear that includes you bastards. Soon have ya arse in the fire now, boys! Eat hearty!" And the hatch was jerked from Haldor's grasp to clang back into place.

Ulf reached for the pot-lid. "Beans!" he said disgustedly. "Fucking beans! Again! For grown men! Odin's balls!"

"That right, *leder*?" asked Skallagrim, "They downed Zoe, you reckon?"

"Doubt it" replied Hardraada. "Dunno what's been happening while we've been in here, but if it's anything like before they grabbed us, not a chance. She's too well guarded and too well-liked. That fuckwit Calaphates knows that, even if he knows bugger-all else. Nah – just the Scythians getting pissed-off with Haldor."

"Sounded pretty bloody certain to me though" came back Skallagrim. "Don't think that bonehead Poxy could make that up. There was a lot of noise las' night, an' even more today – an' if there wasn't fighting among it, I never walked a battlefield in m'life."

"Don't let it worry you" said Hardraada. "If Poxy's pulling your tit there's no need to, an' if he's not – well, there's nothing you can do about it 'cept be grateful you're not one of the bastards who've gotta get us out of here. Because I tell you, I'm not going to provide fun an' games for the fucking crowd. I'm going to take as many Scythians as I can, right here in the cell. Now get stuck into your beans."

"Fuck the beans!" said Skallagrim. "I'm sick of beans."

"So's he" said Haldor. "So're we all. But ya got a duty to eat your share. Stops Ulf eating his then yours, see, 'cause the more he eats the worse he farts, and I'm sicker of that than I am of beans. So, eat up like Harald says."

Throughout the slowest afternoon any of them could remember, the noise from outside rarely abated and they took turns standing on each other's shoulders to crane for a glimpse of crowds of people surging to and fro, but the window was too small and too high up for the effort involved, and the four took to lying quietly on their beds.

"You know" said Haldor reflectively, "that bastard Maniakes—" but Hardraada heaved himself off his bed and snapped "Listen!"

Down the corridor again came the ring of nails on stone, and the four looked at each other. "Not feeding-time" said Hardraada. "Bare hands it'll have to be."

"Unless we c'n get a weapon from the first we drop" agreed Ulf.

"I think we'd be better goin' hard for the doorway, weapons or not" said Haldor. "they won't expect that, an' that corridor ain't very wide."

"Right" said Skallagrim. "No room in it for anything longer than daggers. Bit more man-to-man than in here."

"Agreed" said Hardraada as the tramping of feet got louder. "Me in the middle, an' as the door opens I'll go straight out, hard, and take out the man in the doorway. One of you grab his weapon, use it real quick an' try to get another one." They nodded, flexed arms gone soft over four months' captivity and began to draw deep breaths as the footsteps crashed to a halt outside and there came the jangle of keys.

The crackling tension in the cell was palpable, and too much for Ulf for, just before the key turned in the lock he broke wind loudly and mightily, and there came a hoot of laughter from the outside.

"In a world of constant change" came a call in familiar tones, "it's nice to know that some things are forever. How are you, Ulf?" And the cell door swung open to reveal the Scraeling and a grinning escort of heavily-armed *varangers*.

The Chronicle.

*T*heodora's orders were of little use at the Kadirga Tower, and the varangers I had collected from here and there were obliged to fight their way in – and if any were unhappy at that, it didn't show – but fortunately the Tower was manned only by a skeleton garrison due to the calls on Scythian manpower elsewhere.

Hardraada lost no time in arming and equipping as many varangers of both kinds as could be found, and once word spread of his release a steady stream of them emerged from the myriad places where they had either taken refuge or been imprisoned. Some had even gone beyond the City precincts, and these now returned to swell the force at Hardraada's disposal to something over two thousand blades. He performed miracles with them and, not for the first time, I marvelled at his abilities as a soldier.

Splitting his force among Haldor, Skallagrim and Ulf, he told them to sort out some competent under-officers while we, he and I, divided a map of the City into areas for the attention of the four sections so formed. For himself he retained the immediate area of the Palace for the Scythians would tend to fall back to what would be the centre of their power – the emperor and his household. They nodded, three of the most ferocious warriors in anyone's world, completely in thrall to someone who had yet to turn thirty, as he explained that the first objective was to kill as many Scythians as they could in driving them back on Hardraada's group. In turn, the idea was to entice Michael into making a run from what had to strike him as an impossible situation as he saw his troops cut up. It was time for the Landwaster to wave over a battlefield again.

The Hippodrome, Constantinople, 19 April 1042.

Hardraada was laying down the law. "We've got to get this little arsehole out of the Palace" he insisted, "before people get iffy about the idea of fighting the emperor. He ain't a real emperor of course – but, fuck me, are any of 'em legal? – an' he's no soldier. He'll go, all right – an' when he does, we'll have him. Zoe'll have him."

Night was approaching, so he sent his commanders to their areas with instructions to quarter and provision their men as best they could, but to observe a strict propriety concerning their use of the civilian population. "Pay for everything" he commanded, "everything. Use my name and Zoe's – tell 'em, their empress and her general will see 'em right once the Little Mother's got back what belongs to her. Put it that way, an' we'll win the people – that's what this's all about according to the Scraeling here. Anything else? No? – stations, then. An' tell off three runners each to keep me up regular with what's going on in your area – that's the Scraeling's job."

But as dusk fell the streets became clogged with people moving towards the Palace. The Scraeling would not know until later that the magistrates had decided to present their concerns to the emperor in a group, nor that Zoe's faithful had, in their dozens, scores and hundreds, taken it into their heads to see it done. The result was a river of humanity moving through the streets to collect in a vast and noisy pool before the Palace as the magistrates presented their demands to an imperial chamberlain.

That worthy announced to the crowd that the empress had decided to retire from public life voluntarily, and that her decision to end her days in a convent had been hers alone, and prompted only by her confidence in the emperor's hands upon the reins of power.

After an incredulous moment's silence, there was a cry of disbelief from near enough four thousand throats and a spontaneous surge forward to the railings. Someone began to chant "Zoe! Zoe! Little Mother! Little Mother!" and in an instant the crowd was in full voice and the chant echoed and bounced from building to building. It was clear that, short of a miracle, the crowd would roll either over or through the railings and, at the moment when it seemed inevitable, the miracle happened.

Through the colonnaded porch of the Triconchus Palace and on to the broad platform at the top of the steps came a diminutive figure in the cowl and black robe of a nun. She stopped at the centre of the top step and stood facing the crowd, her cowl up and her face lost within it.

"My people!" came from her, and only those in the front row could have heard before a herald stepped from the colonnade and to her side. "My people! What does this mean? Why have you come in such numbers and in such disturbance?" and only those in the front row could hear the lack of conviction in her voice. But it was enough, and it was from there that the chants of "Little Mother!" began again.

Zoe held up her hands for silence and into the stillness she began to repeat what the chamberlain had said, and the herald echoed her words. "I have decided" she said, "to pass the burden of office to younger hands. Not because I love you less, my people, but because my love for you dictates that a person of greater strength assume the burden of caring for you." She paused, and into the silence came a voice that the Scraeling remembered very well, saying the self-same thing,

"We people of this City don't want the cross-trampling Calaphates as our emperor, but you, Zoe, mother that you have been and are to us. Who but you can do this? Who but you will do it? No low-born and common fellow, but you – you, niece of Basil of blessed memory, descended daughter of kings and emperors, mother of our City and our state. All hail Zoe, daughter of kings and mother of her people! Come back to us! See, your people kneel before you!"

"Zoe! Zoe!" her name crashed and thundered again round the square, and like a great wave dashing itself upon the shore, a great ripple came as a thousand people sank to their knees before the tiny black statue standing on the steps.

The figure's head, still cowled, drooped forward as she began to weep and the voices tailed away. Then a lone voice called "Look upon your people, Little Mother. Look upon us, bless us, and show us the light that shines from you!"

Slowly and hesitantly the hands went to the cowl and paused there a moment before jerking the folds back and away from her face. A thousand people gasped as one and then came a roar of such fury that the very buildings of the palace, old and huge as they were, seemed to quiver. For Zoe's hair had not merely been cut; her head had been shaved and the torchlight reflected from her white and naked scalp.

Ever after, the Scraeling held that to be the moment when an emperor lost a throne. Michael had gambled on Zoe's appearance being enough for the crowd, and he had lost. A people willing to accept his coup and tolerate both his taxes and his incompetence, found his spite in treating their beloved icon as a fallen woman insupportable and, again like a wave on the shore, the crowd spilled over the railings and surged for the steps. Soldiers appeared from within, whisked Zoe and the herald inside and slammed the great bronze doors closed before the first of a crowd intent on doing murder was halfway up the steps.

Then squads of Scythian Guards came round the sides of the palace at a trot and smashed deep into the throng in the forecourt of the palace. There was no pretence of holding a line with their shields nor of pushing back the crowds whose attention was on the doors now barred to them; the blades were out and being used with a vengeance, and cries of "Zoe!" turned to shouts of warning and screams of pain as the masses melted before the fury of the Scythians.

"Odin's balls!" snarled Hardraada, where the *varangers* stood at the back of the crowd. "That's it! The call, now!" and he ripped his sword from its scabbard and swept it forward to point at the Scythians as the double note of the charge split the air. The lines of *varangers* leaped forward with a roar and, as long as he lived, the Scraeling believed that the Scythians never saw the lines of Norsemen behind the crowd they were set on decimating. People falling back from the Scythians became aware of the threat of armed men behind them and fought to get out of the way, with the result that bare hands and street clothes were replaced by gleaming steel and mailed coats, and the Scythians faltered a moment – a vital moment, for during it they took the full impact of the *varanger* charge.

Hardraada's men blew the Scythian ranks apart and in a twinkling those who survived the onset were struggling hand-to-hand with men who had months of hatred and insult to avenge. The contest was as brief as it was uneven, and not a Guardsman survived.

"Scraeling!" bellowed Hardraada as he wiped his sword on a Scythian cloak, and the Scraeling stepped forward. "Get runners away to the others – tell them it's on, and Scythians are fair game wherever they're found. This is our chance – Michael the Fuckwit might've talked his way out of it before, but not now. No holding back – force the bastard's hand.

Kill them all! Got that?"

The Scraeling acknowledged and turned away to find the group of messengers he had assembled.

The city centre, Constantinople. 20 April 1042.

The Scraeling looking up from the table he'd covered with pieces of paper. "It'll be all over by mid-day at this rate" he said. "They can't go on losing men like they're doing."

"Yes they can" grunted Hardraada round a mouthful of bread and cheese. "Doing it, aren't they? Must say I'm bloody impressed – they're hanging on, and there's no surrender."

"Not that you'd take it anyway!" returned the Scraeling.

Hardraada grinned. "Not that we'd take it anyway!" he agreed, and the Scraeling snorted.

"There you are then - that's why they're fighting!"

"Don't care" said Hardraada. "More of them we get now, the less chance of another go Michael has later. The Scythians'll never make their peace with Zoe now, an' it's time to show them what happens to naughty and rebellious subjects. Remember Russia? Remember the Bulgars? The scraelings among the Greek islands? The Bedu? Nothing changes, Scraeling, – 's called ruling. Don't be so soft!"

The Chronicle.

*T*he ravens' call in those seven days of spring was loud and harsh. For whatever reason the Scythians died to a man in the most vicious hand-to-hand fighting imaginable through the streets, squares, courtyards and alleyways of the Imperial City. That very day we received reports of a contingent of Scythians newly returned from Sicily on rotation and hastening to lift the siege of the palace. I had eighty archers standing by from the fleet, and I took them up to the rooftops of the most direct route from Galata with six quivers each; we wrought such slaughter that barely half of them survived to meet the charge of Penda's axemen, who offered no quarter.

Slowly, and despite the doggedness of the Scythians, the noose tightened around the palace and Michael fled with his uncle Constantine in the evening of the 20th to claim sanctuary in a monastery. There we left him for the time being, with three companies of marines surrounding the building.

It was then that Theodora showed steel of an order that amazed me at first, for she was insistent that Michael suffer the harshest of punishments. While this was in part to prevent his ever challenging again, the greater part of it, I believe, was that very religious lady's utter belief in the doctrine of an eye for an eye. His treatment of Zoe was, she held, reprehensible and Zoe's position as Theodora's sister was by no means a consideration. No – Michael had laid hands upon one born to the purple, and there was an end of it. Thus this gentle and pious lady stepped from her voluntary seclusion to do what one of her station and family saw as her duty; she ordered Michael's blinding and castration.

She would not order the death sentence, for royals were expected to take their own lives if it became needful, but she acted as she did to prevent either Michael or his seed from adventuring in the future. To her, the issue was clear and that might be why she ordered the Guardian of the Peace to carry out her decree. She also ordered that it be done without delay, and certainly while the position of Zoe, elder sister and empress as she was, was in limbo and Theodora was ruling as the magistrates had asked her to do.

So it was that I accompanied Hardraada and half a regiment of the Varanger Guard to the Studite monastery where Michael and Constantine had taken sanctuary. In fact we were only just in time, for a sizeable number of enraged citizens had beaten us to it and were set upon tearing the fugitives to pieces in defiance of Holy Church and its traditions.

Hardraada put a stop to that by showing his orders and requiring the citizenry to stand back so that the edict of the ruling empress might be carried out according to the word of her law rather than mob rule. Turning to the monks, he also pointed out that his orders had been countersigned by the Patriarch of Constantinople and that the fugitives were therefore outside the sanctuary of the Church.

What followed was brutal, but in fairness to Hardraada his were only the hands that executed it. He had irons heated and a physician standing by, but he insisted upon doing the deeds himself that the responsibility might be his and his alone. Constantine was stripped and spread-eagled before him and Hardraada knelt, thrust his thumbs into the man's eye-sockets and gouged forth his eyes with a motion so swift that the eyeballs lay on the ground while the first anguished scream still echoed.

Then Hardraada had the physician gather tightly the slack flesh of the man's scrotum and secure it with a ligature before he took a keen knife and sliced the uncle's testicles from him; whereupon the physician applied a red-hot cauterising-iron. The stink of charring flesh caused many to gag, and that may have been what set Michael off, for where Constantine had borne his agony as well as any might, Michael suffered his doom less well. He plunged, thrashed, screamed, wept and twisted in his captors' grasp and I have little doubt it merely prolonged his agony, for his blinding was a drawn-out affair and in no wise as quick or painless as his uncle's. But his agonies took his senses from him so that his castration was equally swift and efficient.

Hardraada stood, at the end, and pronounced sentence executed before leaving them in the care of the monastery for life as monks. Constantine lived out his days there, but the ex-emperor lingered in shock and died only four months later. And by then we were elsewhere.

The Dowager's Apartments, Buceleon Palace, May 1042.

Zoe put down the hand-mirror. "The wig helps" she said with a tremulous smile, "but I won't bother with the dye when my own hair grows back in."

"Why not?" asked Kia, her head on one side, "Black hair really suited you. And you've got such thick and silky hair anyway."

"Why? Well – we really need to talk about that. And we might as well do it now, because . . . because time's pressing. You know what I mean?"

Kia nodded and began to pluck at a loose thread on her sleeve. "Yes, dearest Zoe. It's not going to work. Our beautiful and clever plan's not going to work."

"Not since that little bastard stripped me off in front of the Court when I was supposed to be four months pregnant" snapped Zoe. "I'm glad Hardraada took his balls – he never knew what they were for anyway!"

"Yes, that ruined things" mused Kia. "Can't spring a pregnancy on people now, can we?"

"Hardly" said Zoe, and they both fell silent until Zoe asked, "What, ah . . . what have you decided to do?"

"Mmm? Oh – I'll have the baby" said Kia. "Yes – I've decided."

"Dearest, you don't have to" said Zoe earnestly. "There are ways around it."

"I know" said Kia. "But, as I told you, he's of royal blood. For one thing. For another, his father's quite a story. Oh, why don't I tell you? Want to hear an interesting tale?" And she told it as the afternoon shadows lengthened outside.

When she'd finished, Zoe rose and walked to a window. Gazing out, she said "Kia, dearest, I'm not religious. I've sinned too much for that, and I daresay I'll pay for it one day, down here or up there. But I can honestly say I've done what I've done because I felt my position demanded it, and you know that. Anyway, now and again God reaches out and taps you on the shoulder, just to remind you He's there. And this is such a time. Your baby was supposed to be mine, precious friend. But he'll be yours now, and there's every chance he'll be a king at least. More likely an emperor, just as we planned – because I've got an idea."

She turned from the window. "Let me put a few things together, Kia dearest, and think out the fine details. In the meantime, keep healthy and keep eating for our little prince!"

The Chronicle.

*T*he weeks after the overthrow of Michael and his uncle saw Hardraada at the very height of his powers in the imperial service. As Commander of the Varanger Guard no man in Constantinople might say him nay, for both Theodora and Zoe saw him as the natural protector of the imperium and he was charged expressly with 'the protection and preservation of this our state' by the sisters, now reigning together in a partnership as uneasy as it was unofficial. In keeping with his nature, Hardraada launched a wave of terror that sought out and punished any and all whose loyalty had wavered during the last days of the previous reign and the imperial headsmen were kept busy indeed. The only rebel of any note who escaped him was, ironically, the one he most wanted to secure. But Maniakes was then far away in Sicily and up to his armpits in Turks.

Also in keeping with his nature, Hardraada used his position to levy substantial fines and many of those who escaped the headsman did so only through their ability to meet his demands. By this time we of his inner circle knew that the wealth he had accumulated and held in Constantinople was the equal of that which he had deposited in Kiev over the years, and that more would merely be a hindrance.

Perhaps that was why Hardraada sent for me in the middle of 1042 and instructed me to begin planning for a permanent return to Kiev. There was, he said, no place for him in the City of the emperors and no function for him to discharge as Zoe had recently decided to end the unofficial dual monarchy with her sister and marry the noble Constantine Monomachos, who would be crowned as Constantine IX.

And that had surprised me as much as any, for I had had no foreknowledge of it. Kia disappeared in the middle of May and even Comnenos did not know where, he swore. I had come to think more charitably of the black-eyed Russian during my illness, for the intimacies we shared each night could not, I had told myself, have been feigned. I was aware that Kia, Zoe's handmaiden in all things as much as Comnenos was her strong right arm, used her body in her mistress' service but I had persuaded myself that her appetite for me during the time of uncertainty was some proof that she regarded me as something other, for what could I have that she or her mistress sought? And she had never made any demand of me that I was not more than willing to grant. She might, I had thought, have returned to her family's roots in the Rus for I could discover no word of her in the City – though why she should have done so was beyond me.

But disappear she had, swiftly and completely, and even in that there was a puzzle. It was only Penda's casual request of me to know how my writing stood in these days of great endeavours that made me search high and low for it before concluding that it had gone with Kia – perhaps bundled up in haste and error with something else. Well, no matter. My days were now certainly as full as any might wish, and if I thought about her a good deal in the early days of her absence I had no doubt at all that she didn't think about me.

Hardraada thought a good deal of Penda, who had attached himself to the leder during the fighting around the Palace. "A complete and swift axeman" was his judgement "and not one I'd care to face, Scraeling" and that was high praise from a man as vain of his prowess as Hardraada. For his part Penda admired Hardraada as soldier, leader and warrior, but the perceptive and intelligent Saxon confided to me that he thought little of him as a person worthy of trust in matters where his own interests or desires were concerned.

In those days, then, we stood at something of a crossroads. On the face of it there seemed no good reason for Hardraada to remain longer in Constantinople, for he had attained all there that any foreigner might and I could see the signs of impatience in him, or so I thought. When I found out what those signs really

portended, I was as shocked as any of his lieutenants, for Hardraada had kept the
most momentous news to himself.

The Buceleon Palace, May 1042.

Zoe, stared out of a window and spoke over her shoulder. "I knew Hard Harald wouldn't stay by me" she said.

"Why not?" asked Kia, "You can give him what he wants – for my money that includes wealth, power and his own way. That's all any man wants!"

"I told him that, almost exactly, ages ago – before Michael died in fact."

"And?"

"Less than enthusiastic" said Zoe. "Which means those things aren't all he wants. Hardraada wants excitement – challenge – risk and danger. He wants to look death in the face and beat it. That's what Harald's about." She paused, struggling to find the words.

"For Hardraada, the game's more than the prize. He'd be happy with five gold pieces if he took them in battle. Give him the same five gold pieces and he wouldn't want them. You see what I mean? He's not interested in being the emperor. Emperor of anywhere. That's about routine, you see; it's about administration, courts and their rituals, dispensing justice, having to deal with things other than soldiering."

"So – offer him all the soldiering he wants. At least the frontiers would be safe!" suggested Kia, and Zoe turned to face her.

"If Hardraada were emperor, my dearest, we'd be constantly at war even if the frontiers were mouse-proof – because he'd be looking for fresh wars all the time, and he'd have no interest beyond the next enemy – not even in running and ruling what he'd just won! No, my Kia – deep down I've always known the throne of Constantinople, or Miklagaard as they call it – isn't for him. Just another thing to fool myself about."

"But I'm not doing that any more, Kia. Young Michael's haircut got rid of all that for me. It's all about reality now, and practical things – and that brings me back to you and our baby."

"Zoe, dearest friend – you needn't concern yourself with me. Not now – not with all tumbling about you like this."

Zoe waved her to silence. "Nonsense. You and our dream are the best of all I have to think about now." She began to pace, head bowed as she spoke. "You see, our plan's failed; there'll be no prince to be regent for – but there's no going back. We'll finish what you've begun for us, my Kia, and we'll do it. You, and me. I won't see the end of it, but you will my dear. Oh yes."

"Now – let's look ahead. I may marry again, just to give the people an emperor. Then, who after me? Theodora, I suppose. After Theodora? I'm going to instruct Isaac Comnenos. Yes, Comnenos. He'll spend Theodora's years serving her as he's served me – and quietly doing what he needs to do to ensure he's in a position to take over when she dies. And Isaac, my good and faithful Isaac, will hold the throne . . . until your child, Kia, is of an age. I've thought carefully about this, and Isaac can – will – hold the throne until a strongman emerges to take it. That'll be your child, Kia, our child. The child you'll bear de Lannion. You'll see him crowned, as I said."

"Zoe, my Zoe – what can I say? Are you . . . are you . . ." she swallowed.

"Am I sure? Yes, Kia, I'm sure. You have served me in every way possible these ten years past, and your blood will serve our people even beyond us. And I'm very sure of that. So let's be practical." She held up a finger.

"One – the child must be born in wedlock. Two – he must be watched over by strong and clever people. Three – he must have the path to the throne prepared for him."

"When we last spoke of this I asked you to give me a little time. I've used that time to make sure of a few things. Kia, I have a father for our child. He's a Paphlagonian, son of a provincial governor. Now, we haven't had much luck with the Paphlagonians, I know, but all we need of this one's his name and not his juice, because you've done that. He's well-born, a widower, not given to politics very much – although that'll be taken care of in ways you'll have a bit to do with – and most important of all, well-enough connected to put our boy exactly where we want him one day, whatever his 'father' does or doesn't do with his career. So that's my first condition met."

"My second requirement is much easier. With you as his mother, tucked away in the country and Isaac Comnenos watching over him, he'll grow up both educated and safe. And finally – the legacy that Isaac leaves will see him safe on my throne because if Isaac has to, he'll . . . cancel . . . any and every possible contender or challenger before he abdicates, because that's how our boy will come to the throne."

Suddenly Zoe sounded tired. "So, my Kia, my faithful Kia – much of what we planned will come to pass after all. The child you bear for me will indeed reign after me – although I'll never know the thrill of holding him and pretending, even for a moment, that he came from my womb. But that's little enough compared with the knowledge that we will, you and I, shape and control the destiny of our state and people even as we said we would. And I – I shall have done my duty by that state and people as best I could. And when you think of the task I was given and the dice I was given to roll in doing it – it doesn't take as dear a friend as you to acknowledge that I haven't done badly?"

Zoe crossed to Kia and, holding out her hands, an empress knelt, the tears coming as she did so. "Mother of an emperor, beloved friend of an empress. I greet the child who is yours and ours, and I salute you both." She pressed her face again to the younger woman's stomach as Kia soothed and comforted her.

Zoe raised a tear-stained face. "Will you tell de Lannion – the Scraeling – of his child? Of what his child will be? He'll go from here in any case if his purpose holds, won't he?"

Kia considered. "No" she said at length. "He doesn't need to know, for there's no saying what he'll do if he does know. Although he's intelligent enough to see things our way, I'm sure. No – as we said, you and I my sister, on a day long ago – men think with their genitals and he's a man. You and I have what we need – a child of royal blood from a father who's intelligent, educated and courageous. We can do the rest. We can make a king and an emperor."

The Brazen House, July 1042.

The fist thumped on the table to emphasise the speaker's point. "It's over" said Hardraada. "It's been nice at times, exciting at others but mostly bloody dangerous. We're away, my men, any time now, and we're going to settle how and when today."

"You sure, *leder*?" asked Skallagrim, "Got these scraelings by the balls, we have, an' you're top dog again. That not worth hanging on for?"

Hardraada shook his head, slowly and definitely. "No, old comrade, it isn't. I'm top dog now, aye – and I was once before, and look how quick that changed. Nah – when I think what we've seen here, an' what some of us have done and been part of, that we still shouldn't talk about – makes you realise we're bloody lucky to be still alive, let alone cock of the walk. All I could think about when I cut Michael's nuts off him was how close we were to the same thing three days before. You were in the dungeon too. Remember how desperate we were? If the Scraeling hadn't laughed at Ulf farting the day they came to get us, they'd still be putting him back together."

Haldor stirred. "Harald's right" he pronounced. "Said it before, right at the beginning – these scraelings're oily, smooth, slippery. I like a man who tells you to your face he's gonna have a go at you. I c'n understand that – we can all understand that. But these bastards'll smile at you, offer you a drink, an' poison it between pouring it an' handing it to you. No. I'm with the *leder*."

"So what's the problem?" asked Ulf. "About going, I mean?"

"Zoe" said Hardraada heavily. "I've told her I need to go back to Norway to look after my interests there. The Magnus thing, I mean." The lieutenants nodded, for they knew of the election of Magnus, Hardraada's half-nephew and son of Olaf, to the Norwegian throne. "She said she couldn't spare me, and that—"

"At her age" scoffed Skallagrim. "Still chasing pork at her age. Randy old trot, eh?"

"Not that!" snapped Hardraada. "I can't be spared from the City's defence forces is what she said."

"Why not?" asked the Scraeling. "There's no threat closer than Sicily, and she's got Maniakes making a good job of it there, at long last. So what's her concern?"

"Don't know what her concern is, but I can tell you mine" replied Hardraada, and even he lowered his voice. "Maniakes was closer to the mark than he knew when he accused me of spying for Yaroslav. Yes, they know in Kiev about our strengths and dispositions, 'cause I've told them. Told them not to bother, too, because the City's too strong for 'em. And Yaroslav believes me – he's got enough going on to keep him happy being Yaroslav the Wise. It's not him, it's his son. It's that fucking little would-be, Vladimir – not going to be king, he thinks, so he'll be a soldier. And he's going to start at the top – going to have a slap at the City."

"You serious?" Haldor was bolt upright. "Miklagaard, for fuck's sake?"

"No-one's ever said so in my hearing" said Hardraada, "but anyone can read that little softcock like the Scraeling here reads books, an' I told him what he wants to know to make him realise he'd have more trouble than a nun in a knocking-shop. But he's thick as well as a dreamer."

"A horrible combination. And you don't want to be military commander of the city or Guardian of the Peace when your future brother-in-law lays it on you" said the Scraeling, nodding.

"You're onto it" said Hardraada. "So it's a straight race – Zoe against us, but we have to win it before Vladimir turns up to piss in the wineflask. Scraeling, you're never short of a thought or two . . .?"

The Chronicle.

*T*hree drakkars would be enough to carry Hardraada and those who would come with us. One, I was pleased to discover, was Penda for I had come to think much of the big Englishman for reasons other than our supposed kinship. Penda had that calm that goes often with truly big men, men secure in their strength and physical prowess, and that calm allowed him to view any situation dispassionately and thoughtfully. His views on the matter of Kia's disappearance, when we discussed it, were an earnest of that.

Kia, he suggested, had ever done what she did according to her own wishes and ambitions. Despite all protestations, only two people knew where and how she had gone and as those two were Zoe and Comnenos there was little chance of discovering anything further. But why bother? Unless Kia had become dear to me, I had lost nothing that would cause me to stand back from a return to the Rus.

No, I decided, I had not. I owed Kia nothing while she, from the manner of her going, clearly felt the same. Still, it rankled somewhat – but less so with the passing of the days.

For I was busy in many other ways. Hardraada's own drakkar – which he was conceited enough to name Sleipnir after Odin's steed – was carefully and secretly loaded with the wealth he had accumulated over the years of his imperial service, and there was so much of it that it took a carpenter half a day to chock and wedge it against shifting at sea so that when he was finished the craft lay snugly, if deeply, in the water.

We purchased two more drakkars, again secretly in case word of our intentions *reached Zoe's ears. She had refused again to part with Hardraada even though he was no longer welcome in her bed, and day by day Hardraada's conviction that the Palace knew of, or suspected, a Kievan invasion in the spring hardened ever more into certainty.*

At last Hardraada set the date. We would sail in the first week of November on the pretext of carrying out a reconnaissance in force on the Bulgar shore, where a tax-party had lately been ambushed, despoiled and slaughtered almost to a man and where rumours persisted of a war-band several hundreds strong. I was well aware of the rumour, for Hardraada had had me embed it in the monthly intelligence report he presented at the palace in October and which had been the culmination of several such reports before then.

A tax-party had, in fact, been attacked at that place and only the arrival of a band of mercenary varangers en route to relieve the garrison of the nearby imperial fortress had caused the bandits to take flight – with the coffers, unfortunately, but leaving behind a surprising number of weapons and articles of clothing dropped in their haste to be away. These, with the reports of the surviving members of the escort and the varanger officers, had confirmed that the attackers were indeed Bulgars, doubtless emboldened by the recent troubles in the Imperial City. However, the coming winter promised to be a cold one and in recognition of that it was remarkable how quickly the members of the 'Bulgar bandits' grew their beards and moustaches again afterwards . . .

The Golden Horn, November 1042.

Four hefty *varangers* heaved their way along the length of their sweeps in response to the order "Pole off" and the strip of water between quay and *drakkar* widened in the faint light of the new day. The oars went home in their rowlocks with a bang and the longship spun across the ebbing tide to shiver and straighten as the sweeps bit and she changed from a lump of floating wood to the beautiful and living thing she was under power.

Hardraada ordered the sail crew to stand by and four men spat on their hands and took hold of the lines that would jerk the furled and heavy linen at their feet up the mast and spread it along the great yard. The Scraeling looked across to the other *drakkars* and saw that they had leaped to speed just as quickly, the white waves foaming back from the forefoot and the sweeps rising, twisting and dipping with what was possibly the only regard for discipline that these fierce warriors ever showed.

He felt the morning breeze strong on his cheek, and in the same instant Hardraada's voice snapped "Hoist!" and the blood-red square sail rose swiftly up the mast to swell and tighten with a loud crack. The dragon heeled a little, then settled before the wind and the oars slowed at Hardraada's bark, stilled and came inboard.

Hardraada turned to the Scraeling. "Free and away, Scraeling – say farewell to Constantinople and the cunning lot of double-dealing bastards they—" but the Scraeling cut him off, pointing to one side of the harbour.

"Look, *leder*! Look there!" And following the direction of his pointing finger, Hardraada saw a series of twinkles and flashes from the summits of the dawn-lit dark hills behind them. The Scraeling spun to look ahead, and was in time to see answering flashes from the eastern darkness dead ahead of them and he cursed.

"Heliographs!" he exclaimed. "Heliographs ordering the chains back up. Zoe's onto it – she knows we're away, and she's ordered us stopped!"

"Well we're not stopping" said Hardraada grimly. "Not for her or anyone else."

"Those chains won't be very deep this time of day" said the Scraeling, his mind racing. "But the deepest they'll get will be in the middle of the gap between the islands. How fast can we get there?"

"Let's see" said Hardraada. "Out oars! Dig, sons of the raven, dig 'f you want to live!" And the *drakkar* seemed to leap in the water as the oars swung and bit to send them forward under the combined thrust of sail and sweep.

"Wind's freshening – thank Loki it's full astern" said Hardraada and the Scraeling nodded absently, his concentration on the chain of islands dead ahead, those very islands they had marvelled at when they had passed them inbound for Constantinople a lifetime before, each with a signalling-tower atop a winding-station where slaves laboured on a treadmill at dawn, dusk or whenever else they were bidden bring up the huge and heavy chain that sealed the Bosporus.

"Fuck me, it'll be close!" snapped the Scraeling, watching the ends of the chain from the nearest island as they rose, dripping and weed-slimed, from the depths. "*Leder*, can we lighten the front?"

Hardraada saw at once what he meant, and bellowed for everyone not manning an oar to get back aft. "Double-bank the oars to halfway up!" he snapped and men leaped to the benches, sliding on to them and grabbing hold with only the slightest stutter in the rhythm. "Pull, you bastards, pull!" And the stout ash sweeps seemed to bend before the Scraeling's incredulous gaze.

The activity hadn't gone unnoticed aboard the other two *drakkars* and the Scraeling saw men scramble to do the same and the dragon prows lift perceptibly under the increased pressure of the sweeps and the lessening weight at the stem. He tore his eyes back to the front as the dripping chain, a monster of heavy steel and slimy weed, seemed to leap towards them and in the heart-stopping moment of its disappearance beneath their forefoot he felt his heart hammer until it seemed fit to burst from his chest and the roaring of the blood in his ears was all he could hear.

Then the *drakkar* hit the chain with a crash that shook the world and hurled the Scraeling to the deck. He scrambled to his feet, dazed, hearing a voice scream, "Forrard! Get forrard!" and obediently he scrambled forward dragging the nearest body with him. The deck beneath his feet tilted, hung – and dropped forward to an enormous groaning and scraping that seemed to come through the very planking under his feet. But the chain was crossed, and from a distance he heard Hardraada's voice bellowing time for the sweeps and again the longship leaped forward.

Looking back, the Scraeling caught a glimpse of something he would never forget as Ulf's *drakkar* hit the chain at full speed and bounced into the air far enough for him to catch sight of the weed-slimed bottom and the shallow keel that pinned it together. The longship hung in the air for what seemed an eternity before smashing back down on the seaward side of the chain but, seaman that he was, Ulf had her back under control and the oars beginning to move as one within seconds of hitting the water. Arngeirr's longship, though, had chosen the same segment of chain as Ulf and had moved further along its bight to allow Hardraada's lieutenant the centre, and it was enough to be fatal.

The third drakkar ploughed into the lifting chain under the full power of her driving sweeps, and it caught her at the base of the snarling and gilded dragon on the prow, snapping the stem and splintering the timbers that supported it so that the waters of the Bosporus rushed into a longship that split apart like a gutted fish. Still under the impetus of her oars, she filled and sank almost immediately and only the very quick managed to leap over the side before she plunged at racing speed down into the depths of the waterway.

Horrified, the two survivors backed oars and lines snaked out to the men struggling in the water while other vikings leaped to the bulwarks to scour the waves now glittering in the light of day for heads bursting the surface. But there were few enough of those, and as the last man was hauled from the water, the Scraeling said quietly, "I make that twenty, *leder*. No more. And there were seventy on Arngeirr's *drakkar*. That's fifty gone."

Hardraada nodded, his face bleak. "Fucking Zoe. Fifty good men gone, just like that. Old comrades too – Arngeirr, Thorkill, Sweyn and more. I've a mind to take that tower and nail its garrison to their own walls!"

"She wouldn't even twitch, *leder*. But Imperial galleys're probably coming after us now – is there time?"

"No, no, you're right Scraeling. But . . . ah, Odin's balls and belly!" And he raised his voice to call across the water. "No more, Ulf? Right – set course down the Horn. We're away."

The Chronicle.

*T*hat was how we left Miklagaard, city of Constantine. To the end of his days, Hardraada treasured the honours he had won there and none could blame him, for he had arrived as a near-penniless varanger mercenary and left as the Commander of the Varanger Guard, lover as well as soldier of the Empress of Constantinople. His energy and ruthlessness were legend, and Zoe's debt to him should have earned him more than her spite at the end. But if a woman scorned is a woman to be watched, an empress scorned is to be avoided altogether. And if the scorned empress is also a Byzantine . . . then thank our Father that Zoe never knew of Hardraada's intention to marry Elisabeth of Kiev.*

For he did – eventually. Yaroslav welcomed him as son-in-law with open arms, his doubts over Hardraada's suitability apparently set at rest by his reputation as the foremost warrior of the Inland Sea and its empire – though some suggested his wealth had more than something to do with Yaroslav's change of face. However, and surprisingly in view of her earlier and girlish feelings, Elisabeth proved to have a mind of her own and that mind was nowhere nearly ready to accept Hardraada. In part, the marriage was postponed because of the utter failure of Prince Vladimir's attack on Constantinople which did, indeed, go in during 1043 but with which Hardraada resolutely refused to become involved.

But the tall and golden-haired beauty married Hardraada towards the end of that same year. As a result, Hardraada's journey homeward to try conclusions with his kinsman Magnus over the throne of Norway was held up for all of 1044 by the revelation that Elisabeth was with child, and she was delivered of a daughter in the autumn of that year. The journey to her new home in Norway would begin in the following spring, and as that time drew nearer it was my opinion that Yaroslav found himself torn between reluctance to part with his dearest daughter and the wish to get an idle – and therefore dangerous – Hardraada away from dominions much weakened by Vladimir's disastrous and foolish assault on Constantinople.

For myself, I often wondered what I was about with my life. Hardraada seemed able to do nothing wrong, nothing that would bring him within leagues of anything I might do to justify my vow or to bring its resolution any whit closer, and in those days when he waited, rich and triumphant, to marry a princess I fell back more and more upon reminding myself that when Maniakes had Hardraada under lock and key with the prospect of his vengeance looming, I had felt even greater despair. But it was cold comfort nonetheless, and I confess that I looked forward to journeying to Norway with no little foreboding.

Penda was a source of great comfort to me, for it was ever my belief that he not only sensed my turmoil but stayed longer with us because of it than he might otherwise have done. The stalwart Saxon waited patiently through the days of 1043 and saw, with all of us, Hardraada married to Elisabeth before leaving for home in the autumn of 1044 with promises that we would, somehow, meet again one day.

One day he drew me into conversation on the subject of Hardraada, and then confided in me that he could never serve a lord such as Harald the Ruthless. In England, he said, and among those who were of the rank of hus-carl, it was customary to serve a lord for love of him and not for money alone. A hus-carl was sworn to bring his lord to victory or to die on the field of battle with him and this, he maintained, could not be a matter of money.

I agreed, but sought of him why he would not serve Hardraada, and he told me that, peerless warrior and soldier though Hardraada was, there was something in him that told Penda that Hard-counsel fought for the lust of battle and not for principle, nor cause, nor for the right. "There is no mercy in him, cousin" he said, "no thought of offering quarter to any living thing, because he does not seek it himself." He had paused a moment, searching for the words, then finally,

"Hardraada is in love with death, cousin, but also with cheating it so long as he can. Not because he fears it, for then he will feast with Odin for all time, but because the more often he triumphs over it the more he triumphs over those with whom he will one day sit in Valhalla. Aye. He whom you call 'leder' wants no mere place at the table of heroes – he wants to dominate it. He wants to be Odin. He is a bad man, no Christian, and I would not serve such a one" he ended, and thereby gave me no small amount to ponder upon, for I had as much respect for Penda's intelligence as I had for his leadership.

I had watched Penda in action during the savage fighting around the Imperial Palace in those days of April when all between us and Michael had hung on a spear-point. Then, I had seen not only the battle-prowess of the giant Saxon but also how men rallied to him and around him, leaping to do his bidding in their confidence of his direction, his cunning and his power. And, perhaps most of all, because they liked and trusted him as leader, champion and friend.

"Hold to your vow" Penda said eventually. "Hold to it, for you do right. The world will be better without such as Hardraada, and we in England fear them as much as any. Oh, we have them too, never fear, but . . . but not so many, I think. So hold to your vow, Ranulf, and trust that God will place him within your power one day. And if ever you need the arm of Penda Raedwaldsson, whether to shelter or to strike, cousin, comrade and friend – it will reach out to you from Hell itself if need be."

I received his promise with bowed head and part of me noted his use of my own name, a name I had heard only rarely in my life. Was it a sign that the days of my darkness were coming to an end?

But were they so, it was not likely to be soon for in the days after his departure I missed the cheerful Englishman most sorely. Time hung heavily upon me until it was time to busy myself with the task Hardraada set me, which was to set in train all the preparations for a return to Norway and a future, for me, that remained as dark as any in my life.

BOOK FOUR

OF THE KING
1042–1063

"In arms 'tis right the common man
Should follow orders, one by one, —
Should stoop or rise, or run or stand,
As his war-leader may command;
But now to the king who feeds the ravens
The people bend like heartless cravens --
Nothing is left them, but consent
o what the king calls his intent."

"Harald, who till his dying day
Came off the best in many a fray,
Had one good rule in battle-plain,
In Seeland and elsewhere, to gain --
That, be his foes' strength more or less,
Courage is always half success."

"Severe alike to friends or foes,
Who dared his royal will oppose;
Severe in discipline to hold
His men-at-arms wild and bold;
Severe the bondes to repress;
Severe to punish all excess;
Severe was Harald — but we call
That just which was alike to all."

The skald, Thiodolf, in 'The Heimskringla'

The Chronicle.

*I*f I write little of Hardraada in this time it's because there is little to be told. For twenty years after his return from Kiev in 1045 Hardraada was fully and even happily engaged in warfare either within Norway or beyond it, and if any found cause for wonder that one of the greatest warriors of our age took all that time to subdue his enemies, I can say it was because such a delay suited him.

For as empress Zoe well knew, Hardraada found the rewards of kingship as exciting as he found its duties boring. He might indeed have brought his enemies to decisive battle much sooner than he did – but to what end? Keeping Norway on a war footing suited his preference for battle, slaughter and danger. It suited the merchants also, the smiths who made arms and accoutrements and the mercenaries who plied their trade through them. It even suited the farmers, for Hardraada knew full well the value of protecting his food sources.

It did not suit the folk of coastal villages or of border townships, for these were ever wont to suffer from raid and foray. It was less than attractive, also, to those churches and splendid places that a Christian king was sworn to protect, but all that meant to Hardraada was a demonstration of why Holy Church needed to bless his arms and designs.

And that forces me to remark that it was never very clear what Hardraada's designs were - and I, as close to him as any and closer than most, admit that. He began by claiming the throne of Norway as half-brother of Olaf, slain at Stiklestad and now St Olaf of blessed memory. But Olaf's son, Magnus, had been acclaimed as king by the council of electors, the Althing, in 1035 and there seemed no good reason why he should make way for his uncle who, as the son of Queen Aasta and her second husband, Sigurd Syr, was but half an uncle at best.

Now Magnus was a well-regarded king, wise in counsel for one of such tender years and as doughty a warrior as his father had been, but he was childless. In fact he was womanless, for most of his six-and-twenty years had been passed in upholding his right to his father's thrones of both Norway and Denmark against the host of contenders and challengers for them – chief among them the pretender to the throne of Denmark, Svein Estrithson – and he must have greeted his uncle Harald's return as an unsought and unwanted complication.

On one hand the Commander of the Varanger Guard and the empire's foremost warrior was the very shield that Norway needed, but on the other Hardraada's help would not be bought cheaply. While Magnus laughed off his uncle's outright demand for the throne, he thought long and hard before proposing to his redoubtable uncle a joint kingship whereby Hardraada would succeed him should he die childless. Magnus, at twenty-six and in his prime of his young manhood and virility must have thought the bargain at least worth making, but I have always thought it only sealed his fate, for he knew little of his uncle.

But perhaps he learned during a joint kingship that was marked by tension and quarrel, for when he died suddenly and mysteriously in the last days of 1047, he had the last word in naming, on his deathbed, Svein Estrithson to succeed him in Denmark.

Hardraada regarded that as the provocation it was intended to be, and before Christmas of that year he had the Althing proclaim him king of Norway – with all the ambitions and intentions that had gone with St Olaf and with Magnus. If anything was inevitable, it was the reappearance of the raven banner.

Hardraada's capital — Nidaros, Norway, February 1048.

Confidence rang in Hardraada's words. "They will, you know" he said to his lieutenants. "May I never see Freya's left tit if they don't!"

"They don't give a bugger whose tit you see, play with or suck on" said Haldor, blunt as ever. "A Norwegian *jarl*'s not a scraeling – you won't frighten him. You'll have to beat him – over the head and often!"

"Granted" said Hardraada, the soul of good humour. "And the more I do of that early on, the less I'll need to do later. What's the problem?"

"Practical ones" said the Scraeling. "Look – you've only just been named king and even your home area, the Uplandende, is lukewarm about it. Haldor's right – what I hear is, Magnus had the *jarls* by the balls and squeezed till their faces turned blue, and they never respected him – just feared him. Now you've got it all to do again. How'll you improve on that?"

"Something you said, smartarse" said Hardraada, "and I think it'll work."

"Something I said?" asked the Scraeling, "When? And what?"

"About halfway down the Golden Horn as I recall" said Hardraada, looking pleased with himself. "When we spoke one night of what we'd got and what we'd learned from Miklagaard. What you said was how you'd noticed from their histories that every time an emperor had a problem with his nobles, he'd start a war somewhere or grab a bit more land – anything that'd get the stroppy buggers with too much energy using it instead of plotting with it. Remember?" he asked, looking around.

"Not me" said Skallagrim. "Sometimes the Scraeling makes my head ache."

"It was the wine made your head ache that night" came back Haldor. "You got shitfaced – first night out as I recall. Aye, *leder* – I remember something like that. D'you, Scraeling?"

"Vaguely" said the Scraeling. "But it's true anyway. Zoe's uncle, Basil the hardman, that's just what he did – over and over. Everyone thought he was a hell of a fellow, too. Mind you, he had the talent to back it up."

"And we don't?" asked Hardraada. "We know a bit about soldiering ourselves, eh?"

"Look" said Ulf, "speak plain *leder*. What're you on about?"

Hardraada shifted his bulk at the top of the table and leaned forward. "Right" he said. "I'm a new king. I don't know the politics 'cause I've been away for fifteen years. There're a couple – at least – of Magnus' boys who don't fancy me any more than half, and a whole bunch who need their arses kicking, just like the Scraeling says. I'm starting from scratch. What do I do?"

"I say get on with it" said Haldor. "We know all this, an' I say the quicker it's done the better. Anyone else?" and he looked around the table.

"Hang on" said Hardraada. "Think about it. What worked in Miklagaard won't necessarily work here. For a start this is Norway, not a place full of scraelings with arses fit for kicking – or the other things some of 'em got up to with their arses" he added as an afterthought. "For another, it's like you said yourself. Norwegians aren't up for bluffing – you thrash 'em or win them over. And we haven't got the men or the force to thrash 'em; not if they combine. And I reckon they will. So, according to the Scraeling here, we need to find them a war, aye?"

"A war we can win" said the Scraeling.

"Or a war we can drag out a bit" nodded Hardraada. "So they can see how much they'll benefit by following and not fighting me. Us."

"Think I know where you're going" said Skallagrim. "Svein?"

"You've got it" grinned Hardraada. "Cnut's little nephew, the bastard who should've been happy with Denmark when he had the chance. The *jarls*'ll follow us all right when they realise – or when we point out to them – how much Danish land there is for the taking. If I offer them the job of collecting it. Follow?"

Haldor nodded. "So we give them something to do and get rid of Svein too. Fucking good riddance; the little maggot tried to knock you off up at Zealand last year. It *was* him, you know, for all he swore he knew nothing about it. One of my captains heard a story he wasn't supposed to hear in a brothel and pointed out the storyteller to me. Couple of us had a word with him and out came the truth, right after his second fingernail, the bloody girl. But I'm sure he was telling the truth."

"No matter" said Hardraada, "but thanks. It's what we're going to do to him that counts, not what he failed to do to me. But I'll bear it in mind, old friend of mine."

"Now" he said, "a couple of other things an' I want you to hear 'em first. First – the Orkneys. Magnus never did sew them up, and I'm going to – early. People notice that sort of thing, and I reckon it'll be easily done. Old Thorfinn's a reasonable sort of character, but him hanging out there on his own's a bad example for the rest, and I'm not having it. He can name his price if he'll come in – or be the first I make an example of. Won't come to a fight, though, because he's not that popular with the others is what I hear, and he can't stand up to us alone. Give him the options, Scraeling – but make him see he can get off to a good start with me by coming in, right?"

The Scraeling jerked upright. "Me? What d'you want me to do? Who the fuck's Thorfinn? And where's this . . . this Orkney anyway?" to general laughter.

"Yes, you. I want you to go and see Thorfinn, and be back by spring. Thorfinn's the *jarl* of Orkney. Orkney's off the Scottish coast, and Scotland's north of England. Don't worry – we'll send you with someone who won't miss the islands and bump into Scotland" and there was another roar of laughter at the look on the Scraeling's face.

"You're the man, Scraeling" said Hardraada. "You've got the head and the tongue and the wit to be an ambassador, and besides – you're an honest man. Anyone can see that." *So much for what you know* thought the

Scraeling, but Hardraada was speaking again.

"Y'see, Scraeling, I can't spare one of my captains right now – but apart from you being a better bet anyway, you're high enough in rank for Thorfinn to see I take him seriously because you'll come directly from me as my secretary. And people know that. We'll talk in more detail later, but for now there's one other thing you should know. One of Thorfinn's top men in Norway itself is Thorberg Arnesson. He's head of the Arnmodling family, who've had strong links with Orkney for years. To show I mean business, Scraeling, you can tell Thorfinn I'm going to link myself publicly with him and the Arnmodling by marrying Thorberg's daughter, Thora."

The Scraeling jerked upright a second time. "*Leder – leder –* you're . . . what? You're already married! I was there!" which brought another snort of laughter from around the table.

"Can't hide much from you, Scraeling!" said Hardraada genially. "That's why you're an ambassador, aye?" to another roar of laughter.

"Harald, Queen Elisabeth's just had Princess Ingegerd. You can't . . . can't set her aside, surely . . .? With two little girls? I mean . . . Yaroslav . . ."

"Yaroslav's far away" said Hardraada, "and there's nothing personal in this, Scraeling. It's called politics. Elisabeth'll still be queen – but she'll have help. With whatever she needs help in" he added to a burst of ribald laughter, and the Scraeling felt himself blush hotly.

"Scraeling, Scraeling, you don't understand" said Haldor, not unkindly. "Here in the north, a man can take as many wives as he wants. Or as he can support. No, truly – it's the custom. We've always done it."

"The reason is" said Skallagrim, "we fight a lot. You've noticed? Good. That means there's a shortage of men – always has been – so if we couldn't take more than one wife, who looks after the women without one? And what about the babies who wouldn't get born?"

"Well mend your ways!" said a genuinely outraged Scraeling. "Stop bloody fighting so much! How does the Church let you get away with . . . with bigamy's what it's called? How, eh?"

"Church doesn't have a lot to say about it" said Hardraada. "Y'see, Scraeling, if you scratch a Norseman you're likely to find what you followers of the White Christ call a pagan. Even my saintly brother had a bit of trouble with that. Lots of us have a foot in both stirrups, you could say. So the local holy men don't ride their luck about second wives, y'see? Anyway

– tell Thorfinn it's going to happen. He'll like that, and I need all the help I can get. Thorfinn of Orkney, the Arnmodlings – all I can get."

"Hey, cheer up Scraeling" said Ulf, making a rare contribution, "like Harald said – nothing personal. It's politics." And beneath his breath, "Stop fighting, eh . . .? Fuck, that'll never catch on. What an idea . . ."

The Scraeling blew out his cheeks, let out a long sigh and gestured to Skallagrim. "That wine-flask nailed to your hand, Skallagrim, or can I have some over here?"

Nidaros, Norway, April 1048.

Hardraada stretched his arms to the fire on a spring morning that was still sharp and asked, "So how'd he take it?"

"Delighted to be asked" replied the Scraeling. "He's a hard old bugger, isn't he? How old would he be?"

"Over sixty" mused Hardraada. "I remember him when I was a lad – had a face that'd been lived in even then. But they're all hard men down there y'know. Fight at any excuse – when they're not fighting the weather, and that's wilder than any of 'em. But he's happy to come in with us?"

"He is. Even said he'd never dream of staying out, because if you're good enough for the Empress of Constantinople you're good enough for him"

Hardraada threw back his head and laughed. "Why Scraeling, if that means I find old Thorfinn in my bed one night, I'll pick him up and toss him into yours, and that's a promise!"

"No fear, *leder* – I'm sure he was talking about soldiering rather than shagging. Well, almost sure!"

They laughed again, and the Scraeling went on to give details of the men and vessels the Jarl of Orkney could place at Hardraada's disposal at need before he ended with "And lastly, *leder*, Thorfinn sends you his compliments on your forthcoming wedding and begs you give his old friend Thorberg a grandson as soon as you may."

Hardraada grunted. "He's got one of those already from Thora, I hear. She's a lusty wench and always was. Supposed to be enthusiastic in bed, but not very good at it. Still – you'd go a long way to find one as polished as Zoe anyway."

The Scraeling couldn't believe his ears. "That sort of talk's going around?

How d'you feel about that?"

"Freya's tits, Scraeling, that's nothing to get excited about! You're bloody amazing, you are. Look – for a dozen years you lived among the most devious, cunning, two-faced, scheming and evil people that your God or mine ever put on the face of the earth, and became just as cunning and devious yourself. But you can't get over some of our customs up here, can you? Can't you see that we're . . . we're a little more straightforward, shall we say?" Hardraada ended.

"My oath, you're straightforward all right!" said the Scraeling, surprising himself with the force of his passion. "One minute a queen's a queen and then she's not. Next minute a king's got two wives and one of 'em's had a baby to someone else and the whole town knows how she is between the sheets. 'Enthusiastic but not very good.' Fuck me!"

"Not a chance" said Hardraada, laughing at the Scraeling's state. "Not if Thora's offering – and I believe she does offer, quite often. Look, Scraeling, it's like Skallagrim said – we think every woman should have a man to keep her happy and to father her kids an' provide for them. And if he can't, someone else does. And, as far as Elisabeth's concerned, she's still queen till she doesn't want to be. Because that's another freedom our women have – if a woman doesn't want to belong to a man any more, that's fine. And if she wants to belong to someone else, that's fine too. Even the queen."

"But let's go back to Miklagaard. Now don't tell me you never knew any woman there use the honey-trap to her own advantage?" And a picture of Kia watching him erupt in climax flashed into the Scraeling's mind and, watching him intently, Hardraada saw it and chuckled. "Thought so. That's that then. Not saying we're better, Scraeling. Just different in the way we live."

"Look, if you're that concerned about Elisabeth, drop in on her. You'd be someone she knew from, ah, her other life – someone who's not one of her Rus women. And she's educated, like you, and Christian like you – so you'd have a lot to talk about, wouldn't you? Yes, yes, that's a good idea. Do that, Scraeling – I insist!"

The Scraeling mumbled something, his mind still reeling as Hardraada continued. "Now look, I needed to know about Thorfinn before the campaigning season, and thanks to you I do. That's good, but it's not enough. I can handle our opposition inside Norway, and I'm going to do that by setting about Svein Estrithson and his Danes, right? But Svein's related to Cnut the Dane, curse his memory, and so's the biggest man at the English court. He's called Godwin, and he's an earl. A real big noise, 'cause he's the father-in-law of the English king, Edward, as well as a cock-relation of Svein's through Cnut. I'd bet gold that Svein won't have forgotten that, and that he'll be trying to get English help."

"Now, the English aren't much on the water, but they're bloody hard men on land. Their *hus-carls* are the best heavy soldiers anywhere, including the Empire, and – ah, but you know that. Your friend Penda's one, remember? And remember how he fought through the streets of Miklagaard? We don't need a couple hundred like him turning up with Svein, Scraeling. And it's up to you to stop it. You'll have a proper escort this time, mind, something appropriate to your station and your task. And that's to try for an English alliance against Svein. You won't get one, of course, but you've sold enough amber to know that if you aren't in the market you don't sell any. Right?"

"They're expecting you, by the way. So you're off on the horse again, or on a galley at least. To England."

The Chronicle.

*A*nd so again I boarded a ship to journey south, this time with an escort *of two sections of axemen resplendent in matching tunics – red trimmed with the white winter pelt of the wolf if I recall correctly – commanded by my old friend Skuli. We made landfall at the towering chalk pile of Flamborough Head and as the English coast slid slowly by on the right hand I mused on the times when a prowling viking drakkar would surely have attracted bands of mounted guardians riding along the shoreline.*

But we saw none such, and made harbour at South Hampton in that part of the country known as Wessex. Here we made ourselves known to the king's ealdorman and were received, if not warmly, then at least politely and arrangements were made for our onward journey up the great river to the king's court at Winchester. There we were much more warmly received by none other than Penda, who had had word of our sighting off Flamborough and who spared no effort in making us welcome. He saw to the quartering of my escort and entertained Skuli, two of his officers and myself in the evening of our arrival to a meal that was little short of sumptuous.

After, he led us in the consumption of huge amounts of the mead for which the land was both famous and notorious but Skuli, perceptive as that man was in all my knowledge of him, laughingly declined a fourth horn of the potent liquid that was all too easy to drink "while I can still hold on to it, friend Penda". He sensed that our host had things to say that were for me alone, so he wove happily off into the darkness with his section leaders.

Winchester, summer 1048.

Penda returned from the doorway where he had called a last farewell after Skuli, poured two more horns of mead and set them carefully down on the table.

"You've risen high, cousin" he said, "to be ambassador to the thunderbolt of the north!"

The Scraeling looked at him with eyebrows raised.

"Aye" he smiled, "that's what Hardraada's called here. Why? For the speed of his moving against his *jarls*, for his alliances with the Arnmodlings, for cleaning up the mess in the Orkneys that Magnus couldn't – oh for any number of things."

The Scraeling struggled to hide his astonishment. "You're well informed, cousin" he managed, and Penda smiled.

"We take care to be, Ranulf. We take care to be. These are dangerous times."

"Is your Edward so concerned about Norway, then?" the other asked, and Penda shook his head.

"Not Edward" he said. "Edward cares about nothing except buying forgiveness in heaven for his sins here on earth. Godwin runs England, Ranulf, not the king."

The Scraeling spread his hands. "Well now" he said, "this is what I know of Godwin" and he repeated the little Hardraada had told him. Penda listened, sipped at his mead and put the horn down with a click.

"Aye" he said, "but here's what Harald doesn't know. Godwin's not as firm in the saddle as Hardraada thinks. Old Siward of Northumbria and Leofric of Mercia can't abide him. They're old blood, y'see, and they look down on Godwin as Cnut's lickspittle. For his part, Godwin thinks the north'll never be English until it's properly under the control of men from

Wessex – that's here" he added, and the Scraeling nodded. "Too many reminders, too much history of the Danes up there" he went on. "Makes a natural landing-place for invasion from the north."

"So Godwin and the other earls contend" mused the Scraeling. "But isn't he the king's father-in-law?"

Penda puffed out his cheeks. "Aye" he admitted, "and no. Godwin's price for the strength of his arm five years ago when Edward came to the throne was that the king married his daughter, Edith of Wessex. And Edward couldn't refuse. But he's always hated Godwin – blamed him for the death of his brother, years ago, but that's all nonsense. Still –" and here Penda hesitated – "Edward's . . . strange. Once he gets an idea in his head – ah well, you'll see for yourself."

"Anyway. He hates Godwin and all his kind – and while he couldn't avoid marrying Edith, he's not handing over the throne to someone who's even a half-Godwin. So – get this, cousin – he's never taken Edith to his bed, and swears he won't. Amazing – she's a beautiful woman too, by the way. Swears he's taken a vow of celibacy – dedicated his life to God's glory, contemplates Christ's majesty rather than man's, that kind of thing. That's why I said both aye and no."

The Scraeling couldn't believe his ears. "What about the succession?" he asked, "what then?"

Penda shrugged his massive shoulders. "It'll come to a fight" he said flatly. "Nothing surer. Would've come to that before now, though, 'f Magnus hadn't died. Tell me – how did Hardraada manage that?"

"To the best of my knowledge" returned the Scraeling, "he didn't. Could've just as easily been Svein, you know."

"Ah, Svein" said Penda thoughtfully. "You'd be here to ask for Edward's help in that little brawl?"

"I would. How much chance is there?"

"Less chance than there is of that drinking-horn crawling up your arm and into your mouth by itself. Godwin's a relative of Cnut's – which is to say, of Svein's, so he's all for offering the English fleet to Svein. But you're lucky. Edward's not pro-Hardraada, but he is anti-Godwin. So he's going to concoct an excuse – what it is he'll tell you at your audience, but boiled down it's that, while Svein and Hardraada are keeping each other busy, England's northern frontier's safe. See?"

"Completely. And in Edward's place I'd be happy to own a situation like that. But enough of politics, cousin – tell me how a broken-arsed mercenary comes to be so high in the councils of the king of England?"

"Ah" said Penda, "my father, Raedwald, is an earl in his own right. No Godwin, mind you, but an earl just the same. My older brother will inherit the earldom – that's why I could go a-*varanging* and take up with knife-throwing Breton renegades in the first place, y'see – so I have my own way to make, an' I've chosen to make it in the Godwin service."

"Is that wise, cousin? When the king clearly hates the family so?"

Penda looked down at his drinking-horn and said, "But Edward will die childless, Ranulf. Godwin is the power in the land. He has three daughters to marry to three earls, and six sons to rule the other earls, and he can do the job that Edward can't in keeping this land secure. I'm *hus-carl* to his second son, Harold, because no Christian man can serve his eldest, the godless Sweyn. With luck, the devil will take Sweyn for his own one day soon – God knows, the man's outraged enough husbands and fathers and profaned enough holy places for any six others. And when the other Godwin sons rule in name as well as fact, why then, a 'broken-arsed mercenary' may one day find himself high in the counsel of the earls of England!"

He yawned mightily, then stretched until his great arms creaked. "But cousin – it's late, and the king'll see you tomorrow. After that, there're others who want to speak with Hardraada's secretary while Edward considers your master's request for an alliance."

The Chronicle.

*E*dward of England didn't impress me one whit with his majesty, for he had none. A man of middle height, he had a stoop to him that made him appear shorter while his watery and red-rimmed eyes consistently refused to meet mine while we spoke.

No, he said, assistance to Hardraada couldn't be countenanced for that would involve interference in the affairs of a foreign state – as, he was quick to point out, Svein's ambassador had already been told – therefore, while he saluted the Empire's greatest warrior and was flattered to receive his offer of an alliance, the most he might do was to advise Hardraada to beseech God through prayer that

He might send an unmistakable sign of His intentions for the Scandinavian countries.

All the while he was telling me this, my attention was taken by the nails on the hands that clutched the arms of the receiving-room chair. They were broken and bitten, with the skin at the base red raw and bloody on some fingers. They were the fingers of a man of deep and violent passions, and much at odds with his mild-mannered reputation. On a whim I gave it as my opinion that God would certainly reward such a petition of his disciple Harald, for he had acquired much merit both by his conduct in making the arduous pilgrimage to Jerusalem and in his distinguished acts and generous donations there. And I had what I sought, for deep down in Edward's eyes there appeared a fierce and unmistakable flare of jealousy.

So much for the saint-king, I thought – and if that was so, then so much, too, for his protestations of sanctity and the more for Penda's reading of him as a vengeful man of powerful emotions. And that might suit my purpose one day, although I couldn't see how at that time.

Winchester, the same day.

Penda indicated the Scraeling to the visitors. "Harold, earl of East Anglia and lord Tostig, this is Ranulf de Lannion, secretary to Harald Hardraada and leader of his embassy to our sovereign lord Edward. He's also a cousin of sorts, and I claim him as such" said Penda.

"That a fact?" asked the powerfully-built and very blond man before me, holding out a hand. "That'll be a Breton name then, if I'm any judge. Welcome to England, cousin of Penda. He tells me that you shared desperate times in Constantinople towards the end – and but for you they would've been more so."

"Penda's a mighty teller of tales" replied the Scraeling, "who'd surely have been a *skald* were he my size and not his. So treat his tales as travellers' tales, earl Harold, as kin to those of sea-monsters and demons!"

Tostig, as dark as his brother was fair, laughed. "There, Penda – set down by your own cousin. What about that?"

Penda was unmoved. "You can't choose your relatives, Tostig. The Scraeling – as he'd rather be called – is a man of many secrets and well fit to be a *skald* himself for his way with cunning designs and stratagems. Fact is, Hardraada himself refers to him as 'the most dangerous little bugger alive.' Let me tell you what he once did with a castle that had no weakness – they still sing of it among the *varangers*, so you're bound to hear about it. Just remember where you heard it first . . ." and he told on, while Harold poured wine for them in deference to the Scraeling, who squirmed in embarrassment the while.

And once the tale was told and the English earls had done exclaiming at the Scraeling's cunning, nothing would do but that Penda must recount his part in the gathering of Hardraada's prodigious wealth, even over the Scraeling's protests that the stories had lost little in the mouths of the tellers.

"And your master – ah . . . Scraeling" said Harold at length. "What manner of man is he?"

The Scraeling paused a moment to gather his thoughts. Then, "A man, lord Harold, much given to warfare and soldiering. A man who knows his own mind. A man who never shrinks from the most difficult of undertakings or the risk of failure. A man who'd gamble his soul against the devil for the joy of victory. Aye, a bold man and one who well deserves the name others have given him."

"*Hard-raede*, aye" said Tostig thoughtfully. "Is there no softness in him?" and again the Scraeling thought a moment.

"I've known him seventeen years" he said at last, "and can't recall a decision ever made in weakness in all that time. So, no – there's no weakness in him, lord Tostig. He's what the sagas call a 'fell and stark man.' Why? As if I can't guess . . ."

Harold erupted in laughter. "Brother, haven't we just heard of the Scraeling's cunning? Did you think to trap him? And has he set you on your arse or what?"

Tostig smiled thinly. "Aye, Scraeling. We who, ah . . . are concerned with the business of this England, we like to know of those who are our neighbours. Is that wrong?"

The Scraeling shrugged. "Hardraada's only recently returned home from imperial service, and he's got his hands full with the would-be king of Denmark" he said, "so he's no threat to you, surely?"

"No?" asked Harold, but his smile robbed the next words of any malice, "as you say, he's only just returned home – so just how dangerous does the fact he's already challenging Svein of Denmark for two thrones make him?"

"Fair point" said the Scraeling, "but again – if your king has his way, Hardraada won't trouble you for long enough, will he?"

"Look" broke in Tostig, "let's speak plainly. Penda, here, can sort out the detail for you – maybe he already has – but if we get right down to it, Scraeling, our concern's for the future. And we think your man'll win. Question is – what's that mean for us here?"

The Scraeling spread his hands. "Why ask me? Hardraada sent me here because he knew your man would be doing likewise – Svein's your relative after all – so my mission's purely defensive. It's a bit soon to be thinking about Hardraada coming over anyone's border except Svein's. And frankly, if Svein would give up his ambitions as far as Norway's concerned, my master wouldn't even be thinking about Denmark." Which wasn't, of course, true – *and if the gleam in Harold's eye means anything*, thought the Scraeling, *he's worked that out for himself.*

"Anyway" the Scraeling pressed on, "aren't we a little previous in all this? After all, my master's your master's problem rather than yours surely?"

"And who do you think'll have the sorting of any . . ." began Tostig, but Harold raised a hand to interrupt him.

"Truly spoken, Scraeling. Edward's the king and, as you say, the one to deal with the problem. So enough of his business, and let's raise a cup to Penda's cousin and our new friendship. For I trust you'll consider the Godwins friend, Messire de Lannion, not only today but in the future also." And he held out his hand again.

The Chronicle.

*T*hat was my meeting with the sons of earl Godwin and, had I only known it then, it was one of the most fateful meetings of my life as from it would come not only the fulfilment of my life's work but the toppling and death of two kings.

A bold statement? Aye, perhaps so, for the results were far beyond imagining at the time. Then, I went on my way thinking about the most powerful brothers in the country – chiefly, of how correct were the reports given me that Harold was capable of charming birds from trees, for in my mind he was a born leader. But also of how Tostig, neither so handsome nor as relaxed as his brother, was the more intense and even passionate of the two. They were a formidable pair, I thought, combining as they did a shrewd and careful talent for thinking ahead with awareness of the realities of power and statecraft. Not to mention a lack of scruple sufficient to examine, directly, an ambassador on the subject of his own leader and I smiled at the thought of the temerity they had shown.

But then I thought of the military force they could command, and I stopped smiling and began to wish Edward of England success in keeping his nobles and their retainers out of the affairs of Scandinavia. The Godwins, and their pro-Svein sympathies, might easily turn the issue in Hardraada's wars with Denmark and take the prize from me.

And so I thought that I might take Harold Godwinsson at his word and count his family among my friends. Whatever I told Hardraada.

Winchester, two days later.

Penda held up the arrow, squinted along the shaft and slid it carefully into his quiver. "They were impressed with you" he said, picking up another. "Not just because of who you are, but because of what you've done."

"What's that mean?" asked the Scraeling, putting his sound knee into the business of flexing a bowstave. "What'm I supposed to have done?"

"Not 'supposed' at all" insisted Penda, "what you have done. Hardraada and his crew between them ran the Rus and the Empire for a dozen years. They fought battles, toppled kings, ravaged lands and ruled the seas – all as they needed. And who kept that war-machine going? You – the Scraeling. Look at you – five foot five on your tiptoes, one leg useless, not a man for axe and mail but stone-cold deadly with anything you can throw, launch or shoot – and you're a scholar, schemer and planner on top, as well as a master horseman. That's what you're 'supposed to have done', cousin Ranulf."

"And I've got a cousin with a big mouth, I suppose" mused the Scraeling as he notched a bowstring to the stave he'd chosen.

"Never!" exploded Penda. "The Godwin boys knew all about you before they came near me – fact, Tostig mentioned that Harold wanted to meet you while you were here. Don't ask me how they knew – but I'll tell you this for nothing – the Godwins amaze me regularly. Old Godwin might be a left-over from Cnut's day, but his boys – and 'specially Harold – have their hands on things and they're a bit different. They know they're going to run this land one day, one way or another, an' they leave nothing – that's nothing – to chance. Ranulf, they didn't squeeze me to set up that meeting with you just so's they could pour you a cup or two. They wanted to meet you, to watch you, to hear you. They've got plans for you, an' if they haven't, they think they might have plans for you – and for the Godwins, that's enough."

"Interesting" said the Scraeling thoughtfully. "And Harold did make a point of assuring me of his friendship."

"Exactly" said Penda, moving to the rack of bowstaves in the centre of the armoury. "And you know what – I might not be in your class for cunning, but I thought the Godwins might – just might – help you with—"

"Cousin" interrupted the Scraeling, "I do believe I know where you're going. But don't. Don't even think about it. Not a bloody word to the Godwins, an it pleases you. Why? Because if it suited them for some reason to let Hardraada know, one day, that he'd better start having his food tasted, why they would. And given the way they spend their lives and the things they think about, it'd be quite reasonable for them to do that. So no, please – leave it strictly alone."

"But I'll tell you what" he said, looking at Penda's crestfallen face, "it's probably the best idea I've heard since the night I woke up after that Scythian pegged me in Constantinople. I'll never be able to do it alone, Penda, and I've got to face that. Yes – I might be useful to the Godwins one day, but yes also – it works both ways. I just can't see it yet. One day I will, and I'm not going to rush things now. But that day, Penda, when the Godwins' need and mine come together – goodbye Harald."

"Now – our wager. Six shafts each, you said, at seventy paces, your gold ring against my wolfskin cap, yes? Well cousin, if you must . . . I suppose I really ought to shoot left-handed to give an axeman a chance, but I'm not going to!"

Nidaros, Norway, summer 1049.

The Scraeling had high hopes of the colt that circled him on the end of the leading-rein clutched in his fist, and it showed in the way he spoke to the horse between the whistles that changed the beast's gait and direction.

"Ah-*sa*! Such a horse! So quick, so sure, so beautiful! Your mother the wind and your father the thunder. Ah-*sa,* horse among a thousand, horse for the gods themselves, finest of all the herds in the lands of the North ..." And through all its evolutions, thought the woman who watched from the corner of the stable, the colt seemed ever to have an eye on the figure who turned in the centre of the yard and an ear moving to the stream of praise as it listened for the whistle that would send it from walk to trot to canter, from right to left and back again.

The voice fell silent and the colt stopped, standing perfectly still. The Scraeling clucked softly to it, and the young horse moved daintily in towards him to thrust its velvety muzzle into the angle of the Scraeling's neck and shoulder as he coiled the long strip of leather to keep it from under the animal's feet, The man laughed softly and scratched the animal between its eyes as his other hand dived into the front pocket of the smock he wore to emerge with a handful of corn, and the watcher stepped forward as the colt whinnied its delight and took the treat daintily between tongue and lip.

"Beautiful" she said, and the Scraeling spun round, "the colt is beautiful, Scraeling, and you handle him with such love!"

"Majesty" said the Scraeling, bowing to her, "I apologise for not ..."

"Needlessly" interrupted the woman who had been Elisabeth of Kiev, "for you were about a most serious matter. The training of this wondrous animal. And how well you do it!"

The Scraeling bowed again. "He's quick to learn, Majesty, and well-bred" he said.

Elisabeth nodded. "That's easily seen, but I see also that he reflects the training he's had. Surely you've trained many horses?"

"Fewer than I'd have wished, Majesty" said the other, stroking the soft muzzle that was seeking entry to his food store, "for there's been little time, and even less of late."

The golden head nodded as Elisabeth ran her hands over the muscles beneath the silken skin. After two daughters, thought the Scraeling, she was still the slender golden beauty he had seen married in the cathedral of Kiev, but the smudges under her eyes and the lines beginning to show on her high forehead were much more recent.

"The demands upon you are many, Scraeling" she said and, lifting her face to him, "for I know the king depends much on you."

The Scraeling shrugged and spread his hands. "Nothing I haven't done before, Majesty."

Elisabeth looked at him curiously over the note in his voice. "You sound as though you regret it" she remarked, and the Scraeling covered his confusion by adjusting the colt's bit and bridle. "And you needn't address me as 'Majesty'" she added. "Save that for Queen Thora. She enjoys it because she's not used to being treated as royalty, although now she's had a young son she'll probably get more of it." Her voice was coldly matter-of-fact and the Scraeling glanced at her as he turned the colt towards the stable entrance.

"No" he replied neutrally, "Queen Thora's rather newer to all of it than your Maj— than your, ah, Highness."

Elisabeth laughed. "Scraeling, 'Elisabeth' was good enough for my family, and it's good enough for me when we're by ourselves. As we're going to be, I hope, for I seek a favour of you."

"I'm bored, Secretary. The nurses have my daughters, Thora has my throne, my bed and my husband – and I need what I used to have in Kiev. And that is – a lot to do with horses. Now, Norsemen don't appreciate horses as anything but a way of getting about. But I'm told you do, and what I've seen today more than bears that out. Well, Scraeling – will you be my horseman? Say you will!" And at the last, the longing was there in eyes and voice so the Scraeling inclined his head as they passed into the dimness of the stable.

The Chronicle.

It was easy to accede to Elisabeth's request. Queen Thora repelled me for she was large, loose, loud and coarse but those very attributes won her the hearts and minds of Hardraada's companions, while being brought to bed of a long-desired son did her no harm either.

Elisabeth was as lonely as I had ever seen another human being, but she was a queen who had been a princess – like Zoe, she had been born to the purple – and she suffered the humiliation Hardraada put upon her with regal dignity and carriage. She lived for her daughters, Maria and Ingigerd, and for the bloodlines she had vowed to build among the shaggy and hardy horse-herds, and I was happy to help her in that. For her part she always seemed to be happy in my company and to count the hours passed in stable, yard or riding in the open countryside with her women and myself as time well spent.

And there was an increasing number of hours so passed, for the war of that campaigning season was one of movement, feint and parry. Hardraada invaded Denmark and Svein invaded Norway; the armies circled each other like Byzantine wrestlers seeking a hold and the war went nowhere, it seemed – and certainly not anywhere that my team of secretaries and clerks could not send it without me. I had learned in the imperial service of the folly of attempting to do everything myself, and Hardraada had never demurred at my building of teams because, I considered, it made him appear more important even though he preferred to believe that it gave me more opportunity to plan the advancement of his designs.

But, and as I have written elsewhere, it was frequently difficult to understand just what those designs were – if you press me to say why, I answer that this was because Hardraada looked no further ahead than the next battle. Warfare was what he did and why he existed, and each battle was to be enjoyed for its own sake and nothing else. Whatever the reason, I found myself in that campaign season of 1049 with more and more time to devote to our shared interest in horses.

And then things changed.

That autumn

Elisabeth smiled her pleasure as she turned from the colt. "You speak to him" she said, "and I know he understands. Why d'you do so?"

"Well" said the Scraeling, "it's no bad thing to have a horse understand you, surely?" and they both laughed before he said, "but apart from that, my lady, I cannot control a horse with my knees, as you see. So I ride as you and your ladies do, in this saddle I had made a long time ago, but I ask more of a mount than a lady and so I speak and whistle to him where another would use his knees."

"But that's wonderful!" exclaimed Elisabeth, glancing behind again to where the colt, still not broken to the saddle, followed at the end of a leading-rein and just ahead of two of her ladies. "And so clever of you. Did you train your other horses so?"

"One other" said the Scraeling. "A long time ago, Elisabeth. He was a colt like this one behind us, as clever and as beautiful and he was as swift as the wind over the ocean. When he ran, his feet seemed never to touch the ground, and my mother claimed that he danced on the wind. So we named him Dancer. Then . . . my life changed."

Something in his voice made Elisabeth glance sideways and what she saw in his face led her to stretch out her hand and lay it over his bridle fist.

"Scraeling, what is it? What changed your life?" she demanded, but he pointed to a thick grove of trees a little way from the road.

"There, my lady. Let's rest the horses and eat. And then I'll answer your question."

They swung from the way, and in a glade screened from the road the Scraeling saw to the tethering of the horses on reins long enough to allow forage while the ladies set out the cold meat and ale from the saddlebags upon a cloth on the ground before they took some food and moved deeper into the trees. The Scraeling looked his surprise, and Elisabeth said.

"I've told them to leave us, Scraeling, for I saw the unhappiness in your face and I alone would hear your story. If it pleases you to tell me." She busied herself with bread and meat while the Scraeling laid his bow and quiver by him and sat, awkwardly and heavily.

Elisabeth did not meet his gaze while he told how Les Trois Étoiles had died and of how Dancer, the horse who rode the wind, had had its legs broken on a leather rope and its skull cleft by a viking axe, but as she handed him the food she had prepared, her hand shook and the tears ran from her. "He's an animal" she whispered, "an animal. But animals cause pain and suffering only when they kill to eat. He might have taken the food they needed without . . . without any of the rest."

"He did none 'of the rest' himself, Elisabeth" said the Scraeling. "Not that I saw. Nor did I see him do so on the voyage that brought us to the great rivers of Russia."

"He might have stopped it" she said fiercely. "And he a Christian baptised! But no. It's part of him" and the tears came again. "He fouls all he touches. Aye, when I grew to womanhood something told me the tall warrior-hero I'd worshipped as a girl was a cruel and stark man. So I put him off as long as I might but my father . . . my father would . . . oh Ranulf, I'm so unhappy . . ." and saying so she cast herself into the Scraeling's arms and sobbed as if her heart was breaking.

The Scraeling soothed her as best he could, with part of his mind conscious of the closeness of her maids. As if she had read his mind she raised a tearstained face to him, sat up and made the best smile she could, and explained shakily "Fear not. My women know of my despair, Scraeling, and they're also of the Rus. They're faithful to me and will say nothing. Your forgiveness, I pray you. I thought I had no tears left, but your story of Dancer . . . will it ever end? The Church teaches that the meek shall inherit the earth, Scraeling, but will they? In the presence of the evil that men make for their own ends, is there anything left for the meek but suffering and death? Is there?"

The Scraeling reached out his hands to her intending nothing but the comfort of a human touch, but she moaned as if in pain, leaned forward and in an instant had slid into his arms to take him in a fierce embrace, her lips full upon his in a passionate kiss. For a moment he responded, then twisted his head free.

"Elisabeth, Elisabeth" he managed, "this is folly. You are . . . my queen and I'm the subject of the king your husband! We cannot do this, my lady!"

"Ranulf, Ranulf, I've thought of little else these weeks past" she whispered. "This is no folly, my man. You're not as they are, and God be thanked for that. I . . . I . . . long for a gentle voice, for . . . for the touch of a hand in understanding. You, who are so different from they . . . if I hear your voice correctly, you know loneliness too, and have known well the harshness of these rough folk. These folk who cannot even say my name, for to them I am 'Ellisif'!"

"Elisabeth" said the Scraeling shakily, "I know how it has been for you, and pray you believe me that you'll be my queen forever – whatever you are to the king. Thora the Slut isn't fit to stand in your shadow, my lady, and believe me, too, that it . . . it . . . would be easy for any man to accept the gift . . . the gift of you, my lady. But there are reasons why I may not" he said desperately as he saw her flinch at the 'but', "and I can't speak of them except to say that . . . that one day I shall be damned before God and man. And that is the path I've chosen for myself. But I won't . . . I can't . . . drag you down it with me. No, my lady and my queen—"

"You speak riddles" said Elisabeth, and there was a world of sadness in her voice. "Ranulf, if you cannot understand what I feel and what I say . . . then I'm truly lost. Damned, myself even. If you won't give me the love and the comfort I seek – then why not? Out of consideration for he who tore you from your home? Who slew Dancer? Who brought ruin and death to those you loved and who loved you? Is this the king you speak of? Is it?"

The Scraeling was silent, and Elisabeth drew a deep and ragged breath. "I don't know why you serve him" she said, "and I fear to ask. But I do ask that you love me as a woman who has no man – for I don't – and whose children spend more time away from her than with her. Scraeling, if my rank holds you back, don't let it, for I'm no-one's queen now. I'm a woman who needs a man to love her, to comfort her, to hold her when she weeps, to tell her it'll be all right. And sometimes, when the mood's on her, just to fuck her."

Elisabeth grinned mirthlessly to see him flinch at the deliberate crudity. "You see what the Norse do when you live among them for a time? Anyway, my horseman – I trust the man I see in you to do these things for me, for you're the only man I'd ask or have. And as for being damned, pray you let me worry about my own soul." She took his hand, and he didn't draw it away as she kneaded it in her long fingers.

Raising the hand to her breast, she said huskily, "Scraeling, my Scraeling, according to their laws I can take any man I like. I don't like any of them, and I like you. I'm twenty-three years old. Must I live, so young, as a woman without a man?"

She released his hand, and it stayed where it was as she leaned forward again to undo his belt.

The Chronicle.

*T*hat *began a chapter of my story in which, at least in the beginning, my mind warred with my nature. It was foolish, I told myself, to let anything come between me and my design for Hardraada – but Elisabeth derived so much from our relationship that I couldn't bring myself to alter it in any way. Thus for almost twenty years I bedded the queen of Norway with some regularity, and as her children grew to womanhood and we ourselves aged, we adapted and adjusted to each other much as, I suppose, any other couple does.*

As I say, my anxiety was greatest in the early days, and what eased it at first and finally caused it to disappear was the gradual realisation that Hardraada actually knew of the relationship between his secretary and his wife, and he did not care. The enormity of that staggered me, but when I could contemplate it clearly and coldly I understood that his setting-aside of Elisabeth was his punishment of her for the year she had kept him waiting in Kiev. In the end he attained her, as he attained all his ends, one way or another, and once attained she was of no further interest – and even less in the light of the two sons, Magnus and Olaf, that Thora bore him.

In fairness I say that he gave every indication of love for his daughters by Elisabeth, Maria and Ingegerd, and Maria in particular, who was as tall, handsome and fiery of spirit as her father – a true Valkyrie. But towards Elisabeth he was no more than polite, and sometimes not even that.

I like to think – and call it vanity if you will – that Elisabeth found in me the love and comfort a wife should find in a husband. Certainly, as the years went by and the land of Norway found a peace it had only rarely known in the past, the occasions when Hardraada demanded the attendance of his queens came to be as unusual, in our minds, as our stolen occasions had been in the beginning. But what made me aware of what I was to her, came through another.

Nidaros, winter 1049.

At the end of the campaigning season Hardraada led the army home and into winter quarters, and the Scraeling hadn't seen Elisabeth for days when one of her Kievan maids arrived at his quarters bearing a beautifully-decorated missal he had brought from Constantinople and had given to Elisabeth.

"That belongs to your mistress, Olga, for I intended that she keep it."

Olga inclined her head and said, "Lord Ranulf, my mistress asks that you take it back, for such things enrage the king and she values it such that she fears to have it nearby should he call on her."

"I see" the Scraeling said. "How wise of your mistress" and held out his hand for the book. But to his surprise she took the hand, fell to her knees and kissed it. He was so surprised that he snatched the hand away, and she mistook the gesture and held up the book to him, still on her knees.

"Lord, forgive me! Don't be angry with me, for my heart is full and it bade me do what I did!"

"It's all right Olga – I was surprised, that's all. I'm not angry. Here – take my hand" and the Scraeling drew her to her feet. "Now, what's this all about? I'm no king, that pretty women should kneel to me!" He made the feeble jest, for he could see the tears standing in her eyes, but her next words astounded him.

"To the ladies of Elisabeth of Kiev, lord Ranulf, you're a king indeed! Aye, in every way! You're wise, you're kind, you're merciful, and you put the sun back in our lady's face and the life in her eyes, my lord. When she's been with you, we see again the happy and beautiful young woman she was before . . . before she yielded to her father. Oh my lord, we, her women, thank you for giving us back the mistress we vowed to serve in her exile. Thank you, thank you!" And she seized his hand again while he gaped like a landed fish.

"Olga . . . Olga, I thank you in my turn for your words. Your mistress is dear to me, for she's my mistress too. Ah . . . that is . . ." the Scraeling floundered, "I'm favoured, aye . . . favoured to serve her . . . in every way she wishes . . . as a subject, of course should . . . should, and you who serve her too . . ." He drew himself up, aware that he was digging himself deeper with every word, and ended "So thank you, and thank your ladies, and tell them that our queen will always come first with me. Ah . . . that is, I mean . . . ah . . . thank you Olga."

Olga sank to a deep curtsey before him, to hide a smile he suspected, then she straightened and laid the missal on a small table. At the door she turned again, and said delicately,

"Lord secretary, there's one thing more. Our lady's husband has returned home, and will be so until the spring, likely. So we . . . we won't see the sun shine from our lady's face again until then, and we know this. We her ladies, would have you know that we . . . any of us, will gladly and happily serve you, my lord, should your needs as a man require it. Gladly and happily. You need only say the word."

If the Scraeling had gaped before, his jaw near hit the floor at that. When he found his voice again, it shook. "Olga, dearest of our lady's maids – did she send you with this offer? Our lady?"

Olga was shocked. "No, lord Ranulf! No! This is the gift of her ladies to you, for the gift of happiness you give to one we love, and any of us would be honoured . . . aye, honoured indeed. Unworthy though we are, my lord, in comparison with her. My lord, shall I return tonight?"

"Tonight?" the Scraeling said around a tongue grown huge and thick,

"Tonight ... you see ... I may be called to ... to council ... with the king, aye. So no, Olga, not tonight. Ah thank ... thank you though."

"My lord" she murmured, and curtseyed again.

The Chronicle.

*I*n the spring the army went out again to harry, ravage and invade Denmark while Svein did no less to Norway leaving me, as before, in charge at the centre of Hardraada's empire and supply train. And 1050 was as 1049 had been, and 1051 no whit different – not for us, although cousin Penda was at the centre of great things in England. But more of that in its place.

For all Hardraada's efforts, however, he couldn't bring Svein to a decisive battle because, though the Norse generally had the better of things when the armies met, the Danes loved Svein dearly and they rallied to him through reverse after reverse in a manner, I suspected on reading the despatches from the field, that the Norse wouldn't have demonstrated for Hardraada.

But let me not suggest that Hardraada was unpopular. On the contrary, and as I've written before, much of Norway benefitted from a war that ran for over ten years – some from the booty won from the Danes, some from the lands that came to them, some from the ending, through the war effort, of the internal bickering that had plagued Norway through so many other reigns. And all of them from the need to supply the army with all that an army needs - and as that was my responsibility I know, as does no other, what it was all worth.

Time passed, then, and Elisabeth and I were happy in a manner that owed nothing, I may say, to her maids, before the second anniversary of Olga's offer brought Penda to my door.

Nidaros, December 1051.

Stretching his legs luxuriously to the fire, Penda yawned and said, "So, cousin mine, it's all turned to shit for the Godwins. Or so Edward believes. Wonderful beer, though!" and he belched.

"And you don't?" asked the Scraeling, "Why?"

"Well, as I said, it was all over a bunch of Normans. When all's said and done, that's what people will remember, and that'll come back to bite

Edward's arse, believe me."

It seemed that the English king, Edward, had banished his father-in-law, Godwin, because the latter had refused either to punish or to hand over some vassals of his who had roughly handled a group of the king's Norman guests. From what Penda said, the Normans had richly deserved their treatment – "Remember how they behaved in Sicily? Well, these bastards were the same – swaggered into an inn at Dover, ate, drank and buggered off without paying."

One thing had led to another, and the Godwins had called out their retainers. And that, the Scraeling could see, had put them firmly on the wrong side of the law and he had said so.

"But whose law?" Penda had asked, "English law or something designed either to protect those Norman arseholes or –" and he paused significantly, "– or to get the Godwins up on their hind legs?"

For it had certainly done that, but Edward had levelled charges of treason at the Godwins, the other earls of England had supported him, and Godwin had gone into voluntary exile in Flanders.

"So, where's it going from here?" asked the Scraeling, and Penda drank, thought, belched again and said,

"Godwin's an old-time Cnut man, as you know. Left to him, he'd drag in some blades from Flanders, raise his host from Wessex and march on Winchester – or more likely London. Kicking someone's arse is what he believes in. But the boys're in charge, and they use their heads. As you also know. So, they're letting Edward get over it – and they will until spring. If Edward moves seriously against their lands or people, that'll be it."

"And then?" from the Scraeling and Penda looked bleak.

"Then they'll go in, no error. The Godwins're quietly organising men and ships from Flanders round to Ireland. And let's not forget how the Godwins' friends in England're busy pointing out how Edward pampers his Norman relatives. That's why I say, whatever Edward might think, it hasn't turned to shit for the Godwins. And I only hope he works that out for himself before it starts raining shit on him."

That evening.

The king of Norway raised his goblet. "Penda of the singing axe. Good to see you again! Looking for work? I can always use an axeman like you!"

"Possibly" said Penda, acknowledging the toast, "and it's good to be among old comrades, *leder*. My cousin, here, will have told you what's going on in England?"

"Yes and no" said Hardraada, stroking the head of a huge deerhound that sat by his chair, its hazel eyes never wavering from the Scraeling and Penda. "He wanted me to hear the details from you, so –"

Penda nodded, and recounted the tale of Godwin's defiance and exile, Hardraada nodding at the points he made. "So, what's your pick?" he asked when the Englishman was done.

"My pick? Godwin to come back; Siward of Northumbria and Leofric of Mercia, the senior earls, to remember they're English first and anti-Godwin second; Edward to get his Norman potlickers out of England."

"And if he doesn't?"

"He will. They'll go – one way or another. Look, the earls jumped in because they don't like Godwin. Now they've cooled off, they're starting to see that the only thing Godwin did wrong was taking up arms against the king. And they have to admit that Godwin broke the law only to uphold it, which is what Edward should have done. Yes – Edward's had his moment and won his battle. But it's winning the last battle that counts. Hear you're doing a bit of that yourself, by the way?"

Hardraada guffawed. "You're well informed, friend Penda. Still, you've got the connections, I suppose! Aye, I need to catch that slippery Danish bastard just once! Just once, and when I do ..." he squeezed the fire-clayed goblet in one huge hand and the crack of it imploding was loud and sudden enough to get the deerhound snarling to its feet. "That's why I need good men" said Hardraada. "Interested at all?"

"Thanks *leder*" returned Penda, "but I'm a little embarrassed, to tell the truth. Y'see, if there's war in the spring, my place is with the Godwinssons. If not, well – there's nothing worse than boredom, so who knows?"

"Anyway" put in the Scraeling, "Penda's not a bad man to have just where he is, surely? Anyone can swing an axe!"

"Spoken like a true bowman!" scoffed Hardraada. "Anyone can't swing an axe like your cousin. But you're probably right in the other thing, because you usually are. Have I told you, Penda, how dangerous this little bugger is?"

"Often" said Penda, "and I've seen him in action. It reminded me that you and I need to get our enemies within four feet or so before we knock them off, but he can knock off his at anywhere around seventy paces. But I know his weakness, if you're interested?"

"Aye?" said Hardraada, "And what's that?"

"He bores easily" said Penda, with a fond glance at the Scraeling who lifted his fingers in a rude gesture. "He needs to be kept busy – preferably plotting."

"Right" said Hardraada, "and I'm going to. He's going to keep me in real close touch with you, Penda, and you won't find me ungrateful. I want to know what you know about everything going on in England, so I need you to share it with my secretary and your cousin, here. Then he can share it with me. He's good like that – why you'd be surprised what the Scraeling and me share. Eh Scraeling?" he added, and the Scraeling knew with utter certainty what he meant.

The Chronicle.

*P*enda and I kept the feast of Christ's Mass together, and I realised how much I had missed the stolid calm and great common sense of the big Saxon. He was a reminder of a world beyond Norway, a world that didn't include Hardraada and which never would, in my mind – for I thought I knew what was in Hardraada's.

We ate well and often, drank likewise in the evenings, and hunted the wolf in the short and dark days. And we talked much while we did these things and I came to be greatly impressed by Penda's total dedication to the cause of England and the Godwin family, which he held to be much the same thing. For he held also – and he blamed me for putting the idea in his head, although I couldn't recall having done so – that the manifold changes of kings and dynasties in England since the days of Cnut had only made his homeland a weak and feeble playground for those of ambition, and that the strength of the Godwins would put an end to that. At the time, I envied my cousin his simple and uncomplicated path to fulfilment.

It seemed natural to tell Penda of Elisabeth, and even more natural for him to meet her once my cousin had recovered from his shock. In the event, that was easy for Penda had known her as Princess of Kiev and had of course been part of her escort to her new home. It was no surprise that they took naturally and easily to each other for, as Elisabeth mused once while we lay drowsing together later during that summer, each of them had me, while I had had no other close to me since the night of death and ruin on the coast of France. I bade him farewell with deep regret, although we arranged to remain in contact – I with Hardraada's winking connivance and he as a cousin.

I next saw Penda when I attended his wedding in 1053. Following the upswing in the Godwin fortunes in 1052 when the magnates of England had seen things as Penda had forecast, many landowners made haste to ally their families with the land's leading house, and for Penda this meant betrothal and marriage to Gytha, an heiress orphaned by a hunting accident that had broken the neck of her earldorman father.

Gytha was dark and pretty, as slight as her man was huge, and we got along from the first as well as Penda had with Elisabeth. She was curious about my home in Nidaros and of Elisabeth in particular, and I could see that Penda had told her enough to whet her woman's curiosity. In particular, she professed herself amazed at the freedoms that Norse women enjoyed, and Penda laughingly cautioned her not to dwell on them overmuch lest she were disappointed. But Gytha gave back as good as she got in advising her husband that she was the only wife he would ever need – or, indeed, have. So, I ruled the contest a draw and invited them to Nidaros when chance allowed, that the lady Gytha might see for herself.

Reading, August 1053.

Gytha put the big pitcher down on the long table with an ease that belied her tiny frame and smiled at her husband and his guest. "There, my lord and man. One to end the day, perhaps? Lord Ranulf has walked far today, for I cannot think that the tally of rabbits the servants brought back simply cast themselves upon his arrows!"

The rumble of Penda's laughter echoed in the room as the Scraeling lifted his cup to her, and she bent over her husband's chair to peck him on the cheek. "I say goodnight, then, husband, and do not keep Lord Ranulf from his dreams of the lady Elisabeth!"

The Scraeling raised his cup again as the door closed behind her, but this time to Penda. "You're a lucky man, cousin. We both are."

"My pledge on that" returned the blond giant, raising his own cup. "Would that all we do were to such good effect! Is there an end in sight to Norway's war?"

The Scraeling shook his head gloomily. "No, Penda. The longer it drags on the more and more clear it is that Hardraada prolongs it on purpose, for these days he puts forth no more of a strength that's grown enormously than he needs to keep Svein on the run. If he wished to, he could launch a series of devastating thunderbolts to bring the Danes to heel. No – it's clear he's building for a purpose and that his mind is elsewhere. In fact, from his repeated requests after your doings and thoughts when he comes home from campaigning, I'm certain I know exactly where."

Penda nodded, his eyes across the empty fireplace full of sympathy. "Your time with Elisabeth must then be the dearer to you, Ranulf. Cherish it."

The Scraeling nodded in his turn. "Aye, cousin. This dreadful war over nothing serves its purpose for Elisabeth and me, and whatever the cost in the misery of others, it's no fault of ours. The years when Hardraada's campaigning are years . . ." he paused to seek the words, ". . . years in which we've come to share all that any marriage offers. You see, if our situation is uncertain, each day is the more piquant because of it, and because all might end at Hardraada's whim. Whatever freedoms commoners enjoy, queens are and still something else – we live every moment as we watch her girls grow to young women. Aye, every moment is cherished indeed. But you too know what it is to live on a knife-edge, cousin."

"And never a truer word, Ranulf. Edward took back the Godwins in the spring of last year, much against his will but because he had no choice. Oh, he's still on about Old Godwin's supposed part in his brother Alfred's death – I told you he'll never let go nor forgive, didn't I? – and when the old man died of a stroke last year, Edward pronounced it divine justice and a judgement! And of course, Sweyn the godless Godwinsson died the year before in the guise of a pilgrim – now *that* was probably divine justice for blasphemy – so now my master and lord, Earl Harold Godwinsson has succeeded his father as Earl of Wessex and the true force behind the

English throne. A throne that he'll surely occupy on Edward's death. And that's where your master comes in, eh?"

The Scraeling looked into his cup. "Aye. Hardraada's interested already."

The Chronicle.

*F*or by the early 1060s Hardraada was the complete master of Norway. The powerful jarls who had troubled Olaf, Cnut in his turn and Magnus had been brought to heel by force, by bribery or by treachery; the Church was humbled in the face of Hardraada's insistence that his kingdom would have only one master; Norway's empire in Iceland and the Orkneys was restored by good kingship, marriage alliances and naked terror where necessary, and the common folk, except those who remained within the ever-shortening reach of Danish Svein, enjoyed full bellies, safety, and the prosperity that went with it.

Time and chance took its toll of Hardraada's old comrades of Byzantine days. Haldor – who had grown prodigiously stout – spoke his mind once too often in council and Hardraada had me draft an order for him to govern Iceland until the leder thought better of it, with Ulf succeeding to Haldor's position as marshal. Skallagrim and a fifty-strong reconnaissance party were caught at the Gotha River by an overwhelming force of Black Danes and, being Skallagrim, he charged. The few survivors were honoured by the Danes for their bravery and charged with bringing home Skallagrim's body.

New men took their place – Hardraada's nephew, Guthrum Gunhildsson returned home from the imperial service, even as his uncle had done, and was welcomed, while Haakon, son of one of Hardraada's oldest comrades, Ivarr, but long estranged from him made his peace with his father and took service under him against Svein. The young man's advancement was assured when Hardraada saw him and two spearmen hold a ford for half an hour against all attackers, to allow half a regiment to retire in good order and later counter-attack.

These men, and the new ones in particular, fought in the last battle of the war in 1062, when Svein caught Hardraada off the mouth of the River Nissa with a fleet double that of the Norwegian king. But Hardraada didn't hesitate, and sent his longships into the very heart of the Danish formation where a savage mêlée of hand-to-hand fighting raged across the decks of ships rafted together. In the end, sheer numbers must inevitably have doomed Hardraada for all the ferocity of his axemen, but the arrival of Haakon Ivarrson and thirty drakkars from a long sweep to the south changed all that, and his longships knifed into the Danish fleet so that Svein found himself menaced from both sides. Haakon himself got aboard Svein's flagship before a desperate bodyguard rallied and bought Svein's escape with their lives.

A portion of the Danish fleet got away, and as fighting stopped and the Danes threw themselves on the mercy of the Norwegians, Svein himself vanished into the growing darkness – true to his nature, he lived to fight another day.

Thus, Hardraada had caught his "slippery Danish bastard", only for Svein to prove too slippery for him in the end. But the Nissa had been a victory that took the attention of all Europe, and established Hardraada as its greatest fighting warrior, even if those of us closest to him knew just how loud the wingbeats of the ravens had been.

And then Hardraada hurled his true thunderbolt. He sent me to open negotiations for peace with Svein, and he was sincere for once, as he proved through the many provocations that Svein seemed to feel were needed to test Hardraada's resolve. At the Gotha River, in 1063, the kings of Norway and Denmark agreed that one would continue to be king of Norway and the other to be king of Denmark. Sic transit gloria.

And what had been gained by a decade of war? If any looked at the results, not much. But any looking behind the results might see that Hardraada now led a prosperous and united country that no longer feared its exhausted neighbour and, strong in its battle-hardened military capacity, was happy to follow where its warrior-king led. It was easy to understand that Hardraada no longer sought the land and people of Denmark, for a richer prize called the ravens to feed elsewhere.

BOOK FIVE

OF THE CONTENDER
1063–1066

"Where battle-storm was ringing,
Where arrow-cloud was singing,
Harald stood there,
Of armour bare,
His deadly sword still swinging.
The foeman feel its bite;
His Norsemen rush to fight,
Danger to share,
With Harald there,
Where steel on steel was ringing."

"And should our king in battle fall, —
A fate that God may give to all, —
His sons will vengeance take;
And never shone the sun upon
Two nobler eaglets; in his run,
And them we'll never forsake."

The skald, Thiodolf, in 'The Heimskringla'.

Winchester, England, autumn 1063.

The king's voice rose to a shriek and his face suffused with anger. "No! I will not name a successor, Earl Harold! Doing so would be an affront to God's hidden purpose for us all as well as an inducement to every ambitious and ragged-arsed outlaw to take it on himself to alter my design. No, I say!"

"Majesty, we hope for many years of your rule yet, but simple prudence—" began Harold Godwinsson, but Edward broke in, waving a forefinger bitten raw.

"Do not lie! Secretly, Earl Harold, you want me gone for the betterment of a family that has already carried all before it, if not for yourself! Admit it! Admit it before God!" And Edward snatched up a crucifix from the dresser and thrust it into Harold's face.

"Very well, sire!" snapped an earl quite out of patience. "I admit that I want no war in this realm when your majesty . . . goes to his reward. I admit that I would keep the peace of this land above all else. I admit that God and the kings He has placed over us – yourself included, sire – have smiled upon their servants, my family, and made them strong enough to shield and defend this realm against those who would despoil—"

"Hah!" shouted Edward, "You admit it!"

"I admit" said the earl of Wessex, deliberately lowering his voice, "that I will willingly swear to place the strength and the power of my arm behind the successor your majesty chooses. Saving only that he be an Englishman."

Edward's eyes nearly started from his head. "You would . . . would dictate to me? *Me?* Of who should be king? Godwinsson, you tread a dangerous path! If my concern for the safety of this realm leads me to choose a strong king – say, the king of Norway himself – what then? What then, sir?" And the flecks of foam flew from his lips as his hands balled themselves into claws.

"Then, sire," said Harold wearily, "then there will be civil war. It is not the temper of the English folk to suffer foreign rule again. They have had—"

"The people? The people?" mocked Edward, "What do the folk of England matter? God sets kings above the folk to lead them, direct them and to make their decisions for them! How dare you, Godwinsson? Leave me! Leave me, I say! Work your disaffection elsewhere!"

The most powerful earl of the realm bowed. "Majesty, I have reports to consider from the Welsh border. Where another of the scheming, ambitious and self-serving Godwinssons patrols your majesty's frontiers to the great detriment of his own estates. Now I have your leave to withdraw . . ."

Nidaros, December 1063.

He must be closing in on fifty thought the Scraeling as he looked at the figure at the head of the table, *because I am, and he's a year older, so let's see . . .*

". . . no doubt about it" said Ulf, "They'll follow you wherever you want to lead them. Fact is," he added, "once they've got over the Yuletide, drunk all the beer their missuses've got laid up and made a bairn or two these long nights, they're going to need something to do in spring."

"Well" said Ivarr, "I dunno about spring, Ulf. Ten years, near enough – takes its toll. Know I'm about stuffed, and I reckon the Company –" by which he meant the old comrades of the imperial service, now all regimental commanders – "the Company'd be about the same if they're honest, an' they're the guts and the drive of the army. Next spring now, not this one coming – c'd be a diff'rent story, sure enough."

"A year lying quiet" mused Hardraada. "A year fishing, farming, hunting, boatbuilding . . . eating more than's good for them . . . shagging themselves silly?"

"That too" put in young Ivarrson, proudly sitting in the army council alongside his father. "That won't do them any harm. Not for a year. In fact, a year of all the things you just mentioned'll put 'em back in the mood for . . . for whatever you want 'em to do, *leder.*"

"And what's that, *leder?*" asked Eystein Orri, son of Thorberg Arnesson and the betrothed of Hardraada's first daughter, Maria. "Shall you tell us?" and a hush fell around the table.

"What makes you think I've got a plan at all?" asked Hardraada, but the lift of his crooked and scarred eyebrow told its own story.

"Ah" replied the young man who was a particular favourite of Hardraada's, "anytime the Scraeling disappears for days at a time, something's going on. And when he does appear but spends all day in the stables shoeing his own horses 'cause he won't let anyone else near them, well, that means there's not only something going on, but it's half over. And since the Scraeling does your bidding before you know what you want him to do y'self . . .'s not too difficult really" he ended, to laughter and a slapping of the table from the others.

"Odin's balls!" exclaimed Hardraada, "Scraeling, you've got an apprentice here if you ever want one. Wasted leading the Viken regiment, is our Eystein – he's nearly as cunning as you! Taller, too . . ." he added, to more laughter, but the Scraeling merely shrugged.

"Only means his brains're in more danger from the sun" he retorted, and smiled at the young man, whose sunny nature had made him popular with everyone in Hardraada's immediate circle.

"As it happens" said Hardraada when the laughter had died down, "the Scraeling suggested I get your opinion about what I'm going to say next. It's not to be repeated outside this room, and you'll see why when I tell you what it is. Eystein's right – the Scraeling'll soon be on his travels and busier than all of us, and you of the Company know what that means, right?" He looked at the hard faces around the long table and nodded. "But it can't happen without you – that should tell you a little more."

"Right. Get hold of this, but remember – not a word outside this room. Drunk, sober, praying or fucking. Not a word. Here it is . . ."

The Chronicle.

Eystein was correct. I was off somewhere, and that was to visit those jarls of Norway that Hardraada had identified as key to a successful invasion of England. Briefly, my task was to convey to them that the king would contemplate an invasion in pursuit of his 'just' claim to the English throne as successor of Cnut the Dane, who had ruled England as well as Norway and Denmark. In Hardraada's eyes, the story went, ruling over one-third of Cnut's dominions gave him the right to lay claim to the others, but he sought the advice and counsel of the key men of the realm before deciding whether or not to proceed to the planning stage.

For the most part they were those who had the most manpower, but three or four were on my list because their loyalty was suspect enough to make Hardraada reluctant – not afraid, just reluctant – to turn his back on them for a while, and we had decided that my story would make the latter feel important enough to come aboard.

And that, just as briefly, was what my retinue and I did in travelling through a cold and snow-driven January and half of February to visit the leading men of the land. And if my escort grumbled at being separated, in that dead time of the year when the very earth turned to white iron, from the warmth of home and the pleasures of the marriage bed, I did not for, with Hardraada home, Elisabeth was a stranger to me. "If you can't take a joke" I would point out to them unfeelingly, "you shouldn't have joined. That's what they say in the imperial navy!" And the muttered answer was usually, "Well, fuck the imperial navy too!" Which never failed to get a snort of laughter from unsympathetic comrades.

But we were back in Nidaros six weeks later, weary and saddle-sore. I had pushed the pace more than a little, for if Hardraada and his council acted upon the information I had gathered, I thought, there would be much to do that year. The scheme, as I reported to Hardraada, was received with favour everywhere I had gone and I had pledges of men and matériel from each of the names on my list. It was made clear to me, I reported also, that the land to be had in England was a major draw to the jarls of an overpopulated and harsh landscape that suffered a harsher climate, and Hardraada remarked that the ancient sagas had always held England to be favoured in that respect. But whatever their reasons – land, loot, glory or just adventure – the magnates of Norway were ready for it, just as Ulf had predicted.

The Welsh border, autumn 1063.

Tostig swung a heavily-strapped ankle onto a stool with a grunt of pain. "A master-stroke, brother. Having your *hus-carl*s lay their armour aside, I mean. How'd you manage that?"

"Just an idea" said Harold, busy with goblets and wine-flask. "I had the notion, y'see, that training and discipline were likely to be what wins us this miserable bloody place. Right – so the best-trained and most disciplined troops either of us have are our *hus-carls*, yes? So instead of waiting until God drove the Welsh buggers onto our best in battle, I'd send the best into their valleys after them. But they couldn't do that wearing their armour. So I asked for volunteers, and I got them. Now all of 'em want in on it."

"Won't need to much longer, if what I see of the body-counts is right" said Tostig, accepting a cup and nodding his thanks to his brother. "There can't be many more of the bastards left. Your armies drove them like sheep – right onto our swords. And your 'no prisoners' policy's the right one."

"Well, they started it" said Harold, "and I've the idea it was Gruffydd's doing, that. I've had peace feelers, you know – even before this last business." By which he meant the rout and slaughter of close to a thousand Welshmen caught like nuts between his army of south Wales and Tostig's coming down from the north.

"That a fact?" asked Tostig with interest. "What'd you say?"

"Told them to come back when they had Gruffydd ap Llywelyn's head to show they meant business. I said I was sick of seeing bodies without heads; that they'd started it, and I wanted it to end with one more – Gruffydd's. And that was the price of peace – and now, thanks to our hammer-and-anvil trick, they've lost a thousand more."

"You'll get that head all right" mused Tostig. "What then, though – we leave garrisons here?"

"Not if it's up to me, brother" said Harold. "They've lost so many men I doubt if it's necessary. We can't spare the garrisons anyway. You know what we're up against at home. And what might make it worse."

"Aye" said Tostig moodily. "How long's the old bugger going to live anyway?"

"Shame on you" laughed Harold. "No way to talk about your brother-in-law. Must be that ankle playing up. How'd you do that anyway?"

"It's this fucking country" said Tostig with great feeling. "I slipped on a wet rock. The rocks are always wet, here – like everything else. Because it never stops raining, does it? Why do we want Wales anyway?"

"We don't." said Harold. "You know that. If the buggers would leave our western marches alone and stick to shagging their sheep, no-one'd be happier than me. But they won't. So – Gruffydd's head it is."

"Short-term though" said Tostig, shifting his ankle again. "And we can't stay here forever, can we? We've got this year to sort out Wales once and for all, because next year's the Norman business. And no-one can do that for you, because if Edward won't name an heir, you'll have to. So, back to my question – what happens long-term?"

"Good question. I reckon – intermarriage" said Harold. "I'm offering the land we've taken to English settlers provided they marry the widows we've made. That's really long-term. In the meantime, we take heads until they ask us to stop. Got any . . . yes, Oswald? What is it?"

"Sorry, Earl Harold, lord Tostig" said the officer of the bodyguard who stooped into the tent doorway. "Bloke outside here called Cynfor insists on talking to you – says you've spoken already. He's carrying a bag he won't let go, and if I'm not mistaken something inside it's been bleeding. Can you be bothered with him, or it, or whatever he wants – or shall I kick his arse through the camp?"

Nidaros, May 1064.

The Scraeling spread his hands to make the point. "Twelve thousand" he said. "At the least. The very least." His words caused a startled hush and then a hubbub of talk. Hardraada slammed a hand on the table, and the hubbub died.

"I'm not going to ask if you're sure" he said. "You do things properly, Scraeling, and all here know that."

The Scraeling inclined his head to acknowledge the compliment. "Thank you, *leder*" he said, "but yes, I've checked. Three times actually. Twelve thousand is – well, it's the least we can put together, and my feeling is that we ought to plan for fifteen, because if we can assume that the interest your proposal got among the *jarls* I spoke to will be the same as interest elsewhere, well . . . you've had my report."

"Right" said Hardraada "and we'll get on to that in a minute. But so many raises a question or two. Want to point 'em out for us, Scraeling?"

"Preparation" said the Scraeling. "We're going up against the richest kingdom in Europe, and one that hasn't been at war since Cnut and Edmund fought it out. It's an island, which means we've got to get ashore in the face of their *hus-carls*, the best heavy troops in the world. We need to organise and take our own food supplies 'cause we can't guarantee they won't burn their own grain or kill their own beasts to stop us getting them – and I would, in their place. And finally – we need ships for fifteen thousand. Comrades, last time I spoke to this meeting someone asked if it was wise to let our men spend a year fishing, farming and fucking."

"Well, if we make as many ships as we need, which is some three hundred by my reckoning – and we can't buy them without tipping our hand to any Englishman with half a brain – and salt down or smoke as much meat as we'll need to feed that many people for the week it'll take to get us ashore and in battle order – anyone care to tell me when he'll have time or strength this year for shagging?"

North Norway, early autumn 1064.

Hardraada looked down to the northern end of the valley and the wall of brightly-coloured shields that blocked it, spat and turned to Eystein. "Send forward a messenger – hold on, what's that?"

The shield wall parted and a small knot of men came through, paused and came forward. Hardraada spat again and heeled his horse into motion, his long legs dangling nearly to the heather beneath. The Scraeling clucked to the elderly mount that had been the colt Elisabeth so admired, and followed with Eystein and four of an escort.

Hardraada drew rein five yards from the knot of men on foot and waited for the one in front to speak while the frown between his eyebrows deepened. At last he said, "Finn, son of Thorkel, I would pass on my way and your host blocks my road. Is there reason for this?"

The man in front looked up at the towering figure on the horse and nodded slowly. "I had thought, son of Sigurd—" and I heard Eystein's quick intake of breath at insult and tone "—that you had come to offer apology and *mulct* for your outrage of my wife. Am I wrong, in that you come with an army at your back?"

Hardraada looked down at him. "Son of Thorkel" he said, "I don't know your wife, and my men accompany their king on his travels as he has bidden them."

"Ah" returned Thorkelsson, "in the right of things, Sigurdsson, she was not my wife when you used her so foully. But she was my betrothed, and she journeyed to her wedding."

"She was stranded on the road" said Hardraada impatiently, "with a cart that had broken an axle and night approaching. I took her under my protection and sent her safe on her way next day."

"You took her to your bed!" snapped Thorkelsson, "And used her worse than a common whore!"

Hardraada shrugged lazily. "That may have been what she told you" he answered, "but – Scraeling, what's that French term we spoke of again?"

"*Droit de seigneur*" said the Scraeling unwillingly, for he recalled the incident – and the sobs and cries that had come from Hardraada's tent – only too well.

"There you are" said Hardraada complacently, "Believe it means the right of the man who owns everything, to enjoy what he owns. That's fair, surely? Anyway – she enjoyed it. Every inch of it, every time. Couldn't keep her off me, matter of fact. No, I wasn't her first. Well – maybe her first royal one . . ."

Thorkelsson took a snarling step forward and two of his men seized him by the arms. "Sigurdsson, I defy you and term you no king of mine – or of any other honest and law-fearing man" he ground. "This road leads to the Jamtland and I, its *jarl*, say we want none of your kind there. Nay – you are no king of mine!"

"Then your lands are forfeit" said Hardraada crisply. "I give them, now, to my man Eystein Orri, who rides at my side. What do the Christians say, Scraeling – the Lord giveth and the Lord taketh away? Something like that, isn't it?"

Fuck me, thought the Scraeling, *is there no blasphemy bad enough for God to strike this man down*? But Hardraada was speaking again.

"Clear the way, Thorkelsson. Last chance. You're deposed now, and a sensible man would let it rest there. Resist me and you'll be dead too. But if you should fancy your chances, I promise I'll give you decent burial – so I can have your wife again, on top of your grave!"

Thorkelsson swayed and went pale with rage, and the Scraeling truly pitied him. Then he cursed Hardraada standing, sitting, lying, living and dying while the thunderbolt of the north laughed in his face. When he had finished he turned back to his own host and stumbled blindly away. Hardraada turned likewise and led his party back to the columns on the road behind.

"Eystein, take the Viken regiment through those who bar their king's path" he commanded. "Spare none you can catch, but if you can take Thorkelsson alive, I have an end for him that will be spoken of wherever traitors gather. The rest of you – let's give Eystein a little room, shall we?"

The staff pulled their mounts aside as Eystein rode down the column shouting orders that resulted in companies of archers shaking themselves loose and trotting forward to fan out at the head of the column where they paused to string bows and nock a shaft each. Thorkelsson's men set up a mighty shout at sight of them, and the Scraeling clearly heard "Cowards! Gutless bastards! Meet us man to man!" But the archers trotted forward another dozen paces before settling themselves at the shout of their leader and sending the first flight whistling down upon Thorkelsson's men.

It did no damage, for the men before them simply raised their shields and in an instant the front rank bristled with shafts. The archers broke ground and trotted forward another dozen paces, but this time they came to rest in three groups for behind them came Eystein, trotting at the head of two columns of *byrnie*-clad and heavily-armed footsoldiers, and the Scraeling guessed what they were about.

The columns paused behind the ranks of archers, who redoubled their efforts to send shaft after shaft across the intervening space until they stood thick in the shields. "With me, Viken!" bellowed the young commander, and he brandished his axe by the throat and broke into a trot. The regiment gave a mighty roar and swept after him, keeping in ranks of three so that none strayed into the archer's line of sight, yet rolling forward at a pace that built steadily as the shield-wall loomed.

As they neared the wall the heads of men bracing themselves to meet the charge began to appear from behind it – only to clutch at faces and throats as the arrows found their mark. The Scraeling saw Eystein change his angle and head for a section of Thorkelsson's shield-wall where four men had gone down within heartbeats of each other, and men from the rank behind stepped into the front just as Eystein hit the wall with the momentum of his column behind him, his axe whirling around his head. The wall bent before him, bent still further – and shattered, with the mailed column powering through Thorkelsson's host like a shiny steel arrow.

"Quite a boy, that" murmured Hardraada from beside the Scraeling. "Left, left about now my boy, left, support your —Aaahh! Just right. D'you see how he's split his column to cover himself against what's left of his target? He'll take the left-hand file against Thorkelsson's centre now . . ." and Hardraada talked his staff through what Orri was doing as if it were a drill or a training exercise, and the Scraeling reminded himself that men were being maimed, killed or hewn asunder at the end of a pretty valley on a fine day because Hardraada had determined to teach a nobleman a lesson.

The end was never in doubt, for Thorkelsson's men were largely farmers and Orri's battle-hardened veterans of the Danish wars, and when they had seen their comrades smashed to the ground as they attempted to seek quarter, men began to break from the fringes, singly and then in pairs and finally in groups to run for the safety of the foothills. But by then Thorkelsson was dead and his bodyguard with him, for they had honoured their oath not to leave the field unless their leader did.

That evening Hardraada raised a cup to the new *jarl* of Jamtland. "*Vess-heil, jarl* Eystein, *vess-heil!*" and the others present echoed the salute. "Well" commented Hardraada at the end of the night when only the Scraeling and Haakon Ivarrson were left, "can't have a landless man marrying a princess of Norway, eh? No matter how handsome he is, or what Daddy'll leave him one day!"

"That what it was all about?" demanded the Scraeling in disbelief, "you wanted to make Eystein a *jarl*?"

"That's part of it" slurred Hardraada, whose cup had rarely been empty throughout the evening. "Part of it. Thork– Thorkelsson's had it coming anyway. Part Danish, see? His mother . . . or gran'mother, I forget, doesn't matter . . . the last one, Scraeling. Last one. They'll all do what they're told now. Eystein did it well, eh?"

"A wonderful job" returned the Scraeling, but the others were too far gone in drink to catch the irony in his voice, for Haakon simply nodded and Hardraada belched.

"Now" said Hardraada, "want you off home. To Nidaros, Scraeling, an' get ready to go see y'r cousin. That big bastard, Penda. Good man Penda!" and he tapped the side of his nose with a forefinger. "Got to know . . . know what's going on in England, Scraeling. The latest, y'know? Whatever Penda wants f'r his infor . . . no, don't insult him like that. Jus' make him a present. Oh, go on Scraeling – off home with you. Rest your saddlesore arse. Whatever other part of you gets a thrashing!" And his coarse laughter turned into another belch.

The Chronicle.

*F*or he enjoyed it, you know. He enjoyed the knowledge that his wife and I were lovers, enjoying too the fact that we never knew what he might decide to do about it at any time. Beyond that, though, I think that having me enjoy his largesse – or so he thought – after he had finished with it tickled his vanity. That Elisabeth and I might share something more than lust never occurred to him, for he viewed highborn women as political pawns and lowborn women as handy receptacles for his relief. And women of the station of a jarl's betrothed as an interesting and enjoyable dimension of a problem he had already decided to solve anyway.

But at any rate Finn Thorkelsson was spared the fate Hardraada had had in mind for him – I later found out that he was to have been deprived of hands and feet and left overnight for the wolves – and I went home to Nidaros and Elisabeth's love, which was the warmer for my early homecoming.

You, who have read my story and know that two other people knew my secret, may think it strange that Elisabeth never knew of my design for Hardraada, but in fact I never told her because of my respect for her Christian conscience. And I never knew whether she guessed what I would ultimately do, for she never asked what I had meant by my remark concerning my own damnation on that day in the clearing when we knew each other for the first time. No, if she knew, it was not from me – and that made her patience and forbearance the more wonderful as she lived her life, a discarded queen with no prospect of anything else, day by day. She never wavered in the promise she had made me, that she would love me as a woman who had no man, and I counted myself fortunate in it.

So we had our idyll in the late summer weather, and just before Hardraada led his army home to get in the harvest I bade Skuli choose a score of lusty young men who had never seen England, and follow me.

Reading, England, autumn 1064.

There was still a slight limp, noticed the Scraeling, watching Penda stoop to the ball his son had played along the ground.

"Aye" grinned Penda. "know what you've been putting up with all your life, cousin – but mine'll get better, so I'm not complaining! Your turn to be hit all over the place by this ex-son of mine, so catch!" And the ball came through the air to the Scraeling's hand.

"Ex-son? Hey?" came from the slender Osmund, as dark as his mother at nearly eleven years of age and poised like an axeman with the bat in his hand.

"Yes" said his father. "Tonight I'm giving you away for the torment you've caused your uncle and me – if I can find anyone silly enough to take you."

"One more chance" said the Scraeling. "You'll never handle this one anyhow" and he made a great show of swinging his arm in a warmup before asking "Ready?" and on receiving the nod he swung his arm, checked it as he saw the boy's feet move and dragged it backwards to release the leather ball underhand. His timing wildly out, Osmund slashed helplessly as the ball shot past to rebound from the slab of wood he was guarding.

"Hah! Told you!" said the Scraeling, scuttling crabwise to field the ball.

"Well ... missed it on purpose ..." said the boy and the Scraeling could see the twinkle in his eye from where he stood on the mark, "if Dad's going to make threats like that. I mean, who wants to be given away? Before dinner too, I suppose?"

The men guffawed and Penda dragged the boy to him in a rough embrace. "Off with you, seagull" he said. "Spend a bit of time grooming that pony of yours and Uncle Ranulf might – just might – look it over for you when we've had a chat. You've worn us out anyway."

The boy clung to his massive father for a moment longer while the Scraeling marvelled at the love in his eyes, then moved away to the stables. Osmund turned to the Scraeling and smiled. "Good ball though, Uncle Ranulf. It beat me fair and square!"

"It's called 'cunning', my boy" smiled the Scraeling in his turn. "Don't get too much of it, too soon. And I needed all of mine to get past the speed of your feet, Osmund. You'll be in your father's class as an axeman one day. I'll be round directly – don't spare the brush, will you?"

They watched the boy skip round the corner and Penda said quietly, "That's what it's all for, Ranulf. A chance for all the land's Osmunds to grow and get grandchildren. You once asked why I served a house the king hated. He's why, although he wasn't born then. He's why."

The Scraeling nodded. "*Vess-heil* the idea, Penda" he said. "As someone we know might say. If he thought of anything or anyone but himself."

"And what's he thinking at the moment?" Penda asked, moving to the pitcher of beer sitting in the shade out of a sun that was still warm for autumn.

"He's thinking about becoming king of England" said the Scraeling. "Fact, he's doing more than thinking about it – he's planning it now. You can wager on that, 'cause I know who's doing the planning – and he's a cunning little bugger, I've heard tell – so often!"

Penda guffawed. "Good God!" he said, "And He is, Ranulf, He is good to give us Hardraada's right hand as the friend of England at this time. Hardraada thinks he's sucking me dry – by the way, what am I worth this time? It's all going to Harold's new church at Waltham Holy Cross, y'know – wouldn't that curdle friend Harald's pagan soul if he knew?"

The Scraeling greeted that information with a snort of laughter and Penda held up his cup in salute.

"Anyway – tell me what he's up to and we'll work out something to confound him. The boss wants to meet with you again this trip, but before you do I'll tell you what he's been up to this year. It's all true, I may add – I couldn't make up something like what I'll tell you, and that's another fact."

The Chronicle

*A*nd that was no more than the truth, for the tale he told me was little *short of amazing. For him it began in spring when he was thrown from a horse while hunting, landing awkwardly enough to break his right thigh some five miles of rough country away from home.*

What was worse, he said, than the journey home was his inability to accompany the oldest Godwinsson on a journey to the Continent. Aye, he said seeing my eyebrows rise, to the Continent – there to discover, in person, what such as the Count of Brittany and Baldwin of Flanders thought of the English succession and whether or no they would countenance the fourteen-year-old Edgar, called The Atheling, King Edward's only blood relative, succeeding him.

Foul chance and fouler weather had shipwrecked him on the rocky coast of Ponthieu, a part of France ruled by one Guy, the brother-in-law of Duke William of Normandy. 'William the Bastard' had lost no time in arranging for Harold's transfer to his 'protection and hospitality' in Normandy, but once there he had lost even less time in pressing the English warrior-king to accompany his forces in a punitive expedition into Brittany, where Harold had won great laurels in battle.

On their return to William's capital at Caen, William had admitted Harold to knighthood and then demanded of him that, as a vassal, he would support William in all things and against all men. This, said Penda, Harold had willingly done, laying his hand upon the reliquary offered him – which was opened by William at the conclusion of the ceremony to reveal the relics of St Ouen, the patron saint of the dukedom.

Now as Penda pointed out, the Saxon kind set great store upon the swearing of oaths and Harold's credit would be much diminished by what had happened. But for myself I saw no force in an oath made through trickery, even if holy relics were indeed involved, and I said so. However, Penda's story was food for thought because it signified the interest of yet another contender for the English throne.

In the north was Hardraada and in the south the fiery and impatient duke of Normandy. Somewhere in Europe was Edgar, with perhaps the strongest claim and the least chance of realising it – for there was little doubt that the accession of a fourteen-year-old would bring invasion from north or south or even both. Aye, food for thought and the result of that thought was a sleepless night and a request to Penda, early the next morning, to bring forward my meeting with the Earl of Wessex as much as he could.

An exchange of messengers saw Penda and I bidden attend Harold the day after, and when we entered the presence of the most powerful lord of the kingdom I saw at once how the burden of a kingship that was not a kingship had weighed upon the young and vigorous nobleman I remembered. The blond hair had thinned and the high forehead was as lined as the corners of his eyes and mouth. But the smile was as brilliant as ever and it was much in evidence as he came towards me in greeting.

Waltham Holy Cross, outside London

Harold Godwinsson's greeting rang through the room. "Lord Ranulf!" he exclaimed, holding out hand and arm so that the bow the Scraeling had begun halted midway, and even as he took both the Scraeling found himself applauding the ease with which the Englishman turned a simple act of greeting into an apparent act of favour. Harold, he decided, had lost none of his charm.

"Welcome back to England, my lord, and I'm sorry only that my brother Tostig can't add his welcome to mine. And his appreciation of what you've shared with your cousin here over the years." Harold said that with no hint of the curiosity he must have felt. "His cares in the north are many, my friend, but as he'd wish me to add his welcome to mine, let this cup come from him!" and he poured wine for us with his own hand so that the Scraeling offered a pledge to the Earl of Northumbria, as Tostig had been for ten years at that time.

"Earl Harold" said the Scraeling when the pleasantries were done, "Penda has told me of your recent misfortune in France, and while it grieves me to add to your burdens, I fear I must. My king is in the planning stages of an invasion of this land. The decision has been taken and the preparations are in hand as we speak. The timing is yet undecided, for I doubt if he'll move while Edward's alive, but Hardraada is coming, my lord. He's coming."

His words hung in the room like clouds between the lightning and the thunder and the Scraeling saw the puzzlement in Godwinsson's eyes as the shock receded and he flicked a glance towards Penda. "Cousin" said the Scraeling, "tell Earl Harold what you heard the night I awoke in Constantinople. Come – it's time, for your master puzzles over why he should be hearing this from one such as I."

Penda nodded, and shot the Scraeling a grateful glance as he waved the others to seats and began the Scraeling's tale. Harold listened in silence, glancing at the Scraeling from time to time until Penda was done, and then he asked, "Is there more, lord Ranulf?"

"Nothing of substance my lord. Penda's told my story faithfully and well and I say plainly to you that my purpose remains what it's been since my sixteenth summer – the destruction of Harald Sigurdsson and all his kind, that God's earth may be a cleaner place after."

"And you've worked all these years – more than thirty years – to emplace yourself for that." It wasn't a question and the Scraeling inclined his head.

"For that, aye. But truthfully, Earl Harold, I can't do this alone. I might slay Hardraada at any moment – and watching, over the years of his excesses, I've come close to doing it, for the relief of my immortal soul. But what then? Haldor Sturlsson or Ulf Ospaksson would have taken his place then. Now, it would be Guthrum Gunhildsson, or Haakon Ivarrson or Eystein

Orri – men in Hardraada's own mould, for no other kind advances at the court of the raven-feeder, the Landwaster. So again I say – what then?"

"No, earl of Wessex. Hardraada without his host won't do. By my count – and no man living knows these figures better - he'll strip the icelands of warriors to bring fifteen thousand northern wolves against you."

"And you seek English help to destroy him." Again it wasn't a question, and again the Scraeling nodded.

"Yes. But there's another way of putting that – I offer England my help in destroying him, for aren't our wishes one in this? I seek the destruction of Hardraada and all his kind for the sins he's wrought upon the world, and you must encompass it if the land you protect is to be safe from the north evermore."

Godwinsson rose and walked to the window. "Lord Ranulf, I admit freely that had this come to me from you alone, I'd not have believed it. There's something about someone plotting revenge for thirty years that . . . that chills a man. It's not natural. And it speaks of a greater burden of hate than's good for any man."

"Lord Harold" returned the Scraeling, "if it comes to that, Hardraada's not good for any man. He does as he wishes, and the only guide in his life is what seems good to him at the time. Let me tell you something, earl of Wessex. Hardraada doesn't seek power as you or I might, for he was offered that in Constantinople. He might, now, be the husband of the Empress and lord of a mightier empire than we – with all respect – can imagine. But he isn't, because kingship bores him."

The Scraeling paused to sip from his cup. "If Hardraada invades this land and beats the earl of Wessex to win it, he'll have an empire of the northern lands – just like Cnut. But he'll need to go one better, because that's his way. Forget an empire at peace under the mightiest warrior of the north. As soon as he's discovered the military capabilities of England – and he'll probably have me draw them up for him, come to think of it – he'll take on William of Normandy. Why? Just because he can, and because it would please him to feed the ravens yet again."

"Harold of Wessex, I tell you Hardraada is darkness, war and ruin. He's kept his own land at war these ten years when he might have ended it the year you and I first met. And none knows that better than I."

Harold nodded. "Ranulf, I don't dispute your knowledge of Hardraada nor the information you bring. And I believe all you say, because Penda vouches for you and Penda's the sort of man I can build an England upon. So, aye – I accept all you say, my friend, and I offer you all the assistance you need – we need – for what you say of our common cause is true. And my hand upon it, lord Ranulf."

Later that day.

The Scraeling took the scroll from Penda's hand, unrolled it and read:

To the Earl of Wessex, Greetings.

Dearest Brother,

I cause this report to be made on the anniversary of my elevation to this earldom, as we agreed and as is usual, and I thank our sovereign lord Edward through you for that appointment.

Would that I had more pleasing matters to report, brother, but as you know I care little for the half-truths and niceties of the diplomat. I am a soldier, and I learned that with you, who are even now soldiering in France, thus you will understand my preference for plain speech and straight dealing.

I have entered my tenth year as earl over the folk here, and still they have not learned that I will brook none of the lawlessness or corruption that grew unchecked here under Siward; nor will I tolerate a situation where the king's peace is broken by powerful families who are wont to settle their quarrels – of which there seems a never-ending number, for they dispute as readily as other men breathe – in ways that involve recourse to the sword rather than to my law courts. But they will learn, brother, for I am resolute in that, even to the infliction of the death penalty where I deem it needful.

Since we last spoke I have felt it necessary to add to the seven-score huscarls of my personal guard, for keeping the peace, collecting the king's taxes and such other duties as are necessary for the administration of this earldom, requires so many with no other consideration. Thus I have added three-score to their number, good men of sound Wessex stock, and in truth their voices put me much in mind of our home in the south and is much to be preferred to the harshness of the tongues I hear about me in this, the Danelaw. This has, of course, added both to the burden of taxation and to the volume of complaint. But what would you?

I prepare as best I can for a settlement with the Scot, Malcolm, but this is the worst of times to contemplate it. When other matters allow, brother, you and I will visit upon the Scot the lesson we taught the Welsh. In the meantime it is meet only to allow him to retain possession of Cumberland, much though I am criticised for this by those sons of Aelfgar, Morcar and Edwin, who covet my lands and possessions. Why, they say, should the men of Northumbria pay taxes to a Wessex man who cares nothing for the protection of the north? I could tell them, would they but listen, that the divisions they cause and foment within this earldom are the first and best of Malcolm's weapons against us here.

The Abbey of Durham begins to flourish under the Judith's interest, and the Church, at least, now judges the Godwinssons less harshly than many of its flock for the many bequests and beneficences they give. And in that, brother, I pray that the goodwill we earn will continue and spread from the vicars of Christ to the citizens of this city, and beyond to those of this earldom of Northumbria, and I pray also that God the Father will smile upon you and offer you His wisdom.

Your loving brother

Tostig of Northumbria
York
July 1064.

The Screaling read the document again, and then picked up his cup and sipped while he read it a third time. "Thank you for showing me this" he said at length, and Penda shrugged.

"It was the quickest way of showing you how things are in the north of this kingdom" he said, "and the north's important because that's where Hardraada needs to land if he's going to get ashore at all."

"Aye, he's worried about that. I've put the idea in his mind that landing in the face of your *hus-carls* won't be pleasant. He's not worried about your fleet, but the heavy axemen've got him in a sweat. Know what I'd do?"

Penda lifted an eyebrow and the Screaling went on, "I'd capture a port. You can't land fifteen thousand men on an open beach, and Hardraada's too good a soldier to miss that. If we assume he'll do that, doesn't it make sense to assume also that it'll be a northern port?"

"That should help some" said Penda. "It'll cut down the places we need to guard, anyway."

"Not sure you need to do that" said the Scraeling enigmatically. "But look – humour me for a minute, cousin. Let me tell you what I think Tostig's all about, eh?"

"Tostig?" asked Penda, the frown lines appearing on his forehead, "What's Tostig got to do with anything?"

"More than you might think" answered the Scraeling, pushing the report this way and that with a fingernail until it lay perfectly squarely before him. "May I?" Penda shrugged and opened his hands in a gesture more eloquent of bewilderment than words could have been.

"Now – I've met Tostig once, in your company. So I can't say I know him, right? But this is how I see him from his own words in this report. Tostig Godwinsson's a man who respects the letter of the law above its spirit. He's capable, thorough, organised, determined, and a lot harder of mind than his brother Harold. He doesn't mince his words, and he's doing a job there in the north that he'd rather not do – but his sense of duty means he'll do it in the face of the Devil himself if needs be. Harold can't have anyone other than him hold such a sensitive and dangerous post, because he guards England's northern frontier against Scots and Norsemen alike. He's not a native northerner, of course, so that gets him no points from those who are – and if my poor knowledge of your politics serves me well, the Aelfgar he mentions is – was – Aelfgar of Mercia, and the others, as Tostig says, are his sons. Probably his disappointed sons, disappointed in not being confirmed as earls of Northumbria and Mercia; so quite ready to be the centre of local opposition to Tostig. Who doesn't need any help at all in getting squarely in people's faces, because by his own admission he's doing fine in that. How'm I doing, cousin?"

Penda's jaw had dropped further and further during the Scraeling's recital, and now he muttered, "Jesus!", blinked twice and emptied the goblet he held. "How're you doing? I think you know Tostig better than I do, cousin! You c'n tell all that from . . . from that letter?"

It was the Scraeling's turn to spread his hands. "It's all here, Penda. Truly. Look, I've spent half my life reading what people *aren't* saying when they write reports. This one's easy because, as I say, Tostig Godwinsson's an honest man who doesn't mince his words. Shall I carry on?"

"There's more?" asked a disbelieving Penda.

"Well, yes. There's what I can read into the way Tostig's expressed himself – this is guesswork I suppose, but you might be able to say whether it's far-fetched . . .?" Penda sat down heavily and waved at him, so the Scraeling continued.

"Tostig's not one for bending. In fact, because he hasn't got Harold's way of reading people, he lacks the flexibility that anyone in the business of ruling needs. He believes in rules for everything, and he can't understand why people don't follow the rules. He knows there's a problem in that, but his solution – and this is revealing – his solution is to beef up his *hus-carls* – his enforcers if you like. So he's not going to compromise, see, Penda? He's going to compel. And that'll get him deeper in the shit than ever because, being a West Saxon and a foreigner he *is* shit as far as the people of the Danelaw're concerned anyway."

Penda just stared at him, and the Scraeling ended, "The rest's fairly straightforward. He's had his battles with the Church, but he's making progress there. Probably because he went to Rome in person to secure the archbiship's *pallium* from the Pope for Ealdred of York – oh yes, I know about that; even if Hardraada doesn't recognise the pope's authority in Norway, some of us keep up with things – and that won't have done him any harm. But it doesn't mean he's softening, by the way. It means he did his duty in a way he saw to be right – and being Tostig, it'd take a better man than the Pope to convince him otherwise. That's about it, I think."

"No" said Penda. "No. None of it's far-fetched. Witchcraft, maybe, but not far-fetched – that's Tostig, living, breathing and farting. You know, you're bloody frightening, you are. I'm impressed. Let me pour you another cup of wine, and ask you – where's all this going, cousin?"

"Going? It's going right back to Harold, because it can't wait. Your credit good enough to arrange another meeting, father of my nephews? Aye? Well, listen to this and then pick the bones out of it for me . . ."

The next day.

The Screaling shook his head. "It's not a matter of guarding the coast, lord Harold. How long d'you want to watch the mist for a fleet of *drakkars* to come nosing out of it? And even if you had the men – what if Hardraada made Ireland his base and then came ashore among the Welsh? Or what if he hits the north while the Bastard comes over from Normandy? Stranger things have happened – ask Penda to tell you about Hardraada and a chap called Maniakes some day."

Harold frowned. "You paint a grim picture, lord Ranulf" he said tersely. "Can you paint us an answer also?"

Penda glanced at Harold and spoke up. "Perhaps we can, earl Harold" he said. "Ranulf?"

"No, cousin" said the Screaling gently, "it's your privilege to offer counsel to your lord. Pray you, ease his mind."

Penda thought a moment then cleared his throat. "We know four things" he said. "One – Hardraada will attempt the throne. Two – William will attempt the throne. Three – nothing will happen until Edward dies, for neither Hardraada nor the Bastard wish to be seen as usurpers, but as men pursuing legitimate claims – William because, he will say, Edward promised him the crown. And Hardraada will claim it because, he will say, it was once Cnut's – and he is now Cnut's heir."

"And your fourth – if there is one?" asked Harold.

"Oh, there is. It's likely to be the most important consideration of all" returned Penda, "for Hardraada prides himself on his cunning. In fact, all the Norse do – they take delight in it. Oaths forsworn and promises broken litter their sagas and their stories. Were he to discover that during your stay in Normandy, earl Harold, you promised as a vassal to uphold him against all men, he would certainly strike first to deprive William – and his excuse would be that by doing so he spared the land from a long and bloody war between Saxon, Norseman and Norman. This is the man – we have Ranulf's word on that."

The Screaling nodded as Harold's eyes swung to him. "How, then, does this knowledge help us with our answer?"

"It helps us" said the Screaling, taking over, "in leaving open the door to the sheepfold so the wolf can come through. Lord Harold, within a year – two at most – England will be beset in the north and in the south. But it need not be so beset at the one time. Call in the wolf, my lord. Call in Hardraada and destroy him. Then turn to your south coast and hold it against those others who must cross the seas to land on another hostile and watchful shore."

Harold said nothing for a long, long time and his gaze went much further than the meadow that lay outside the window. "Will the wolf come to the trap?" he asked at length.

"Should the bait be juicy enough, aye" answered Penda. "And Ranulf's been thinking about that too."

"I'd never believe it" said Harold ironically, but the brilliance of his smile softened the remark. "Go on, lord Ranulf."

"My lord" began the Scraeling, "I mean no criticism of lord Tostig in what I say now, but well is it written that a man should know his enemy – and I hold it even more important that a man should know his friends in like manner. Lord Harold, what if the wolf saw the sheepfold riven by dissent, where royal authority is mocked, scorned and spurned, where the people are Norse by descent and temper, where they have rejected the House of Wessex in favour of their own ancient house. What then?"

"Do you speak of Northumbria?" frowned Harold, "The Danelaw? But that's preposterous – that's the very thing that Tostig's there to prevent, and he's doing the very finest of . . ." but he broke off as he saw the Scraeling glance at Penda and both of them begin to smile.

"My lord, I spoke a moment ago of bait, and juicy bait" said Penda. "Listen to Ranulf here, as he tells you what he read of lord Tostig in a report I showed him."

The Chronicle

In that way, what I had worked for throughout most of my life came to pass. I say, proudly, that on that day I wrought Hardraada's doom, and all that happened from that day onward only brought it closer and made it more certain. I was then able to turn my mind to how I might best ensure the deaths of enough of Hardraada's host to fulfil my vow that my vengeance for Clothilde and her sisters would be no less than the end both of Hardraada and his world. For that to be so, and for the souls of my murdered aunts to find rest, his followers needed to hear the scream of the ravens themselves.

So it was a well-content Scraeling that Skuli and his companions bore back to Nidaros, where I found Hardraada, restless as ever, on the point of leaving to investigate Orkney as an assembly-point and forward base for his assault upon England. He was eager to hear all I could tell him, so I regaled him with accounts of my visit that dwelt much upon the unsettled condition of Tostig's Northumbria – some of it was even true – but also of how Harold Godwinsson was so occupied with the threat from Normandy that his eyes were closed to the thought of invasion from the north.

And I told him of what I'd had from my well-connected cousin, of Harold's ill-fated venture to the Continent on what I assured Hardraada was a mission to discover what support existed for his seizure of Edward's throne. Even a blind man could have noticed how Hardraada's interest quickened at mention of how the Bastard had tricked Harold into swearing fealty to him. But his greatest interest was reserved for the preparations Godwinsson had made to meet the threat from over the Narrow Seas, and I assured him that the bulk of his hus-carls were permanently along the Saxon Coast of South Sussex, while Tostig's were stretched so thin in the turbulence of the huge earldom of Northumbria that he had been driven to employing Danes among his hus-carls. And that, I believe, he knew from other sources for aye, he said, he had heard whispers that many of Svein's former army were looking elsewhere.

Perhaps that convinced him, for I have always noticed that a grain of demonstrable truth sweetens and lends credence to any lie. However it was, he swallowed easily enough my assertion that, with the professionals on the frontiers, the midlands were dependent on the fyrd, the militia of farmer-warriors for their defence.

All told, it was easy to convince Hardraada that Harold Godwinsson inhabited a house of straw that would collapse when Edward's death caused the winds to blow – but that a wise man and a good soldier would prepare to the smallest detail for that occasion. At which he nodded, and I knew his doom was sealed.

In the years since that moment of triumph I have often wondered why it was so easy, and while I cannot say with certainty, I believe it was because I had told Hardraada what he wanted to hear. I had told him of the ease with which he would conquer England, and that was what he wanted to believe because he *had won every battle except his first – and winning in all that he ventured had become his favourite habit.*

Again, he trusted me. As I have written before, it never occurred to him that I would harbour resentment at the manner of his acquisition of me, and the Norse conceit held that I would accept my destiny as the Norns had spun it. Perhaps that was only another example of his belief in himself; that his wish and will would always prevail. But however it was, it doesn't matter now.

What mattered then was that his departure for Orkney brought Elisabeth to my bed again, and she gave it as her opinion, one night as we lay lost in each other, that we might be more assured in that from then onwards, for Hardraada had told her – obliquely to be sure – that he would have one further use for his queens, and one only. Which use she assumed to be his crowning in the English capital. And then, she thought, she dared hope that he might release her altogether – and there she stopped, my lady and my love, waiting for me to take up the drift of her thought and meaning.

So I did, of course – and with only a tiniest nagging of guilt at the knowledge that I would make her a widow and had chosen not to involve her. But would we not inherit a better world after? Had I only known it, one of the last patterns in Hardraada's wyrd would soon be spun in a conversation taking place far to the south of where my lady and I lay fast in each other's arms.

Waltham Holy Cross, February 1065.

Morcar scowled and Harold Godwinsson spoke sharply. "Let's not beat about the bush, lord Morcar. You were passed over because your ability to do the job was in question."

"Only in your mind" retorted the thickset and dark young man before him, "and the fact that the earldom went to your brother had nothing to do with it I suppose? Christ's bones – you're a creeping blight, you Godwinssons, and no mistake!"

"It ill becomes the son of a man who allied himself with the Welsh to cast insults" said the other, "but if what you say's right, things are likely to get worse before they get better, so take care they don't get worse for you personally. And while we're speaking of it, know that my brother was twice the warrior you were when he was made earl, and reflect on the fact that he who sends a boy to do a man's job will surely regret it. No, just listen –" he said as Morcar snarled in fury, "because if you do you'll hear something to your advantage."

"Now" he said, placing a cup of wine on the table by Morcar, "I have no quarrel with you, Morcar Aelfgarsson, despite what your father did. There's been too much quarrelling in England these many years, and while families have been rising and falling like a harlot's skirts, the power of the throne has been the weaker for it."

"Oh aye," he added, "I see the look on your face, and you'll get no argument from me that we of Wessex have risen further than any. But put aside your dislike of my family and me, Morcar, and believe me that I serve England before myself. Your chance to do the same may be closer than you think, and if I'm any judge, you'll also serve England before yourself. Wessex isn't England, any more than Northumbria's England, Morcar. We must work together!"

"Why?" shot back Morcar, "Your family has both earldoms – and most of the rest of England as well. Why must I work with you?"

Harold passed a hand over his forehead. "Because, Morcar" he said, and even to the other he sounded weary, "things . . . may not always be that way. The time may not be far off when . . . when you have the chance to show the world how well you might have seized the chance to be the earl of Northumbria."

"What's this all about?" said Morcar harshly. "For fuck's sake, speak plainly Godwinsson – have I ridden all these miles through weather that's shit only to listen to riddles? Say what you mean!"

"Very well" said Godwinsson. "All that I said concerning my brother is true. He's an honest and good man, and I've seen enough of him in battle to know his worth as a soldier. But I'm Edward's *subregulus*, as you must know, and charged with defending this land – and it's no easy task."

"Don't look to me for sympathy" snapped Morcar. "You and your father before you worked manfully to pick that up!"

"You don't make things easy, do you?" returned Harold. "I'm not asking anything of you – except that you consider accepting appointment as Earl of Northumbria."

Morcar gaped, his surprise evident. "Earl of — and what of Tostig?"

"Leave Tostig to me. Morcar, I'm going to say something now that I shouldn't say to you – but I'm saying it to show my good faith, and my wish to work with you for the good of our kingdom. And if any word of this ever comes back to me, look for my vengeance right behind it. That's a promise, Morcar, not a threat."

"Right. Tostig's a southerner, and the bulk of his estates are here in the south. That doesn't sit well with his duties in the north, although he does a good job. But – doing that good job sets him at odds with people like you. People who are, shall I say, less than enthusiastic about a Godwinsson in Northumbria and who can't stop scratching the itch."

"So after a decent interval, during which I'll require his presence more and more for consultations here in the south, I'm going to bow to the inevitable, move him home and give him something else to do. Then I'm going to give you Northumbria."

"If you're half as popular as my reports claim you are, you'll unify the earls there, stop them plotting treason and keep them facing north, which is where most of Tostig's troubles come from. That ungrateful Scotch bastard Malcolm's habit of nibbling off bits of English land is starting to annoy me as much as it encourages the view that our kingdom's coming apart. It's not, Morcar, believe me – and you're going to show me that by the manner of your keeping of the northern frontier against all men. So, here's the chance you've been waiting for. Want it?"

Morcar thought, smiled, picked up the wine-cup and raised it silently in acceptance.

York, late March 1065.

Tostig put down his cup and asked moodily "And when's this all going to happen?"

"Sometime this year" replied his brother. "Depending on how hard you turn the screw here in the north. You need to keep on doing what you're doing – not giving anyone an inch, rubbing their noses in your expectations, pumping up taxes. You want 'em thoroughly disaffected, and ripe and ready for revolt by summer. This can't look like a simple shift in responsibilities, because Hardraada will see through it. You need to be nursing a grievance – the north's going to reject you and turn to Morcar. I'm going to accept a situation I can't alter and rule, as *subregulus* responsible for the weal of the kingdom, in their favour and make Morcar earl in your place."

"Makes me look worse than useless though" muttered Tostig.

"I know, brother. But I can't ask anyone else to do this. Look – you know, 'cause we've been over it often enough, that I'm going to take the throne when Edward dies. I've no option. We've got Hardraada in the north and the Bastard in the south, and the only proper heir is Edgar, a fourteen-year-old boy. So the Witan will ask me to take the crown and we both know that. That'll draw our enemies in on us, and if we can get Hardraada to move first – and my information is that he will, because he's planning it this minute for he knows about my so-called oath to William – we can fight them one at a time."

"Hardraada'll be a big enough task on his own" agreed Tostig. "But why's my part in it necessary?"

Harold held up a finger. "Hardraada's the sort of man who likes to be right" he said. "He likes to have a cause to fight for – and in this case, it'll be restoring peace to England, a country he thinks he's got a claim to in any case. So you make your way to him as the mighty arbiter of the north, the only man of stature great enough to be listened to. His vanity's such that he'll intervene on your behalf – mind you, later on he'll do you over too. That's his way – right hand and left hand?"

Tostig grunted.

"The other thing" said Harold, "is that it'll look as though England's riven and about ready to fall apart, and that'll tempt him almost as much as having a Godwinsson on his side. So, you see now why I can't quietly replace you with Morcar?"

"Ah, Morcar" said Tostig malevolently. "How much does that backstabbing little shit know about all this? Isn't his big mouth a risk?"

"No" said Harold, "because he doesn't know enough to make him a risk. I've taken care to bring him into my confidence, you see, over how royal policy in the north isn't working under you, how the job's a big one – hinting that you're not up to it despite your many fine qualities, because northerners aren't Welshmen – that sort of thing – and suggesting that if his balls are as big as he pretends they are, he'll do the job in fine style. Northern family, you know. Confidence of the locals, that sort of thing."

"I'm impressed" said Tostig grudgingly. "but how'll he get on against Hardraada?"

"He doesn't know Hardraada's a threat – unless he's got sources we don't know about" said Harold, "but ours is the best there is. No – I've pointed Morcar at Malcolm the Scot and told him his task is the keeping of the northern frontier against all men."

"But you haven't told him that includes Hardraada" nodded Tostig as light dawned. "But my question again – how'll he stand up against Hard Harald?"

"Well enough to slow him down" returned Harold, "and that's all the use I have for Morcar. I can't be watching the north all the time, Tostig. I need Morcar to take the first shock to give me time to swing the army away from the Channel and up there to the north. He's good enough for that – and frankly, brother, the more of those northern shit-stirrers Hardraada kills, the less trouble the next earl of Northumbria will have, so good luck to him."

"And who's he going to be?" asked Tostig, holding out his cup.

"Not you" replied his brother, picking up the wine flask. "You're going to be the next earl of Wessex, my boy. Strong right arm of the king, your brother."

"Where's all this coming from, brother?" asked Tostig curiously. "Is it Penda and the Scraeling? It is, isn't it? 'The best there is' you said – that's the cripple, yes?"

"And you're probably wondering why" nodded Harold. "So I'll tell you, and that'll make four of us who know everything. Don't talk in your sleep, do you?"

Tostig smiled and sipped from his cup.

The Chronicle.

*B*ut the people of Northumbria were slower to reach their limits than the sons of old Godwin calculated, and only in October of that year did word reach us in Norway that they had taken advantage of Tostig's absence in the south to rise in rebellion and invite their favourite son, Morcar, to make himself available for election as earl. I say 'election' because their assertion of that ancient right was a deliberate provocation to the royal prerogative of appointment, but it showed the temper of the north. And as it happened that was all grist to Harold's mill for, after making an exhaustive show of investigating the issues and considering the claims and contentions of both Tostig and the Northumbrians, he advised the king, with every outward sign of reluctance, to let the matter lie and confirm Morcar as earl.

For his part, Tostig angrily rejected every offer of compensatory positions in swearing that he had been shamed before all men and betrayed by king and brother both. He took himself off to the Flanders court of his father-in-law, Baldwin, where he waited for a while before leaving his wife, Judith, with her family and making his way to the court of Hardraada at Nidaros.

For myself, my moment with Penda came when Tostig's first audience with Hardraada was done. Then, as was only natural, I could meet my cousin as a cousin and I made sure I chose for our conversation a room that was at the end of a corridor, and I left the door open. For all that, we spoke in low tones as we pretended to punish a keg of heather beer.

Hardraada's court, February 1066.

The big Saxon smiled as the Scraeling said "Good idea to turn your coat and come with Tostig, Penda."

"All a thinking *hus-carl* can do, cousin, when his lord breaks the oath he's sworn to those under him. Couldn't avoid it, eh? With us, oaths're a two-way thing, y'see. Harold should've upheld his vassal." He said this with such a guileless look on his face the Scraeling was hard-pressed not to smile.

"But how'd you think that went?" Penda went on, 'that' being the audience at which Tostig had formally asked for Hardraada's assistance in being restored to his earldom and offered to place himself at Hardraada's service in the matter and thereafter.

"Pretty well, on the surface, because Hardraada can't be seen as anything other than the all-powerful monarch. Underneath, though . . ." and his voice tailed away.

"Yes? Underneath?" from Penda.

"Well, Ulf's definitely not keen. Now not only's he the marshal and Hardraada's top soldier, he's his oldest surviving comrade. So he's listened to, often when others – including me – are dismissed."

"So what can we do about Ulf?"

"Not a lot. He's almost unassailable, but if anyone can, I think I can. He's not well, and I take a bit of interest in him. Some of my horse liniments give him relief from the joint pain he suffers – he's broken more bones than most men've got – and everybody jokes about him going to the horse-doctor. I think I can persuade Hardraada that Ulf's gloom about things is only his joints playing up and souring him. It's probably true, come to think of it. The English venture will be the only one Hardraada's begun without Ulf at his side, and the old bugger knows it. He knows, too, it's his time for staying at home by the fire – and he hates the idea."

"You know best, Ranulf. That's one of the reasons Harold sent me with Tostig. You know – but he wants me to make it absolutely clear – that the whole thing's in your hands, and Tostig and I are to be guided by you. In everything." The Scraeling nodded and Penda continued:

"How'll you get round Ulf? He's a hard old bugger in all my knowledge of him – 'f he said a prayer for everyone he's killed, I'd say he could be Pope in a week, eh?"

"You're right there" nodded the Scraeling. "He used to move like lightning – you should've seen him training Yaroslav's foot-soldiers. Going up against any three steppe barbarians was nothing compared to going up against Ulf. It's a judgement on him that he can only move with a stick now. But your question – as you saw back in the City days, Ulf's a man of action rather than words. I'll put it in his mind that Tostig should show his mettle somehow and he'll mention that to Hardraada. That should do the trick."

Penda raised an eyebrow. "What, cousin? You want us to beat up some Norsemen then?"

The Scraeling laughed. "Nothing so crude. Look at it from Hardraada's viewpoint. What's he seen of Tostig so far but someone asking for help? What's in it for Hardraada? Lots more than Tostig realises, Hardraada being who and what he is. But what's Tostig risked? Why couldn't this be a deep-laid and devious plot? Which of course it is! No, father of my nephews, getting Ulf onside will need a bit of cunning and a demonstration of Tostig's commitment."

"So—" prompted Penda.

"So, I want you to get Tostig to offer the kind of demonstration Hardraada and his cronies will appreciate. He needs to spit in his brother's eye by falling on Wessex and ravaging it. Burning towns. Killing and looting, taking slaves. Yes, yes I know, cousin –" as Penda's jaw dropped, "it's a lot to ask. But there's a lot at stake. And when Harold's solidly in the saddle, he can always see that justice's done. Believe me – that's the only way for Tostig to win Hardraada over, and the whole plan depends on convincing him that the brother of the king of England's ready to become his man– hand, heart and totally."

"Can't fault a word of that" said Penda slowly as he thought it over. "But – phew! – it's up to me to sell Tostig the idea. You know he's going to be earl of Wessex after all this?"

"That can't get in the way" said the Scraeling impatiently, "and if it does, it'll be up to him, or Harold, to make things right eventually. Look, pick an area where the damage can be confined if you like – but wherever's hit, it needs to be hit hard and well." The words had hardly passed his lips when the thought came to him and he swayed a moment.

"What's the matter?" came Penda's voice from a distance, "Ranulf, what is it?"

"Hit hard" said the Scraeling, and his own voice seemed to come from far away, "just like Les Trois Étoiles. See, Penda? Hardraada hit my home to impress his warriors – now I'm having someone else's home hit to impress Hardraada. It comes to us all in the end. What a desperate fucking world we live in."

Westminster, England, January 1066.

The man's breathing was slow and laboured and his face had sunk in upon itself. The watchers stood or sat around the great bed, each lost in his own thoughts and only the face and the gaze of the sole woman present betrayed any feeling for the man who lay at its centre. She put out a hand and dabbed gently at the man's forehead with a dampened cloth, the action speaking more eloquently of affection than any words might have done. At the gesture, the thickset man at her side took the kerchief from her other hand and wiped as gently at the tears that escaped her eyes to roll down her cheeks.

"Courage, little sister. Can't be long now, and he feels nothing" murmured the earl of Wessex. The woman nodded, but still the tears came and the man dabbed again until she turned her face away.

"A woman should weep for her man" she whispered, "and a queen most of all, for she has others but herself to consider. And it must be a hard thing to . . . to lie there, feeling nothing and . . ." Her voice died away, and her brother nodded his agreement, for the man in the bed had lost all control at his final stroke the day before, and though he had eaten nothing for days the stench of his voided bowels filled the room.

Harold looked up at the churchman across the bed and nodded towards the censer that lay on a table nearby. "Stigand?" he said, and the cleric moved to the brazier that kept the January chill from the room where a king lay dying, brought back a burning taper and applied it to the powder that lay within the vessel. The scent of incense spread through the room and it may have been that which brought the bloodless eyelids open as Edward looked for the last time at the men of his world.

The burning eyes settled upon the oldest of Godwin's surviving sons. "Earl Harold" he said, his breath rasping at each syllable so that all present needed to crane to hear the words, "to you ... I commend this kingdom ... to guard and protect it against ... against all manner of men ... until the Witan shall choose my successor. To you also I commend ... this lady, your sister, and charge you with her protection ... in like manner. Take not from her anything I ... have given her, but see her always in the condition that befits her rank ... I charge you now ... bring forth Archbishop ... Stigand."

"I am here, majesty" spoke the priest, and he moved within the king's line of vision.

"Stig ... Stigand, I would now make my confession. Bless me, for I have sinned ..." and as the age-old words of the ritual rasped from the tortured throat the cleric shushed him, leaned over the dying man and traced the sign of the cross on the pallid forehead.

"Edward, *rex, pater Anglorum, ego te absolvo. In nomine Patris, Filii et Spiritu Sancti*—" and as Stigand spoke the words of absolution Queen Edith's hand tightened on that of her brother. For his part, Godwinsson fought to suppress a surge of elation at his naming as successor to Edward the saint and he strove to keep his face unmoved as the breath rasped ever less loudly through the tortured airways of the king. At the end, there came a choking rattle and the physician thrust forward to seize the king's tongue and draw it from the straining mouth. Edward convulsed, strained upward a moment and died.

The physician lowered his head to the narrow chest, felt for the pulse at the side of the neck and shook his head. "The king is dead" he pronounced, and Queen Edith turned to her brother and knelt before him.

"Long life and wisdom to your majesty" she said, and Harold bowed his head a moment to the still figure in the centre of the bed before drawing his sister to her feet.

"Sister, you must never kneel to me again" he said gently, "for you were royal before I. Indeed, I call all here to witness that I am not yet royal, for the Witan must pronounce upon that tomorrow, even as our sovereign lord Edward, but now departed, has said. In the name of the Father, the Son and the Holy Spirit."

"Amen" echoed the great ones of England.

Nidaros, February 1066.

Tostig stamped circles with the bottom of his cup in the droplets of wine spilled on the table. "It's hanging there like a plum, I tell you" he said. "The north hates the Godwins – didn't they kick me out, the ungrateful bastards? – Leofric's sons won't turn out for Harold, even to save the north from my ally, Malcolm of Scotland, and in the west, the Welsh're only waiting for the chance to revolt – which'll come if you land in the northeast and give 'em a start."

"But you'll lose the chance if you fuck about, Harald – you know as well as I do, the Bastard of Normandy's got the idea that Edward and Harold both promised the crown to him. Come on, man – you'd never have hesitated when you commanded the Varanger Guard. You're still a legend in Constantinople from what I hear!"

"What you hear, Tostig" said Ulf wheezily, "Is what bothers me. You're well informed for a man who's been kicked out of his own earldom an' who's turned his back on all his sources, eh?"

"Who says so?" demanded Tostig, "I might've left England, but that doesn't mean I've got no interest in what goes on there. I'm going back, friend, so I take care to know plenty, believe me. I'm only telling the king here what you should be telling him as his marshal. For both of you – England's there for the taking. Want it? Cnut didn't hesitate, Harald. Why do you?"

A telling blow thought the Scraeling. Comparisons with Cnut were always calculated to bring out the bellicose side of Hardraada's nature, and this one did just that.

"I'll pick my time" said Hardraada, "just as Cnut did – but I'll do it better. When I take England, I won't be sharing it with anyone like Cnut had to."

"Exactly!" said Tostig. "So why not now? Get in first, and show the Bastard your arse. Grab Harold in the spring, I say. Look," he said, leaning forward over the table, "here's an idea. What say I show you how easy it'll be? I'd be happy to take a half-dozen ships and light up any part of England you name – yes, you choose – an' just singe brother Harold's arse, just a bit. A little taster for him, let's say?"

"Tostig, why should my king pull your fucking chestnuts out of the fire for you?" demanded Ulf, "your earldom's your problem – you've got half a dozen ships of your own – so why should he?"

"Because he can" said Tostig, ticking off the points he made on his fingers. "And because he's the greatest warrior of the north, and there's not been a commander like him in Constantinople in the twenty years he's been home. Because if he doesn't, the Normans will. Because he's a soldier who's fought for his throne and not a stay-at-home blanket-warmer; because he's vigorous enough to do it. That answer your question?"

Skilfully done thought the Scraeling *and just as we spoke of it*. Flattering enough to keep Hardraada happy, insulting enough to piss Ulf off but not so much that Hardraada stepped in for him. *Well done Tostig!*

"Why you cheeky English shit!" erupted a flash of the old Ulf, "that a dig at me or something? Odin's balls, I'd like to . . ."

"Nothing of the sort!" interrupted Hardraada. "Settle down, Ulf. Tostig didn't mean you at all – he's just speaking generally, eh Tostig?"

"Of course, majesty" returned Tostig, all smoothness and poison. "Why would I have a go at you Ulf? You're the marshal of Norway and the king's right-hand man. Have been for years, and if he's the man I think he is, he'll be the first to say how much he's relied on you for all those years. But it's important he keeps on getting good advice, see – because which Hardraada will the *skalds* celebrate? The young man who took every chance he was offered to become the greatest soldier of our time, or the man who grew old in caution and came second to the Bastard of Normandy? 'Cause Harold's not in the race, I can tell you."

Tostig paused to empty his cup. "My offer stands – send your most trusted with me, and let me show them what half a dozen ships might do.

And if they're not impressed, let them say so and I'll see if Svein is. You've kicked his arse square, Harald, but even he'd have enough grunt left to topple brother Harold."

"Why a broken-arsed effort like Svein?" asked the Scraeling, doing his bit as they'd agreed, "Why not your father-in-law? Surely Baldwin of Flanders has even more – grunt – as you put it?"

"Because, secretary" said Tostig with heavy politeness, "Baldwin's got his own troubles with the king of France. Who wouldn't be averse to taking advantage of him while Baldwin's invading England. Or of allowing the Bastard of Normandy free passage through his dominions so he could take advantage of Baldwin. No – I'll look to the north for help because – and I'll say it again – England's half-Norse anyway and has been since Cnut."

The Scraeling nodded thoughtfully to acknowledge the truth of Tostig's reply, aware as he did so that Hardraada's eyes were on him. There was silence around the table, until Tostig said, "What d'you say, king of Norway?" and the Scraeling caught Hardraada's eye as he looked up.

"*Leder*" said the Scraeling, knowing that what he said next would probably be the most important thing he had ever said to Hardraada, "Earl Tostig's got a lot of common sense on his side. So's Ulf, though. Tell you what – if Tostig's offer finds favour with you, I'll go with him. If I do that, I'll get some idea finally of the things that'll be required for an undertaking we've spoken of anyway, but from the soldiering point of view I'd like Styrkar here, and Eystein. If they'll come. What about it?"

"I'm in" said Eystein, and "Me too" came Styrkar, and the Scraeling cocked an eyebrow at Hardraada.

"Done" said Hardraada. "Which part'll you hit?"

"Well" said Tostig, "the Danelaw'll be easiest, so let's make it hard for ourselves. What about Wessex itself, Penda? Let's kick my brother fair in the balls!"

The Chronicle.

A nd Hardraada let us do just that for, Ulf notwithstanding, he had already decided that England would be his and while we were away he pressed ahead with the provisioning of Orkney as the base from which his ravens would fly to Harold's lands.

But as the cattle were slaughtered and salted and the fish smoked and packed into kegs we were far to the southeast, set upon devastating the island the ancients had known as Vectis and which others know as the Isle of Wight. Call it what any wished, it was still part of what Romans and Britons alike had called the Saxon Shore, and it was in the very heart of Harold's earldom of Wessex.

So our ships prowled the great waterway that separates the island from the mainland, and the islanders knew the terror that came by night on three nights running, for by day we hauled away and waited below the horizon – sleeping, examining the loot we had taken and amusing ourselves with the women we had torn from their homes. Neither prayer nor entreaty, not tears and certainly not fight softened the hearts or changed the minds of men set upon a good, old-fashioned rape and I even saw coin change hands in wagers made, won and lost on the matter of how long a given man would last.

I saw, too, a woman who could not have been more than fifteen – a girl, rather than a woman – and who had been foully used in just such a manner by six men, drag herself from where they had finished with her, to the side and rest there a moment, dry-eyed for she had no tears left. With what must have been the last of her strength she hauled herself upright, glanced wildly about her and caught my eye before she toppled silently over the side. And no man moved to prevent it, though there were many closer than I.

And the worst of it was that I was part of it, although of course I took no part in it. I, who could not now close my eyes without the dreams that had haunted my young manhood returning, now saw those same dreams enacted again before me daily. Oh, Tostig's selection of the Isle of Wight was a deliberate one, for it limited the scale and scope of the devastation he wrought to satisfy Styrkar, Eystein and the other observers aboard, who were all hugely appreciative of his outrageous bluff in staying in the area for three nights. Deliberate, aye, but there were moments when Harold's brother looked as white about the gills as I felt at the doom he visited upon his own countrymen and the fleeting conversations I had with Penda only confirmed that.

In the end, then, we hauled away to the north, landing and ravaging wherever caught our fancy – but mercifully, Tostig convinced the observers that a policy of hit, take and run would best show how Harold's defences could be stretched until they snapped asunder. So we pillaged our way up the east coast until we could put into the great estuary of the Humber, in Tostig's earldom of Northumbria, where we put as many fighting men ashore as we could to ravage the town of Lindsey. Morcar, warned of our progress along the coast, rose to the challenge and led a powerful force against us, but after nothing more than a skirmish that allowed him to estimate the size of the force that Morcar could raise in a hurry, Tostig ordered a retreat to the ships and we weighed for Norway to where Hardraada, well enough pleased with the results of our foray, would order us into final planning for his enterprise of England.

Nidaros, July 1066.

Hardraada shook his head. "Nothing's changed. The bulk of his heavy forces're still in the south, facing the Narrow Seas, 'cause he's more worried about the Normans than us. And that's going to bury him, because Morcar's not up to facing us anyway – even if he wants to, and there's some doubt about that. Tostig? Penda?"

Tostig nodded. "As I've said in this room before, the north's different. Northerners are different. Morcar's got what he wanted, but I'd be surprised if it made him any more loyal to Harold, because he's never been anything but a twisted little shit in all my knowledge of him. Morcar's for Morcar, and if he sees it in his interests not to oppose us, he'll welcome us ashore and chuck in his daughters too."

Styrkar laughed. "Word is, he's married his sister to Harold?" he asked and again Tostig nodded.

"That's right. Proves my point, eh?" he said, "But for those who don't know, she – Ealdgyth - was once married to Gruffydd of Wales. Three years ago, Harold put out the word that Gruffydd's head was the price of peace in Wales, and he got it – I was there when they tipped it out of the bag – now he's married the widow he made, 'cause he's trying to cuddle up to Morcar. That tell you anything?"

"It tells me he's worried about the north" said Styrkar, scratching thoughtfully in his beard, "and Ulf thought so too, 'cause we discussed it just before he died."

"Exactly" said Tostig, and he looked at Hardraada. "*Leder*, I'm going to suggest that you and the bulk of the army get ashore in the Humber and drive straight for York. That might – *might* – bring Morcar and his brother Edwin down on you, but I'd bet my life it'll only be a token before he surrenders. If not, and he finds some genuine balls from somewhere, smash him anyway. Same result."

"Spell it out?" came Eystein, who was looking intently at Tostig.

"You get control of the north that way, whatever happens" said Tostig, returning his stare. "Then you roll south, with me and the fleet flanking you and supplying you on a daily basis just like the Scraeling here tells me you did in North Africa, until Harold's got no choice but to give battle. And when he does, I come ashore wherever I like and we crush him between us." Whether by accident or design, the goblet in Tostig's hand snapped as he ended. Around the table the hard faces nodded, but not that of Eystein Orri, the youngest of them.

"Tides" he said. "Shoals, currents, contrary winds. Communications. No. Not for me. Oh, if you want to carry supplies in the ships, fine – no problem about that because we c'n go two, three days on short rations if we have to. But if we need your troops, Tostig, we need 'em under our hand there and then. Not a day or so away 'cause the wind's wrong. Harold's no bunny, and he won't stick his head out for us to chop off."

Guthrum Gunhildsson stirred at his words. "Eystein's right" he said. "What worked before might work again, but I wasn't there and I'd rather trust to what we know."

"Fuck's sake, man, you Norsemen've been sailing since God made water!" said Tostig. "What's the problem in working with a fleet?"

"Since you ask," said Eystein, "raiding's one thing – invading a country's another, lord Tostig. Given Harold's skill as a warrior, we might need to react bloody quickly and – I'll say it again – half an army a mile off the coast's half an army Harold doesn't need to worry about right away, and half an army we can't use."

He's not wrong thought the Scraeling watching Hardraada covertly as the argument raged round the table. *He's got the leder half-convinced, because he's saying nothing. Is he letting Eystein put his case for him? Jesus, that's it! Eystein's his boy all right, and Hardraada's watching the others to see how they're reacting. But that's buggered things. Tostig's going to come ashore when battle's imminent all right, but in behind him, not Harold. The cork in the bottle. Has Hardraada seen that? Does he suspect treachery after all? Bet he does – it's what he'd do!* And in an instant of blinding clarity, the Scraeling knew what he must do.

He cleared his throat during a lull and eyes turned to him. "It's not one or the other" he said. "We can do both. Lord Tostig here and his retainers can indeed march with the host, but the fleet can still supply the army under another – say, myself – so we still gain speed through being unencumbered, speed enough to cut down Godwinsson's options, just as lord Tostig intends. *Leder?*"

Hardraada nodded slowly. "I'm happy with that" he said. "Keeps our strength where we want it, but lightens our burdens. We won't be looting anyway" he said, "Because I'm not going to start being king of the English by pillaging them. That'll come later!" he added to a shout of laughter, and in that the moment of danger passed.

Later that day.

Penda loosed, and grunted as the shaft leapt seventy paces to stand in the centre of the butt. "I'll be as good as you one day soon, cousin" he said, "and then I'll win my ring back!"

"Too late, my man" said the Scraeling, sighting along his own shaft and loosing smoothly. "I've promised it to Osmund when he comes of age. Ah . . . how's that?" he asked, indicating his arrow quivering beside the first.

"My son's getting my ring?" came Penda, and the Scraeling reached up to put his arm around the other's massive shoulders as they walked to the butt.

"No, cousin. My nephew's getting my ring. Dry your eyes and get over it. I promise you, a boy like Osmund will surely look after you in your old age!"

"Least he'll live to see my old age if what we're doing comes out right" muttered Penda, with a glance around him.

"That's why we're out here" said the Scraeling, noting the glance. "No-one to overhear what I need to tell you. And that is – tell Tostig that Hardraada may suspect treachery. Not because we've done anything untoward, but just because that's the nature of the beast he is. He'd pull one, so he assumes everyone else would too."

"That why you came up with the idea of you taking the fleet and Tostig marching with the army?"

"Aye. And why I was at pains to underline Tostig's wish for speed as a reason for advising it."

"Noticed that too" nodded Penda. "My imagination, or is young Orri Hardraada's mouthpiece?"

"Well done" said the Scraeling, reaching up to work the shafts free. "That's how I see it too. He's the one to work on, so tell Tostig that too. Now – we need to work out a way of getting you and Tostig out of trouble when the clash comes . . ."

The Chronicle.

*A*fter that events took on a momentum of their own, and the days became *long and full as the greatest fleet ever assembled in Scandinavia came in twos, threes and in the end, dozens to the great port on the Norwegian Sea. But for all the bustle and apparent confusion of men and vessels in the great basins of the harbour, there was no chaos, for every boat coming near Nidaros was intercepted and assigned a number, a place to berth and a time limit to stay there before moving to a more permanent location where it would be watered and victualled for the voyage down to Orkney.*

All that was the work of my clerical team, grown huge and all-powerful, and just directing it kept me busy through all the hours of daylight. Aye, and it would have gone beyond that had I not given orders to the guardships that none were to be admitted through the headlands other than in daylight. Believe me, then, when I say that the Norwegian fleet that left Nidaros after Hardraada named the older of Thora's sons, Magnus, as regent for him and then performed the ancient Viking leader's rite of clipping hair and nails, numbered three hundred and fourteen, with most of those crewed by sixty men apiece, so that the warriors that Hardraada disposed of personally totalled some eighteen thousand men. And none were sailors only – all were warriors who rowed when needful. Truly, it was a force fit to give pause to any foeman under heaven and when Hardraada sailed through the ranks massed outside Nidaros on the day of departure at the end of August the crash and roar of the "Vess-heil!" salutes when 'Sleipnir' passed shook earth and sky themselves and deafened those aboard.

And those included Elisabeth and her daughters as well as myself, for Hardraada had decreed that his womenfolk would travel with us to Orkney, there to wait until the enterprise of England was brought to a successful end. To my knowledge he never said why, but I believe he feared the intentions of Thora, the regent's mother, towards a woman she could never emulate, bawd that she was. But again – it may have been because of his love for his daughters, and in especial Maria, his favourite child.

But it doesn't matter now, and if I'm truthful it didn't matter then for it meant that Elisabeth and I might meet daily, however circumspectly, and enjoy the closeness of each other. And part of that, for me, was the wonder of how such a woman could care for me, because even in her forties and the mother of two grown women, Elisabeth of Kiev was yet slender, golden, beautiful and cultured beyond anything or anyone else in the ice lands of the north. How much any other apart from Hardraada knew or guessed I have never known, but then I have never cared. As long as I was of use to Sigurdsson – and I took care to be everything to him and his scheme – I enjoyed an immunity that, for me, was worth more than gold in offering me the company of the woman I loved and who loved me always as she had promised all those years before.

Sometimes, now, in the hours of a dark night when there have been one or more cups too many and I look back on a life that has been uncommon by the standards of other men, I reproach myself for the falsity and deviousness that has marked most of it. But in the end, I come to the thought that had it been other I would never have found Elisabeth and her love. At those times, and in that state, I find it easy to convince myself that Clothilde, who knew so much of suffering, had looked down upon us from heaven and drawn us together.

We sailed down towards the Orkneys, then, rolling easily along in the knowledge of our overpowering strength with the ocean aboil wherever one looked with the wakes of the army of the north. There we were joined by yet more warriors and freebooters, chief among them the sons, Paul and Erlend, of Thorfinn Arnesson, and Hjalmar, the crown prince of Hardraada's longstanding ally, Iceland. Hardraada held a great council at which he outlined again for the benefit of all his commanders and allies the arrangements for landing in England and what would follow.

And that night I took my farewell of a tearful Elisabeth with a promise that this parting was only the prelude to our tomorrows, but for the appearance of things I deemed it better for us not to share a bed.

Down, down we went, down the east coast of Scotland to ravage and terrorise where the fancy led us in search of food, water and amusement. The first major town of England we raided, and that with great slaughter, was Scarborough but at Holderness we routed also the first of Morcar's protecting *troops and Hardraada was quick to point out how easy it had been.*

We came at last to the Humber, to the great estuary where Tostig had trailed his coat that year already, and the former earl of Northumbria returned to his lands and joined us in the afternoon of the same day from a greatly successful search among those mercenaries, landless men and adventurers of Europe who were to be found in Flanders. We had been dogged by some of Morcar's ships for a day by then, but they fled into the bay before such a fleet and took refuge in one of the rivers that flowed into the estuary preferring, doubtless, to take what chance sent them on foot rather than on the element ruled by such sea-wolves.

And there, on English soil, the last part of my design for the destruction of Harald Sigurdsson fell into place.

The Humber estuary, 19 September 1066.

Penda flicked a flat stone across the dancing wavelets of the falling tide. He lowered his voice although we were alone, and said, "Harold's coming. He'll be on the move the instant he has news of Hardraada's landing – fact, he's probably on the march now because I saw the beacon-fires going not an hour ago."

Penda had gone to Flanders with Tostig and while his master recruited soldiers the *hus-carl* had slipped away to England across the Channel to bring Harold up to date with the movements and intentions of the Norse king, but more importantly with the change of plan which Hardraada's caginess had forced upon Tostig.

"Now" said Penda, "Harold's hand-picked twenty *hus-carls* of his brother Gyrth's division – I know 'em all, and they know me – and when battle's joined they'll drive straight for Tostig and me. We'll be under Tostig's personal banner and nowhere else, and they'll overpower us 'cause Harold'll put it about that he wants us alive."

"What about the mercenaries Tostig's bought?" asked the Scraeling, "Won't they have something to say about that?"

"The twenty're for us" said Penda. "There's another twenty for Tostig's Flemings, but no-one's said anything about taking them alive. Too bad, eh?" He flicked another stone away into the gathering dark.

"Harold's not delaying, cousin" he said, "He's coming north with all he's got, he's coming fast, an' there's two reasons for that. First, he doesn't trust Morcar to stop Hardraada – well, who would? – and he's hoping the earls can slow him, at least. But second, Harold's a good man, Ranulf, and he's not grabbed the throne for nothing. He's . . . he's the king of England. All of England, and he's not having anyone – Norman or Norseman – ravage it unpunished. He's going to defend it, come what might. If he can get here before the earls give battle, he will. But if he can't, he'll be here before Hardraada can scratch his arse after. Now, what's he want?" he asked, nodding at a soldier making towards them along the beach.

"God knows. What about the Saxon Coast?" asked the Scraeling, covering his wary glance around by stretching and yawning as he did so and Penda grimaced.

"Wind's been solid from the north for a fortnight" he said, "same wind you and Hardraada rode – but dead foul for the Bastard. Every day that passes brings the autumn gales closer. If William doesn't get across in the next three weeks he can forget it until next year. And that means he can forget it altogether, cousin."

"So" mused the Scraeling, drawing his light cloak about him, "that wind's getting keen. Hardraada first and the Bastard . . . perhaps not at all. Let's hope, Penda. Let's hope. Did you see Gytha and the family?"

Penda smiled. "An afternoon, an evening and most of a morning. Then a hard ride back to the harbour. But they're well, and you're to know you're in their prayers – and Osmund's helping the grooms saddle-break the yearlings. He asked me what I thought Uncle Ranulf would think of that – which means, I think, he wanted me to tell you but didn't want to say so . . ."

The crunch of feet sounded on shingle, and a man loomed out of the gathering dusk. "Lord secretary, lord Penda" he said, "King Harald wants to review the order of march for tomorrow and wishes your presence. If you'd follow me please?"

The same evening, in the city of York.

Edwin of Mercia pulled at his nose. "That's it then, brother. He's here" said. "What'll you do?"

"As one of Godwinsson's earls, or as a Northumbrian?" returned Morcar. "In the matter of the first, I've no option. I'm sworn to defend the north 'against all men', remember?"

"Against the fucking Scots, yes" agreed Edwin hotly, "but not against Hardraada – Christ's sake, he and his are related to half the earldom! Besides, d'you want to face the Landwaster across a battlefield? Eh?"

"No" admitted Morcar, "but I don't have a choice. Either way, after this I want to keep on being earl of Northumbria whether Harald or Harold's on the throne, and neither'll turn over the north to someone who made no effort to defend it."

"Well, we're in shit street then, aren't we?"

"Not necessarily. Look, I'm going to have trouble raising many more than my household troops – most of the *fyrd* will eat shit rather than turn out against their own, and by the time your people get here from Mercia, it'll all be over. So – we make the gesture."

"I can think of one or two I'd like to make" muttered Edwin, "Specially at Godwinsson. Dropped you right in it, didn't he? Cunning bastard – don't tell me he didn't foresee this."

"You're probably right" agreed Morcar, "but we need to deal with it, not regret it. Look – Hardraada's first target will be York, and I'm going out to meet him. As I must. But I don't expect to stop him, not with 300 longships behind him. But I must be seen trying, yes? So, I'm going to offer battle. And then I'm going to fall back in the face of superior force. Hardraada will take York anyway, but I'll have tried – what happens next's up to Godwinsson and the southerners."

"Fuck Godwinsson and all his kind!" came in Edwin like a benison. "We'd be better off making our peace with Hardraada, I reckon."

"Amen to that, brother" returned the earl of Northumbria. "It'll probably work out that way in the end."

Fulford Gate, a mile from York, 20 September 1066.

Hardraada demanded "What'd you see?" and the scout showed yellow and gapped teeth in a smile.

"Not too much to bother you, lord king" he said. The two roads we've been followin' come together into one again over the brow yonder and down the hill. The English're lined out across the road, their right on the river, an' their left sittin' on the swamp – it's all downhill there, an' we can't get round on our right – too boggy, aye?

"But they've got depth?" asked Hardraada and the scout nodded.

"Aye. We'll have to go through 'em though, 'cause we can't go round. Ah, no archers by the way."

"Good. Numbers? What's their war-gear like?"

"About fifty ships' worth – maybe sixty, but no more. Bit more'n half are *hus-carls*, but the rest – *fyrd* militia, an' not the best of them at that; no *byrnies*, no weapons that don't come off a farm. Oh, an' the *fyrd's* all on the flanks."

Hardraada dismissed the man and turned to Tostig, who had listened intently. "How's that, Tostig?" he demanded.

Tostig shook his head decisively. "They should've raised more than that" he said, "way more than that. They've known about us, probably since we hit the first town in Scotland and certainly since Scarborough, and even a fuckwit like Morcar should've worked out where we'd land. No, he's not serious, because if he was he'd be on that hilltop this minute."

Hardraada smiled at him. "Go on" he said, and Tostig spread his hands.

"Morcar's not going to die for anyone's cause but his" he said, "and especially not for a Godwinsson. He's going to put up a fight, just for the look of it, and then he's going to fall back on York and surrender. Look – he's given himself no room at all. He's penned between his position over that hill and the gates of the city, so he's not hoping to duck and weave and slow you down until Harold gets here. No – it's all on this fight, and when we blow him away, that's it. He'll make his peace with you then."

"That's how I see it too" said Hardraada. "But d'you want his head, or what?"

"Haven't thought that far ahead" said Tostig easily. "If I'm right about this, Morcar's head won't be on offer during this battle anyway, will it? But anyway – I'm not that keen on being earl of Northumbria, to tell the truth. Wessex, now, if my king thinks I'm worth it . . ." and he smiled.

"Later" said Hardraada, returning the smile. "All that make sense to you, Screaling?"

"Completely" spoke up the Screaling. "Lord Tostig knows these people better than any of us, and if he says we can take this rabble without Eystein's reserves back at Riccall, that's enough for me."

"Good enough" said Hardraada. "Let's have a look for ourselves." He dismounted and strode off up the slope.

The Chronicle.

*A*nd in fact, I wasn't far wrong. Hardraada put his hard men in our centre and left, and that simple action won the battle before it began, for it made clear to any – except Morcar, apparently – that the Norsemen would pull off a flanking movement at some stage, roll up Morcar's right and power through his centre. Tostig's mercenaries and some of the Icelanders were good enough to hold our right, where the lines petered out in a marsh treacherous enough to drown the unwary.

But our right, surprisingly enough, saw the best English effort of the day when Morcar's fyrd, showing more dash than the scout had suggested, made progress against their former earl and his mixed force. Tostig showed his class as a commander by twice rallying his staggering forces and leading them under his personal banner in a wild counter-attack to regain ground lost. However the English, too, were heartened at their success in that most unlikely of sectors, and when Tostig's line began to bend a third time, fierce eyes on top of the hill marked it.

Hardraada's ox-horns screamed, the Landwaster banner swooped down the hill and the leder's personal praetorians crashed into the English fyrd to send them staggering and reeling back into the embraces of the marsh. Once the deed was done, though, and Tostig's mercenaries had rallied, the horns pealed again and Hardraada's veterans disengaged long enough to see Skuli's division launched like a dart along the firmer banks of the River Ouse at the English right before they buried themselves, a huge steel arrowhead, in Morcar's centre.

Then Hardraada's wedge began to spread in the manoeuvre he termed "the wings of the raven" as those warriors on the outsides of the wedge, chosen for their strength and reach, turned to the foemen on their outsides and began to hew at an angle to the line of advance so that the Norse front spread sideways in an expanding torrent of steel. At the same time Skuli's division bore inwards and away from the river, and those caught between him and the Landwaster found themselves unable to wield their weapons for the press.

Suddenly – and from where I watched it was like the snapping of a rope – the English line collapsed and Skuli simply rolled it up as I had been wont to roll up my cloth after an afternoon's amber-trading in Miklagaard. Resistance before him ceased as none could raise an arm in defence or attack, and the ravens gorged and gorged as axes and blades rose and fell and the battle dissolved into knots of figures struggling to surrender to those too drunk with slaughter and blood-lust to take any heed.

Perhaps fifteen minutes had passed between Hardraada's thunderbolt charge to Tostig's aid and the English rout and as I watched the final stages, sickened, a growing stream of figures ran, staggered and stumbled along the road back to where the walls of the city were just visible in the distance. Dark figures leaped in pursuit with the energy and vigour that comes from triumph, but Hardraada's ox-horns wailed for the last time that day and, reluctantly, the dark figures broke off and turned back.

Oh, I knew why – and it had nothing to do with mercy. Nothing urges surrender quite so dramatically as the visible presence of a bleeding defender, and the remnants of a shattered army would tell their own story. The Rus again, I thought – leave a few to tell the tale.

And across the field in a day that was not yet ten hours old, came striding Hardraada, dread lord of the North, acknowledging the "Vess-heil!" salutes of his warriors who were despatching the dying, and looting them ere they stopped twitching. But neither he nor they knew that the Landwaster, the most famed soldier of our time, had won his last fight.

City of York. The afternoon of 20 September 1066.

The Screeling spread his hands and spoke soothingly. "Look" he said, "to begin with, let's understand he's not going to be overly hard on you. There's a lot of goodwill towards York and the north among us, but you must know that. Penda?"

Penda translated, and the Screeling was glad to note that his English was well up to the task of understanding what his cousin said and what was said in reply. The city fathers looked at each other, shuffled a bit, and the one who couldn't avoid it asked, "Very well, ambassador – ah – what does the king of Norway want of us?"

"First," said the Screeling, "your friendship. My king regrets what was forced upon him this morning. He is aware of the blood ties that exist, and welcomes them. He has chosen to send me rather than to come in person because he doesn't wish to come as a conqueror, but as a liberator. I'm here today, only hours after a battle he'd no wish to fight, to explain that. Second, and in token of that, he wants you city fathers to invite him to enter York. Penda?"

God forgive me for the lies I'm telling thought the Screeling, with one ear on Penda and the rest of him wondering where the northern earls were hiding. *All I want is a secure base behind me* Hardraada had said, *and if they think York's going to be my seat of government, well, let 'em. First things first, eh?*

"We understand" said the greybeard who seemed to be the city's principal man, "and we are grateful for the king's forbearance. We ask you to convey our invitation to his majesty King Harald to enter York, or Jorvik if he would have it so, and to convey to him also our readiness to co-operate with him as he wishes, for the sparing of our city." *Not to mention your possessions and fortunes* thought the Scraeling when Penda had finished, but he smiled and said,

"My king – and yours now – will soon require provisions for his march of liberation southwards. He would also welcome your young men allying themselves with his army, and from what I understand of the blood ties that already exist and to which I referred before, surely there will be little problem there."

The Scraeling allowed Penda to translate, then he leaned forward and said, in an English deliberately slow and thickly-accented, "My king . . . understands . . . that your young men had to stand . . . against us today. And he understands why also . . . but no more of that now, aye?" The words were hardly out of his mouth before he realised that he had struck exactly the right note, for the city fathers beamed with gratification and broke into a babble that he patiently endured before turning to Penda again.

"Of course" Penda spoke over the babble and it died away, "of course, our king will require the usual hostages from the city." There was a stricken silence, and the Scraeling took advantage of it to have him add, "But only for form. King Harald will exchange one hundred warriors, one for each hostage, to show the people and the fathers of York that none has any reason to fear him. The warriors have already volunteered to remain among you, unarmed, while the army marches south."

At that there was further babble, and the end of it was that the city fathers would be pleased if the Scraeling would convey their thanks and devotion to the king, and their assurances that, given a few days' grace for selection and collection, all would be as his majesty desired . . . and so on . . . and on . . . and on. In short, they were almost pathetically grateful that their city, their lives and their fortunes were to remain intact and not become the prizes of war. *Nor,* thought the Scraeling as he and Penda collected their escort and swung back into the saddle for the twelve-mile ride to the anchorage at Riccall, *can I blame any for that.*

Later that afternoon.

The Scraeling washed the dust of the road from his mouth and lowered the goblet. "Just as we agreed" he reported. "I pushed the line that you came as rightful lord of the north and as a friend, not as a conqueror. You're cut up about their battle losses; don't want any more bloodshed among people you regard as kin; not going to take advantage of a wide-open York – that sort of thing. And when you come to York in response to their kind invitation, you're coming in fellowship and friendship."

"And they really believed that?" asked Hardraada, toying with his dagger; "buggered if I would!"

"Ah, but you're different" returned the Scraeling. "You haven't got all you own wide open to a viking army, and you're not pissing yourself with fear that the new king of England will begin by making an example of you just to get your countrymen thinking right. Are you?"

Hardraada raised his eyebrows and nodded. "Fair enough" he said. "Got to see it from their end I suppose."

"I've found it helps" agreed the Scraeling. "And, while we're looking at it that way, I think it'd be a good idea to go to York on Sunday unarmoured."

"Unarmed?" said Hardraada, "Bugger that, Scraeling! The army doesn't feel dressed without its weapons. What're you thinking of?"

"Not 'unarmed', *leder*; I said 'unarmoured'" returned the Scraeling. "It's all in what the people of the Danelaw see. Armed and armoured, you're an army that might turn on them any minute. Armed, you're what they'd expect – but going without *byrnies* shows them clearly that you're not intending violence. You'll take a big step towards easing their minds, if you take my meaning, by giving up a bit of your undoubted advantage. That's what they'll think. And don't forget – you'll want 'em happy because they'll be at our backs when the army turns south, aye?"

Hardraada scowled. "See what you mean" he said, "but what happens if Morcar turns up?"

"He won't" said the Scraeling confidently. "If Morcar had any intention of disputing our progress, he would've done a better job at Stamford. In fact, he wouldn't have fought Stamford at all. He'd have sent messengers flying for the south, retreated into York, and told us to get fucked. But he didn't do any of those things, because he knows where his people's loyalties lie – and your going to York as a friend, an ally and the rightful king is only going to underline that."

Hardraada thought a long moment while the Scraeling held his breath, then nodded. "All good sense, Scraeling. What'd we do without you?"

With any luck, thought the Scraeling, *you'll find out sooner than you expect. But that's the best I can do, Harold – by all the bones of all the saints, get yourself up here quickly. No time like now . . .*

Riccall anchorage, 7am Sunday 25 September 1066

Hardraada flexed his mighty arms until the muscles cracked. "Got it then, Scraeling?" he asked before his assembled lieutenants, "We still doing the right thing?" and the Scraeling nodded.

"I think so" he said. "It's the appointed day, and it's time their new king met his people and –" he pulled a face – "graciously allowed them to do him honour!"

Guthrum Gunhildsson guffawed. "D'you think, majesty," he said in the same affected tone, "you can get any of your loyal people to do one or two of your officers honour as well? No-one's done me honour since the night before we left Nidaros!"

"I should think so" said Hardraada, winking at the Scraeling. "You pick out any of the city fathers that takes your fancy, Guthrum my man, and I'll have the two of you shown to a quiet chamber!" There was a shout of laughter, and jeers at Guthrum's expense.

"Thanks very fucking much" he said when the laughter died away, "but I was thinking more of the city daughters than the fathers, aye?"

"Let's see what we can do" promised Hardraada, "but if there's any of it on offer, I'm telling you – I'm first!"

"Now keep your mind on business, boys–" admonished the Scraeling, thinking *God in heaven, nothing changes, does it? Do these people keep their brains entirely in their breeches? Still – if it helps convince them . . .* "– because we want to leave these people happy, right *leder*?"

"Aye" confirmed Hardraada, "you're right, Scraeling, as usual. We've shown these English who's boss an' they're halfway to welcoming us with open arms. So I'm telling you – if anybody gets welcomed with open legs today, it'll be because she wants it. Or 'he', in Guthrum's case" he added, to more laughter and Guthrum's discomfort. "So get it through to your men, all of you – anyone fucking things up today'll answer to you first and then me."

"That why we're not going in *byrnies*, then?" asked Haakon Ivarsson and Hardraada nodded.

"Aye. Scraeling's idea, to show good faith and how we're all northerners together, not conquerors. I like it, myself."

"Too bloody hot for mail and helmets today anyhow" came Eystein, and Haakon snorted.

"You won't be worrying – looking after the base today'll be all about lying on the riverbank, you lucky bugger" and the day was, in fact, cloudless and warm even in the early morning.

"A rotten job, but someone's got to do it" retorted Eystein. "But since you're my friend, though – you can have anyone in York who might want to do a handsome viking honour. Course, you'll need to tell her about me first, 'cause you don't match that description." Haakon's rejoinder was short, incredibly obscene and drowned in general laughter, for the Norsemen were in the highest of spirits.

Hardraada was to lead the bulk of the army to York to receive the formal surrender of the city, to outline his requirements for food and other provisions and to exchange hostages, all as the Scraeling had negotiated on his visit after Fulford Gate.

"Quicker we get this over with the better" noted Hardraada, "because, day after tomorrow we're moving south. There's a king to kill and a kingdom to win, so make the most of today – but mind you tell your men what I said!"

"Now" continued the Landwaster, "Eystein's staying here, an' he won't be lying on the grass till he's had a report from each ship that seams are tight, rigging's sound and she's ready to take on the food we'll bring back with us today and tomorrow. The Scraeling's overseeing all that, working on the order of sailing and anything else that takes his fancy. Olaf's in charge, of course." And he waved at his younger son, who had hardly been seen on the entire expedition thus far – not that the reason was far to seek, thought the Scraeling, given the presence of his larger-than-life father.

"Questions? All clear? Yes? Right – let's not keep my good subjects waiting.'Specially those who might want to do us honour ..."The Screaling caught Penda's eye where he stood, and knew that his cousin was thinking, wondering and weighing the same thoughts as himself.

The Chronicle.

*W*here was Harold? By my reckoning the Norsemen hit Scarborough on 15 September, ten days before. Penda told me that Scarborough was *some seventy leagues or two hundred English miles from Harold in London. How quickly had the news travelled?*

Quickly enough, more than likely, for Harold had always expected a Norse descent on the North Sea coast of the Danelaw, and if his prudence had not extended to setting up relays of riders to bring him news – and I would have wagered it did – he also had a chain of hilltop beacons.

So – assume that Harold knew of Scarborough the day after it had happened. What then? 'Harold's coming' Penda had said, 'He'll be on the move the instant he has news of Hardraada's landing'.

And that was the 16th, realistically. Mobilising his best troops and swinging them back from their watch on the Channel to London – two or three days, say the 19th or the 20th – the very day of Fulford battle. On remounts already procured and standing by, say four days to cover two hundred miles from London to York. Difficult, not impossible, but leaving soldiers saddlesore and in no condition to fight. Best possible position? Harold could be here, with a tired and sore-arsed army ... well ... that very day.

But in order to do that, I gloomed, still conscious of Penda's gaze on me, the king of England would have to move like lightning and drive his soldiers like a galley-master. More likely that we should look for him in two or three days more, for he would surely need to rest his men. And before then I would be standing out to sea with the fleet while Hardraada's host, rested, fed and "honoured" rolled south in all its awesome power and mailed strength.

I groaned inwardly but managed a smile that didn't, I suspect, fool my cousin for a moment – and if the look on his face meant anything, his calculations were no more cheerful than mine. No – we had done all we could, and my suggestion of the day before to Hardraada that his men go unarmoured to York for the look of the thing and to reinforce my remarks to the city fathers was only a final, desperate refinement that depended upon an English army catching the wolves in the open.

So I clasped my cousin's hand and arm, bowed to Tostig who had come up by then, wished them both a pleasant journey in the sunshine and promised them a welcoming draught or two on their return that evening.

Riccall anchorage, Sunday 25 September 1066, two in the afternoon.

Olaf paused and said, "My father's lucky to have you", and the Scraeling jumped in alarm. Buried in a pile of papers as he was, sitting at a table in the sunshine, he had not been aware of the young prince's presence until he spoke.

"Highness" said the Scraeling in confusion, "my apologies – I didn't hear you approach, I –"

"No" said Olaf, "for you were completely lost in your task. That's what I mean, lord secretary. I've watched you these two or three days past – you're always busy, aren't you? He's lucky to have someone who can deal with so many things, and so well if it comes to that. Your cares are many, and that this fleet has come here as smoothly as it has, says much for you."

"Oh, practice, Highness, practice" said the Scraeling, "I've been with your father now for . . ." but the scream of an ox-horn brought him scrambling awkwardly to his feet even as it brought Eystein to his from where he dozed under a tree, to swing wildly around as he scrutinised the placid Humber anchorage.

"That's the alarm . . . what . . . where . . .?" began the young commander, but the horn sounded again and this time there was a soldier running towards them for all he was worth.

"Lord Eystein" he panted, skidding to a halt and ignoring the prince and the Scraeling both, "three riders coming hard down the York road . . . an' they're ours, too. Going like Thor's hammer, sir. Can you come?"

Eystein broke for the barricade at the road entrance to the anchorage like a hound after a rabbit, with Olaf and the soldier behind him, and the Scraeling turned to put his papers back in a box with a sudden fierce thrill running through him. *If Hardraada hasn't forgotten his favourite comb,* he thought, *something's happened that requires Eystein's reserve,* and the Scraeling had an inkling of what it might be – enough to make his lips move in prayer as he stowed the box and made for the gate at his best scuttle.

The third rider fell off his horse in the gateway as the Scraeling hobbled up, but Eystein and the prince were deep in conversation with the other two. Eystein swung to the Scraeling, his face ashen.

"The army's been caught by the English, Scraeling" he said without preamble. "This man swears he saw the Dragon Banner of Wessex itself, and the king sent three riders to urge us to come at once. He can hold, he says, until we come up."

"Not mailed?" said the Scraeling, "We can't lose time, Eystein!"

"We, not you" said Eystein. "You, man!" he barked, "sound 'Assemble' and keep sounding it until I tell you other! Now –" he said, taking the Scraeling by the arm and leading him aside, "Harald left me here to save the fleet at all costs. It's clear he needs me up with him, so I'm handing on that duty to you. Lord secretary, I charge you with the defence of this anchorage and the fleet with the troops I leave you. I've heard of your cunning and your wisdom ever since I came to serve the king, and I know you'll do all that needs to be done."

"One other thing – the prince Olaf is also your charge, for if evil befalls the king today, Olaf's second in line to his brother on the throne of Norway. Got any questions? No? Good. I'll thank you tonight when we bring the king back." He fetched the Scraeling a buffet on the shoulder that sent him staggering, spun on his heel and bawled for the men tumbling out and up from all directions to get armed and to form in column. For flankers to get to the sides, for scouts to get out in front, and where the fuck were the ponies for the scouts? In twenty minutes the area behind the gate witnessed the formation of a long, coiling double line of Norse warriors, each man armed, armoured and helmed.

"Listen, sons of the raven!" Eystein bellowed, and a hush fell. "The English have caught the king at a bridge up yonder. He c'n defend his position, but you all know your brethren only have personal weapons and a few shields – no mail, no helmets an' fuck-all shields really – so they're going t'be pushed until we get there to make a difference. We're gonna do this at the double time – run a hundred, walk a hundred, run another hundred. You've done it before, but you've never needed to do it as much's you do today. You c'n stop when I do, right? Run till you drop, you bastards – an' if you do drop, roll out of the fucking way! After me!" And that amazing young man turned, slung his shield on his back and set off at a jog-trot to run what the Scraeling later discovered would be eight miles and fight a battle at the end of it.

The gleaming column unwound behind him and passed through the gate like a great glistening snake and when the last man had gone the Scraeling looked about him helplessly. The soldiers left behind were mainly those who had taken wounds at Fulford Gate, but here and there able-bodied men stood among them watching the tail of Eystein's column disappear up the road. The Scraeling gestured to the soldier with the horn. "Sound 'Assemble' lad. Twice." The soldier looked at him, nodded and put the instrument to his lips.

When the last man had shuffled into rank the Scraeling looked over what was only his second command, nodded and raised his voice. "Prince Olaf has commanded me to put this place in a condition fit for its defence" he said. "When I'm done speaking to you, he wants this barrier doubled in height all along its length with timber cut from the woods – there, and over there – and while that's going on he wants tree branches lopped and piled in front of the barrier, thick and deep as you can make it. You four on that end, get up to the top of that high ground and take an hour each looking up the road. Everyone else on the barrier. When that's done, get back to the ships and finish checking seams and rigging. Top up the water and report to me how much food there is on board. And lastly – single up both anchor cables so that one cut's all's needed to get free, then do the same with the reef points on the sail."

He paused and looked hard at them. "The prince doesn't know any more than you about what's going on over yonder, and me neither. But we can't rule out having to move in a hurry later today, maybe with wounded, maybe having to hold that barrier while the wounded're loaded aboard. That's what we're about, so do it properly. Do it all properly. Any more, Highness?" and he turned to Olaf.

"No, lord secretary. Very good, thank you. When you're ready."

The Scraeling turned back to the ranks and dismissed them with a reminder of the need for haste. He and Olaf watched them scatter.

"That was well done, secretary" said the prince. "I had no idea I was such a strategist."

"We all have to learn, Highness." And it was on the tip of the Screaling's tongue to add *and your father should offer you the chance now and again* but he contented himself with "Please feel free to order them as you wish – they'll expect it, and they'd rather see you commanding than wondering. It's good to have something to do at a time like this, so they'll happily do whatever you ask."

The Chronicle.

I fought to hold in my joy, for there was no doubt in my mind that Godwinsson had caught Hardraada unarmoured, partially armed and in the open, and when I thought of what hundreds of hus-carls like Penda would therefore do to the flower of Norway's military I realised that there could be only one ending. In truth the issue was closer than I had thought, largely because of the greater Norse numbers but at the time my only prayers were for the safety of Penda and Tostig, who at least had opted for going armoured and armed "just to remind them who I am" Tostig had noted, to Hardraada's great amusement.

So, we put the anchorage in defensive order, and the task kept the men at work and their bodies and minds occupied until early dusk brought the first survivors stumbling in.

Riccall anchorage, 25–26 September 1066.

The hilltop lookout hailed the encampment "Sir! Men coming down the track. Wounded, by the look."

And indeed they were. Some limped, some were supported by comrades, some staggered, fell and got up to drag themselves another few yards and fell again. It was clear that catastrophe had overtaken the army, and that was borne out by the first words of many men who collapsed at the gateway. "King's dead." "Harald's slain." "Guthrum's gone – saw an axe split him shoulder to hip." "Hundreds – no, thousands – in the fucking river." "Eystein? Too bloody late – gone – arrow got him, same's Harald."

Not a man of them was able-bodied, and the Screaling would discover that this was because the able-bodied had formed themselves into companies that covered the retreat of their hurt fellows, falling back sullenly before the tides of English who pressed them back to the anchorage that we guarded.

It was a token, certainly, but as the Scraeling also discovered that evening, Harold had ordered pursuit but no engagement to save further English casualties in a cause already lost to the viking army.

One of the last in was Styrkar, Hardraada's marshal, who paused in the gateway to spit in the direction of York. "That's it, then. Whole fucking army's gone. Eystein was the last chance to save something – but what'd he do, the little bastard? Flung his men in to get back the king's body. 'S if it mattered, eh? Should have rallied on me – might've fought for a draw then, 'cause we hurt them right enough, we hurt them, aye. Still – gutsy little bugger, give him that. Heart's in the right place – what about his head, though? Eh?" He glanced again at the Scraeling.

"You in charge?" and the Scraeling shook his head mechanically.

"Prince Olaf is. I'm advising him."

"Well, advise him the English're right up our arses an' if I was them I wouldn't miss a chance like this, Scraeling."

The Scraeling glanced around to where Olaf stood, white-faced and swaying, and stepped swiftly to his side. "Highness" he said, and the youth blinked, "with your permission, these men need to get aboard the fleet as soon as possible. The English will be here at any moment, and that barricade needs to be manned."

Olaf blinked again and returned from wherever he was. "Aye, secretary, order it so" he said, and the Scraeling set about ordering the transfer of the wounded from the bank to the vessels of the fleet. "Furthest-out ones first" he ordered the officer he put in charge, "fill 'em up and send a helmsman who knows what he's doing to each one. Move!"

Darkness came but the English did not as the streams of men – pitifully few, though, in comparison with the hosts that had left the anchorage throughout the day – clambered into the boats that took them through the fleet to the outermost vessels and returned for more, and the business was over well before first light.

"Sir!" came the hail from the hilltop in the growing light, and the Scraeling acknowledged. "Rider coming forward, not armed" and the Scraeling went to the gateway to order the logs that blocked it dragged aside.

The horseman drew rein and looked down at the Scraeling. "I seek the secretary, the man known as the Scraeling" he said. "By the look of you, I've found him. Right?"

The Scraeling looked up into a face that was oddly familiar. "Right. And you are?"

"I am Gyrth Godwinsson, brother to Harold. And Tostig. There are things you should know, Scraeling. Will you come with me a short way?"

"I will, brother of Harold and Tostig, and I will come now." He turned to the officer at the gate. "Tell Prince Olaf I am bidden to the English camp" he said, and turned back to the Englishman.

Godwinsson swung down from his pony, took hold of its reins and fell into place at the Scraeling's side as they walked off up the track. "I will not keep you long, secretary" he said, "but Penda suggests that I summon you that we may speak privately."

"Penda?" asked the Scraeling joyfully, "Penda is alive?"

"Oh yes" said Godwinsson, and the Scraeling glanced at him again. "And lord Tostig?"

"Unfortunately not" said Gyrth neutrally. "My brother chose to die on the field. That Harold isn't here instead of me is due to his search for Tostig's body and its preparation."

"I'm sorry" said the Scraeling. "I hold your brothers in high regard as brave and good men."

"And you could say that's why we're talking now" said Gyrth. "At Penda's suggestion, I'm asking – how d'you want to be treated when we take possession of your base back there? Are you still Hardraada's right-hand man, or d'you want us to acknowledge how much we owe you, lord Ranulf?"

The use of his name brought the Scraeling's head up and he blinked. "Ah – ah, no" he said. "been thinking a little about that, and I'm not through it yet. Not quite. But at least for now – I'm Hardraada's secretary, and adviser to his son, Prince Olaf. That all right?"

"Perfectly" said the young Godwinsson as they rounded a bend in the road that shielded them from the hilltop overlooking the anchorage. "Harold'll want to know, and we'll tell him that when he arrives later. Now – you two know each other?"

The road before him and the meadows on each side of it was one big English encampment, and standing before all of them was the massive figure of Penda, a bloody cloth round his head and strain lines etched in his face. But they vanished in a huge smile as he stepped forward to engulf his cousin.

Riccall anchorage, 26 September 1066.

The king of England looked at what many of his predecessors had considered the worst sight they could envisage – hundreds of longships anchored in an English estuary. "How many did you lose?" he asked, and the Scraeling cleared his throat.

"Well, we've filled thirty *drakkars*" he answered, "and there might be another four or so to go, depending on what prisoners you've got, majesty. And we brought three hundred ships."

"Prisoners?" echoed Harold, "We haven't taken any. Partly because they wouldn't surrender, partly because I'm off back to the south coast, and what'd I do with prisoners? It's a bloody old business is war, I tell you lord Ranulf – prisoners? I couldn't even take my own brother prisoner!" The Scraeling bowed his head at the bitterness in the king's voice.

"My sympathy, majesty. Earl Tostig was a brave man and he played a brave man's part in this matter."

"Thank you, Ranulf. Come to the tent – we need to talk." He turned and led the small party consisting of Gyrth, Penda and the Scraeling to the large leather tent that had been set up inside the enclosure.

When they were seated inside and servants had put food and drink before them, Harold turned to Gyrth. "Olaf and the senior commanders – under guard?"

"On that longship yonder" said his brother, nodding to the nearest large *drakkar*. "Want them?"

"Soon. But I need to hear of this from every side. I've no idea, for example, of what Hardraada was doing wandering around enemy territory on a fine day in his bloody shirt. I think we need to tell our stories. Shall I start?"

What he said confirmed the Scraeling's thinking in the matter of when Harold had set out from London. "Hard miles all right" said the king, his eyes far away, "and many of them. But we needed to get here quickly to confine the damage to where it didn't matter, see? Fifty miles a day, dragging in whoever we could, whatever mounts we could find."

The English army, five thousand strong, had reached Tadcaster, just outside York, at dusk of the 24th and, realising that the speed of his advance had taken Northumbrians and Norsemen alike by surprise, Harold had sealed the area tight before advancing to York in the pre-dawn darkness of the next day and learning what that day would hold.

"Once I'd reminded them of who I was and who they were" he said, "they came to their senses and told me all I needed to know. After that it was a matter of deciding whether Hardraada or the fleet should be the target. I chose Hardraada, and he walked into it. Yes, he did. Penda? Your story?"

"We left here" said Penda, "in fine spirits. Or the Norsemen did – Tostig and I were wondering where you were, majesty, and by the look on his face I'm sure Ranulf was too. We got eight miles up the road to Stamford Bridge and about quarter of us were across it and on the other side when we saw your dust-cloud and the light coming off the spearpoints. Hardraada said, 'Now why's Olaf sent Eystein and the reserve up to us?' He'd no idea you and the army were close – that's worth thinking about, majesty, because any who wanted to could've warned him about you, easily."

Harold grunted, and Penda continued. "Then someone caught sight of the Dragon Banner, and that got things moving. Hardraada sent riders back here to Eystein, and called the army back across the bridge to hold the hillock on the other side. That's when the Icelander stepped up and offered to hold the bridge."

"The Icelander?" frowned the Scraeling, "not the big one? Fynn the Tall?"

"That his name? That's the one" said Penda. "He's – was – a berserker too. You saw him" he said, turning to the Godwinssons – "only a couple of inches short of seven feet tall. Bloody huge, with an axe to match. Anyway, Ranulf, he started stamping, howling, tearing off his clothes till all he had on was a helmet and his boots. And in between times splitting heads like firewood, helmed or not – no-one could get past that axe with a reach like his. He killed thirty, maybe more, singly or two at a time, didn't matter. And he gave Hardraada time to form his shield-burg on the hillock."

"Didn't anyone think of arrows?" asked the Scraeling and Harold stirred in his chair.

"Didn't seem right" he said. "We offered him his life for his bravery."

"And?" prompted the Scraeling, looking at Penda.

"Told them to fuck off. Yelled there wasn't a man among the English fit to go near him. Grabbed his cock and waved it at them, laughing. Then he split some more heads. In the end, someone found a boat on the riverbank, a couple of spearmen got in it and floated down to beneath the bridge. Waited their moment, and one time when he stepped back – ppssstttt, up between the planks, right in the crutch and down he went."

"Wasn't very happy about that" said Harold, stirring again. "But it had to be done I suppose."

"Getting on for mid-afternoon then" said Penda, "by the time you got across, and remember no-one knew how long Eystein would be. So you waded in right away, and it wasn't long before the lack of armour began to tell. The shield-burg lasted about ten minutes before the weight told, then it fell apart. Tostig and I looked at each other – we were together under his banner with the Flemish mercenaries around us – and both of us saw what happened next." He paused, and his eyes were fixed on a river-meadow eight miles away.

"Go on" prompted the Scraeling gently, and Penda came back to himself.

"Hardraada lost his temper" he said. "Rushed forward out of the shield-burg screaming something about betrayal, and cowards and treachery – I'm not sure about much of it, 'cause a battlefield's not a good place for a chat – but he was really laying about him and raving about a warrior's death, and men were going down before him. Then he staggered, stepped forward again then dropped The Nibbler and sank slowly to his knees. When he fell over, I saw the arrow standing out of his throat. But he didn't die at once. The group that rushed to him included one of your scribes, Ranulf."

"That's right – Ulfvar. Lad from Stiklestad way. And?"

"Saw him writing something while Hardraada's bodyguard stood over him. Thought it was his will, but it wasn't." Penda paused, then said, "It was a bloody saga. Man's dying, and he dictates poetry." He shrugged his big shoulders. "No idea what it was about, of course – can't do that on a battlefield. Anyway, that's when it happened."

"What happened?"

"Tostig. Y'see, with Hardraada gone, he was in command. Lord Tostig could've surrendered, or made terms. But you know what he did? He turned to me, grabbed his personal banner and thrust it into my hand. Then he said . . . he said, 'Earl Penda Raedwaldsson, you will not move from the spot where you stand, and you will give up this banner to none until it is wrenched from you. This is my command as your lord, and by your oath to me I enjoin you to heed my word.' That's what Tostig said, and I'll never forget it." And as he spoke the words, his eyes filled and the tears slid down his cheeks. Angrily he dashed them away with the back of a huge hand while the king filled a cup with his own hand and passed it to him.

"Then" resumed Penda, "Tostig jumped forward to where the shield-wall had been, snatched up Landwaster and bawled for the shield-burg to re-form around it. 'To me, sons of the north! No surrender!' he yelled. 'Eystein's on his way! Hold, you droppings of the raven, hold! Strike! Smite! Slay!' And I stood there in the middle of his Flemings, as much use as a nun in a knocking-shop, and I'd likely be there yet but Gyrth's picked *hus-carls* came crashing through, aiming for Tostig's banner and us."

"I beat off one go at my head, but someone else took me from the side; I recall going down under a great weight, and then it all went black. When I woke up I was looking at Gyrth here while my neighbour at Reading – remember Aelle, him with the six daughters? – while he poured water over my head and down my throat. Seems one of the *carls* who flattened me landed on my head after the first one knocked off my helmet" and he touched the cloth around his head.

"Anyway, we were in a bit of a backwater 'cause the battle had moved on a couple of hundred yards and the Norsemen were being driven into the Derwent. But they wouldn't surrender, and I couldn't see Tostig anywhere. I called to Gyrth – least, I tried, but nothing came out my mouth – but Aelle got him and he came over. Told me Tostig was dead – he'd seen him go down." The tears were back, but he made no effort to wipe them away.

"But why? How? You and Tostig were marked men. You were—" The Scraeling stopped as he realised what had happened. "But Tostig wasn't under his banner, was he?" he said slowly. "He was holding Landwaster. Yes."

"And rallying the Norsemen" put in Gyrth. "Don't forget that. And in the heat of battle, when a Norse *byrnie* looks just like a Saxon mail coat—?"

"But why?" asked the Scraeling again. "Why didn't he stick to the plan?"

"You know the answer to that better than any man alive" said Harold, rising and coming to lay a hand on the Scraeling's shoulder. And at his blank look the king of England asked gently, "Tell me again why you didn't slit Hardraada's throat on any of the dark nights of the last thirty years, Ranulf?"

"Hardraada? Eh? What ... ah, killing Hardraada wouldn't have changed anything, sire. Someone else – Ulf, Haldor, Skallagrim – any of a score of others, would've taken his place. And they're as bad, or maybe even worse, 'cause Hardraada did his best to out-viking any of the ones they sing the sagas about. You know – I told you – his world had to die with him, or there wouldn't be ... oh. Oh."

Harold squeezed his shoulder gently. "Tostig knew that, my friend. With Hardraada gone, another would take his place – if the viking world lived beyond today. And if it did live beyond today, it would return tomorrow. Or next year. Or the year after. How many more Ionas? How many more Les Trois Étoiles? How many more Fulfords? Most of all, Ranulf – how many more Clothildes?"

"Tostig wouldn't surrender" said the Screeling, "because he saw that you'd be forced to let them go home – beaten, but not destroyed – because you've got business on the south coast. And that the Eysteins, the Haakons, the Styrkars and the Guthrums would prevail on Magnus to lead them back again. Or they'd depose him and choose another from among themselves."

"That's why" said Gyrth, "I told you my brother had chosen to die on the field. You recall?"

"Aye" said the Screeling. "I do recall how you put it. What a ... a kingly man. How he served England!"

"And that's the curse of it" said Harold. "England knows Tostig Godwinsson as a tyrant driven out by his people and who turned renegade against his own brother and his own country in leading the Landwaster here." He sounded old and tired, but then he lifted his head.

"But mark this, all of you. I stood over Tostig's body today and swore to him that word of what he had done and of how he died would go from my court to all the corners of this land. At Christmas of this year, my great church at Waltham Holy Cross will be dedicated, first to the glory of God and then to Tostig Godwinsson. And this I swear to you and before you, as I have sworn it to him."

"Amen" said the Screeling, and crossed himself while the others echoed the blessing.

"Now" said Harold, "Your story, Lord Ranulf, if you please." And the Scraeling recounted what had passed at the anchorage, ending, "A much poorer tale than either yours of your march, or Penda's of lord Tostig's great courage, sire." But Harold shook his blond head decisively.

"Not so, Ranulf, not so. Yesterday's battle turned on one thing and one thing alone – that Hardraada's warriors were not mailed as they might have been. Only that enabled us to overcome their numbers, and but for your advice to Hardraada, he would now be sitting here with the road to London empty before him instead of lying stark under the skies. It's another of the many ways you've served us over the years, and I want to know how England might reward you."

"Lord Ranulf, there's a place among my advisers for you. That place is at the head of them, as my Chancellor. Will you serve me, advise me, smooth my path for me? And for England?"

"Sire, nothing would please me more, and I'll gladly do that. But in a different manner. We spoke, just now, of the end of the viking world. Each of us, for his own reasons, brought that about yesterday. But, lord king, when a building is torn down it's as well to build another in its place, is it not, even if only to prevent weeds from growing there?" Harold's brow furrowed, and the Scraeling hastened on.

"Norway has a new king, a good and honest young man who, like his brother presently awaiting us over yonder, has played no part in a land governed by *hard-raede*. Yes, I sought the end of all his father stood for but I also fear his mother and her influence upon that young man. Majesty, good is more than the absence of evil. Good is itself a way of life and it must be taught, guided, fostered – as much as any child needs these things, for without such care only weeds and evil grow." The Scraeling paused and took a deep breath.

"Lord king, all I want is to return to Norway, to serve a new king and make a new beginning. In doing that I can serve England's interests by turning *drakkars* into trading ships and pirates into merchants. No longships will prowl your coasts by day, and those who live close by them will sleep soundly of nights. And if England must strive against Normandy – and I pray that it doesn't – I can ensure that your northern flank is forever secure. Do you approve, majesty?"

Harold of England stood and offered hand and arm to the Scraeling, who took them silently.

"Gyrth, let's have the Norsemen in now" he said, "and this is what'll happen. I'm going to tell them that I was minded to blind all of them for their ruin of our land, but that Lord Ranulf – never 'The Scraeling' again, not in my presence nor anywhere else in England – has convinced me of the need for new kings to be merciful as well as strong, and so to show my goodwill for the new king of Norway I'm going to return his brother and his retainers. Without taking hostages, by the way. And I'm going to add my own *hard-raede* that Lord Ranulf is well worth listening to, because England has every confidence and faith in him, and will deal with and through him evermore. How's that? Lord Ranulf?"

"Much more than I deserve, majesty" returned the Scraeling.

"You think so? I don't. In fact, I'm going to suggest what I suggested at our first meeting, Ranulf. What I said then was, 'Let's raise a cup to Penda's cousin and our new friendship.' Once more, I think!" Cups were raised and drained, then the king of England spoke again.

"Right, Gyrth, let's get this over with. We've got a coast to guard, and it's a long way off."

The Chronicle.

*A*nd so I led Hardraada's fleet home, or rather Olaf did. But I used the voyage to Orkney to speak to him at length of what his place in the new Norway might be, and of how he could help his brother with the burden of kingship. Perhaps it was as well that I did, for all the world knows that the ever-sickly Magnus reigned a bare two years before the crown of Norway passed to the youth who voyaged homeward with me. Olaf ruled for quarter of a century as Olaf the Peaceful, giving his country the longest period of peace and prosperity it had ever known, and I'm vain enough to believe that I played some part in that, even as I'd promised Harold Godwinsson.

But that was all in the future as we watched Orkney take shape out of a weeping Scottish morning. Then, I knew only that I was returning to the place I thought of as home – and that she who waited for me in Orkney was she who made it so.

Penda had reminded me, at our parting on the shores of the Humber estuary, of why a man who had taken the heaviest of blows to the head in one battle was *now about to push his body through a punishing ride perhaps to take part in another. When I chided him over his intentions he smiled and reminded me that the task to which he had set his hand was only half-done, but that when the gales of autumn closed the Channel for that year he would consider it fully done. Aye, I thought, I was sailing away from a land still under siege, but I could do no other for the sake of my own new task. Having torn down Hardraada's world I was obliged to put another in its place, and I could not allow a gap to occur between intent and execution, for fear of who or what might fill it.*

I'd been cheated, I mused, of seeing Hardraada's death in the end – but then I hadn't seen Clothilde's death either. Nonetheless, I had brought about his downfall and in that I'd had my reward. Was it enough? Penda fought for a real world, a world that held Gytha, Osmund and his other children; whereas my fight was for a world that might be.

But no, I told myself, my fight was for a world that needed to be, though it would contain no children of my own. I would face that as I counted the blessings I yet possessed in my wondrous Elisabeth. And then I would put it from me in a moment, I told myself, when I had finished thinking of the love for a father I'd seen so often in Osmund's face when he and Penda were together. And I would share it with them when the Bastard of Normandy had been thwarted and Elisabeth and I might journey to Reading, whenever it might be. No – the Norns of Hardraada's world had not spun children into my wyrd, but in many ways I was none the—

"We left in power and might, but come home in sorrow, lord Ranulf." Olaf's voice broke in upon me, and I smiled.

"Highness, that might almost be the first line of a saga" I replied, and he turned to me.

"You think so? My father loved the sagas. You think he might have written such a one?" And I thought again.

"No, Highness. Not he. Not Harald, son of Sigurd, the Landwaster."

***

Epilogue

Constantinople, Easter 1067.

The slightly-built woman, reached up to embrace her son. "Michael, my darling, you made me as proud as any mother can be today" she smiled at him.

"Mother, mother, you must be used to these occasions – you're an empress" he teased her. "Not the first coronation you've attended. What about yours and Constantine's?"

"It wasn't the same" she replied, smoothing a lock of curly dark hair back from his forehead and smiling up at him. "Anyway – I was your mother before I was an empress and I was proud of you then, too. It's silly, I know, but I wish Constantine could have been there today to see you, so grown-up and so confident when you spoke the oaths to the Patriarch. He was always proud of you too in every way, even though he wasn't—" She broke off as the door flew open and a girl tumbled through it, skidded to a halt and drew herself up to her full height before walking gracefully across the room on coltish legs and curtseying to the young man.

"Your majesty" she said, her head down in the depths of the curtsey, "may you live forever and rule us wisely in that time" and she straightened to smile up at him.

"Thank you Zoe-Zobabs, little sister" he smiled back at her, "I've never seen my bratling sister curtsey before – in fact I've hardly seen her wear a dress before! – and I'm more honoured by these things than anything else that happened today!"

"Well, you've never been an emperor before" Zoe replied with all the crushing certainty of a ten-year-old princess, "so there" and she rather spoiled the moment by sticking out her tongue to clinch the last word.

"Oh Zoe!" said her mother, collapsing into laughter, "you've worked so hard on that curtsey this week – now you've spoiled it!"

"No, she hasn't" said Michael, scooping her up in his arms to plant one kiss after another on her head and face as she squirmed and squealed, "In a world – where a man can – wake up a citizen – and go to bed an emperor – it's good to know that Zoe – will be Zoe-Zobabs forever! Getting tall though" he added as she struggled free and tried to stamp on his foot, "look at the length of those legs! Ow! All right, I give up!! Peace!"

"She gets those from Constantine" said his mother, looking fondly on at the love between her first-born and her youngest, "certainly not from me!"

"Ah, never mind, my little mother – you're just proof of the saying that wonderful things come in small portions" he said, enfolding her with his other arm as she snuggled into him.

"Tell me, mother" he said, as he stood with his women in his arms and his chin resting on his mother's head. "I'm not tall. Not for a grown man. But you're tiny. Do I take after my father, or you?"

"Oh, after him, I'd say" she said, looking up at him. "Yes. Oh yes. You're very like him to look at – same eyes, same hair, same ears and you've got his nose. You've got his nature, too. And best of all, you've got two sound legs, my love."

"Hey?" he asked, and frowned down at her. "Doesn't everyone?"

"No, darling. Your father didn't. Well, he was born with two sound legs, but – excuse me a moment." She freed herself and went to her bedchamber, where she took a leather-bound book from a chest and returned to the pair in the other room.

"Here you are" she said, offering her son the book. "It's a new beginning for you today, my darling. Today you became Emperor Michael VII of Constantinople, and it's probably as good a day as any to read about your father. In his own words, my son."

The new emperor smiled at the love in his mother's black eyes, kissed her forehead and turned away to the light, his sister moving to the couch with him and sniffing the soft leather of the book's binding as children will. Placing the book on the table, the two of them opened it and began to read the first page while their mother glanced at them once more, smiled her secret smile and quietly left the room.

'If it is true,' Michael read to his sister, 'that what we survive makes us *strong in the same manner as repeated heating and hammering tempers a blade, then adversity is to be welcomed and I must include within these pages my belief that I have known more of it than many others. Am I, then, stronger than others? I write these words in order to discover whether a case can be made for that.*

I have been 'the Scraeling' among my companions these many years, although I was christened Ranulf Denis Chrétien Nominoe de Lannion, first son of Ranulf, Sieur de St-Brieuc in that part of France that men call Little Britain and descendant, through my mother, of its ancient kings. . . . . . '

***

House of Sigurd; Norway

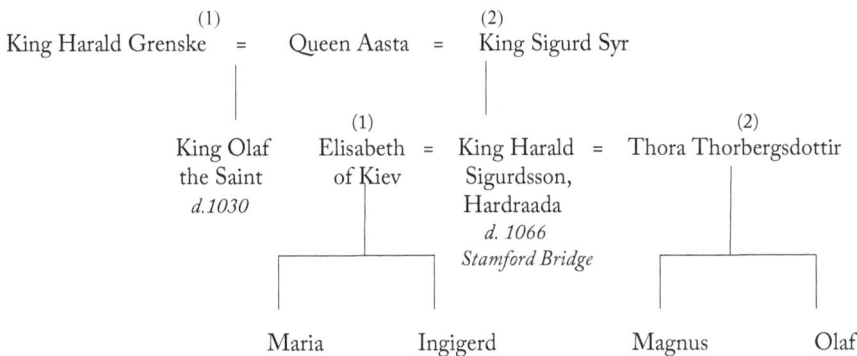

```
                    (1)                        (2)
King Harald Grenske  =   Queen Aasta   =   King Sigurd Syr

                         (1)
        King Olaf    Elisabeth  =  King Harald  =  Thora Thorbergsdottir
        the Saint    of Kiev       Sigurdsson,
        d.1030                     Hardraada
                                   d. 1066
                                   Stamford Bridge

             Maria        Ingigerd       Magnus        Olaf
```

House of Godwin; England

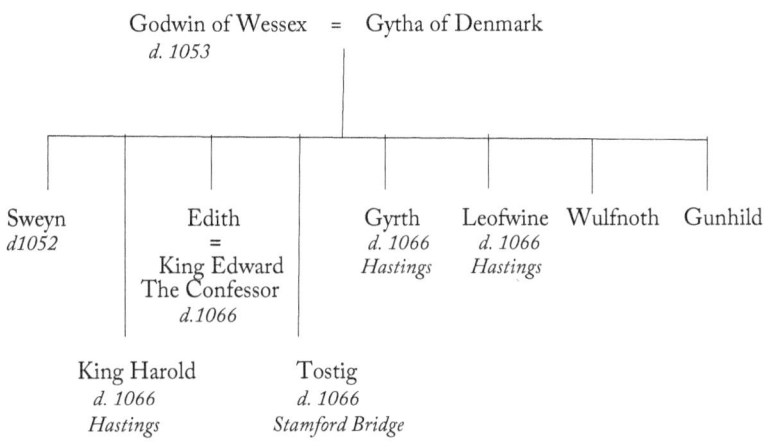

```
        Godwin of Wessex  =  Gytha of Denmark
        d. 1053

Sweyn        Edith         Gyrth    Leofwine  Wulfnoth  Gunhild
d1052          =           d. 1066  d. 1066
           King Edward     Hastings Hastings
           The Confessor
           d.1066

     King Harold       Tostig
     d. 1066           d. 1066
     Hastings          Stamford Bridge
```

Author's Notes

1. Harald Sigurdsson, 'Hard-raede'

His is the story of a Viking adventurer who rose, a penniless refugee from the wreckage of his half-brother's reign, to become arguably the finest soldier of his time. As mercenary, commander and king, Harald Hardraada was a brutal exponent of *realpolitik* who lived in an age when brutality was not only characteristic of a ruler, but expected also. Widely celebrated as "the last Viking" he is also properly seen as a man born too late for the kind of life he wished to lead. Where Harold Godwinsson and William of Normandy, his great contemporaries, took some care to maintain good relations with Church and Pope, Hardraada cheerfully insisted upon having the last word in all matters, religious as well as civil, within his realm. One of the reasons for this attitude was that, philosophically, Hardraada was an out-and-out pagan whose Christianity was no more than a front that enabled him to marry a prince's daughter as a benchmark of his success and to succeed to a saintly brother's throne.

But fresh and constant challenge was irresistible to Hardraada, for as Zoe noted, the game was everything to him. His journey along the well-trodden path of the Viking trader to the lands of the Rus was a venture that he quickly abandoned in favour of a much bloodier one. His rise to greatness in the armies of the Eastern Empire took a mere eight years and left him still a young man with worlds to conquer, and the return to Norway marked the beginning of the challenge to become the pre-eminent sovereign of the North. And when the Landwaster had reduced the *jarls* of Norway to submission and Denmark, at last, to co-existence, he turned – as so many prominent men do – to consideration of what his enduring place in history would be.

For this restless, ambitious, ruthless, unprincipled and by then fifty-one-year-old adventurer, the morass surrounding the English succession was a game fit for a viking bent on either success or an honoured seat in Valhalla; probably the last adventure of his life, and one that he lost only at the last throw of the dice.

Essentially, the Hardraada of my story was a completely self-centred and ruthless man who was born two centuries too late; who achieved great things in life nevertheless, and whom, one suspects, left it laughing.

'Landwaster' is not a sympathetic nor flattering portrait of one of the greatest men of an age rich in great men, because in anyone's estimate his bad deeds outnumbered his good. In fact, it's difficult to think of anything Hardraada did that wasn't motivated by self-interest or avarice, but no such subjectivity can, or should, obscure the fact that Harald Hardraada, the Landwaster, blazed across the eleventh century as spectacularly as did Halley's Comet in the last year of his life.

2. Other Characters

This story has its origins in the stories of the people who appear in it, for most of the characters of 'Landwaster' are real.

Hardraada, of course, Yaroslav the Wise, his wife Ingigerd and their daughter Elisabeth who did, in fact, marry the Landwaster; Empress Zoe and her sister Theodora; Emperors Romanos, Michael IV the Paphlagonian, Michael V Calaphates and Constantine X Doukas; John Orphanotrophos the Eunuch; Isaac Comnenos; Harold and Tostig Godwinsson, Eystein Orri, who arrived at Stamford Bridge too late to save his king but in time to die with him – are all historical characters and their attitudes, concerns and viewpoints mirror reality as my researches reveal it to have been.

Even Ulf Ospaksson and Haldor Snorreson, Hardraada's lieutenants, actually lived, and it was one of Haldor's descendants who wrote 'The Heimskringla', verses from which open each book of Hardraada's story.

My reason for using real people is that history is frequently more real and often vastly more entertaining than fiction, because history is about people and their reaction to events, and people's motivations tend not to change over time whatever else does.

I may, however, have taken liberties with earl Tostig Godwinsson's motivation for allying himself with Hardraada. Old Godwin's third son was a hard-fighting, upright and loyal servant of the English crown through two reigns and was much favoured by Edward 'the Confessor'; to the point, some historians suggest, where he was not only the sole Godwinsson for whom Edward had any time at all, but was the king's unofficial choice to succeed him. Whatever the truth of that, there is little doubt that Edward's reluctant acquiescence in Tostig's banishment sorely taxed the remaining energies of a king who by then had precious little left.

So how does one explain Tostig's incredible fall? What I've presented as the Screaling's 'Tostig Deception' probably never happened, but I'm unrepentant because I struggle to accept what historians of the period tell us – that this capable, faithful, and honest servant of king and country, a highly-principled and very moral man, in a blinding fit of pique tossed it all in and betrayed the brother he loved and whom he had served loyally as a comrade-in-arms.

What do you think?

And finally, the tantalising thought remains – how do we know that it *didn't* happen as the Screaling tells it, given that Harold Godwinsson and Saxon England perished only three weeks after Hardraada, leaving events of the year 1066 to be written by Norman propagandists such as William of Poitiers, all of them determined to present William of Normandy as God's avenging arm?

What's more fun than History? Only, perhaps, History's 'what ifs'...

3. So what's he about?

Writing historical fiction offers lifelong teacher MJ Burr the chance to indulge his deepest passions – the study and story of ordinary people in sometimes extraordinary situations.

"The people whom Kipling wrote of as 'Captains and Kings' may create the extraordinary situations," he says, "but they're stage dressing. Joe and Jane Ordinary provide the legends and the fascination in how they react and adapt to those situations. We need to remember that, because you can train a parrot to recite the regnal dates of kings and queens. That's not what history's about, but it is why dozens of people have told me that school put them right off History. It's my aim to offer a counterbalancing view, namely that History-as-story can be as entertaining as it's informative."

That view is dependent upon thorough research, a scrupulous regard for the historical record and the practice of keeping an eye on the realities of how ordinary people ordinarily behave.

Michael Burr
Oakura
Taranaki
New Zealand.

Glossary

althing	(N)	a Scandinavian parliament or legislative assembly
byrnie	(N)	a mail coat extending to the hips
cataphract	(G)	heavily armoured Byzantine cavalryman
centarch	(L)	leader of ten Byzantine soldiers
destrier	(F)	heavy European warhorse
drakkar	(N)	Viking dragonship
dromon	(G)	cargo ship
earldorman	(OE)	royal official
fyrd	(OE)	militia soldiers
hagle forfekte	(N)	all's in order
hauberk	(F)	mailed coat reaching to the calf, slit to enable wearer to ride astride.
hetaireiarchos	(G)	Byzantine rank approximate to colonel
holmgang	(N)	duel
hus-carl	(OE	professional soldier and personal retainer of a Saxon magnate
jarl	(N)	earl
krøpling	(N)	cripple
leder	(N)	leader
manglavites	(G)	Byzantine title of nobility
nithing	(N)	low and contemptible fellow
Norns	(N)	those who spun the wyrd (below)
pallium	(L)	Roman Catholic vestment, denoting bishop's rank
pentarch	(L)	leader of five Byzantine soldiers
qarib	(A)	fast-sailing, lateen-rigged small ship of shallow draught
scraeling	(N)	native
skald	(N)	minstrel
spatha	(L)	Roman-type cavalry sabre
thrall	(N)	slave
valkyrie	(N)	maiden who carried the souls of heroes from battlefield

varanger	(G)	foreigner OR 'those sworn'; mercenary in Byzantine service
Varanger Guard	(G)	élite corps of axe-bearing Scandinavians (initially) directly retained by the Emperor of Constantinople
vess-heil	(N)	all hail; (OE) wassail
wyrd	(N)	the destinies of all mankind, spun and woven by the Norns

Arabic; (F) French; (G) Greek; (L) Latin; (N) Norse; (OE) Old English

Chronicles of The Scraeling

The Landwaster

Russia, the Eastern Empire, Norway and England 1031–1066.

The Scraeling

Norway and England, 1066–1072.

The Varanger

The Eastern Empire, 1072–1075.

The Scraeling

Welcome to the world of The Scraeling . . .

'The Landwaster' is the first of these three books about the eleventh century as Ranulf de Lannion, The Scraeling, viewed it. The second book, 'The Scraeling', opens on the morning after King Harold Godwinsson lost the battle of Hastings, just three weeks after he'd beaten Hardraada at Stamford Bridge.

The story moves between the Conqueror's struggles to consolidate his rule over post-Conquest England and a Norway where the Scraeling, now first minister to Hardraada's son and successor, Magnus, is happily looking forward to becoming husband to Elisabeth of Kiev while he steers Norway down the path of peace and co-operation with the other North European nations.

None of this happens and, his dreams dashed by political expediency, a heartbroken Scraeling journeys to England to pick up the pieces of a previous life. Here, he finds a relative widowed at Hastings discovering her own suffering through political expediency in being married off to one of William's divisional commanders – the Conqueror's settlement policy in action. This brings him into contact with the Norman army of occupation in general and the Fenland Rebellion of Hereward the Wake in particular.

Again, most of the characters in 'The Scraeling' – Magnus, Olaf, Morcar, Hereward, all the Norman commanders including Giffard and the Conqueror himself of course – actually lived, and behaved pretty much as the story suggests because Truth often beggars fiction. And the Conqueror's assimilation policy did actually work as the story has it. To that end the people in it, and two very strong women in particular, assume pride of place over great events.

Thank you for reading 'The Landwaster'. If you enjoyed it, you may find this excerpt from 'The Scraeling' of interest…

Senlac Ridge, Hastings, East Sussex, 15 October 1066.

Minstrels and poets might write of the thin drizzle of an October dawn being tears for yesterday's fallen, thought the young warrior as he picked his way among the mounds and heaps of the slain. As far as he was concerned, though, the film of rain was nothing but a nuisance – just another cross to bear on top of the stench of his days-old and soiled underclothes and the weariness that consumed him, flesh, bone and soul, after the short and fitful night's sleep in his *hauberk* at the edge of the Senlac battlefield.

"Jesu!" came a voice from his right, "I'd give half the land the duke's offering for a couple of day's sleep. 'Slong's I can have it now."

The first warrior tried to spit from a mouth that was still dry from his awakening. "You've got to be alive to be tired, Odo" he said, "so look happy. None of these buggers do" and he fumbled at his belt for a water-jack. What a dreadful place a battlefield was the day after, he decided as he swirled the tepid water round inside his mouth before swallowing gratefully. Yesterday had been noise and fury, charge and retire, hack and slash, thrust and parry amid the screams of stricken men and gutted horses from early morning until the twilight, but at least there had been movement, purpose, life and comradeship among the men who had assaulted the ridge and those who awaited them at its summit. Most of all there had been blood hot with the determination to do it to the enemy before he did it to you, but now there was nothing.

And nothing disturbed the early morning where a near-vanquished army lay abed, mortally weary and licking wounds that had nearly proved fatal, and nothing disturbed the heaps of the slain where another army slept its last sleep in ruin and death. Across the field the only things moving were the half-dozen in helmet and *hauberk* stumbling out to search among the slain for the body of a king. "Find me Harold" had been the duke's command, "and mark the spot, for I will raise an abbey on it in thanksgiving."

"Shouldn't be so difficult, Leo. We all saw the Fighting Man banner yesterday. Some of us saw too bloody much of it" Odo's voice broke in, and the warrior fought back the waves of tiredness to answer him.

"Won't help, Odo" he said, "Ponthieu brought that in last night as a gift for the duke."

"Didn't help him explain why he cut into a dying man's crotch though. William's expelled him from the army. Fucking silly 'f you ask me. A dead Saxon's a good Saxon, an' the duke was glad enough t' send Ponthieu in after Harold in the first place rather than go himself, eh?"

"Jesu!" exclaimed Leo, darting a glance all around. "That mouth of yours Odo! Shut it, would you? No, no, I don't want to talk about it – just shut it! It's dangerous!" And he moved away as swiftly as his aching legs would allow, uphill to the ridge that ran across the top of the field; the ridge that had been held to the last the day before and the one along which he had himself ridden in charge after charge once his *destrier* had scrabbled its way to a toehold on the flat ground.

Here the dead lay in even thicker heaps, Saxon *hus-carl* and Norman knight indistinguishable in their helmets and *hauberks*, and he paused a moment while the roar of battle filled his head as it had filled his world the day before in this very place. Then his world had been the reach of the lance from his *destrier*'s broad back until the sweep of an axe had lopped its darting head from the shaft so that he smashed the ash staff down upon a snarling face and reached . . .

There – yes, there. Further along the ridge than he had remembered. Had his *hus-carls* been trying to get him from the field? No matter. It was Harold all right – or all that was left of him, and Leo shook his head as he looked at the remains – mere meat, hacked worse than anything he had seen in the shambles stalls of Rouen. The headless torso gaped open in a tremendous chest wound and the slit in the *hauberk* that allowed a mailed man to mount a horse was lost in the welter of black and dried blood that had burst from the groin after the passage through cloth, flesh and muscle of the sword hard-swung from the high Norman saddle. *You wouldn't butcher a pig that way*, thought Leo, feeling his own groin contract involuntarily.

He shook his head again and reached for the water-jack to wet his lips before he took the horn from his sword-belt to send a note pealing through the drizzle. The searchers made their way to the horn as quickly as their own stiffness allowed and stood a moment silently looking down before Leo's gruff suggestion that they get on with it brought the offer of the only cloak they had between them.

What was left of the last Saxon king of England was hefted onto the cloak, and as it was swung clear of the surrounding carnage one of the searchers whistled. "Look at him" he commented, nodding sideways. "Care to face that?"

'That' was a huge *hus-carl*, well over six feet in height and lying five yards from his king with a dead hand still fast around the haft of a four-foot double-headed axe. His face was clotted with his own blood, and a shaft standing from the right eye-socket revealed how he had died.

"I did" said Leo into the silence. "His name's – his name was – Penda. That blood on his leggings isn't his, either. When he took the head off my lance, he'd turned from over there – aye, that pile of our dead's due to him – to face me. He must've been wading in blood. No jest. Wading in it."

"Shit!" said Odo. "Some axeman, to take the head off a lance. You're a lucky man to be standing here then. How'd you manage it?"

"I hit him with the stump" said Leo, his eyes far away, "and threw his aim off. Still, the blow he struck took my horse's leg off – clean as a whistle, right through the shoulder – and it screamed, threw me and bolted somewhere on three legs. All the while he was bellowing his name to rally his own kind, and all I could hear as I hit the ground, trying to get my sword out, was 'Penda! Penda! Penda!'" He shuddered at the memory.

"Thought I was done, and no error" he said. "When I stopped rolling – no shield, no sword, no helmet, no breath after I hit the ground – I saw him against the sky. And – believe this or not; I don't care – he held his hand, waiting for me to get up. Aye, he did."

One of his companions whistled. "Jesu – what then?"

"Then" said Leo slowly, "I got to my feet, clawing for my blade. Scared shitless too, and I don't mind who knows it. He was like a mountain standing there – a mountain who'd just cut the leg off a warhorse and made it look easy. He whirled up that axe, and took a step towards me, and . . . and I pissed myself. I'm not joking."

"But then his head snapped back and he screamed. And I saw why. The arrow was sticking out of his eye and he was swaying there like a tree in a gale, one hand to his face but the other still round that fucking axe. Then something hit me from behind and I fell over again. I think it was one of Count Eustace's four, 'cause then they were past us and into the group round Harold. I must've bounced off someone's leg, or his shield or . . . something. I don't know."

"So, you saw Harold go down?" asked one of the group and Leo shook his head, his exhaustion coming in waves.

"Not really – couldn't tell one from another, and every fucking bell in the world was ringing inside my head by then. But I remember being glad I didn't have to face that monster. All I could think of last night, and what kept me from sleeping was, if he hadn't stopped; if he'd stepped forward to take me on the ground – Christ Jesus, I would have and no mistake – if he'd taken me on the ground, the arrow would've missed. And he'd be alive and I wouldn't. Aye, Penda. *Vale*, my friend."

He shook himself and stooped to the corner of the cloak. "Now come on. Let's go and see if new kings are more generous than old dukes used to be. Eh?"

The royal Court of Norway, Nidaros, January 1067.

"It's important to begin as you mean to go on, majesty' said the Scraeling doggedly. "Look – please excuse my presumption, but I'd be doing less than my duty to you and the throne if I didn't point out that you're a young king, and therefore vulnerable." He paused, aware that Magnus' brows had come down.

"And that" he said hastily, for this was Hardraada's son he faced after all, "that'll lessen over time. Of course. But at the moment – at the moment I say – everyone's waiting to see which way the Landwaster's successor will jump, and that's why things are dangerous."

"Who's 'everyone', lord Ranulf?" asked the king, his free hand scratching the ears of the huge wolfhound that had been his father's, "who in particular?"

"The *jarls* of the north" said the Scraeling promptly. "Our Icelandic 'allies' for another. And outside your majesty's realm – Svein Estrithsson, King of Denmark. And he's perhaps the most dangerous of all."

"I think I see where you're going" said the young king, "but please explain your thinking, lord Secretary."

"Well" began the Scraeling, "Svein ended the wars between himself and your father profoundly lucky to have hung onto his throne. Only your father's decision to pursue . . . ah, other avenues of foreign policy, prevented . . ."

"You mean his idiotic pursuit of the English throne, don't you?" broke in Magnus, and the Scraeling spread his hands in deference.

"We must always remember, majesty," he said, "that things seem different viewed within their proper time and . . . ah . . . context. At the time, the Danish wars had served their purpose in uniting the land and providing practice for the army, and so . . ."

"Yes, yes, very well" said Magnus. "So, what's changed?"

"A great deal has changed" said the Scraeling, hoping that Magnus' question was a rhetorical one. *Jesu – he can't be serious about not knowing. Can he?* he thought.

Aloud, though, he said "To begin with, the loss of your majesty's father, King Harald, and nine out of ten of Europe's most formidable army with him – that's changed a good deal. Now Svein's the most powerful man in Scandinavia. In fact, given that Scotland's in its usual state of turmoil and the Bastard of Normandy's hanging on to England by his fingernails and eyebrows, it's probably not stretching the case to suggest that at this moment, Svein commands the greatest military force between here and the kingdom of France. Even though the arse is still hanging out of his breeches."

That brought a snort of laughter from the others in the room and Magnus joined in. "And how d'you see Svein?" he asked, "Leaving his breeches out of it?"

The Screaling pursed his lips. "He's had time enough to rebuild since your father let him off the hook" he said. "But I never saw him as an ambitious man, not in all the dealings I had with him on Norway's behalf. However – and this is important, majesty – things were very different then, and I'm sure those in this room who served King Harald then will agree with me." There was a buzz of agreement and the Screaling continued,

"For a start, he was only a petty king then, and he knew it, for all his bluster. He was lucky to avoid death in battle several times, and nothing he did contributed to our king's decision to break off the war. Well, all that's changed too, majesty. As far as Svein's concerned, I'd say that what we need to do is offer him assurances of our neighbourly intentions towards him – show him he's no need to fear us, open trade negotiations – that sort of thing."

"If he's half as shrewd as he ought to be, lord Ranulf, he'll have worked out already that he's no need to fear us, surely?" returned the king, and the Screaling nodded.

"A point well made, sire" he acknowledged. "I believe that, militarily, Norway hasn't been as low as this since King Harald returned from the Rus. Styrkar, here –" nodding towards the marshal of Norway "– can tell us about that in detail. But you see, that's just why we should bend every effort towards starting off a trading relationship. Trade is what the Danes're good at, and they're greedy buggers – pardon me – so especially if the terms of that trade were to favour them – oh, not obviously, but pitched in such a way that the potential was there for them to exploit us just a bit – they wouldn't miss the chance, and they'd enjoy it. And they'd want to keep *that* going as long as they could, so . . . I'm sure you can see the benefits. All of the benefits."

Styrkar shifted in his chair and eased the shoulder that had taken a sword-cut in the retreat from Stamford Bridge. "I'd agree" he said. "Screaling's right. We'll come again, majesty, but we need a breathing-space and Svein's turn to gloat a little – that'll give it to us. But Scrae— lord Ranulf, can you work out those terms of trade you mentioned? It'll take a bit of doing. I mean, we'll need to balance Svein's greed against our merchants' losses and that. I'd not know where to begin."

"But I do" said the Screaling smugly. "Been thinking about it for a while. We'll work something out, never fear."

"Very good" said Magnus. "And do you have something worked out for the northern *jarls* and Iceland too?"

Again the Scraeling spread his hands. "Well majesty" he began, "now you mention it, why . . ." But the rest of his words were lost in the hoot of laughter that swept round the long table.

"Knew it" chuckled Styrkar to his neighbour, "Old One-Eyed Skallagrim was a good friend of mine. He c'd never make up his mind whether the Scraeling was more've a cunning little bastard or a dangerous little bastard. But one thing he did know, he allus said, was he was glad the Scraeling was on his side."

If only you knew thought the Scraeling, who had heard the remark. *I was never on Skallagrim's side for one moment of one hour of one day of the thirty years I suffered him. But I won in the end, and if I have anything to do with the new Norway, it won't be long before I have you so bound about with restrictions, marshal, you'll take up fishing for a living and give up war-making forever. There's been altogether too much of that, and I'm just the man to put an end to it, so laugh while you can, marshal of Norway, laugh while you can. Fuck you and your warmongering both. Your day is over.*

"Well" came back Magnus, "since lord Ranulf's been giving the matter some thought, perhaps we can leave the matter of the *jarls* and our Icelandic friends until the next council meeting. Till then?" and as the table arose, he added, "Lord Ranulf, a word if you please . . ."

The Chronicle

*I*n fact, *I played up the menace of Svein, who was actually a man I admired and liked. All courtiers do, because proving their indispensability guarantees their employment. And it was the time to do so, for the lost battle of Stamford Bridge had decimated the biggest viking army that had ever left Scandinavia.*

No, I'm wrong there – decimation takes away only a tenth, and Odin's ravens had called nine-tenths of the Landwaster's last host. Aye – three hundred ships had sailed to England, and thirty had sufficed to bring the survivors home. The ice-lands were stripped, purged and laid bare of warriors and leaders alike. Women farmed the land and boys fished the seas, and if there was a home in Norway, Orkney or Iceland that had escaped the loss of a father, son or husband

– I didn't know of it. And I would have known of it, for among my other duties I had been Hardraada's secretary, a job whose functions were as loose as the word implies.

I felt I could offer something to fill such a void for, though a man with only one sound leg might neither farm nor fish, I could do things much more valuable. Magnus, the Landwaster's elder son by Thora Thorbergsdotter was, I'd always felt, a disappointment to his Valhalla-filling father for he was sickly and inclined to be studious. He had little idea of how to deal with the kingship that had been thrust upon him in the wake of his father's death, for his appointment as regent for his father had been nothing but a formality in everyone's mind.

His brother Olaf was little more fitted to become king, as Hardraada's daughters by his first wife, Maria and Ingigerd, had been the apples of their father's eye even though their mother, Elisabeth, was regarded merely as another piece of treasure he had brought home from Kiev. In consequence, the two boys had little knowledge or experience of the craft of kingship, and it was there that I saw the part I might play in making Norway the friend of all and the enemy of none.

But a sheepfold with a neglectful shepherd only invites the wolf. I could think of several – both within and without – who would covet the throne of Norway if they saw it weakly held, so my advice to King Magnus Haraldsson was designed to alert him to that . . .

***

www.ingramcontent.com/pod-product-compliance
Lightning Source LLC
Chambersburg PA
CBHW071046250626
47159CB00002B/377